PAPERLESS

A JULIUS BARLOW MYSTERY

Phil Robinson

Heather
All the best to you
and your family

2017-11-22

Paperless

web: paperless.milltown.ca
twitter: @paperlessnovel
email: paperless@milltown.ca

Tellwell Talent
www.tellwell.ca

ISBN
978-1-77370-247-6 (Paperback)
978-1-77370-248-3 (eBook)

This story was inspired, in part, by the atrocities against children and their families that took place between 1988 and 1995 in the United Kingdom. The ensuing scandal, labelled as the Alder Hey Organ Scandal, initially focused on the Alder Hey Children's Hospital in Liverpool but quickly spread to include a majority of the hospitals governed by the National Health Service. The scandal led to the Human Tissues Act of 2004. The primary perpetrator was never criminally charged.

Acknowledgements

A much-used traditional African proverb states: "It takes a village to raise a child". So it has been with the creation of this novel. Fibers taken from childhood, education, experience, and inspiration are woven by the imagination into a tale comprised of intriguing characters and rich images that magically emerge from mere words and phrases. To the many 'villagers' who invested in my life I extend my sincere thanks.

Modern technology greatly simplified the research required for this novel. Google provided search results, Google Maps and Google Earth offered a bird's eye view of unfamiliar terrain, a wide variety of web sites provided background material, and Wikipedia provided welcomed knowledge, otherwise elusive. The internet provided the connective tissue that bound the various technologies together. The author is grateful to the vast army of individuals who make and keep this technology available at little or no cost.

To those who helped me work through the plot, those experts who reviewed the technical aspects of the story, those who worked so diligently to locate and correct typographical and grammatical errors, and the editors who made it readable, I offer my thanks; the book really couldn't have been completed without you. Any remaining errors are strictly mine.

For the brave who freely offered their time to read and comment on the story as it developed, I have nothing but admiration. Your encouragement was the fuel that powered its completion.

To those who teach and example faith in our lives I am eternally grateful.

Notice to the reader

This novel includes scenes involving aviation, information technology, and the practice of medicine. These fields use technical terms and acronyms, some of which may be unfamiliar to the reader. Rather than interrupt the flow of the narrative by explaining each of these *in situ*, the author has elected to provide a Glossary of Terms at the end of the novel for those who wish to sate their curiosity.

Prologue

THE PAGER ON HIS BELT BUZZED SOFTLY, ROUSING HIM FROM THE trance induced by the professor's hypnotic voice as it droned on about how to prevent incisional hernia during a small bowel resection. Not that the information wasn't important, but the schedule Niele Kaupas was keeping had reduced his body to a mere machine fueled by caffeine and his mind to a wasteland devoid of structure and focus. His body lay almost horizontal as he slouched in the lecture theater seat, the dark bags under his lidded eyes broadcasting to peers and professor alike that he was tired and on the edge of collapse. Later he would brush up on the surgical complications being discussed. With some effort he gained the professor's attention and apologized for the interruption, his Lithuanian accent clearly betraying his birthplace, "Dok'tor, I am sorry but I have just been pag'ed and have urgent surg'ry to attend. I will read topic and come to office if I have some questions." He excused himself to the other eight interns in the class while gathering his belongings, and left the room.

Dr. Wambua Omondi was in the middle of lecturing the third year class on Hodgkin lymphoma when his pager chirped. Ignoring it, he continued speaking. Moments later, it chirped again. He paused and said, his rumbling voice booming out a lilting Kenyan inflection, "I must apologize, class. I have been called to the operating theater.

Please spend the remainder of our time today reading the article I distributed to you. Put particular attention on the diagrams—they are very helpful. I will answer any questions you may have the next time we meet and then will move on to other topics. Again, I apologize." After gathering his notes and extra handouts, Wambua left the classroom then turned down the hallway toward the operating rooms. He was fortunate to have been assigned a conference room in the operating wing for this class, making his trip to the OR shorter than the usual trek from the teaching annex.

As he approached the security doors, Wambua fished around in his pockets for his key card. Sliding it into the reader he impatiently put his shoulder to the door. It wouldn't budge. A second later the lock clicked in response to the security system that had verified his identity. The door soundlessly yielded to the continuing pressure of his shoulder, ushering him into the hallway leading to the operating suites. After elbowing his way through the doors of scrub station 'B', he began his routine: he removed his outer street clothes, the wedding ring from his left hand, and the class ring from his right; he took the tiny diamond stud from his left earlobe. He placed these personal items, together with the papers he had dumped on the floor, in the only locker with an open door. He scanned the linen rack for a pair of XL scrubs then dressed, making sure the tie on the waistband was secure. On the adjacent shelves he located a surgical cap, beard cover, and mask, applied them carefully and secured their ties. He placed a pair of lightly tinted safety glasses on his face, tucking the arms behind his mask as he shuffled over to the sink. He then executed from memory the scrub routine: hands, nails, forearms to two inches above each elbow ... He glanced at himself in the mirror opposite the scrub station, verifying his face was totally obscured—following the prescribed procedure to the letter. He crossed the room and raised one knee, using it to knock on the windowless door to the right of the lockers. A scrub nurse emerged in response, similarly garbed and equally obscured. In silence they walked back to the scrub station. Wambua continued to hold his hands in front of him, allowing the assistant to apply surgical gloves and check the ties on the various elements of his operating attire. The assistant left the same way he—or she—had come. Wambua thought perhaps the scrub nurse was male by the size of the hands, though he wasn't certain. It was not his place to attempt an identification.

In spite of his physical and mental condition, Niele moved quickly through the halls of the teaching annex to the main lobby, caught the elevator, and stepped off at the fifth floor. He pulled out a pass key from the back of his wallet and inserted it into the card reader. The large doors that stood guard over the operating suites clicked, allowing him through. As instructed, he located scrub station 'A', entered, removed his street clothes, donned a sterile gown, cap, and mask, and conducted his scrub routine by following each item on the posted checklist. With his right foot he tapped the door to the left of the lockers. A fully gowned scrub nurse walked through the door, applied his gloves, and then checked his gown and mask, her delicate hands confirming her gender. She left via the door from which she had arrived only minutes before.

Niele and Wambua entered the operating room a few moments apart, from opposite sides, gowned and masked. Not much more than their eyes were showing, and *they* were all but invisible behind tinted safety glasses. They did not speak. Each knew his duties precisely, and executed them with practiced efficiency.

The patient was a child, around five years old, body draped, readied for surgery. There was no need for a respirator or an anesthetist; the child's brain had ceased to function several hours earlier from complications associated with a fall. The full complement of hi-tech life support equipment, the only thing sustaining breath and heartbeat, had been removed just before their arrival. They did not read the child's chart. They did not see the child's face.

Wambua made the incision, exposing the organs. Niele packed the body cavity with sterile ice and prepared the infusion equipment. After gently chilling each organ of interest with the appropriate solution, Wambua carefully removed it and placed it into one of the specialized containers Niele had prepared. The kidneys were placed into the largest of the containers and connected to the integrated pulsative infusion device. Niele closed the body cavity, cleared the operating room and placed the sealed organ containers on the two-level stainless steel cart along the far wall.

Each man returned to his respective scrub station after less than two hours in the OR, removed his surgical clothing, donned his street clothes, gathered his personal effects, and left the operating suite. Neither would know for certain who the other was. Neither would speak of the surgical event to anyone. Each would check his bank account at the end of the day.

Chapter 1

STAINLESS STEEL ELEVATOR DOORS CLOSED SOUNDLESSLY BEHIND Tess as she stepped into the carpeted hallway leading to the administrative offices. She was in Tower C, the Ludlow Belk Memorial Tower, which had been erected just three years earlier, funded by a large endowment from the Belk family foundation. The executive offices of the Parks Hospital for Children had been moved to the seventh floor of Tower C, allowing for a new Imaging Unit on the ground floor of Tower A.

Tower C was an artistic wonder, its irregular geometric shape pleasing to the adult eye and fascinating to the imagination of a child. Approval seemed universal for its award-winning, yet daring design.

The building's east side formed a sharp vertical edge, the apex of a triangle housing the stairs and the elevators. Massive glass panels played prismatically with the sunlight. Cartoon-decorated fire doors formed the triangle's base, beyond which a hallway stretched crookedly, sprouting offices and conference rooms.

Tess walked through the open door of the third office on the left and inquired, "Good morning Kathy. Is he in?"

Kathy looked up from her computer and said, "Ah … Tess, he's expecting you. Go right through."

Tess knocked lightly on the tall natural oak door displaying **James Koehler, CIO** on a polished brass engraving. She took the muffled response as an invitation to enter and, pressing on the lever-style handle, opened the door.

Despite the number of times she had seen it before, the room's odd shape continued to intrigue her. As certainly as artful architecture is beautiful on the outside, it spawns strange spaces on the inside. To her left was a dimly lit alcove separated from the rest of the space by a tall curving structure sporting six large computer screens, each dispensing a cold, multi-colored, vaguely eerie glow. As if in defiance, a lone incandescent lamp sat on the large rosewood desk facing the monitors, spreading a pool of warm light revealing several neat piles on the left, partially hidden by Jim's shoulder, and an open document in front of him. Behind the structure, all but invisible from the doorway, was an extensive library, bright with fluorescent ceiling lights, housing a small round desk and two opposing sofas. To the right along the windows was an oblong conference table with eight swivel chairs. Perhaps not your average administrative office, but it seemed to suit Jim's management style perfectly.

In one smooth motion, Jim made a quick scan of the computer screens, rose, and gestured toward the conference table, saying, "Morning, Ms. Rivard. What have you discovered about this alleged breach?"

"I've made some progress," replied Tess as she sat, "but I don't think we're out of the woods yet." Referring to her notes, she continued, "I *have* confirmed that on the Wednesday in question someone did hack into our system and steal some data—"

"You mean you've been able to prove this breach is real?" Jim cut in, his voice controlled but instantly taut. Tess's head snapped up, her gaze fixed on him. "But our network security is tighter than a brandy barrel. We put millions into preventing this very thing. How can data just escape into the outside world like so much ... vapor?"

"Luck," replied Tess cautiously, "just dumb luck, I guess. During the last couple of weeks I explored every possible security scenario and found nothing. Then in the middle of the night this weekend something hit me.

"Early that Wednesday morning, the hardware guys were implementing a new server. They stuck to protocol, populating it with sanitized disc images. At two o'clock, the very moment the machine was powered up, before the anti-virus protection could be installed, it happened ... best I can figure from the time line, anyway.

"Where they screwed up was not removing the external network mapping like they should have. Whether they missed that specific item on the checklist, or thought it wouldn't matter given the time of day and the short vulnerability window, I don't know. What I *do* know is that in just a few milliseconds a virus found its way into the new computer, extracted data from our MX103 server, then deleted itself."

He shoved his chair back roughly and began pacing behind his desk. "Have you been able to actually *confirm* any of this?"

"Yes, I'm afraid—as much as possible. I'm still guessing at some of the details, but all the stars align on this theory. The exact moment the server was vulnerable matches with the time stamp on the log that detected the breach. I can't think of anything else that would allow access to our servers, particularly MX103—as closely guarded as we both know it is."

Tess paused to assess Jim's reaction. He had stopped pacing and was gripping the back of his chair with both hands. Any CIO worth his salt would have the same doubts: Had the security not been their top priority? Could all this tireless effort amount to nothing, simply because of an unchecked line on a list? Similar questions swirled through her mind.

"This will not go well for those involved if any real proof surfaces, I can promise you that much." His gaze seemed to bore right through her, making her squirm. "Is there any way to be certain?" he rasped.

"I doubt we will ever find 'legal' proof. The virus was smart enough to spoof the IP address of the breach, so to the log it looks like MX103 was the culprit. But I can't bring myself to believe it. I've gone through its logs and the resident code; MX103 is water tight … as expected. Internally it looks like a regular data transfer. If the logger on the external IP address hadn't flagged this, it would have gone unnoticed."

Jim's knuckles were turning white, the implications transforming his carefully guarded business countenance. Staring blankly at the edge of the desk, he muttered, "And if I hadn't caught that particular warning on the monitor, even the log anomaly would have gone unnoticed. Dumb luck that it happened; dumb luck that it was caught."

Tess simply nodded, looking directly at Jim's downcast face.

After a long pause Jim sat back down, placed his fists on the desk and looked directly at Tess. "So … to summarize … someone on the outside has plucked sensitive data from MX103 due to human error on the part of *our* hardware group, and we can't do a bloody thing about it."

Tess responded with a more positive tone in her voice, "Well … almost. We know where the data went."

Jim leaned further forward, his face becoming stern and hard. "Really? Does that mean we know who did this?"

"We know the IP address that collected the data; a far cry from pinning down the *who*. Even if we could identify the route it took, we still wouldn't know who was sitting at the other end."

His voice stronger, Jim replied, "But you *can* find out, right?"

"Perhaps. This is a brand new lead and if we think it's worthwhile I'll get started on the tracing. It's what I wanted to get your approval for this morning. I didn't want to put this in writing, so I asked Kathy for a face to face."

"I appreciate your keeping it under wraps for now. We can't let even our security staff know about this until we have it figured out. This could be an *internal* breach, in which case everyone is suspect—even you."

Tess's neck muscles tensed as the words hit home. She knew exactly what Jim meant. In her head she knew it wasn't personal, but it stung anyway. Relaxing a little as she put his statement into perspective, she said, "I understand. I'll get right on it."

Tess stood to go. She hadn't quite reached the door when Jim shouted, "Wait! … Do we know yet *what* was stolen?"

Tess turned toward him but didn't get a chance to respond.

"Perhaps if we knew the *what,* we could look for motive and maybe get closer to who did this. On the other hand, maybe the data was … well … just data, and we're getting all riled up over nothing. If so, we don't really care, do we, other than to take the warning that our internal procedures might need some tweaking?"

Tess found her voice, "I don't think we'll ever know, Jim. The log file gave us a beginning and ending memory location—like a partial memory dump, I suppose—and the logging system made no attempt to capture the data in-between. What we do know is, with MX103 being the billing server, the transfer contained billing information and some patient data. Apart from insurance and Medicare codes, it doesn't work with any other patient history, so I think it's fair to say patient confidentiality has *not* been compromised. That's why we segregate the servers, after all."

Jim replied with a wave of his hand, "You're right, of course. Keep me posted. Face to face only. My door is open for updates any time."

The way Kathy looked at her as Tess passed through the outer office made it clear the poker face she feigned had failed miserably.

Jim waited several minutes before picking up the phone. As much as he wanted to keep this a total secret, it was his duty to report it. As CIO he dealt with sensitive information every day, and because he had access to *all* the hospital data, he reported directly to the CEO, and only to the CEO.

"Noah, we have a potential problem I need to discuss with you in person. Do you have a few minutes?"

"Sure, Jim, I have a brief gap in ten or so. I'll contact Kathy when I'm free."

Jim broke the connection.

Standing, he walked over to the window and stared at the wispy clouds as he continued to think through the implications of the breach. How serious was it? Did it really matter? Could anything be done about it? Are they getting strung out over nothing? Would the breach put the hospital in jeopardy of any kind … legal maybe? His mind was whirling, but for the moment at least, he could not zero in on anything specific. Security was such a fragile thing. One could take measures only against those threats known to exist, yet new ones appeared all the time; it was a mug's game. The amount of energy and money spent, and the amount of time wasted, was appalling … and, in the end, for what? Tomorrow some new virus or hack will rob precious time from important tasks—like saving the lives of innocent children, to name just one.

As he let this percolate a little, he grew confident a resolution would be found, and with that realization came a releasing of the tightness that had crept into his shoulders.

Kathy knocked on his door and reported Noah was ready to see him. He walked briskly down the hall and, entering the CEO's outer office, said good morning to Noah's assistant. He walked straight in, closing the door behind him. Noah Jackson's office was as misshapen as Jim's, but it had been decorated in an entirely different manner. Noah's desk was across from the windows, and artwork of various kinds populated the nooks and crannies. It was warm and all business—a reflection of its occupant.

"Noah. Thanks for seeing me on such short notice." Sitting on the edge of the leather chair positioned opposite the desk, he continued, "I'll get right to the point." Pleasantries were not necessary between the two men. They had walked through many administrative fires together and, over time, had developed a deep respect for each other. As a team, they had a good success rate, albeit imperfect. "We have confirmed the data breach we spoke about previously. Some of our hospital data has been transmitted to the outside world by a lucky virus that penetrated our defenses in a moment of vulnerability. Our confidential records are OK as far as we know at this point. The data was extracted from our billing server. We have no idea what left the hospital, and we may never know. We are just now trying to discover where it went. If and when we find its destination we may be able to determine what was taken, and why, and if there are any residual implications for the hospital."

Noah looked at Jim intently for a moment then stated, "I see. Nothing definite yet—so this is a heads-up?"

"Right. I'll keep you in the loop as things develop."

Jim was almost to his feet when Noah said, "Thanks, Jim. I would like you to bring Atchley in on this."

Jim froze. Supporting himself on the arms of the chair, he snapped, "You have got to be kidding, Noah." He sank limply back down.

"He *hates* me! At the best of times he's arrogant and short-tempered. In fact, he hates everyone in this hospital except himself. For two years I've had to tolerate his hostility, and, frankly, I'm tired of it. And you want me to bring him into this mess so early in our investigation? He'll crucify us both and laugh all the way into *your* office as he puts *his* family pictures on *your* desk."

"Jim! Jim! Hang on a minute. Let's not go all squirrely over this. Look at what he's done for this hospital in the last couple of years; he's put our name on the map in several medical arenas, he's hired great staff, and, let's face it, he brings in a lot of revenue. I know he's not the most pleasant guy to work with, but hey, we're all professionals here. As Chief of Staff, if we don't keep him in the loop, we risk his running us up the pole for *that*. Which is worse, a little cursing now over a problem at the staff level, or a lot of cursing later over incompetence in the executive suite?"

A curtain of silence hung between them.

Finally Jim replied, his voice stretched and low, "OK, I'll do it as soon as I can get a moment with him. But, just for the record, I don't like the idea, and I can almost guarantee it will come back to bite us somehow, somewhere—it's just who he is."

Jim left Noah's office, slicing through the tension as he went.

Slamming the phone down, Dr. Blake Atchley bellowed for Erika. As she came through the adjoining door he commanded gruffly, "Erika, right after this next surgery I need to meet with doctors Torres, Reed, Perry and Gomez. Work out a suitable time. Clear schedules if you have to. I need 15 minutes tops. And if you can reach Garret, I want him here as well."

Chapter 2

Tuesday

HEY, PIERRE!" SHOUTED JULIUS, TRYING TO BE HEARD OVER THE snapping of the three flags whose halyards clanked in the breeze against the commemorative flag poles, two of which were beginning to show the rusty scars borne of cutbacks over the past several years. The Stars and Stripes stood proudly on the center pole, flanked on the left by the veteran's flag, and on the right by the Louisiana nested Pelican, each framed by the stunning blue of a cloudless Louisiana sky.

Pierre glanced over his shoulder to confirm that he had been called, then spun around in recognition of Julius, his unlaced work boots scoring the worn and pebbled blacktop. Breaking into a broad grin, he began walking toward Julius with long strides made possible by his six foot four frame. Their hands met in a friendly grip of camaraderie. "Julius," he said excitedly, "it's been a while. How y'all doin', anyway."

"No complaints here, Pierre. You've been away I hear? How was it?"

"We had a great time, my kids especially, but you know, in a strange sort of way, I'm glad to be back. I missed the smell of aviation fuel, the unrelenting demands of you pilots, and the weird hours of course. I could have used another week, but I was scheduled back for Monday and here I am, one day in, and looking forward to the weekend already," said Pierre warmly with a hint of his typical sarcasm. "Anything I can do for you today?"

Julius returned the smile, welcoming his friend back to the airport and its duties. "I need a top-up on both tanks and check the oil all around, if you don't mind. I'm heading to Houston this afternoon expecting to be back by evening. The kids are coming over, and I don't want to miss dinner if I can help it. You know how it is; seems harder each day to get everyone together in one place at one time."

"Tell me about it … and my kids are still young," flipped Pierre.

Julius paused for a moment, his face turning serious. "Say, we seem to have a new aircraft in here today. Quite a beauty. Any idea who owns it?"

Pierre lifted one shoulder, "Not sure really. It landed early this morning. I assumed it's someone doing business at the mill, but now that you mention it, I didn't see anyone leave the terminal. I've been fairly busy this morning, so I may simply have missed them."

But Pierre never missed anything.

Worry began to nip at the heels of Julius' mind. Behind a forced smile, he said "See you in a few minutes." Casting another glance over his shoulder at the airplane, he sauntered to the FBO to finalize his briefing and file his flight plan. He did most of his planning before leaving the house; getting a preliminary weather report and checking for TFR's. Guided by the oil-stained pathway carved in the ancient carpet of the wartime hangar housing the FBO, he headed toward the pilot's lounge. As he passed the front desk he said "Good day, Ava. Still forecasting clear and a million for the rest of the day?"

She replied, "And good afternoon to you, Julius. Looks like a great flying day. A little breezy, but based on the weather charts I've seen, the wind is steady at 25 knots aloft, forecast to diminish as the day progresses, so the ride should be smooth."

Julius winked at Ava, and leaning over her desk, quipped "I think I'll get that information from a slightly more reliable source." Ava made a face and called after him, "Do you want a cup of coffee to go?" Julius made a 'thumbs up' sign as he marched down the hallway.

His attention was focused on the room at the end of the corridor. Over the years he had come to the realization it was best not to look up or down while walking this hallway. Looking up would reveal heating pipes with peeling insulation and what seemed like miles of old cloth-covered electrical wires intertwined with modern computer cables. He mused that if one could peer into the dingy crevasses they would host knob and tube wiring from a bygone era, and perhaps a deeper look would reveal one of Edison's original light bulbs. Just above eye level the walls took on the appearance of a bunker, with gray-green paint curling from cement blocks, most of which displayed concentric rings of white powder from decades of taking on moisture.

Looking down was perhaps, if possible, even worse. Along the walls were old display cases strewn with aviation charts and books from years long gone, their glass stained and finger-printed, with the odd yellow-brown-ringed puddle that Julius could only hope was the result of a leaking roof. Peeking out from under the cabinets were wrappers, crumpled newspaper pages, and dust bunnies—colonies of them.

The FBO kept a dusty computer and an aging dot matrix printer in the back office, allowing pilots access to the internet so they could obtain current weather information and file flight plans. After replacing bits of deteriorating foam still stuck to slivers of deep green naugahyde curling off the seat, Julius sat in the metal swivel chair and placed his elbows on the huge oak desk that must have been scavenged from government surplus decades, if not generations, ago. Its stained, worn surface had exchanged the papers, rubber stamps, and index cards of a former time for items essential to the modern aviator: the computer, its keyboard and mouse, an old black rotary phone, and paint-bare metal bookends flanking large printed volumes of FAA regulations, an Aeronautical Information Manual, the AOPA airport manual, and the smaller green Airport Facilities Directory. Scattered in the back corner were scribbled work sheets, idly discarded by previous not-so-litter-conscious pilots. Perhaps, Julius sometimes thought, if he rummaged through them, he might find one in Amelia Earhart's own handwriting. And, of course, there was the dust, years of it, disturbed in various spots where pilots had hastily dropped their flight bags and kneeboards. After many visits to this room, these artifacts were familiar to Julius, but his amusement lingered.

Deftly loading the browser, he entered the address for the DUAT web site, typed in his credentials, and entered the designators of his local and destination airports. The ancient computer screen flared with an area map marked with lines and symbols which, to the uninitiated, looked like third grade doodling. But to Julius it represented information critical to his flight. A quick glance at the hieroglyphics and Julius understood the weather picture; he would benefit from the winds aloft pushing him to his destination, saving time and fuel. The weather system would move off to the east during the day, leaving in its wake a calm area of high pressure, yielding light winds but relentless heat and scorching sunshine. A large stationery front to the south west was creating nasty weather west of his destination, but would not affect his flight, or so he hoped.

The computer prompted him to enter his flight plan, but, enigmatic as it was, Julius hadn't yet learned to trust this critical part of his planning to an inanimate flow of electrons, so, taking the handset from the old black desk phone, he dialed the local Flight Service Station, intent upon talking to a real person. Dialing 1-800 on a rotary dial was no picnic, but after the clicks and taps subsided, the connection was made, and a briefer came on the line with a professional greeting.

Julius responded, "Good afternoon. This is November Seven Three One Papa Tango, Piper Navajo looking to fly between Springhill, Kilo Sierra Papa Hotel, and Lone Star Exec, Kilo Charlie X-ray Oscar, this afternoon, leaving at twenty fifteen Zulu, IFR, about one hour ten en route. I have the current and forecast weather for the trip, the local AWOS, and the published TFR's and would like to file a flight plan." The rapid-fire conversation continued as he gave the step-by-step information required by the ICAO.

"Thank you," said the flight service specialist. "Looks like a great day to fly. If you are going to return today be sure to check the weather before you do. The front that will precede the high pressure is not behaving as expected, so our forecasts may not be entirely accurate. Your flight plan will be filed with the Springhill tower within the next ten minutes. Have a good flight."

"Thanks, I'll be sure to keep my eye on the weather, and you have a fine day," said Julius, breaking the connection.

Julius gathered his scattered papers, bundling them into his kneeboard as he headed out to the apron where he hoped his aircraft would be fueled and ready to go. Passing the front desk, he threw a smile at Ava, snatched his coffee, and wished her a good day.

He was not disappointed. Pierre knew his job and did it well. Julius looked around to see if Pierre was within ear shot so he could thank him, but he was nowhere to be found. Although hating himself for it, he let the thought skim through his mind that perhaps it was for the best. Pierre could get talking on almost any subject, and unless you knew how to politely cut him off, he could make a mockery of one's schedule.

The Navajo sat proudly on its tripod of struts waiting for its commander. This was the part that played to Julius' ego. He loved the thought of being *in command* of his faithful bird; not *his* term, but one used by the FAA to designate the warm body generally in the left seat behind the controls, whether truly in command or not. However juvenile, Julius liked to be 'pilot in command'. He loved the freedom of flying, and being *in command* was just one perk that contrasted the general patina of his daily life.

He executed the external pre-flight with precision. Walking slowly around the aircraft, he checked control surfaces, fuel levels and quality, tires, engines and props, cargo bay doors, skin, and antennae. It appeared just as it had been left after his last trip. The bird was ready to fly.

Approaching from the rear, Julius climbed onto the left wing using the engine nacelle for balance, then opened the pilot entry door. Suspending himself from the upper door frame, he swung over the pilot's seat into the center aisle. He slipped between the leather club seats to the passenger door at the rear, verifying it was locked and secure. As he returned to the front, he noticed the heat building from the midday sun, knowing there would be no relief until after sundown. Even in a Louisiana autumn, it was a hot start to almost every flight, but Julius had long since steeled himself to this discomfort as he prepared the instruments. It would be short-lived. Once he had both engines warmed up, he would throw the switches to activate the air conditioning, and the entire cabin would cool rapidly. He propped open his door to get some cross-breeze and pulled out the checklist that was beginning to show signs of wear, faithfully going through each item in its turn. He checked that he had the necessary documents for himself and the aircraft: air worthiness certificate, license, and radio certificate. He verified that all the instruments were serviceable and checked the position of the electrical breakers. He knew this airplane intimately, and he would recognize any item that was even slightly out of place or defective. But he would not allow himself to become complacent. His caution had saved his life numerous times and he worked hard to keep vigilant when preparing for a flight. While reaching under his seat to touch the fire extinguisher, he also verified ready access to the smoke hood, shuddering at the thought of ever having to use it in flight. It intrigued him that the smoke hood was the only consumer item he knew of where, if the item were ever used, the company would replace it free of charge. He mentally noted his disinterest in ever exercising that guarantee.

After pushing the mixture levers full forward, he made sure the props were feathered, then set the right throttle at one fifth open. Pressing the start button for the right engine, he observed the prop as it strained to turn. The engine coughed, fired, and settled into a smooth hum at 1200 rpm. He pulled the throttle back gently until the engine purred at a smooth 1000 rpm. Repeating this procedure, he started the left engine. It was his practice to allow the engines to come up to temperature before taxiing, using this time to set his radios, GPS, and autopilot.

At last everything was set. He pulled the door closed, making sure it was latched and locked. Once more he went over the panel, touching each instrument and piece of equipment, methodically double checking the settings. The machine was ready to fly. He inched it to the end of the apron, stopping just short of the taxiway.

Julius keyed his radio. "Springhill tower, November Seven Three One Papa Tango looking for IFR clearance to Lone Star. Over."

"This is the tower. Wait a minute."

Julius' brow knotted involuntarily.

"'N 7 3 1 P T', cleared via runway heading to Lone Star; vectors to V 13. Squawk 22 19. Climb, maintain 3000. Higher in 10 miles. Departure 123.7. Over." Fumbling with the clearance as he wrote its essence in his own shorthand, his anger flared. He had taken hundreds of clearances, yet today he seemed to be all thumbs. He had to hope the rest of the flight would not find him this incompetent. His life would depend on it.

Julius read back the clearance. "November Seven Three One Papa Tango; cleared Lone Star; runway heading; vectors Victor One Three; three thousand; higher in ten; one two three point seven on departure. Uh, say again the squawk. Over". There it was again. He hadn't had to beg for a repeated clearance since his student days, and the heat that skimmed his neck seemed to fuel his anger.

"22 19," barked the tower.

"Two two one niner on the squawk," repeated Julius, somewhat meekly.

"7 3 1 P T, read-back correct. Taxi alpha and hold short of runway 18. There's some traffic on its way in." The words were clipped and spoken with an effort as if perhaps to hide an accent, not Texan, not Cajun …?

"Seven Three One Papa Tango taxi alpha, uh, hold short one eight for landing traffic. Over," repeated Julius.

He verified the frequency set in the second radio, knowing from experience what the hand-off frequency would be after takeoff, but double-checking to make sure his clearance did not contain something unexpected.

As Julius taxied the Navajo he felt uneasy. Something was wrong. He knew all the controllers at Springhill, and had a pretty good handle on changes that took place from time to time, but he hadn't recognized the controller's voice. And there had been no "howdy", or "how are the wife and kids", before getting serious about the task at hand. Perhaps someone was sick and a substitute controller had been called in for the day. But that didn't sit right. And his embarrassment at botching the clearance irked him. In one final check, Julius chanted the mnemonic 'IMSAFE', thinking through each item: Illness, Medication, Stress, Alcohol, Fatigue, Eat. Perhaps he had misjudged his personal readiness to fly.

But there wasn't time for all this now. He was at the edge of the runway, the nose of the plane a few inches behind the hold line. He found no faults as he rehearsed in his mind the sounds and feel of the aircraft when the engines had been put through their paces on the apron prior to taxiing. He radioed, "Tower, November Seven Three One Papa Tango, holding short one eight, ready to go".

"P T, hold short, traffic is almost down".

Julius watched the Cessna 150 wobble over the runway threshold. A last minute drop of the remaining eight feet of altitude caused him to wince, as he recalled those early days of trying to gauge airspeed, altitude and attitude, and how many of his 'arrivals' had been pure torture for both the training aircraft and his instructor—and, not to be left out of the reminiscence, the buckets of sweat collected by his shirts while he was learning those skills.

His radio snarled as the tower took the frequency. "1 P T, cleared for takeoff. Wind 200 at 9. Altimeter 2 9 2 2". That voice again! Why was he bothered by it? But not now. He had an aircraft to guide safely to 8000 feet before he could explore his concerns.

Julius taxied onto the runway, aligning his front wheel just to the right of the center line. Quickly scanning the instrument panel, he verified, almost subconsciously, that all the controls and needles were in their correct positions. He pushed the throttles forward while maintaining proper pressure on the rudder, and began his take-off roll. Watching the airspeed carefully, he pulled back on the yoke as the aircraft approached rotation speed. Gracefully the Piper left the ground. The propellers had not yet been synchronized, evidenced by the steady slow beat broadcasting that the engines were strong and healthy. Almost without thinking, he flipped the auto-sync switch, the beats slowing until there was a single hum; one engine indistinguishable from the other.

The runway fell away beneath him, changing from a black surface immersing him, to an ever-thinning ribbon attended by its entourage of miniature buildings and cars and disappearing people. This metamorphosis always amazed him. It was one element of the magic that charmed him each time he flew.

As the Navajo gained airspeed and altitude, he checked for a positive rate of climb then lifted the gear switch. The whirring retraction of the landing gear mechanism terminated with a familiar thud as the wheels found their homes and the covering panels snapped into place. He then flipped radios and pressed the push-to-talk switch. "Shreveport Departure, Piper Seven Three One Papa Tango off runway One Eight, passing through twenty eight hundred."

"Piper November Seven Three One Papa Tango, roger, cleared to Lone Star airport as filed. Climb, maintain eight thousand."

Julius gave himself a mental high-five as he accepted this clearance. They were not always so simple.

Reaching 8000 feet, Julius set the manifold pressure, engine RPM, and mixtures. He activated the auto pilot, and relaxed as the computer gently settled the airplane into cruise. On course, at altitude, and everything trimmed for a smooth flight, he felt the tension in his muscles seep away. Up here, Julius was in his element; the ground seeming to slowly slip beneath the aircraft, the deep blue of the sky his canopy, the haze of a warm summer day enveloping him. He felt safe here in this amazing cocoon, where technology, physics, and the ingenuity of man, all melded together in a miracle guided by his own hand.

As his mind began to slow its pace, from the rigor of the takeoff duties to the pure freedom of the flying experience, he began to analyze his interaction with the tower. Analysis was both a boon and a bane to Julius. Sometimes he over-analyzed things, making it difficult for him to accept events and people at face value. Other times it served him well.

That voice still bothered him; the accent, the unconventional language of the tower controller. This was overlaid with his own humiliation at missing the clearance. Related? Not related? Just an off day for both himself and the controller? His thoughts spun with the propellers, but, unlike the props, they didn't seem to move him forward.

After several minutes, Julius decided he was being silly. Turning his attention to the flight path and the terrain over which he flew, he began lazily scanning for emergency landing spots, hoping the need would not arise. Looking at his kneeboard to ensure the autopilot was programmed correctly, the bungled clearance seemed to jump off the page at him, and the rough edge of his discomfort began to return.

Then it struck him. The clearance was not in the expected sequence. That's why his practiced shorthand hadn't worked. His pulse quickened. Both the routing and the squawk code were misplaced. That was what led to his confusion. He had not been at fault after all. The controller had delivered his clearance incorrectly, unprofessionally in fact, not using proper terminology or phonetic conventions. This controller was incompetent or inexperienced, or worse, and Julius intended to find out what was going on.

Chapter 3

AFTER JULIUS LEFT THE HOUSE, SHERI'S DAY MOVED INTO FULL swing. Although they shared Cora's care, swapping duties as necessary, Cora's medical needs were generally left in Sheri's hands. It was always easier when Julius was home; it afforded Sheri time to catch up on paper work and confirm or rearrange Cora's various appointments, an unrelenting job aggravated by the rapid progress of her disease.

What they did know was that it was degenerative, but, beyond that, the medical community seemed baffled. The symptoms paralleled those of Friedreich's ataxia, but that disease usually attacked those much younger than Cora. It was thought initially to be Huntington's disease, but Cora had shown no signs of mental regression or dementia. There was talk of it being a deterioration of the insulation around the nerves in the spinal column, leading to the theory that it was related to muscular dystrophy. Some had suggested it was an immune disorder. The truth of it was that current medical science couldn't pinpoint its source, so treatment was erratic and experimental.

The primary focus was on keeping Cora alive and comfortable. Each day it seemed, the symptoms manifested themselves in different ways, mustering a cadre of specialists, each handing the baton to the next as needed. The responsibility for coordination was shared by Sheri and Benjamin Garret, Cora's primary physician. He was an impressive man with an entire novel of letters behind his name. But, more than that, he was intuitive, a quick study, an accurate diagnostician, and an avid researcher. Everyone understood he had other patients, and duties at a variety of hospitals, but he made it seem as if Cora were his only charge; his compassion and bedside manner admirable. Of all the physicians Cora had seen, he was the only one with even the faintest understanding of her illness, and *that* was precious little. If it were not for Dr. Garret's involvement, Cora would have died years ago, and that death would have been unspeakable.

The *gong clock*, as the family so fondly nicknamed it, struck the hour, heralding yet another round of pokes and prods as Sheri charted Cora's vital signs. There was a computerized machine in the corner with coils of wire and various connectors, pincers, dials, and knobs, that would do the same thing and also keep the information digitally for later analysis, but it was used only on special occasions, when Cora's condition was at its lowest ebb and frequent monitoring was essential. Cora, Julius, and Sheri agreed that being hooked to all those wires robbed Cora of the little dignity remaining her, generally causing more discomfort than benefit.

Sheri didn't mind the extra work. It kept her in constant physical contact with Cora. Sheri was a strong believer in contact therapy— humans needed contact with other humans—which, when administered appropriately, gave hope and comfort. She knew it to be a clinical fact that contact often hastened recovery. It also saddened her, since regardless how much contact she had with Cora, it would not speed *her* recovery. But it *was* comforting, and it provided hope—if not for Cora, then for herself.

Sheri had grown attached to her charge. She struggled daily with the injustice of it all. Just four years ago Cora was a vibrant woman in her prime, five feet eight inches tall and athletically fit; beautiful in mind and character to those of even brief acquaintance. Eddie was already off to college by then, and Brittany was finishing high school. Julius worked hard, finding a niche for his talents that brought him into contact with defense contractors, medical instrumentation companies, pharmaceutical labs, and government agencies. And he loved aviation. His career provided a comfortable income, offering Cora the opportunity to engage in community work, where she earned a reputation for being a leader and organizer in charitable projects that benefited her community and, more often than not, beyond her community, sometimes spilling over into nations abroad. To look at her now, hardly able to function … Sheri worked hard at trying to make sense of it.

Her negative reaction to Julius' plans to go to Houston for a late afternoon meeting had been out of character. Julius often had appointments out of town and, whenever possible, he flew. She understood that he also needed this time away from Cora's care; one of the reasons her contract had been extended to full-time. But today seemed different. She was uneasy about his being away, and although he promised to be back by early evening, she wanted desperately to beg him not to go.

When he said his good-byes and the latch clicked behind him, she slumped against the door to evaluate her mood, trying as she might to force her mind back to the tasks at hand.

Chapter 4

SHREVEPORT, PIPER SEVEN THREE ONE PAPA TANGO. REQUEST. OVER."

"One Papa Tango, departure. Go ahead."

"Shreveport, One Papa Tango. I have a strange request. Could you check with the tower at Springhill and make sure everything is OK. My clearance wasn't handled well and … I don't know … something just doesn't feel right."

After a longer than usual pause the controller responded, "Uh … OK, One Papa Tango … Uh … we'll give them a phone call and check it out. Do you want us to let you know what we find?"

"Yes please, if you don't mind."

Departure frequency was seldom quiet. A variety of pilots were checking in, asking for alternate routing, and verifying weather conditions. Several minutes passed, making Julius wonder if the controller had taken him seriously. Maybe *he* shouldn't be taking himself seriously. He began to think he had just asked a busy controller to waste his valuable time on a meaningless errand.

The earth's surface effortlessly slid beneath the Navajo. From 8000 feet the terrain took on the look of a clown's britches; large patches of dark green forest, swatches of light green crops, raked sections of golden stubble, and dark patches of freshly tilled soil. Farm houses came and went like tiny sequins, while roads threaded through the landscape binding the patches together. Livestock grazed in Morse-coded clusters amid veins sculpted on the fields by ground water. Towns had the appearance of—

The radio crackled and Julius heard his call-sign. "November Seven Three One Papa Tango, departure. Over."

"Departure, One Papa Tango, go ahead. Over."

"One Papa Tango, thanks for calling us earlier. No one was answering at the tower so we asked the airport manager to check on things, and he found the duty controller lying unconscious on the control room floor. No one was manning the tower. The police have been called but I have no other information. When you land, please contact the County Sheriff and tell them what you know. I've given them your tail number."

"Departure, One Papa Tango, wilco."

Julius tried to process this information. He thought about Carlos, the controller who should have been on this shift. Was it Carlos who was lying on that floor?

And what about the strange plane that was at the airport this morning. Could these two events be connected?

He needed to know if there was foul play involved.

Carlos was known to Julius only through their interaction at the airport, although, from time to time he had noticed Carlos at community functions with his young family, always looking trim and fit. His mind arrived at the conclusion almost immediately; this was not a freak medical event, it had been violent.

During the next heartbeat everything changed. Julius knew this was about *him*; that *he* was being pursued, and that at least one person had already fallen under the shadow of that pursuit. From the day it happened he knew the time would eventually come when he would have to answer for the virus he had unleashed, but he was not prepared for the sudden seizing of his muscles and the nausea that swirled through his gut. He was in trouble, real trouble.

He needed to penetrate the thickening adrenalin fog, analyze his situation rationally, and form a plan that would keep them away from Springhill and at the same time keep himself out of their clutches—whoever *they* were.

He needed facts, but how could he gather facts while in the air? The radio seemed his one and only resource. Because his conversation would be heard by all aircraft monitoring local frequencies, he couldn't contact Departure, Center, or Approach. He needed a flight service station that would not be the normal choice for a pilot on this route. But would there be one within range? Julius pulled the chart out of his flight bag and began looking for a distant, but not too distant, station. Locating one that looked promising, he dialed the frequency into his second radio, and, lowering the volume on the main radio, tried to make contact.

"Flight watch, November Seven Three One Papa Tango, request. Over." He waited.

"Flight watch, November Seven Three One Papa Tango, request. Over."

A distant voice responded, almost overcome by static, "November Seven Three One Papa Tango, your transmission is very weak, go ahead. Over."

"Flight watch, One Papa Tango. Did a Pilatus PC-12 depart Springhill airport, say about 10 minutes or so ago, with a route that matches my flight plan?"

"One Papa Tango, stand by."

It seemed that an eternity passed before the radio hissed.

"One Papa Tango, flight watch. Affirmative. Do you have further instructions?"

"Flight watch, One Papa Tango, thank you and … uh … no further instructions at this time. Over."

Julius swallowed back the panic. This was no coincidence. He was willing to bet that his clearance had been issued by one of *them*. He didn't know much about the Pilatus aircraft other than it was fast and expensive. If he were right, he would find trouble waiting for him at Lone Star. Instinctively he knew what they wanted, but this was the first time he knew, without doubt, he was being actively hunted. It was clear his secret had been discovered, and he could only imagine what destruction would lie in the wake of that discovery.

His vulnerability was clear. The air space controllers that were normally a pilot's lifeline were no longer his allies. He was entirely on his own. If he stayed in the system, anywhere he went would be broadcast over the airwaves, open to the public, but more specifically, to his trackers. He couldn't run and hide; he was in an airplane, a flying prison, on a fixed course, with a filed flight plan. He needed to get his brain functioning.

Ideas arose and were immediately abandoned as too compli-
cated, illogical, or too risky. But the seeds of a plan were sown.

On he flew. Sticking to his original flight plan he proceeded
toward his destination, known by his assailants, a place of almost
certain death. No, it wouldn't be that easy. Until he spit out what he
knew, there would be pain, perhaps to the brink of death, but never
quite over that edge, an edge he would most certainly crave.

He was approaching the Belcher VOR, the first turn of his route.
He needed to formulate at least a rudimentary plan … and soon;
the details would have to wait. The Pilatus would likely fly direct
to Lone Star without using the Victor airways, cutting about fifteen
miles off the route, and of course, they would be travelling at about
twice his air speed. Mentally mapping out the actions of his enemies
after they landed, Julius figured they would have at least a half hour
to prepare. They would secure the Pilatus, make their arrangements
with the FBO for fuel, and wait for him; one in the pilot's lounge
and, if there were two of them, one in the public waiting room, and,
if there were more … perhaps there were more, how could he know?
… But there would be at least two.

Julius watched as the autopilot made a smooth left turn to a
heading of 204 degrees just as he crossed Belcher. Then, out of habit,
he dialed in the Lufkin VOR frequency and set his heading into the
OBS. The CDI centered nicely. In spite of the GPS navigation system
in the Navajo being state-of-the-art, Julius liked to use the legacy
navigation techniques for backup, and, he had to admit, because he
wanted to keep those older navigation skills alive.

Shreveport Departure handed him off to Houston Center.

His plan began to take root. It would require backtracking
almost all the way to Springhill, picking his way between communication towers, risking his life and certainly his license as the
violations piled up. Those bridges would have to be crossed when
he got to them.

As he approached Lone Star, Center made the handoff to
Houston Approach control. Having already entered the frequency
into the second radio, he flipped radios and made contact. After
checking in with Approach, he performed the duties associated with
landing, but did not trim the airplane, leaving it clean and under
power. He was subsequently handed off to the tower and given a
landing clearance for runway one niner. It was now or never.

His finger trembled as it pressed the talk button on the yoke. "Lone Star Tower, One Papa Tango, on approach, cancelling IFR, request clearance for over-fly at 500 feet. Over."

"One Papa Tango, tower. Uh, you were cleared to land. Confirm you are *not*, I repeat, *not*, landing. State your intentions."

"Tower, One Papa Tango. Confirm not landing. Permission to overfly and leave the circuit to the North. Right turn."

"One Papa Tango, tower. Understand you are not landing. Permission to overfly and depart the circuit to the north via runway heading then right turn, wind one six five at ten, gusts twenty-two, contact Houston Departure on one one niner point seven."

"Runway heading, right turn, one nineteen point seven, One Papa Tango".

Brushing at the beads of sweat forming on his forehead, Julius guided his Navajo skillfully at 500 feet over the center line of runway one nine. He looked to his right and saw the Pilatus parked at the FBO. He could visualize its occupants scrambling. Having heard he was not landing they would realize their plan had been thwarted. They may have been lucky in tracking him so far, but if he had anything to do with it, their luck had just run out. He was going where they could not follow.

Usually Julius flew by the book and stayed out of trouble. Today was going to be different. Dialing Houston Departure frequency into his main radio, he listened. He did not check in as instructed. He coaxed the Navajo into a shallow climbing turn to the North East and leveled off at 800 feet. Checking the chart, he verified that Houston controllers didn't own the airspace below 3000 feet, and he hoped he was below their radar as he skimmed over the trees and fields. He scanned his charts looking for high towers or other obstructions at this low altitude. There would be none in the immediate vicinity of the airfield, but as he left the Lone Star airspace he would have to be very careful. Many towers reached well over 800 feet, with some extending their reach to 1000 feet and beyond, just waiting to pluck an unsuspecting pilot from the air.

Departure did not call him. Because he had cancelled his IFR clearance, the handoff from approach had been informal, and departure would expect him to initiate contact. If he didn't pop up on their radar they wouldn't be the wiser. If he did show on their radar, he hoped the controllers would assume he was a training flight or a crop-duster. Although he knew he was now flying on the ragged edge of the law, he had no other options.

At this altitude things looked very different from his previous view from 8000 feet. Trees, fences, and houses flashed beneath him. Cows sprouted heads and tails. Cars crawled along roads. Farms bristled with drive-sheds and tractors. Clotheslines had house-wives stringing laundry. Fields were spotted with pickers, bent over in their labor. Power lines clawed their way through the countryside, devouring trees and brush, leaving neatly trimmed corridors in their wake. Towers had menacing guy wires that reached out at all angles ready to snag a wing or catch a prop.

Julius shook his head to clear his thoughts. His reverie had pushed the panic aside momentarily, leaving a gap wide enough for a plan to emerge. Julius now knew exactly where he was headed. He could only hope no one else did.

Chapter 5

CORA WAS UNCOMFORTABLE AFTER A RESTLESS NIGHT, THE LITTLE movement afforded her having rubbed shoulder blades and vertebrae raw. It would be a day of bedsores and treatment, and she dreaded it all.

The restlessness of Cora's body had become a language to Sheri. A characteristic squirm or lifting of a hip, an attempt to lie more on one side than the other, told her volumes about what was going on under the covers. This morning she knew the signature wriggle indicating the onset of bedsores. Today would be hard work, both physically and emotionally.

Sheri treated the irritation as best she could, but just after lunch Cora became very agitated, communicating to Sheri that the cursory treatment she had been providing would not be enough.

Some months ago Julius, in partnership with a medical equipment company, created a device that would bring relief to ulcerated skin. It consisted of a plastic bed-sized pad, pressurized with circulating warm water. Over this was placed a soft covering, impregnated with a moisturizer. Antibiotic salve was placed in the areas that would contact the sores. The pad was then placed under Cora for several hours. The warmth was incredibly soothing, the resilience of the water relieving the irritation. The moisturizer refreshed and revitalized the skin, while the salve quickly restored the affected areas. If caught soon enough, Cora could be comfortable again in just a few hours, and would be free of the sores for several days unless something unforeseen happened.

Sheri, not looking forward to the effort of this process, knew her reward would come in the expression of relief that would soon be evident on Cora's face.

The task was much easier when Julius was there. Now, without the extra pair of hands, the struggle to position Cora on the device left her muscles stretched and sore. Maybe some sense of this had prompted Sheri's earlier foreboding, but she was almost certain it was something more.

Chapter 6

AS THE MINUTES FLEW BY, JULIUS FELT THE TIGHTNESS IN HIS CHEST subside. Although the radio chatter was constant, he heard nothing that pertained to his flight. He skimmed northeast, then north, avoiding communication towers and skirting small airports, all the while attempting to avoid any contact with the air traffic control system that kept a sharp eye on this area of the globe. He dialed Fort Worth Center into his main radio and Long View Approach into his standby. Trying to stay well west of East Texas Regional, he hoped not to alert the tower. Julius was expected checked in, but he did not.

The radio started barking. "Long View Approach calling aircraft 12 miles Northwest of East Texas Regional. Over." Julius recalled hearing this once before, just a few minutes ago in fact, but it had been lost in the mist of his thoughts. A quick glance at the GPS display confirmed he had wandered into a sector monitored by the Long View approach radar. He suddenly felt a chill. The radio hissed again. "Long View Approach calling aircraft 14 miles northwest of East Texas, please respond. Over." Julius knew he had to make a decision that would define how the remainder of this flight would go, and likely the remainder of his flying career as well. His training urged him to respond; one does not just ignore a call from air traffic control. His survival necessitated this break with protocol, but he was not prepared for the immediate sense of alienation that overcame him.

Julius remained silent.

The radio hissed insistently, as if reacting to his silence. "Fort Worth Center calling aircraft 21 miles north of East Texas. Over."

Julius moved his left index finger from its usual position hovering over the push-to-talk switch on the yolk, preventing his deep-rooted training from keying the microphone involuntarily.

Having determined to ignore any calls from air traffic control, Julius clung to his silent resolve, the smooth hum of the engines his only remaining companion.

With instinct guiding the Navajo, Julius allowed his mind to concentrate on landing, and what he would do later. After making the decision not to land at Lone Star, he quickly determined a new destination. Airplanes are notorious for not staying in the air forever—it wasn't like a car that could be parked by the side of the road under a tree and left there for days or weeks. He had to get his bird on the ground, somewhere that would be out of the way, unobserved and unobservable. He had chosen the airstrip at the old fishing haunt, Fish-N-Fly. It was barely long enough, and the runway was like a tunnel through the trees, at least at the northwest end. But it would have to do. In his mind he rewound an image of the lodge and its surrounding area. He had flown over, but never into, the lodge, but had looked down the runway once when he was there fishing. A clearer image of the runway began to form in his mind, and if he recalled correctly, the runway was oil-sprayed dirt, polka-dotted with clumps of grass. And that was almost 10 years ago. Julius doubted the runway would have been maintained much since then, causing him to think twice about putting his aircraft, not to mention his skills, through the ordeal of landing on a narrow strip among the trees with an uncertain surface. Julius chuckled to himself dryly as the thought struck him that the lodge was located in an area known as Uncertain, Texas. Perhaps this was an omen that he should not glibly ignore. The value of his first choice was waning quickly; clearly he had better look for something more suitable.

Pulling out the charts again, Julius scanned the area around Uncertain for an alternative landing site. His eyes fell on Cyprus River, just a bit west of Fish-N-Fly. There was no tower, and it was a public use airport, so it would likely be better maintained, and, more importantly, it was close to the place where he planned to disappear. The chart indicated that it had a 3200 foot runway, which would make for a tricky landing, but if guided skillfully, his bird could land and stop safely in that distance. If he did overrun, at least he would not be facing a bunch of well-rooted trees, whose outstretched limbs were just waiting to remove his wings … without the assistance of a mechanic or his tools, he thought … Or had he misjudged? Perhaps he should not make that assumption so casually. He had flown over Cyprus River several times but never really took note of its details. He recalled there were several buildings south east of the runway and that it was fairly open at both ends. A road ran just south of the field. He also recalled that the airport itself was tucked away in the middle of nowhere, far enough out of Jefferson, itself not much more than a tourist town—no fishing lodges, no civilization—just what he was looking for. Although he doubted he could hide the Navajo in a hangar, he was quite sure it could sit there a long time unnoticed by anyone of significance. After spending a few minutes consulting the charts, his mind was made up.

Immediately severing the escalating requests from Fort Worth Center, Julius changed the frequency on his primary radio to 122.9, the common air traffic frequency for Cyprus River. Surprised at the level of activity for such a small field, he listened carefully to the traffic in the circuit as he painted a mental image of where each airplane was positioned in the airspace above the runway. It wasn't long before he was able to make out each aircraft, wings glinting in the sunshine, and he planned his actions accordingly. There were three aircraft in the circuit; one landing and two doing touch-and-goes, most likely students practicing. Mentally timing their takeoffs and landings, he picked a spot that would allow him to give the airport a wide berth to the northwest, and then land straight in on runway two three without flying the normal rectangular pattern required when approaching a small, uncontrolled airport. Appropriately, his training sounded warning bells so Julius put his senses on high alert, worming his way into the airspace, being careful not to interfere with the current traffic. He did not make the required call to local traffic, maintaining complete radio silence, an amateur move rife with danger.

He set his attitude and airspeed for an immediate approach, set his flaps, dropped his wheels, and configured the airplane for landing. His approach was flawless and his landing was a 'squeaker', wheels gently striking the white numbers painted on the tarmac.

Braking hard, he brought the Navajo to a stop just short of the end of the runway, then taxied to the parking area on the asphalt pad north of the apron. He shut down and secured the airplane. He walked into the office fully expecting to be met by an angry airport manager, or a fellow pilot cursing him for approaching and landing without any radio contact and without flying the usual pattern.

He wasn't disappointed.

The airport manager met him at the door. "What in the world were you thinking, man? This is *my* airport and we follow the rules here. Your actions put every one of the pilots sharing this airspace in danger. Radio or no radio, you could at least have joined the circuit properly. You look like you should know better!" He paused to ensure his words sunk in.

"I'm assuming you're the flight that was supposed to land in Lone Star Exec, but overflew instead?"

"Uh … yes?" Julius managed sheepishly and somewhat perplexed. "How … how do you know the details of a flight a hundred miles away?"

"Everyone has been worried about you. ATC was tracking you on radar, so we knew you were still in the air, but there was no response when the controllers tried to contact you. When they saw you approaching Cyprus, they called me on the phone and asked me to keep an eye on your landing … just in case you were in trouble, I mean."

Feeling the heat climb his neck and rest on the tips of his ears, Julius stuttered, "Th … thank you for your concern. I really appreciate it … and I'm sorry for the botched approach. It's good to know the system is watching out for us air jockeys," immediately regretting his choice of metaphors. "I was having some issues and wanted to get away from the heavy iron while I sorted it out. All I can do is apologize for any inconvenience I caused. Do I need to make any official calls?" The dread of the last couple of hours lingered at the fringes of his mind, but he was free for the moment, knowing it was a reprieve of only a few days at most. He had had nightmares in which this day was foreshadowed. Now that he had slipped through the net cast by the Pilatus crew, he needed time to think about his next move. How would he protect his family—and friends, for that matter—against this threat that lingered in the shadows? How would he escape the consequences of the secret he carried with him?

"No, I think things are OK I guess. Just a suggestion … perhaps you should carry a hand-held radio for occasions like this, just so you don't go completely nordo," the manager broke into Julius' thoughts. "I'll call ATC and let them know you've arrived safely."

Julius allowed a smile to slowly drift across his features. Although he hadn't specifically said he was flying without a radio, the manager had made the assumption, and that suited him just fine. As he turned to leave the building he could hear the manager's fragmented conversation with ATC. "Cyprus … manager … Tango … safe … had a chat … Over."

Julius' hand froze on the handle of the door leading to the apron. He could taste bile at the back of his throat, his bowels loosening, and for a moment he couldn't remember what he was doing or what he needed to do next. Convention dictated the manager phone ATC, but he had *radioed* instead. The whole aviation world, and more specifically, the guys in the Pilatus, now knew exactly where he was. Suppressing the fear, he tried to gather his thoughts.

Swinging his head around, his plan shattered, he was uncertain of his next move, convinced he needed to get away from the airport as quickly as possible. Spinning on his heels he walked quickly to the manager's office, willing his knees to hold him up. In a raspy voice, barely in control of his breathing, he managed, "Excuse me … uh … I don't mean to be any more trouble, but do you have a courtesy car I can borrow for …" He took a gulp of air. "… for an hour or so?"

"Yup, we have two available," the manager said in a slightly more conciliatory tone. "We have an old Jeep Cherokee that's on its last legs and a relatively new Corolla. Neither is busy, so I guess you have your choice."

With the sleeve of his shirt he scrubbed at the moisture gathering on his forehead while he tried to process this information. Finally he responded, not wanting to tip his hand, "I've been enough of a klutz for one day. How about I take the old beater just in case I'm on a roll." He turned to leave, then swung back to face the manager. "Oh, by the way, do you happen to have a local area road map? Not sure my memory will do the trick; it's been a while." His voice sounded to him like it was coming from across the room.

The airport manager located a crumpled map from under the counter and, pulling the keys from their hook on the board behind the desk, tossed them to Julius. "You might need these, too. Just leave the map in the Jeep when you return it.

"Do you want anything done with the Navajo while you're away?" the manager called after him, hesitation in his voice.

"Yes, of course, I don't know what I was thinking," Julius chanted, half turning. "Top off both tanks please, 100 low lead, and tie it down, if you don't mind. It's possible I'll be here overnight."

"Will do," the airport manager assured him. "Hope you get things sorted out."

"Me too," Julius murmured as he reached the door.

Not wanting to appear ungrateful, but desperate to be on his way, he left the building and walked quickly to his airplane. He threw open the cargo door, retrieved his emergency kit, dumped the contents into a heap onto the cargo bay floor, and sifted through the articles, setting aside those he felt he would need. He stuffed the resulting items quickly into the emergency bag, closed the zipper, and slung it over his shoulder. He slammed the cargo door, locked it then briskly walked around the building to the parking lot where he found the Jeep. Just as the manager said, it was an old beater, but it looked like it had a few miles left in it. Besides, it was a four-wheel drive, and where Julius was headed that may well turn out to be an asset.

Chapter 7

TODAY WAS BATH DAY. CORA LOOKED FORWARD TO HER BATHS FOR many reasons, other than the obvious. She had 3 baths scheduled per week; Sunday, Tuesday and either Thursday or Friday. The regularity helped her pace the week, with something pleasant to look forward to every few days. Oddly, the mystery of whether it would be Thursday or Friday, provided her with a bit of excitement as the week drew to a close.

Bath day meant getting out of bed and a change of position. It wasn't always easy or painless to do, but to Cora, any effort or discomfort paled in comparison to the privilege of being able to stand upright, walk about, and enjoy different surroundings. She couldn't do these things alone of course; she had to have help getting her feet on the floor and it required a strong arm to keep her upright and steady. Having grown accustomed to the humiliation many months ago, she now savored these moments.

As her disease progressed, it became difficult for her to sit in the bathtub. The unforgiving ceramic pressed on her bones, and compressed her flesh in total mockery. They tried showers for a while, but her increasing weakness soon put a stop to that. Julius had found a manufacturer of custom sporting goods who could build a special air mattress for her. The bottom layer of the mattress was about an inch thick, filled with compressed air. It provided a buffer between Cora and the tub. The top layer was a series of rounded pyramids made of foam rubber, inflated with low pressure air. These soft but firm bumps suspended Cora as if on a cloud. Each pyramid could be pinched as necessary, to release the air pressure inside it, allowing gaps to be created to match any areas of Cora's body that were inflamed or raw on any particular day. The entire mattress could be cleaned easily, deflated, and stored in a small drawer. Cora had been using it for the past year or so, and it was very much responsible for the extra pleasure she received from her bath.

But today she would *not* be having her regular bath. The numerous sores she had rubbed raw last night would make her uncomfortable in the water and leave her susceptible to infection. Perhaps tomorrow. Disappointment showed on her face, but she had learned the hard way that life didn't always go according to her plan.

Cora should have been bitter. The talents and gifts she loved to share with others had been stolen from her by a disease she didn't want and hadn't asked for. Without warning, out of nowhere, she had been incapacitated, her energy levels diminished, her ability to function stripped from her without her permission; surely a form of violence like no other.

Her discomfort today, compounded by the absence of Julius, began to gnaw at the edges of her resolve. In her head she knew he had to spend some time away from home in order to provide for the family, but in her heart she just wanted him close. Not in a selfish way, but his presence allowed her the luxury of letting go, of distancing herself from issues that arose over the course of a regular day, whether with her health, or the house, or the family in general. The tiniest thing seemed to exhaust her. Pure and simple, she needed him around; she relied on him for her next breath, or so it seemed. Although such dependence was not in her nature, she had come to terms with it … or at least so she thought.

Chapter 8

JULIUS HAD NOT BEEN BACK FOR MANY YEARS. HE HOPED THE roads hadn't changed dramatically.

He didn't know precisely how this was going to play out, but he did know his Pilatus 'friends' had his location. And they would be on their way as fast as they could alter their course. They would not likely risk landing on the short runway at Cypress River, so Harrison County would be their next logical choice. After renting a car, what would they do exactly? They would have no idea where he would head from Cypress River, so what would be their next tactic? Whatever it was, he wasn't going to take any chances. This time *he* had the advantage of a half hour head start; he could use every minute of it.

Pulling onto Route 134, Julius headed for the lake. He would be taking a risk skirting the boundary of the Caddo Lake State Park, but what choice did he have? He needed to drop off the Jeep somewhere inconspicuous and then head into the swamp. Although this territory was familiar to him, he sincerely hoped it was foreign to his pursuers. Having been raised here, Julius and his childhood friends often played in the bayou: hide and seek, games of war, cops and robbers, and anything else kids could imagine. They learned the unobstructed paths, the colors, the smells, the insects, the birds, the snakes. They knew a million good hiding places. They knew the itch of bug bites, the bruising of leeches, and the sting of nettles. They also knew, for the most part, how to avoid them.

When Julius was nine or ten, a neighbor died in a tragic farm accident. Marty, who belonged to the ever-together band of *marauding* pre-teen boys of whom Julius was second in command, was not the same after the death of his father. While being shown how to operate the farm tractor, Marty's foot had slipped off the clutch, crushing his father beneath the rear wheel, which, just moments before, had casually supported his Dad's right elbow. Within a few months the remaining family decided to move to the city, leaving behind the farm with its painful memories. The economy was poor, the farms were poor, and the homestead didn't sell for many years. It wasn't until Julius went off to college that he heard the land had been sold to a farming conglomerate. The farmhouse had not been lived in since the family departed, and Julius had not heard from Marty since.

Navigating by memory, looking for landmarks which had survived the twenty-five or more years since Julius had been in the area, he barreled down the poorly maintained county roads, kicking up a rooster tail of dust. The jeep sped by the old stone schoolhouse on Swanson Landing Road. Suddenly remembering that the turn he wanted was just past the schoolhouse fence, he slammed on the brakes, fighting to keep the Jeep between the ditches. Backing up, he choked as he re-entered his own dust cloud. Approaching the schoolhouse again, this time in reverse and very slowly, he squinted through the dusty murk, looking along the road's edge for the culvert that would mark the entrance to the old farm driveway. The brush had grown up over the years, and the average person would never have known the lane led anywhere.

Turning the wheel as he backed across the road, Julius put the Jeep into four wheel drive and pressed slowly through the brush. The nettles noisily scraped along the Jeep's doors, and as the tires dug into the red soil, it inched forward through the growth. He knew he would leave tell-tale tire marks but he hoped the brush would spring back sufficiently to cover his tracks.

Once past the initial undergrowth, the Jeep moved smoothly along the lane, the long grass and the odd bush slapping at the undercarriage. The old farm house was a few hundred yards off the road, the wood gray with age, the roof sagging as if it were burdened with the full weight of the tragedy it had witnessed. It occurred to Julius it wouldn't be long until the buildings were nothing but a pile of rubble, erasing forever the stories of love and laughter and heart-break that had been engraved on the soul of these old structures.

The drive shed stood on his immediate left and he suddenly had what seemed at the moment to be a brilliant idea. Swinging wide, he pulled the Jeep close to the old drive shed doors. The grass was deep, and he wanted to leave distinct tire marks that appeared to lead into the drive shed. If anyone did discover the lane, they would be distracted, adding a small margin to his head start. The barn, standing 50 feet or so beyond the drive shed, had all but collapsed. Julius eased the Cherokee through what used to be the barnyard. Its stone slabs would give nothing away, its periphery overgrown with weeds and thick with bushes thriving in the manure-rich soil. Several trees had taken root, providing great cover. Julius forced the Jeep into this thicket hoping it would not be seen, but if seen, then considered part of the general dereliction. He slid from behind the driver's seat and attempted to erase any sign of his entry into the thicket. It was the best he could do. On a day when all allies seemed to have abandoned him, he hoped this old farm would remain faithful.

Taking just his emergency bag, Julius struck out across the field toward the tree line that lay to the west of the farm. His mind raced back to his childhood when he crossed this field almost daily during many hot Texan summers. Envisioning the arrow-straight trails the boys had made through the short grass, crisscrossing the meandering paths made by the cows and sheep, he couldn't help but wonder why animals never seemed to walk in straight lines. He could almost feel the prickle of the sun's rays on his bare shoulders as he ran carefree through these fields, shirt cast aside somewhere in the vegetation, yelling with delight to his friends in their most current adventure. Julius was a grown man now, with a family and responsibilities, and a terrible secret that was, at this moment, exacting payment for its keeping.

He reached the tree line and paused to look at the Bayou, basking in the scene before him, comparing it to what he remembered, and picked the hiding spot that would provide him with the best possibility of survival. The field was dry, and only a professional tracker would be able to pick out the miniscule alterations left by Julius' footsteps. But the Bayou was different. The soft ground would provide instant witness to his passing, something he could not afford.

As quickly as he could, he picked branches from the shrubs and trees, assembling them into two mounds. He made two flat, teardrop shaped piles about three feet wide by about six feet long, dug some string out of his emergency bag, and began lashing the twigs together. Inspecting his workmanship, he nodded in satisfaction. He gathered dried grass, leaves and small twigs, piling them into the large oval of each teardrop. At last he was ready.

As a kid he had learned this trick; it quickly became the winning card in many of his childhood games. He took off his shoes and socks, placing them in the emergency bag, then secured the pointed end of the teardrops to his ankles so each foot dragged one of the strange contraptions. After a few moments, Julius headed into the swamp. He carefully chose where he placed each foot, and after a few steps, looked back to see if he had left a trail. What he saw impressed even him. Not only were there no footprints, but his track was littered with a covering of leaves and twigs, indistinguishable from the forest floor around it. He knew he couldn't go far, so he chose his path carefully.

Suddenly he viewed the spot he was looking for. It was about a hundred feet from where he stood. For thousands of years the slow moving river had nibbled away the soil leaving a small embankment of just a few inches in height. The water's surface was smooth, but the Spanish moss hanging from the trees, and the dead wood and lilies in the water, created a heavily mottled pallet of colors; the perfect camouflage—or so he hoped.

Stripping off his clothes, Julius placed them into the emergency bag. He would have to do this naked if he were to survive. And if he didn't, he wouldn't be too concerned whether he was naked or not. He tossed the ball of string he had used earlier over a tree limb well above his head, attached it to the emergency bag, and pulled it tight against the branch. The military camouflage exterior made it disappear amid the lichen and moss hanging from the adjacent limbs. Maneuvering the string around the tree trunk, he tied it off as far above his head as he could reach. The trees were not climbable, so he was counting on *them* looking down, not up, for clues as to his whereabouts.

Julius walked the remaining distance to the edge of the Bayou. Removing the tear-drop draggers from his ankles one at a time, he stepped into the water, immediately sinking to his knees in the silt and mud of the swamp bottom. He reached for the draggers, flinging each in turn into the swamp where they floated lazily on the surface; just another pile of organic debris as natural-looking as all the others. He probed with his right foot and found the deep pool his memory assured him was just half a step away. Crouching so his shoulders were barely covered by the tepid water, he was ready to slide into the pool at the slightest sign of danger.

And he waited.

Chapter 9

TODAY THERE WOULD BE SOME EXERCISE AT LEAST, AND A CHANGE of surroundings. Lifting her off the medicated mattress, Sheri placed Cora's feet on the floor. After reluctantly accepting help donning her dressing gown, she slumped in the chair residing beside the bed. The water-filled pad needed to be cleaned, drained, and put away. Cora was happy to sit awhile, even though she fidgeted, trying to find a position where her spine was supported, and her failing muscles would be able to relax.

The chores done, Sheri took Cora by the hand, helping her stand up. Simply taking a step required conscious effort, but Cora executed each with as much grace and elegance as she could muster. It was a demonstration of her former life to both her care giver and, she often thought, to herself.

Her moment of freedom over much too soon, Cora was put gently back to bed.

She had memorized the dining room. It was her constant companion and, although she had lived in the house for 20 some-odd years, she greeted each room in the house as if it were a distant friend. She didn't go upstairs anymore; not for the last 2 years or so. At first she could climb the stairs, but the effort became increasingly taxing, and eventually was more than she could muster. So a motorized hospital bed was purchased and the dining room rearranged to accommodate the bed yet keep the old family dining room table.

That way Cora could be present when the family met for meals, an event which was becoming less frequent as the children spread their wings. She and Julius had considered many times trading in the old dining room table, and, from time to time, they *would* look for replacements, but on each occasion, it was decided too much history was inscribed on the finish of the worn walnut to give it up. Even the bear claw legs held memories, with their corners rounded, grooved by the baby teeth of puppies come and gone.

The matching hutch had been emptied and sold to make room for the bed. Cora's fine china dishes and her collection of Royal Doulton figurines along with the two china Spaniels, her favorites, had been carefully wrapped and boxed, and now lived in the attic far from her admiring gaze. But it was worth the loss to be able to participate in the rituals of her family; this chapter of her life being rife with sacrifice, it was one of the least.

On the wall, forsaken by the hutch, a grouping of family pictures had been arranged so Cora could remain in touch with her former life. She often found herself staring at them, each picture flooding her with deep memories, inundating her with emotion; of faces, conversations, and events, some of which defined the very person she had become. Not her physical self of course, but her inner self; the person she knew herself to be; the person who was confined and constrained, yes, even taunted, by her physical self that grew weaker daily and threatened to abandon her entirely.

The window at the end of the room, at the foot of Cora's bed, looked out onto the street. With the head of her bed slightly raised, she could see past the window sill with its many layers of paint and the pot of begonias perched on the left. Sheri kept the heavy curtains open to their fullest when Cora was awake. The bit of front yard she could see, together with the sidewalk and road beyond, were places where Cora went in her darkest hours. In her mind she wrestled with her six year old son, Eddie, and sat at tea with her four year old daughter, Brittany and, of course, Brittany's friends, mostly stuffed, fuzzy, and very quiet, their button noses turned toward the day's delicacy. She rambled down the street to neighbors current and gone. She pushed Brittany's tricycle along the sidewalk, the image smoothly morphing into a fast forward to Eddie's progress in his love of baseball. The window became a stage on which played out the drama of the bandaging of Eddie's first skinned knee, and of herself, holding a sobbing young woman whose heart had been broken by her first true love. As favorite and some not-so-favorite scenes of her life emerged from the wings, she always had an over-arching sense of Julius looking out of an upstairs window, keeping watch, never intruding, but always ready to help when needed.

What would *he* do when *she* was gone? What would *she* do if anything should happen to *him*?

Chapter 10

IDLY LEANING ON THE LEFT FENDER OF THE TOW TRACTOR, smoking his third cigarette in a row, Vladimir Rusnak watched the traffic come and go on runway one nine, his eyes flitting momentarily to the no-smoking sign mounted conspicuously on the side of the building. He knew the Navajo would be on its approach soon. Fifteen minutes earlier he had set the Pilatus on the tarmac and taxied to the FBO. One of his two passengers, Yakov Travkin, had taken his post just inside the FBO main lobby. He could be seen sitting in a lounge chair facing the reception desk, looking over the top of the local sports section. A keen observer would have noticed he never turned the page. His ears were tuned to the radio chatter and to the friendly banter of the office personnel as they dispatched fuel trucks, ordered refreshments for departing jets, and organized the many activities surrounding incoming and outgoing flights, both business and pleasure. The other passenger, Erik Mukhov, was on the phone giving instructions to the agency whose car they would hire for the next phase of their mission.

Vladimir had been in the special operations division of the KGB when the glasnost liberalization of Soviet society provoked KGB Chairman Vladimir Kryochkov to lead the rebellion that attempted to depose President Mikhail Gorbachev. The coup failed, and the KGB was buried. Those close to Kryochkov were summarily dismissed; Rusnak, Travkin and Mukhov among them. Vladimir took this failure personally and struck out in anger to find some other way to use his skills. Even if it had been offered, he would not have joined the FSB, the new internal state security service, or the SVR, the new foreign intelligence service. *They* were 'modern' warriors, without, in his opinion, the keen survival skills necessary for international espionage, and they did not have the stomach for the brutality that was essential to dominating the world of intelligence. Wimps, in his opinion, all of them, and he would have no part of it.

Vladimir thought he would try being a capitalist, and struck out on his own. He offered his expertise to various operations, overt and covert, clandestine and not. For the past fifteen years he had served oil barons, kings, potentates, and businesses with names well known in the households of America and Europe. He was familiar with killing and plundering for personal gain. His current mission was a serious affair, and, although his body language said otherwise, he was on high alert. The Pilatus was a good investment. It could whisk him to anywhere in the world and he could get in and out of relatively small airports, allowing him to carry out his business without being in the wider public eye.

Yakov rapped on the FBO window causing Vladimir to snap his head around. Yakov indicated with his hands that their target was on final approach. Straining his eyes to the north, Vladimir attempted to catch a glimpse of the Navajo's whereabouts, and, once found, he would not let it out of his sight. Julius would be *his* within a few minutes. His mouth curved slightly in a perverse smile, his heart skipping a beat as he thought of making the kill. He still took pleasure in completing a difficult mission, particularly if it ended the way this one would. The miserable little man in the Navajo had eluded him for the past three weeks. Vladimir put it down to bad luck, since he was certain Julius did not know they were in pursuit, his routine not having changed. He came and went from home as usual, and his business trips were frequent and casual. Vladimir almost had Julius in his clutches several times, but someone, or something, had always been in the way, making it impossible for him to snatch Julius without exposing himself. But today would be different. Julius was flying right into his hands. He would have to park the Navajo, exit the plane and come to the FBO; there were no other options. Once inside the FBO, Julius would be hustled to the waiting car, and Vladimir would have won. After that would come the interrogation, something Vladimir was very good at, as were Yakov and Erik, both equally skilled in extracting information from the most hardened counter-intelligence operatives—Julius would be a snap.

He watched the Navajo descend along the approach path. He couldn't be certain, but it appeared the Navajo's flaps were still in their cruise position … and, squinting his eyes, his landing gear was up. "Maybe Julius is having a bad day," thought Vladimir. "He certainly *will* once he lands and I get my hands on him."

His lips formed the words, "Barlow, wheels down, wheels down, it's time for wheels down, Barlow. Now … Now!" If he had a wheels-up landing the crash trucks would steal this opportunity as well, and that would simply be the last straw.

The Navajo stopped descending, its wheels remained stowed. It leveled out, appearing to start a missed approach. Yakov then came running through the main door of the FBO, and, tripping over the door frame, he hollered, "He cancelled approach and is doing fly-over. Told tower he was heading north. He knows we are here!"

Vladimir slammed his open hand into the fender of the luggage tractor, causing it to resonate, and drawing unwanted attention from the crews servicing the aircraft on the apron. His usual nerves of steel were on edge. Julius had him rattled, and he didn't like it one little bit. Ducking inside the FBO, he quickly gathered Yakov and Erik, and headed for the pilot's lounge. A young student pilot was at the weather computer, and Vladimir commanded "Please leave. We need room for few minutes." The student turned with a defiant look on his face, a look that quickly turned to panic. Wadding his books and papers together, he virtually ran out of the room, staring at the floor as he went. Vladimir closed the door.

They could now speak freely in Russian. "He knows we are after him. This is going to make our job much more difficult," spat Vladimir. He glared at Yakov and Erik, causing them to flinch and instinctively back away. "That miserable little fool has outsmarted us for the moment. But he will be ours soon! I promise you!" And a Rusnak promise could, with very few exceptions, be relied on as fact.

"Erik," barked Vladimir, "call the car and cancel. Yakov, find someone out there and get the plane ready to take off. Do what you need to except draw your weapon or your Bowie. We need to be in the air in ten minutes or less."

Vladimir went to the front desk, and in his best English, employing his best manners, said, "Excuse me, Miss. We have emergency and have to be in air in next ten minutes. Would please file flight plan for me right away? I am needed at airplane to get ready for takeoff." He placed a crumpled flight plan form on the counter top, scribbled out the previous destination airport, and replaced it with Spring Hill, assuming Julius would head toward home. Once in the air Vladimir could monitor the radio traffic, and make any necessary changes on the fly.

It was unusual, but not unheard of, to ask the desk to make flight arrangements. "Yes sir. Certainly. I hope everything is OK?" said the clerk as she took the flight plan from Vladimir, looking at him quizzically. The vicious determination etched on his face stopped her curiosity cold. He turned on his heel and strode to the aircraft, trying to conceal his growing unhappiness.

Vladimir did a quick walk around the aircraft looking for anything out of place, satisfying himself it was airworthy. Settling into the pilot's seat, he soon heard the passenger door close, and the voices of Erik and Yakov arguing. With everyone aboard, Vladimir set his radios, rushed through the checklist, and radioed for taxi clearance. He would take the runway and get his final clearance once airborne. He used only his aircraft call sign and didn't include his aircraft type. If the controller asked for it, he would be obliged to give it up, but he wanted to be careful what he said over the radio in case he alerted Julius to their pursuit. He was in luck this time. The controller remembered his arrival and didn't ask any further questions. Since Vladimir had called the tower using his full registration number without his aircraft type, the controller replied using the same identification.

They were airborne in thirteen minutes. The Pilatus executed a climbing right turn, and headed northeast toward Spring Hill. All three of the occupants had their eyes peeled watching for the Navajo. It was not in sight. Little did they know Julius had headed due north in an effort to stay well west of the traffic around West Texas Regional. Their paths were diverging.

Vladimir became more irritable as the miles passed under the airplane. He should have been able to pick out the Navajo by now, but it had simply vanished. He listened intently to the appropriate radio frequencies while Erik listened to the traffic frequencies of the airports gliding under their belly. Julius was not communicating. They were blind, and he was escaping.

The Pilatus was passing 20 miles northeast of Shreveport when Erik exclaimed in Russian, "I think we have him!"

Vladimir snapped, "What do you mean, 'I think'? Do you have him or not?"

Erik shot back, "I just caught the end of a transmission made by Cypress River. It said the aircraft that went silent had landed at Cypress. I'm sure the call sign he used was the Navajo's. I didn't catch it all but it has to be Barlow."

His mood brightening, Vladimir ordered Yakov to look up the Cypress River airport to see if the runway was long enough for them to land. After a brief rustling of pages, Yakov shouted into the headset microphone to be certain Vladimir heard him over the whine of the engine, "In an emergency, yes, but I wouldn't chance it."

Vladimir shouted back, "This *is* an emergency! Can we get in or not?"

Yakov swallowed hard as he said, "No, we can't risk it."

"Then find me another airport."

Yakov scanned the chart rapidly and said, "Then it has to be Harrison County. Runway length 5000."

Vladimir punched Harrison County into the navigation GPS, and the autopilot began its turn. Vladimir called Shreveport indicating his intentions. It took some sweet-talking, but Vladimir was good at that when the need arose.

A sense of excitement filled the Pilatus as the three assassins contended for the best idea on where Julius was going. Having spent considerable time researching Julius, Vladimir knew where he grew up, where he went to school, where he had worked, and had developed a good picture of his current business interests. Of his home life, of course, Vladimir knew much more than he should.

"If he landed at Cypress then he's headed back to where he grew up," said Vladimir. "That means he's going to head into the Caddo Lake bayous and try to disappear."

Yakov agreed, "Once he hits the bayous we might as well go home. I'm looking at Caddo Lake on the map, and it has a hundred twists and turns and even more bays and bayous and swamps. It will be like looking for a capitalist in the Kremlin."

The Pilatus responded with a momentary drop in altitude as Vladimir struck the yoke with the heel of his hand. "Don't be so stupid. He can't stay in the swamps forever. No matter how well he knows them he can't *survive* in them. And he has his sick wife to think about. He won't leave her to fend for herself. He has to emerge sometime."

Knowing from experience when to keep his nose clean, Erik had been maintaining silence while Vladimir and Yakov sparred. He interjected hesitantly, certain his idea was simply common sense, "The thought just occurred to me that Julius had to get to the lake somehow, probably by car. Let's drive around Julius' old homestead and search the immediate area. He's most likely going for familiar turf."

Vladimir thought about this and said, "That's the first intelligent thing I've heard from you two all day. Erik, get on the cell phone and order us a car. Take whatever you can get. Yakov, as soon as we land find someone with a detailed map of the area. I want roads, parks, picnic areas; everything." Each in turn mumbled their assent. The three fell into silence as they searched for ways of heading Julius off; for where he would most likely go; for what steps he would take to evade them.

Preparing to land at Harrison, Vladimir made the necessary radio calls, received permission to land, and executed a perfect landing on the runway. He braked hard, nearly missing the turn onto the second taxiway. The Pilatus arrived at the fuel farm where Vladimir stopped and secured the aircraft. The three almost stepped on each other as they hurried to leave the plane. Erik stumbled down the steps with his cell phone to his ear. A moment later he said loudly to no one in particular, "We have a Lincoln Mark Five ready as soon as we get to the desk." Vladimir's lips twitched into what could pass as a brief smile. He liked the American luxury cars that were built for speed and handling—a rare combination for the common man in Russia. He would put this car through its paces if the opportunity presented itself.

Yakov almost ran to the FBO in search of a map. As he approached the main entrance he checked himself, slowed his pace and his breathing, cleared his throat several times, and entered with a modicum of dignity. The young man at the reception desk looked at him under raised eyebrows, but was polite when he asked if he could be of assistance. Putting his English to the test, Yakov said, "Good afternoon. Am looking for detailed road map. And please, there are parks or public areas on this side of Caddo Lake?" The desk clerk pulled out a pad from a shelf under the counter, showing Yakov a stylized map of the local area with roads, points of interest, and the public areas marked in bright green. Yakov said politely, "You have regular road map also?" Turning to the wall behind the reception area, the clerk searched among the maps in the rack and, pulling one out, returned to the desk. Handing it to Yakov, he said, "This should get you anywhere in the county. If it isn't suitable, let me know and I'll look for something else."

Yakov took the two maps, nodded his thanks, and said, "We ordered car few minutes past."

Pointing to the rental kiosk across the room, the desk clerk said, "They will look after you right over there. I hope you have a good stay here in the Harrison area." Yakov was already half way across the room.

With the Pilatus secured and the keys in hand, the trio strode to the rental lot and located their car. It was a beauty. With sleek lines and wide tires, it looked like it would be more than suitable. Examining the sparkle in the maroon paint, Vladimir thought he could begin to like America.

"Yakov," he bellowed, "this was your idea, so tell us where to go." Yakov scanned the maps and guided them out of the airport onto Warren Road. They navigated to highway 43, driving north toward the irregular green shape on the map representing a large public area on the south side of Caddo Lake, just to the west of where Julius was raised. Once on the highway Vladimir slowly pressed the accelerator, enjoying the increasing speed with no commensurate increase in road or wind noise—the passenger compartment as quiet as a library. Erik was watching the digital speedometer from the back seat, and said somewhat carefully, "Slow down a little. At this speed you will attract the local police and I don't think we really want to get pulled over for speeding." Vladimir's face took on a dangerous look, its reflection in the rear view mirror putting Erik on notice. But he saw the sense in Erik's comment, and let his right foot relax.

The Lincoln approached the Caddo Lake State Park, a massive area of roads, camp spots, parking lots, paths, green space, and bayous. People from all walks of life were enjoying the park, out with their dogs, jogging for exercise, erecting tents, or biking in groups. Little did they suspect the mission of the three in the Lincoln. Vladimir pulled over onto a grassy edge and barked at Yakov, "This is a big place. Where do we go from here?"

Replying with some confidence, Yakov said, "Let's head toward the fishing piers. We want to go to the park's eastern-most edge to see what's over there. If we separate and walk along the water maybe we'll get lucky."

Vladimir wasn't so fond of 'luck', but he didn't have a better idea so he pulled back onto the park road and headed north. The road snaked back and forth with parking lots and camp spots frequently spinning off from the main road. Yakov was attempting to follow their progress on the stylized map he had obtained from the FBO, flipping it upside down and back again. Eventually he said, "The next parking lot you see, take it. We're almost at the boundary of the park, and the water should be just beyond that stand of trees to our left." Squinting through the dense foliage of the Cyprus trees they could just barely make out the glint of sun on water.

Vladimir parked the car, and the three assassins huddled as they decided how they would split up and when they would regroup. The sun was getting low, the day almost spent, and their mood was deteriorating as the probability of finding Julius plummeted.

Cautiously Erik said, "This looks like too much to cover with just the three of us. Maybe we should head to the east of the park where Julius grew up. There can't be too many roads in that area, and it's very rural so we may find some clues."

Vladimir didn't react violently, as Erik thought he might, given his current mood. Instead he commanded Yakov, "Exactly what's east of the park on your map? Can we cover the roads faster than walking this entire park on foot?"

"There are half a dozen small county roads that crisscross the area. It wouldn't take much time to cover them all."

Vladimir motioned for them to get back into the car. He started it and hastily pulled away, navigating the parking lots and adjoining roadways just a bit too quickly. Several people stopped what they were doing and glared, as if the three ex-KGB agents would somehow care what they thought.

The Lincoln left the park via the Route 134 exit, turned onto the 449 cut-off, almost running over the two dogs napping near the center line, and then left onto the continuation of 134. With great effort Vladimir governed his speed, struggling against his sense of urgency and frustration at Julius eluding him once again.

As they headed east, Yakov exclaimed, "Julius was born in Texas, right?"

Erik responded, "Yes, the research indicated as much. So what?"

"Well, we're in luck then. The Texas-Louisiana border is just a couple of miles east of us, so we have a lot less ground to cover than we thought. If we drive the roads between the park and the border we'll have covered the territory where he grew up."

Vladimir snickered as he began scanning the edges of the road, looking for something; he just didn't know what.

Turning a sharp left onto Route 9, they headed north toward the water, all three occupants of the Lincoln intent on the foliage and farms along the road. They could see the bayou glinting through the trees ahead when the sign for Swanson Landing Road suddenly appeared. Vladimir skidded the car around the corner, the left front wheel barely clinging to the edge of the gravel. Stabilizing the Lincoln, he drove east once again, slowing a little. He had never driven on a road quite like this before. The road was originally paved with black asphalt but had been patched every 50 feet or so with 50 feet of white concrete—or perhaps it was the other way around, he couldn't tell. Neither the original surface nor the patches were in good shape, with local red clay frequently bleeding through. The constant flashing under the car of white … then black … then white … then black, made him think of driving across a chess board, and it was mesmerizing.

Erik was the one to find it. He shouted, "Stop the car!" Vladimir pressed hard on the brake pedal causing the anti-lock braking system to chatter as the vehicle came to a stop. The dust cloud thrown by the car overtook them, enshrouding them and blocking their view momentarily. Erik barked, "Go back about fifty yards." Vladimir threw the Lincoln into reverse and punched out of the dust cloud into clear air. "There, on the right. See the broken branches on that bush. Something has pushed through there recently."

Vladimir craned his neck to see what Erik was talking about. Sure enough, a vehicle had passed through the brush recently, leaving an all but invisible track through the brambles and on through the fence, the tire tracks barely visible in the tall grass beyond the opening.

Executing a three point turn, Vladimir followed the tracks into the bushes, forcing the car through the narrow gap in the fence. The stiff branches screeched along the paintwork like fingernails on a chalkboard. He wasn't thinking about the damage he was inflicting on the Lincoln, but he *was* thinking about the damage he would inflict on Julius, as he squeezed from him the needed information, and then, slowly, his life.

Looming ahead was an old shed with faint, almost imperceptible tracks leading into it. Vladimir steered the Lincoln along the tire tracks and stopped. Jumping out of the car, he drew his weapon and peered into the shed anticipating a trap. He could see nothing unexpected in the gloom; an old piece of farm equipment with large steel-spoked wheels and a huge steel seat suspended by a coil spring had been abandoned just a few feet from the door, leaning to one side on a flat tire, looking like it hadn't moved in decades. He scanned the area looking for another vehicle. Something had made those tire tracks. What, he would like to know, and where was it now? Was it Julius, or tracks made by local teenagers looking for a place to park and party? His mouth set into a hard line as he mumbled an oath to himself, "If Erik has sent me chasing wild geese I'll shoot him on the spot."

His trained tracker's eye examined the drive, the shed, the old yard beyond the shed—every blade of grass, twig, and pebble seeming to slide through his mind in slow motion. Nothing looked out of place; nothing seemed disturbed. Though disappointed and angry he realized he was in a good spot to explore the shoreline of the bayou. This may not be where Julius parked, but it could well be where he entered the swamp. The thought then struck him that Julius may not have a car. He could have hitched a ride and been let off here. But why would his ride have driven through the bushes? Why not just drop him off and let him walk in? As this puzzle was tracking across his mind, his eye caught a broken blade of tall grass just behind and to the right of the old shed. He rushed to it and saw it was freshly broken. Nothing else around it had been disturbed, and he immediately knew he was not tracking just an ordinary man. Although nothing in his rigorous research gave even a hint that Julius had survival training, it was clear he knew how to disappear without a trace—or at least *almost* without a trace. A smile began to play on his lips.

Vladimir shouted at the other two, "He's headed north to the water trying to lose us among the trees in the bayou. Get moving. He was here only five or ten minutes ago. Head to the water and spread out. I'll take the left, Erik, you cover the area straight ahead, and Yakov, you take the area to the right. Look behind every tree, and when you find him save him for me. I don't care what else you do to him but make sure he's alive when I get there."

The three headed for the water at a dead run, splitting up like jets at an airshow as soon as they were a hundred feet from the water's edge.

When they first entered the Caddo region, it had been very busy, and Erik was concerned about what he would do if he met someone strolling along the bayou. He tried his best to look ordinary, although he felt far from it. In his teens he had wandered through derelict parks in his neighborhood, much like he was doing now, except his intent at that time, was to take stock of each person he met, then steal whatever he could. For years he had successfully lived off the loot handed him, generally requiring very little persuasion on his part. One day he came face to face with a middle-aged man who gaped in terror at Erik like he was a common thug—a worm that deserved annihilation under the heel of his boot. Instinctively Erik had hit him ... much too hard as it turned out. The man's head snapped back with a distinct crunch and the body fell backward into a heap on the ground. As Erik turned in panic, two pairs of gloved hands seized his shoulders, roughly pushing him to the ground, face down, manacling his hands. He guessed he would never be able to erase from his memory the incident that began a list of prison stays and hardened him for his career with the KGB. Now, trudging through the tall grass, he could feel those hands again, and he twitched his shoulders to make sure they were free.

Vladimir ducked under the moss hanging on the trees bordering the water, worming his way among the ancient trunks and stumps to the slimy shore. He looked to the left and to the right for any sign of human activity, finding none. Peering across the water, he had to shade his eyes to protect them from the sun reflecting off the constantly moving ripples. He instinctively moved his right foot back as a larger ripple lapped at his boot. He grated at this; he didn't know why exactly. Maybe he was just being protective of the four hundred dollar calf-skin boot, an indulgence he allowed himself as a reward for his last kill. Just as he was lowering his head to give his vision a break from the kaleidoscope created by the moving moss and slowly undulating water, he thought he saw a face staring back at him a few feet from the edge. Shaking his head vigorously, he attempted to clear his vision and jog himself back to reality. Just as quickly it was gone. He stared at the spot for what seemed like an eternity, but the water's surface showed only the reflection of the patchwork sky, the inverted canopy of vegetation, and the odd lily pad stem.

Chapter 11

INSTANTLY, THE SYMPHONY OF SOUND IN THE BAYOU WENT DEATHLY still, as if the maestro, without warning, had dropped his baton. The creatures surrounding Julius sensed danger, ceasing their constant chatter. It was the silence that caused him to suddenly seek the deeper pool. In a heartbeat, Julius' head slipped below the algae-slimed surface. No evidence remained, other than the tiny breathing tube breaking the surface like a leafless stem belonging to one of the abundant water lilies.

Julius was at home here. The local fauna took little notice of him, since his frog-like appearance seemed no threat to the myriad life in the swamp accustomed to creatures of all colors, sizes and shapes.

A sharp pain exploded in his left side as his ribcage caught the upturned point of a broken branch buried in the ooze that slowly swallowed his torso. Julius almost gasped, but it would have been his last, since his tracker, now only a spitting distance away, wouldn't have missed the involuntary thrashing induced by taking in a mouthful of that brackish water.

The sun's fiery orb set ablaze the lichen draping the Cyprus tree branches, making the hanging moss luminescent with an eerie green glow edged with flame, creating massive monsters that hovered menacingly over Vladimir and Julius as if judging between them. Beyond the trees the horizon became a pool of crimson that dripped casually into the water of the bayou, dyeing it with flickering patterns of brilliant color.

As darkness swallowed the remaining light, the ghostly shadows cast by the bearded trees in the glow of a rising moon became his only friends. The water was relatively shallow, but the wide variation in the shading, together with the slow cadence of the vegetation caught in a light, warm breeze, provided impenetrable camouflage. At least it's what Julius hoped. If he were discovered, his escape would be impossible. The warmth of the water could not prevent the shiver that sent out a tiny ripple to the shore, lightly lapping at the boot of his would-be assailant.

Several water spiders danced along the surface just a finger length above his head; shadows in the silvery half-light. Julius hoped their dance was one of deliverance and not one of death. The whiskers of a catfish tickled his skin as it went about its pursuit of food, completely oblivious to his plight. He did not need the reminder that no one knew where he was, that no one knew the danger lurking just a few feet away. But he could not let his mind go there or he would also have to consider the alligators which frequented this corner of the swamp. He saw the results of an alligator attack once, and that was quite enough for him. He had to force his mind past the pending dangers to his intimate knowledge of the bayou and the safety such knowledge could afford to those who, with familiarity and experience, handled it with care. A crayfish scuttled off a submerged limb to sample the tip of Julius' nose, thankfully deciding it could do better elsewhere.

As Julius disciplined his breathing and pulse, ensuring the limited volume of air he was receiving through the tube would be sufficient, he relaxed knowing he was safe for the moment. His mind journeyed to his home where his family would be worried about him—his wife of 28 years and his two grown children and the family cat—although he wondered if the cat ever gave him a single thought, except perhaps at meal time. He had been looking forward to a late dinner with the entire family, a rarity amidst the chaos of modern life, and he could almost hear the front door latch as it clicked behind him, and smell the wafting aromas of his daughter's cooking; the familiar, ordinary things that contributed to making home *home*. He thought about engaging each of his kids in conversation—adult conversation, one of many wonders afforded by this stage of life—finding out what happened at the senior men's college basketball practice, and how his daughter's imminent motherhood was threatening to re-shape a new household established just over a year ago—at great expense to him, if he recalled correctly. His mind wandered to his wife, as she would be in the hospital bed which had been placed next to the dining room table; a tight fit but they had made it work. She would relish the tiny bit of food she would be able to eat, and she would enjoy the banter around the table, chiming in as if this were any normal family. *Normal*, thought Julius—as if his family could ever be considered *normal* again.

The muffled snap of a twig immediately stopped his reverie. The impulse to look was almost too strong to ignore, but he knew that old trick, and wasn't about to become victim to its ruse. Although his surroundings were becoming unpleasant, his skin wrinkling as if he had shrunk within it, they were familiar, and he was willing to wait it out. It would be time soon enough to emerge from his watery, muddy cocoon—but now was not the right time.

Chapter 12

CORA TRIED TO LIFT HER LEFT SIDE FROM THE BED, HER BODY SLUG-gish in responding to anything voluntary, but quick to issue involuntary gasps and sighs. Her back was slowly evolving an unnatural shape as the muscles lost their ability to provide proper support. This put pressure on her spinal cord, which in turn caused pain and intermittent paralysis in her legs. She was unable to get comfortable either in bed or out, the constant stress painting dark circles around her eyes.

But she would not verbalize her distress if she could possibly help it. Her nurse would be leaving just as soon as Brittany arrived—or would it be Eddie who arrived first, she couldn't quite recall, the constant pain seeming to drive the memory from her tired and waning body.

The doorbell chimed, immediately revealing Eddie's six foot three frame. Cora was always afraid he would hit his head on the transom; but he didn't. Ringing the doorbell was a courtesy both Brittany and Eddie offered, just to confirm this was their parents' house, no longer their own, although once through the door, the distinction was lost. They had grown up in the house and knew every nook and cranny, every squeak and rumble, and some of the dust bunnies. Each had written hidden notes to the other during their adolescence. Eddie started it, being the older by two years. There was a decade or so where he despised having a younger sister and wasn't shy in expressing himself in a variety of ways, some of which Julius and Cora were still to discover. Notes in permanent marker adorned the underside of stair treads, and names—mostly uncomplimentary—were carved into the basement stair stringers.

But that was a different time. They were grown now, and although rivals in their youth, they were allies now, jointly engaged in the battle raging in the body of their Mom.

"Mom, I'm home," hollered Eddie, as he had done almost every day for the 19 years he had lived there. "Sheri, I'm here."

Cora was too weak to match his holler, but she knew he would step into the dining room to give her a quick kiss, so a loud greeting was unnecessary. Sheri, on the other hand, wanted to be in the game, so she matched Eddie's volume as she shouted, "OK, I'll be on my way then."

Cora loved the ritual of this routine. It gave her a grounding, roots, something to look forward to, something that wouldn't change with the next appointment, or next medication. Sheri had been her nurse for the past four years. When Cora was first diagnosed, she came by the house for weekly checkups. Cora was still mobile then, keeping house and living large, albeit on a slightly reduced schedule. In the beginning, Sheri was needed several hours each week, then it escalated to several days per week, and now she was full-time at the Barlow home, attending to Cora's many needs, administering the cocktail of medications that kept her alive and relatively comfortable.

Gathering her things, Sheri headed for the front door. As was her custom, if Eddie were there first, she gave him a peck on the cheek and said, "Take care of her tonight, Basil. It wasn't a good day." With that she stepped out the door into the waning light of dusk. Sheri frequently had fun with Eddie's name. He was born Basil Edward Barlow. He didn't appreciate it, so he insisted on being called 'Eddie', hoping his first name would atrophy and its use would fade. With as much flourish as possible, Sheri took advantage of his discomfort any time she thought she could get away with it.

Eddie went to the dining room and sat in the chair that lingered beside Cora's bed. He looked at his Mom for a few moments, quickly assessing the day from her face, multiplied it by two, then leaned over and gave her a kiss on the forehead. "Are we still expecting Dad for supper?"

Cora responded with the best smile she could muster, and clearing her throat in a proper, lady-like fashion, said, "Yes, he left this afternoon for Houston and said he was looking forward to a late dinner with the two of you. I imagine he'll be back soon."

"Great. It will be fun to all be together for a bit. I miss my little sister sometimes—just sometimes, mind—when our schedules get so crazy. Maybe I'll start a food fight."

"Don't you dare, Edward! If I recall correctly, the last time you started one of those, it resulted in you getting the short end of the stick." Cora coughed quietly and Eddie took that as his cue.

"I'll get started on dinner prep. Since we organized this dinner a few days ago I'm sure Dad has already purchased what we need, so I'll just scrounge around in the fridge to see if I can guess what he was planning."

Eddie headed for the kitchen. Cora loved to chat with her kids, but lately each conversation became more tiring. She dreaded the day when she would not be able to participate, and would have to just listen. If that day came, *it* may well kill her, preempting the disease roaming unchecked through her body.

Chapter 13

VLADIMIR WAS GETTING IMPATIENT. HIS TRACKING SKILLS COULD virtually smell Julius, but he hadn't seen any sign of him, and had received no communication from Erik or Yakov. Had Julius slipped past him once again? Vladimir's resumé included hunting some of the most dangerous men on the planet, while in the KGB and since. Failure simply was not tolerated. How could he possibly be foiled by this bourgeois capitalist?

The sun had all but set, allowing the moon to pour its silver coating over the bayou's resplendent vegetation. A thick cloud bank was quickly overtaking the moon, and he knew he was out of time. After gathering his troops, he would drive to the state line and back, in the off chance he and Julius would cross paths on a remote county road. The thought invoked a faint smile, which threatened to transform his dour countenance into something more pleasant, but the murderous look in his eyes confirmed his intent and his resolve.

Pulling out his cell phone, he called Erik, instructing him to meet him at the path where it entered the swamp, and to call Yakov, and make it fast. His mood had turned lethal; something Erik sensed immediately from the short conversation.

Meeting at the path, the three almost ran to where the Lincoln waited, tall grass whipping at their arms and legs, brambles springing back into the faces of those who lagged behind, causing them to stumble and curse.

Erik made it to the passenger door first, staking his claim to ride shotgun. Yakov threw him a barbed glance and reluctantly climbed into the back seat.

It took only seconds to settle into the Lincoln, start the engine, and turn around. Gravel and dust spit from the wide tires as Vladimir blasted down the old lane, punching through the bushes at the road, then turning hard left away from the park. He wanted to cover as much road as possible while there was still a touch of light left in the sky. Daylight was waning quickly; just a few bright spots remained on the western horizon. Clouds obscured the rising moon indicating it would be totally dark in a matter of minutes. Erik and Yakov peered intently, each to a side, into the increasing blackness, looking for any trace of their prey.

They reached the North State Line Road. He came to a rolling stop in reluctant obedience to the bullet-riddled sign pointing left to Cricket's Ramp, half hidden behind tangles of brush and vine, then turned right, south if his sense of direction was intact, and began looking for the next road to the right that would take them west again, back toward the park and Route 134. Once they reached the main road he knew the search would be over for the night and his anger began spiraling upward.

He almost missed it. The state line road had started off as rough gravel, and now opened into a narrow, paved, almost two lane road. Slowing several times to inspect wannabe cross roads, he determined they led to oil wells, some rusty with age and others looking quite new. Eventually he saw the weathered sign announcing County Road 2611 that would take him west, cross country to Route 9, and from there to 134. The T-intersection was obscured on both corners by brush and tall grass. As the headlights arced to shine down the road, he saw it was narrow, unpaved, and perfectly straight. The high beams reflected off the grass and shrubs as if off the walls of a tunnel. From time to time the foliage would thin and he could see the wide, flat, denuded strip to his left. There were no transmission towers, so he thought it may be a pipeline or other right-of-way.

Each foot the Lincoln travelled west marked another girder torn from the bridge spanning the widening chasm separating him from Julius. The weight of his disappointment pressed on the car's accelerator. The Lincoln was fast, engineered with suspension tuned for speed and comfort even on rough county roads. The acceleration was smooth and constant. Erik and Yakov were intent on their search and didn't notice the flaring digits of the speedometer as it passed 80 miles per hour.

It started to rain. Drops the size of marbles hit the windshield like gunshots then ran horizontally across the side windows. The moon's ragged remnant cast haloed pools of light on the vehicle's tinted windows.

Erik was the first to see them. Two glistening orbs on the passenger side; large and getting larger. His mind whirled, searching to place them in his memory. Suddenly he realized they were headlights, distorted by the rain and the speed. His body went rigid. He began to yell a warning to Vladimir, but barely managed to open his mouth when he heard, for just a split second, the agonizing sounds of the impact.

Vladimir caught the lights in his peripheral vision but had no time to react. He hadn't turned the steering wheel, or moved his foot from the accelerator to the brake; there had been no time. He saw the road suddenly veer to the right, the lashing of grass and brush on the windshield, the gobs of dirt mixed with steam and black oil. Seeing Erik coming at him from the right, he reacted defensively from years of training and experience. In a flash, he realized it was not Erik moving, but himself. Erik seemed to be glued to the Lincoln's right side, wrapped in a white shroud. As his shoulder impacted Erik, he heard the familiar snapping of human bone—his or Erik's, he couldn't tell. His vision blurred red and then went black.

In the back seat, Yakov was looking the other way out the left window and saw nothing. The impact caught him relaxed and flaccid. Like a rag doll he was swallowed by the white marshmallow that erupted instantaneously from the right center doorpost. He heard the bending of metal, the screeching of steel on steel, the horrifying sounds of welds stretching and finally separating. He heard the breaking of glass. He heard Erik's head hit the front door post. He heard Vladimir curse as his head and shoulders merged with those of Erik. He heard something in his right shoulder snap or dislocate—a sickening sound—followed by pain that lanced down his spine to his toes.

And then silence … broken only by the hiss of escaping steam.

Chapter 14

JULIUS WATCHED AS THE DISTORTED, WAVY FIGURE OF HIS ASSAIL-ant retrieved his cell phone, mumbled muted words, then turned, and strode away. He paused until he was certain he was totally alone, then slowly emerged from his watery tomb. He had to fight with the sucking mud surrounding his legs and feet, but he knew the swamp's secrets and broke through the bayou's skin barely causing a ripple. He kept his head low in case the assassin turned for a last look.

Retrieving his pack, he dressed and began the cautious trek back to the Cherokee. He could plainly see the boot prints of his would-be attackers, and felt a moment of panic as he realized the Cherokee may have been discovered, his mind madly exploring various scenarios as he worked out solutions and escape routes.

Entering the tall grass at the swamp's edge, he heard, rather than saw, the Lincoln leave. The powerful engine roared and gravel clinked against the old fencing. Unless someone was left to guard the Jeep, it looked like he still had a ride. The prospect of walking any distance was becoming more unsavory by the minute, the clouds inching across the moon as if shuttering a storm lantern. He wasn't certain yet where he would go, but he knew for sure he needed to put some distance between himself and the bayou, and hopefully, between himself and his pursuers.

Julius approached the barn yard with caution, all his senses on full alert. He listened for the foot falls of a guard, the rustling of clothing, the click of a lighter. There was no sound. It appeared the Lincoln had taken everyone with it.

Noiselessly skirting the rear of the old barn, he approached the Jeep from the bayou side of the thicket, peering through the branches and leaves, seeing no one.

He slid into the Jeep, glanced toward the back seat for any sign of an ambush, started the engine, and ensured it was in four wheel drive. He backed from the thicket slowly, trying to make as little noise as possible. The shrieking of the branches and thorns scraping along the sides of the Cherokee made him wince. Clearing the thicket, he turned around in the old barn yard while looking intently down the overgrown lane for evidence of a trap, finding none. He eased the Jeep onto the road, looked both ways and, seeing that the road was clear other than for a wisp of dust or smoke to the left, he turned right, returning to Route 9 and what he thought would be freedom, but likely not safety.

His headlights illuminated the sign for Route 9 and he prepared to turn left. As he did so, the rain started. Large drops of water struck the windshield and exploded on impact quickly covering the glass. He flipped on the wipers, and as he should have expected, they were marginal at best. Chips in the aging rubber blades left streaks that looked like glittering silver lacework as they caught the few remaining rays from the moon. He cautiously accelerated, forcing his vision to focus through the small clearing on the windshield. As he grew more comfortable he increased his speed until he reached 50 miles per hour, watching carefully for oncoming traffic.

The clouds finished devouring the moon, darkness swallowing the remaining light. The rain was increasing, so Julius decided to back off on the throttle as his caution grew. He saw a momentary glint and tried desperately to filter it from the reflection of his own headlights on the raindrops. The details passed in slow motion, seeming to take forever. He saw the side mirror, then the chrome front door handle, the smooth paintwork on the door panel, and then suddenly a wall of white burned his face and arms. He heard every thud, pop, bang, and screech as the Cherokee attempted to bury itself in the belly of the Lincoln, like a kitten in that of its mother.

The violent motion stopped with one final bone-wrenching jolt. While wiggling his toes, Julius stretched each of his hands to convince himself he was still in one piece. He flexed his back and hips, finding he could move, but not without pain. Nothing searing or sharp; that was good. The air bag lay flaccid on the steering wheel which came to rest just a hair's breadth from his chest. Another inch and it would have crushed his ribs, puncturing his lungs and terminating his life. The driver's door was buckled, and the door posts stood at odd angles. Reflexively he tried the door handle. Of course, it wouldn't budge. He checked the dampness on his cheek, discovering it was water, not blood as he feared. The window in the door was completely missing. The windshield was shattered, with large gaps in the mosaic glass admitting the rain and wind and dust and smoke. Smoke! He had to get out of the Jeep! It may have ignited or the other vehicle could be burning. There was no time to lose. Julius peered out the missing side window to see what would greet him if he climbed out that way. The Lincoln symbol on the trunk lid was visible out the window, askew in what appeared to be a field, badly furrowed as if freshly ploughed by a would-be farmer. Scrunching himself into as small a cylinder as possible, he wormed his way out the window, feet first. He landed on the ground with a jar, setting his bruises aflame, while each joint complained loudly to him of stretched ligaments and tendons. Recovering his balance, he took a quick glance at the Lincoln. It was shaped like a horseshoe; the rear faced the county road he had just been on, as did the grill. The Jeep had almost cut the Lincoln in half.

As his mind began to clear, Julius made his way around to the driver's side of the Lincoln and peered through the darkness into the interior. There were three bodies; two in the front looking to be in a lover's embrace, and one in the back. As his eyes became accustomed to the dim light cast by the dashboard, his heart lurched. The face of the closest man was clearly the one he had seen looking at him just minutes before. It was distorted and bloodied. Julius would not have recognized it had it not appeared much like it did earlier, misshapen and bent by the water's reflective surface that shielded him from it. There was no movement and no sound, not even that of shallow breathing. The occupant in the rear sported an expensive leather coat, slightly open, a hand gun partially lodged in a shoulder holster that stood oddly angled.

Julius' first impulse was to check each for a heartbeat, but he couldn't risk reviving any of them. He was certain if he were recognized, he would be shot on sight. Fumbling for his cell phone, he discovered it wasn't in its usual place. He saw one lying on the back seat. It must have flown from the rear passenger's pocket during impact, then bounced off the side air bag. It glowed invitingly. He stretched to reach it but his bruised ribs prevented him. Spinning around, he broke off a twig from a mangled bush ripped out by the impact. He was able to coax the cell phone closer to him, and, ignoring the pain in his chest, leaned through the window making one final effort to retrieve it.

He pressed 911. The GPS symbol flared and a voice came on the line. Julius mumbled, "Help! Accident! Serious injuries!", then threw the phone back onto the seat, ignoring its insistent questioning.

As the clouds opened their floodgates, in minutes soaking him to the skin, he staggered through the broken bushes, torn sod, and mud, and, reaching the road, began limping in the general direction of the park.

Chapter 15

"DAD SHOULD BE HOME BY NOW," MUMBLED BRITTANY TO NO ONE IN particular as she stared out the window into the darkness. Having arrived at the Barlow home a little over an hour earlier, she had settled into the kitchen to help Eddie prepare the finer points of the much anticipated meal.

Her wince caught Eddie's eye, prompting him to quip, "Still kicking up a storm, is he?" as both of her hands flew to her stomach.

"For the millionth time bro, we don't know if it is a *he*! But based on the activity tonight I certainly hope so. I'm not sure I want my *daughter* playing football, hockey, and lacrosse all at the same time." Brittany and her husband were bucking the growing trend of knowing gender at the earliest possible date. Reveling in the anticipation, they took pleasure in picking names for both, neutral colors for the nursery, and gender-indifferent baby clothes. There would be plenty of time to buy sailor suits—does one do that anymore?—or frilly dresses. The nursery could be redecorated when it became a room suitable to a child rather than a baby.

Just then the doorbell chimed and the door opened as Jim stepped through. As a young girl Brittany had dreamed of marrying someone with a simple, regular, easy name. She almost had her wish. Jim was christened James Alexander Beauregard Evenson. As long as she called him 'Jim', she felt she had been granted her wish. Jim's lean frame was strong and athletic. He and Eddie had become good friends, playing late-night hockey once a week at the rink, and pick-up football or baseball whenever possible. He adored Brittany, and had been completely absorbed by the Barlows. Although his background was broken and sketchy, he flourished among the new relationships found in his wife's family. His heart ached for Cora who, in the past few years, had been more of a mother to him than his birth mother had ever been; Julius more of a dad than his father who seemed too self-absorbed to acknowledge his presence.

Running her fingers through her dark auburn hair several times, Brittany repeated, "Getting back to Dad …"

Eddie broke in, "I would have expected him back before dark, but maybe he had delays getting out of Longview. Air traffic can get busy there particularly at this time of day."

"Yes, I suppose it's possible," responded Brittany not the least bit convinced. "We took all that into account when we agreed on what time we would eat. But we're more than an hour beyond that time already and I'm worried. I know he wouldn't miss dinner if he could possibly help it but we can't delay it much longer … for Mom's sake."

Chapter 16

IN MOMENTS, THE LIMPING BECAME STUMBLING. COMPLETELY
spent, physically and emotionally, the adrenalin that kept him safe
in the bayou burning off, he keenly felt the void within him rise,
threatening to consume him. His body had become boneless, each
step a struggle to make his wilted flesh obey him. His downcast eyes,
unconsciously reflecting his defeat, sought for obstacles that might
cause him to fall, knowing for a certainty if he went down he did not
have the strength or the will power to get back up.

The rain was a chilling curtain intent upon impeding his progress, all trace of light devoured by the deluge. Large drops splashed
and bounced on the road's hard surface, breaking into wet tongues
that licked at his shoes. They stung his face and coalesced into rivu-
lets, dripping from his nose, his ears, and his chin.

Julius barely noticed the tiny needles of light exploding into
crystals at his feet; mostly white, sometimes tinged with blue. But
they meant nothing to him. Only when they merged into a beam,
and the blue began its incessant flashing, did he raise his head.
Totally done, his knees buckling, he fell into a heap on the side of
the road, drenched, chilled to the bone, and totally exhausted. He
sought the blackness of death, or at least unconsciousness, but it
wouldn't come. He was mindful of his condition, but utterly unable
to do anything about it.

Like a spectator viewing from the sidelines, he heard the vehicle stop and voices discuss his condition. He felt strong arms lift his head and shoulders. "Are you alright? What are you doing out here? Are you hurt? Have you been hit by a car?" It took a moment for him to realize the questions were aimed at him. Trying to rally his senses, he fought the fog that shrouded his brain, just as it began to break into shifting tendrils. A face emerged, kind but stern, with a wide brimmed hat, and, from the little Julius could see, uniformed shoulders with badges.

"Call for the medics!" the voice commanded, and Julius heard a muffled one-sided conversation with a tone of urgency which seemed to be about him.

Julius whispered to the face, "In an accident … back there on the road … first intersection … two cars … maybe some didn't make it … dangerous … guns."

The face spoke quietly but with authority. "I'm Deputy Patterson from the Harrison County Sheriff's office. Adrian Patterson. I'm here with my partner Deputy Will Turner. We've called for an ambulance."

Julius felt a blanket being placed over his drenched clothing, and immediately his shivering subsided. The rain drops stopped penetrating his shirt and jeans. The streams of water running down his face played a tune on the waterproof exterior of the trauma blanket.

"What is your name?" the deep voice rumbled.

Julius did his best to clear his mind. He very much wanted to make sense and communicate his concerns.

"Julius Barlow," he managed, his voice threatening to betray him. "I was driving the Jeep that hit the car back at the intersection. Dialed 911 and was walking to the park for help."

He forced his mind to consider various scenarios. It seemed an eternity before he recognized the ragged edges of reality emerging. If he told the officer even the periphery of his predicament he would sound demented, and if he told the whole story he could be putting himself in additional danger. He knew he had muttered something when Deputy Patterson had first picked him off the pavement, but he couldn't quite remember what. He hoped he hadn't opened any doors he was unwilling to walk through. He resolved to discuss only the accident.

"I checked the other car and there were 3 men injured … don't know how badly exactly. Wasn't much I could do … so I went looking for help," grimaced Julius, his bruised ribs reminding him of the violence of the collision.

Deputy Turner came into view and Patterson turned toward him and barked, "Julius Barlow. … Get on the horn!"

Julius heard Turner's footsteps slosh rapidly through the puddles, then the closing of a car door. He spoke tentatively, "… don't think my injuries are serious … feeling a bit stronger. Help me sit up … so my ribs stop killing me."

Patterson responded, "Take my arm and move slowly. We don't want to risk any more damage."

The two men struggled as if wrestling, and eventually Julius was sitting more or less comfortably with Deputy Patterson squatting on his heels trying to stay dry, but at the same time wanting to be at Julius' level.

"So … you said something right at the beginning about *guns*. Do you want to explain what you meant?"

"Hey, ignore anything I said until a few minutes ago. There was a serious disconnect between my brain and my mouth, and maybe there still is."

"OK, but if there is something I need to know, now's the time."

"The only thing I'm sure of right now is that I don't want you to leave me here. Well, actually, I'm not sure of that either, since someone needs to check out the other guys in the accident." Through clenched teeth he added, "No, I take it back, I don't want you to leave me."

Patterson chuckled, "Don't worry: we have another cruiser at the accident scene. I called for backup when I saw you collapsed on the road. The ambulance should be here soon and we'll get you looked after."

Julius began to relax. He felt the tension slowly seep out of him. "Thanks," was all he could muster.

Deputy Turner returned from the police car and motioned to Patterson who said to Julian, "Hang on. I have to see what Deputy Turner wants. I'm not leaving. I'm not leaving you … so hang in there."

Following a brief, muted conversation, Patterson returned, squatted beside Julius, and said, "It appears you have an appointment with the Sheriff over in Webster County. He wants to talk to you about a suspicious event at the airport? You know anything about that?"

The muscles in his chest constricted, causing his bruised ribs to scream and his throat to gasp. Julius didn't feel strong enough to take much more, but fighting to bring his voice under control, he said, "I flew out of Springhill this morning and noticed something strange in the tower, so I called Flight Watch and told them of my concerns. They told me to get in touch with the Sheriff's office when I returned to tell them what I knew. As you can see, I haven't returned yet." He immediately regretted that bit of sarcasm, so he softened his tone. "Do you have any more information on what happened there?"

Patterson let out a sigh, "None I can share. So I don't have to cuff you and read you your rights—at least not right now?"

Julius was relieved by Patterson's attitude. He would likely not have to tell the whole story to him. But who *would* he tell? His earlier resolve to let sleeping dogs lie had been shattered in the last few hours, and now his need to tell someone was almost overwhelming. He wasn't sure of the fate of the three men in the Lincoln, but even if they were all dead there would be others to fill their shoes. Clearly his secret was out, and he would be a perpetual fugitive unless he did something, and quickly. But that would have to wait; at the moment he had the accident and his recovery to consider.

The ambulance broadcast its approach with brilliant flashes of red and white that penetrated the wall of rain in a jumble of diamond-like sparkles. Julius and the officers had to shield their eyes as the lights approached, finally coming to a stop beside the cruiser. Two bright spotlights were concentrated on Julius as the medics jumped from the cab, running toward him. The next few minutes were a blur of questions and answers, pokes and prods. Eventually the two paramedics lifted Julius gently to his feet, settling him into the back of the ambulance where it was dry and well lit. Gingerly stripping out of his wet clothes, he put on the jump suit offered by the medics. It felt dry and warm against his skin. He could feel his old self returning. His teeth wanted to chatter when he spoke, but he was on the verge of having his trembling under control. Sitting heavily on the gurney, his body ached, his mind so very tired. Involuntarily the thought of sleep entered his mind, and once it had done so he could hardly keep his head erect and his eyes open. He wanted to lie down on the gurney and sleep for two days. But he couldn't let himself sleep; he had other obligations.

One of the paramedics was about to hop out of the ambulance to talk with the Deputy when he caught Julius in full view under the fluorescent brilliance of the ambulance interior. He stepped back for a brief moment as if to take a better look and exclaimed, "Julius? Julius Barlow? The 'family jewel'? Is it really you?"

Julius was stunned. He hadn't been called the 'family jewel' for 25 years or more. And the only people allowed to call him that, as if he had anything to say about it, were the kids he played with in the bayou when he was nine or ten. He had all but forgotten his nickname, but it invoked such clear memories that he was transported back in time.

Julius looked hard at the face which had spoken those words, and as he did so, it was transformed into that of a young boy who he immediately recognized as his childhood friend.

"Marty, is that you hiding behind that uniform?" stammered Julius.

"Yah, it's me, Marty Goodman. Hey man, it's been so long I didn't recognize you. Actually, time had nothing to do with it; your face is so banged up your own mother wouldn't recognize you. What a heck of a way to meet after all these years."

"Marty, it's great to see you again. I knew you had gone into emergency work, but I always thought you had become a police officer or worked for the FBI or something. But, hey, right now I'm glad you're a medic." The strain and excitement made Julius cough, causing his bruised ribs to shoot needles through his body. He wrapped his arms around his chest, holding tightly to relieve the pain.

The other medic said mockingly, "While you girls introduce yourselves and plan a sleepover, I'll go chat with Patterson and get his permission to leave for the hospital."

Seeing Julius grimace, Marty immediately reacted, getting down on one knee to be at face level with him. "Let me help you lie down on the gurney. If we can take the pressure off your chest you'll feel a whole lot better."

Marty gently lowered Julius, hooked the blood pressure monitor to Julius' arm, the pulse monitor to his thumb, and strapped him onto the bed in preparation for the ride to the hospital.

When Julius was settled, Marty stepped to the rear doors and shouted at his partner, "Let's get this show on the road. Time's a-wastin.'"

Chapter 17

LEAVING THE WINDOW, BRITTANY PACED THE KITCHEN FLOOR, finally plunking herself onto a kitchen stool. Twisting a wayward curl over her left eye, she muttered to the fridge, "I guess we might as well eat."

"What was that you said, sis?"

"I said … you need to do something about finding out where Dad is. This has gone on long enough."

"What do you want *me* to do, Brittany? *I* don't know what's keeping him."

Jim broke in, "Listen, Dad has been in the air what seems like half his life, and I'm sure if there were trouble he would be able to deal with it."

"That's a fat lot of help, guys. If he's not here when he said he would be, then something is wrong."

"OK, hon, if it will make you feel better, we'll do some calling around." Jim gently rolled his eyes at Eddie. "You continue calling his cell, and I'll call the local airport to see if they know anything."

Brittany realized her Mom must also be worried. She pushed herself back to her feet and shuffled to the dining room where the table was set for four; Cora's setting having been placed on her rolling table. Each setting was carefully arranged on a white linen napkin, and, together with the fresh flowers in the center of the table, it looked more like a fine restaurant than a family dining room.

She sat in the chair beside Cora, and asked if she was OK. Expressing her surprise that Julius wasn't home yet, Cora said she wasn't particularly worried. Brittany pondered whether she should raise any alarms with her Mom or wait until they knew a little more. She decided on the latter, and said compassionately, "He's likely running a little late. But if he's not here in a few minutes, he'll be the loser, 'cause we're gonna eat this delicious meal without him." The twinkle in her eye was involuntary, lasting but a fleeting moment, extinguished by her concern.

Eddie reported back, "He's not answering his cell. It doesn't even ring; it goes directly to voice mail, which could mean it's off, or he's currently using it. It's been that way the last couple of times I've tried. I'll check again in a few minutes in case he was on another call. Of course, if he's in the air, he won't be answering his phone, but then it should at least ring."

"Likely it means his phone is off, Eddie, since otherwise it would ring several times on call waiting. Maybe the battery died or he's in a meeting with it turned off."

"A meeting? … That would be a little odd, don't you think? … at this hour?"

Jim offered, "I spoke to the airport manager, and he's not heard from Dad since he took off. He patched me through to the tower and they gave me quite a story. The short version is that Dad left early this afternoon for Lone Star, but didn't land. Instead he headed back north to Cypress River. He also said something strange about having trouble at the tower today—apparently a controller was injured and he said it looked suspicious, whatever that means."

Listening from the dining room doorway, Brittany gasped.

"Take it easy Brit. I'm sure there's no connection between those events, at least none the controller offered."

"Then why did he divert to Cypress River? It's a tiny little airport near where Dad grew up. He and I have flown over it several times but never landed—there didn't seem to be a reason to."

"Maybe he returned to his old stomping grounds to see friends or something."

"Not without letting *us* know, Eddie. He was supposed to be going to a meeting in Houston, and Cypress River is just a little off course, don't you think? … Call it intuition, or maternal instinct, or being silly, or whatever you boys want to call it, but this doesn't feel right.

Dad isn't careless with the plane, and neither is he reckless with his responsibilities at home. It would take something very momentous to keep him from dinner, and even more significant to prevent him from keeping us in the loop."

Jim nodded.

Eddie felt his throat tighten. "I'm going to call Cypress to see what they know."

Brittany stepped over to Jim and he wrapped her in his arms. Tears were beginning to flood her eyes and threatened to spill over.

Eddie muttered goodbye into the phone and reported, "He was there alright. His plane is still there, and he borrowed their Jeep. He didn't say where he was going, but the airport manager said he seemed nervous or in a rush—odd in any case. Apparently he avoided ATC the whole way from Lone Star, getting the controllers quite worried. The manager thought Dad said something about equipment problems."

"That doesn't sound like Dad, does it? He keeps his airplane squeaky clean. If he had equipment problems he would bring it home, not drop it into some Podunk airport without the necessary services. If it had been something serious like an engine or prop, the airport manager would have known about it. Something else is up; I'm more certain of it than ever."

The three of them fell quiet. Eventually Brittany spoke, her voice ragged, "We need to eat. I know all this is hard on the appetite, but Mom should have eaten several hours ago, and we all know regular mealtimes are important to her. If we don't start soon we'll have to call it breakfast, so let's all sit and do the best we can."

As they ate, the empty place at the table was a persistent reminder there was trouble afoot.

Chapter 18

IN SPITE OF THE RELATIVE COMFORT OF THE GURNEY, JULIUS FELT every bump, pot-hole and pebble on the road. He was beginning to realize he was in worse shape than originally thought, but he was still convinced none of his injuries were significant—no broken bones or internal bleeding. He knew the burns on his face would heal, the stretched and torn muscles and ligaments would return to normal, and the blue-red of his bruises would fade into yellow and disappear. It wouldn't be a pleasant few weeks, but he knew he would fully recover. Not so for the three in the Lincoln, he mused. However wrong, he couldn't help hoping—wishing—they were all dead. His pessimistic side reminded him again that, even if *they* were dead, there would be others.

Marty broke into his thoughts, "Since I have you in my custody for a few minutes, you'll have to tell me what you've been doing these past few decades. Are you still married to …?"

"Marty, I'm in big trouble," blurted Julius almost involuntarily. He had to trust someone, and Marty was as good a choice as any.

"What do you mean? … About the accident?"

"No, no. The guys in the other car were after me … hunting me … and I think they would have killed me if I'd given them the chance. Remember how we used to play war games in the bayou, and I almost always hid so none of you could find me. Well, I pulled that stunt on these guys. The ring leader was only a few feet from me and couldn't see a thing. It was pure chance our cars collided back there. And I don't know whether they are alive or dead."

"Slow down, Julius. I understand your words, but haven't a clue what you are talking about."

"It's kind of a long story. I'll fill you in at some point. But I need to talk to a police officer I can trust, and I don't have a clue where to start looking. But I'm sure *you* do. You must rub shoulders with the police all the time. Who can I trust? Who is going to believe a weird tale that may soon have an unhappy ending ... at least from where I sit?"

"Well ... there is a lady detective in Marshall. I've met her only a few times but I hear she has a reputation for being thorough and fair. She has taken on tough cases with good results, but remains very low key. She might be a good person to get you started. If she can't help you herself maybe she has contacts who can. It's probably worth a try."

"In Marshall, you say? What's her name?"

"Rikki Castillo. She's a detective; I guess formally a Deputy, in the Harrison County Sheriff's office in Marshall. She would likely be known by Patterson and Turner, the guys who picked you up. Would you like me to mention this to them and have them organize a meeting for you?"

"No, no, no, don't do that," his voice rattling in his throat as it increased in pitch. "I'll look after this myself. ... I'll try to remember her name. Hopefully when this mental fog clears it won't take everything with it."

"Just in case, let me write her name on my card. Then you will know how to get in touch with me as well. Do you mind if I get your wallet from your wet clothes and put the card in there so you don't lose it?"

"Thanks. How long to the hospital?" He yawned hugely.

"Another 20 minutes or so. Are you comfortable?"

"Almost, but I'll be fine. Do you mind if I sleep? I can't seem to keep my eyes open."

"Not at all. Nighty night. Oh, do you want me to call anyone for you?"

Julius heard the question but it seemed to come from another planet, intended for someone else. He allowed himself to relax and, taking deep breaths, he exhaled the stress of the day. In moments he was fast asleep.

He awoke to bright lights, voices murmuring, and a periodic hum vibrating through him. He tried to focus his eyes but it was impossible—everything was much too bright. He tried squinting. It helped some, but he still couldn't make out what was going on around him. He remembered the accident, falling on the highway, being cold and wet, a police car, and Marty—Marty from his childhood, now a medic—and it all fell into place. He was in a hospital room.

A nurse noticed he was stirring, and said, "Mr. Barlow, you are in an examining room in the hospital in Marshall and we are taking X-Rays of your body to make sure you don't have any broken bones, cracked ribs, or internal injuries. The doctor is in the next room looking at the plates on the computer as we speak. I'm sure he'll be with you shortly to discuss what he's found."

All Julius could muster was, "Thanks, I guess."

Several minutes later he felt a gentle touch on his shoulder and a voice saying, "Mr. Barlow, I'm Doctor Havaris. I've been taking some full-body X-Rays checking for broken bones or swelling organs, and everything looks fine. You don't look so good on the outside, but you look fine on the inside. I expect the cuts and bruises will heal quickly and you should be back to normal in a few weeks. How do you feel?"

Finding his voice somewhere in the void, Julius tried to use it, "I'm very tired and moving even my eyelids seems to hurt."

"That's to be expected. I don't see any reason to keep you, so I'm preparing your discharge papers. You can stay here as long as you want. When you feel like you can stand and walk on your own, check with the desk over there by the door, and collect your things. Take care."

With that the doctor turned on his heel and was gone; probably to more important medical emergencies, Julius quipped to himself.

He lay there gathering his strength and working out what his next step should be.

He was in Marshall, but it was the middle of the night. He would try to locate Deputy Castillo first thing in the morning. Meanwhile he needed to find somewhere to stay for the night—yes, that would be his first task; the rest could wait. Yawning involuntarily, he closed his eyes, just for a moment, while he figured out how he would get to a motel …

… A nurse with hairy arms and a gun approached him, saying she had the perfect place for him to stay—he just needed to follow her. But he couldn't move his arms and legs. He was strapped to a wide board of some kind, and no matter how hard he struggled against his restraints he was unable to make his body obey. No, not a board, it was a block of ice, and he was very cold, not strapped down, just immobilized by the cold … so very cold. The nurse was gone, and he was watching the side of a car get closer and closer until the moment of impact was imminent. But he passed right through the car, if that's what it was, and when he checked himself over, after what should have been a violent crash, he found himself clothed like a cowboy with guns in holsters on both hips. There was no horse, but a police car was standing before him, waiting with its driver's door open. He tried to force his way into the car, but he was too big—it was a toy police car with pedals to make it move. His frustration mounted as he realized he was sitting, strapped, in a dentist's chair. The dentist was huge, with biceps the size of small trees, the handle of a gun protruding from the bulge under his left arm. The dentist had a drill in his hand and he wanted Julius to open wide. The drill started to hammer and spit clouds of steam, and Julius sat bolt upright, ignoring the painful complaints of his muscles. Shaking his head to clear his thoughts, he realized he was dreaming.

Swinging his legs off the gurney, scrubbing gently at his face, he slowly claimed back his balance. He tested his weight, finding he was able to stand without overwhelming pain. After taking a few halting steps, he was pleased to discover he was mobile. Leaving the small examining room behind, he headed for the receptionist, moving slowly, keeping one hand on the wall, checking for weakness or pain that may cause him to stumble and fall. Giving his name, he asked the receptionist what he should do with the jumpsuit he was wearing, since it belonged to the ambulance, and his clothes were still wet and unwearable. The receptionist told him he could deliver or mail the jump suit to the address on the card she prepared for him, and his personal effects were all in the bag she had placed on the counter. She bid him good night, going back to her work on the computer. Almost as an afterthought she said, "Do you have someone to take you home, or can I call you a cab?"

Julius had already turned to go, and cautiously swiveled back to the reception window, saying, "Yes, please, that would help me a lot. Can you recommend a motel close by? I'll definitely not be making it home tonight."

The receptionist pulled a sheet of paper from a neat pile on the desk and said, "Here are all the hotels and motels in the vicinity. Patients and family stay at them all, so I assume they are OK. I could call for a reservation if you like."

"That would be very helpful. Thanks."

She made several calls and finally said, "The Super 8 has lots of room, and from what I hear it is inexpensive, and this one is very nice. I booked you a room under your name."

A bolt of panic shot through Julius. Did he really want his name out there? But the guys chasing him were dead, weren't they? Were there others? The best his tired mind could muster was that it was too late; the motel already had his name. He would have to live with it. In a husky voice he said, "Thanks again, I appreciate your help. Good night." Turning gingerly, he ambled through the automatic doors at the entrance to the emergency room, arriving at the curb just as the cab pulled up. He carefully folded himself into the back seat, then muttered the name of the hotel. If the cabby spoke to him, he didn't hear. He rode in silence until the cab stopped under the portico at the front entrance. Taking his wallet from the soggy clothes in the bag, he paid the fare. He walked into the motel trying to look casual, but the desk clerk started when he saw him and continued to appraise him warily. Julius hadn't seen himself in a mirror yet, but he knew how his skin felt, so he could only imagine how he looked. He thought he would offer some explanation, "Was in a car wreck and just came from the hospital. I need to get some sleep. I'll be fine in the morning."

"Do you want a wake-up call?" the night clerk asked cautiously.

"No, I just want to sleep," rasped Julius, but as his mouth formed the words he remembered he needed to see Deputy Castillo. He said, "Scratch that, give me a call at eight, please." He began to walk away, paused, then turning lethargically to face the desk, handed the clerk a business card and said, "Would you call the home number on this card and tell whoever answers I'm sorry I missed dinner, and I'm alright, and I'll call in the morning. Thanks."

He turned to look for his room. He hardly remembered opening the door and climbing into bed where he fell instantly into a dreamless, restoring sleep.

Chapter 19

THE MEAL WAS FINISHED, THE TABLE CLEARED, THE DISHES DONE and put away, the table cloth brushed and smoothed, the small vase of flowers returned to the center of the table. To keep Cora company the three of them returned to the dining room, taking their places around the table, the conversation broken by long periods of contemplative silence, each playing through their private dreads, and then rewinding. The gong clock continued to chime, but no one was keeping track.

The ringing of the house phone jolted them back to reality, causing Brittany to awkwardly leap from her seat, almost taking the table cloth and its contents with her. Both Jim and Eddie reacted as well, but Brittany was ahead of them. She snatched up the phone and shouted, "Dad?!" There was a pause on the other end of the line.

"Uh … no … I'm calling on behalf of a Mr. Barlow. I'm the desk manager at the Super 8 motel in Marshall, Texas. I was handed a business card with this number on it and asked to call and tell whoever answered, that Mr. Barlow was OK, and he will call in the morning. Who is this I'm speaking to?"

"Sorry," Brittany apologized and gave her name, "Mr. Barlow is my father and we've been worried sick about him. Thank you for the call." Brittany started to put the phone down and then raised it again, shouting in a voice that could have carried several streets over. "Hello? Hello? Are you still there?" She thought for a moment the motel manager had gone, but at last he came back on the line.

"Yes … I'm here. Is there anything else?"

"Is he OK?"

"I think so," the manager replied, "he said he was in a wreck and had just come from the hospital. He looked pretty bruised, and all but asleep on his feet."

"Do you know what hospital he came from? Is there any way I can find out what happened?" Panic was rising in her voice.

"Sorry, he was dropped off by a cab and that's all I know."

"OK, I appreciate your help," said Brittany with a disappointed sigh as she terminated the call, and walked slowly back to the table as if in a daze.

"So? … Don't keep us in suspense!" said Eddie and Jim almost simultaneously.

She relayed the message to them, and added in a raised tone, leaning against the door frame, "I don't understand what's going on. If Dad is OK then why didn't he call us himself? Maybe we should call the Marshall police and see if they know anything. He's been hurt, and there's no one there to help him." Her voice was breaking, her words tumbling out into a ragged pile.

Jim stood quickly, putting his arm around her shoulders, encouraging her to lean into him. He glanced at Eddie and they exchanged a silent warning. "Brit, Eddie and I are here. We'll get to the bottom of this. If Dad said he would call in the morning, we probably should respect that. He was clearly too tired, or hurt, or something to want to talk on the phone, so let's leave him alone. We don't need to get the police involved, since we know where he is, and he's been to the hospital. I know it's hard, but I think we should let this go until the morning."

"I agree with Jim, Sis. Let's wait this out until Dad calls. I don't think there's much we can do tonight."

In spite of her intense weariness, Cora had been listening attentively, examining, when possible, each face as it spoke. Brittany had always displayed good intuition, and Cora was worried because Brittany was worried. But Jim and Eddie were right. If the message delivered by the motel manager had indeed come from Julius, then it would be best to leave it until morning. Clearly something serious had happened, but all they knew at this point was that Julius was alright, and that was comforting.

Over the years Cora had learned how to live with an aviator husband. Stuff happened. Atmospheric conditions, mechanical issues, air traffic, all conspired to frustrate a pilot's best laid plans. But Julius had been good at striking back. He planned his flights around weather, kept his plane in top condition, and paid attention to his gut when making the decision to fly or not. He had experienced 'get-home-itis' but had never succumbed to it—that she knew of anyway. Based on her knowledge of Julius and his flying expertise, she was more inclined to believe that his injuries, if they were injuries at all, were not inflicted by the Navajo but by something more ground-bound—and this worried her more. With effort, Cora tried to sit straighter in her bed, its head previously elevated so she could eat, and raised her voice sufficiently to be heard above the concerned discussion. "Listen to Eddie, kids. Dad may be hurt, we don't really know how badly, and he's been to the hospital and released," she took a labored breath, "so his injuries can't be life threatening. … Let's wait until he calls in the morning." A cough caused her to collapse back onto her bed, a gasp escaping her lips. Three heads silently turned toward her, each feeling some relief, each knowing the cost of the comfort her comment had brought.

Chapter 20

Wednesday

AT EIGHT O'CLOCK, JULIUS WOKE TO THE PHONE JANGLING ON THE night stand beside the motel bed. He had been dozing in and out for the past hour, and was glad for the wake-up call, since it gave him a reason to get out of bed. Drawing back the covers, he lowered his feet gingerly to the floor, performing a self-check as he did so. His mind seemed more intact, and he sensed a small spark of energy, but his body was stiff and sore from his forehead to his toes. Rejecting the impulse to curl up and return to hibernation under the covers, Julius forced himself to get on his feet. An inner voice said everything was going to be alright. He was able to walk and stand upright as long as he ignored the insistent, nagging pain throughout his body.

He had no luggage, so he rinsed his mouth, washed his face cautiously, and dressed. He couldn't remember, but it appeared he had had the presence of mind to lay out his wet clothes in the hope they would be dry by morning. Although wrinkled and misshapen they would have to do. He checked the result in the slightly askew mirror on the bathroom door, deciding it wasn't pretty, but it would allow him to do what had to be done.

Pulling the phone book from the desk drawer, he searched for the Sheriff's office, circling a number with the blue hotel pen. He took the handset from the phone and dialed nine, then the number. A desk clerk answered, and he asked for Rikki Castillo.

"Good morning, this is Deputy Castillo. How can I help you?"

"Good morning. My name is Julius Barlow. I'm a friend of Marty Goodman. I believe you know him, or at least know *of* him. He suggested I have a conversation with you about something rather important."

"Yes … Mr. Barlow … I read the preliminary accident report when it circulated through our office this morning. I know Marty, but only in passing. What is it you wish to talk about?"

"It's not something I can discuss over the phone. I need to see you in person and as soon as possible. I think it will take about an hour or so."

"OK … I'll push some other things aside and see you this morning. Any particular time?"

"How about in a half hour. I'm at the Super 8 near the hospital and I'm going out now to get a cab."

"Alright, I'll see you soon, then. Just ask for me at the front desk." And the connection was broken.

Julius replaced the receiver and immediately picked it up again. He dialed his home number and Sheri answered.

"I see you're in early this morning, Sheri. I guess the kids called you last night?"

Sheri was insistent, "Julius, are you alright?! The kids were frantic last night wondering how you were. The motel manager said your face was bruised and swollen. What in the world happened?"

"I only have a few minutes, so I'll give you the very short version. … I was driving a loaner from the airport and had an accident. The air bags burned my face, and my muscles are stretched and twisted, but, according to the hospital, I don't have any *real* injuries. I'm stepping out right now for a meeting at the county Sheriff's office. I'll start home right after—I don't really know when that will be. Tell the kids I'm OK and I'll be home tonight."

Sheri replied, "OK, I'll let them know. And Cora? What do you want me to tell her?"

"Give her the same scoop. As long as she knows I'm OK, she'll be fine. Thanks Sheri. Gotta run."

Terminating the call, he stuffed the jump suit into the bag that had held his clothes, and left the room, retrieving as he went the newspaper someone had pushed under his door sometime during the night. He stopped at the front desk and payed for the room with a credit card. Stepping into the breakfast room, he picked up a bagel and a cup of coffee then hailed one of the cabs waiting at the curb.

The cab ride was lost in his reverie and his hunger. The weather front had passed, and the expected high pressure system was in full bloom, blanketing the city with blinding sun. He moved the paper out of the glare and found in the right hand corner near the bottom, a short article about the accident.

> Last night about 7:15 two cars collided at the intersection of Route 9 and county road 2611. The collision involved a late model Lincoln and an older Jeep Cherokee. The two occupants of the Lincoln were pronounced dead at the scene. The sole occupant of the Jeep was picked up on Route 9 by Harrison County Deputies and taken to hospital in Marshall. The heavy rain at the time is presumed to be the cause of the accident, pending investigation.

Julius put down the bagel as his pulse quickened. There were *three* in the Lincoln when he had peered into the misshapen car, and yet only *two* were reported. What about the third man? This has to be a mistake! Maybe Deputy Castillo would have some more information.

When the cab arrived at the Sheriff's office, he had eaten and felt considerably stronger. Stepping out of the cab, he paid the fare, then turned to face the building. The office was in the lower level of the Harrison County court house, a three story yellow brick structure lit by wide floor-to-ceiling windows, offset by dark, opaque panels marking the lower third of each floor. The cab had deposited him in a small, dedicated drop off zone close to the entrance on Houston Street. A roll-up garage door stood to his immediate right, followed by six or eight parking spaces for official vehicles. A public parking lot, on the other side of Franklin Street, peeked out from behind the building. Although the windowless, grey steel door was uninviting from the outside, it opened into a pleasant but small room with a combination-locked door, a few chairs, and a reception window.

Reaching the window, he told the desk clerk he was here to see Deputy Rikki Castillo and yes, he had an appointment. The desk clerk reached for the phone and after a few words rang off, motioning Julius to sit in a reception chair and wait to be escorted.

Before Julius could get seated, the door opened and a middle-aged woman about five feet eight inches tall, with dark hair tied tightly at the back in a ponytail and wearing a deputy's uniform, introduced herself, confirmed it was Julius, and ushered him into the large, first-floor workspace which was divided into a maze by partitions; some fabric, some glass. The atmosphere was buzzing with various voices on phone calls, and others discussing cases with colleagues. They walked down the aisle, past windowed rooms containing metal desks, past a nook with a large copy machine, past bulletin boards plastered with notices and pictures, to a small, but adequate, windowed office containing a modern wooden desk behind which stood a table and some filing cabinets, with several chairs scattered around the room. It was certainly nothing elaborate, but it had the air of efficiency, with neat piles of papers, charts and file folders, and a laptop cradled in a docking station.

Julius took a chair across from the desk and asked if he could close the door. Deputy Castillo's eyes flashed something Julius didn't recognize, and after a brief pause she said, "Sure ... and make yourself comfortable."

Deputy Castillo opened the conversation, "Deputy Patterson will want to talk with you about the accident so he can complete his report. But I suspect that's not why you asked to speak to me ...?"

Julius paused for a moment with his head lowered as he gathered his thoughts. Leaning forward while staring at the floor, he offered, "I have a long story to tell you and it's hard to know where to begin. I think it's best if I tell you about yesterday first, then I'll fill in the details. But before I get started I want you to understand I've told no one else this story." He wiped at his bruised face as he looked up to meet her gaze. "No disrespect, but I have no way of knowing if I can trust you. I'm relying entirely on Marty's recommendation." Julius paused to gauge Deputy Castillo's reaction to his statement. The look on her face reflected a mixture of fascination and what may have been taken for pity; he saw no hint of condescension or malice, so he bolstered his courage and continued.

"Before I get into all this, can you confirm what I read in the paper this morning ... there were *two* men found in the Lincoln, both dead?"

Castillo looked directly at him and replied, "As far as I know, the Deputy who dealt with the wreck reported two men dead, both in the front seat. Why do you ask?"

"Because there were *three* in the car when I checked after the accident. There was a man in the back seat who wasn't moving, and didn't appear to be breathing. His shoulder holster was exposed during the impact and a pistol was hanging partly out of its holster."

Castillo straightened in her chair, her eyes taking on an intelligent intensity that intrigued Julius. "OK, you have my attention. Does this have something to do with the story you want to tell me?"

"It certainly does," replied Julius, and for the next forty-five minutes he explained in detail what had happened the day before. He told her about the strange conversation with the control tower as he was leaving Springhill, about aborting the landing at East Texas, landing in Cypress River, hiding in the bayou, and what he could recall of the accident and its aftermath. Rikki made a few notes on a yellow legal pad but said nothing while the story unfolded.

Julius finished and waited for a response. A chirp from the computer on the desk caused Rikki's eyes to flit across the screen and she said hesitantly, "Um ... It looks like Deputy Patterson wants to see you now. ... You said you would take only an hour of my time, but it's obvious to me you need more. We'll talk again after Patterson is done with you." Rising from her chair, she came around the desk, opened her office door, and escorted a bewildered Julius to Patterson's office.

Chapter 21

SHERI IMMEDIATELY WENT INTO THE DINING ROOM TO TELL CORA what she had just found out. Cora seemed relieved, yet not to the extent Sheri expected.

"I'm just glad he's OK," Cora said with some strain in her voice. Her night had not been without its struggles, but the sleep she had been afforded, interrupted more by her concern for Julius than her pain, brightened her mood and strengthened her body.

Seeing right through her façade, Sheri said with a chuckle, "You can't fool me. You were worried sick, and still are."

Cora responded sheepishly, "I can't put anything past you, can I. If Julius wasn't absolutely certain he was OK, he would have called me directly, or at least provided more information in his message, don't you think? I know him too well to even entertain the thought that he could be in trouble and not tell me. It's just ... well ... he hasn't missed a night at home for several years now. He's always made it a point to get back home regardless of where he had to go, and, bless him, he restricted his customers to just the local area so he could do just that. And now it's not true anymore ... that he always comes home, I mean ... it kind of feels like something has been lost forever. Until I see his face, I guess I'll continue to worry."

Sheri looked at her with admiration and said, "You know what? You're one tough cookie." She made sure Cora was comfortable and went to the living room to phone Eddie, Brittany, and Jim.

She was glad Cora was stronger today. It would be a day of doctor's visits and tests, some intrusive; others not. In the beginning, Sheri took everything in stride. She was there as a nurse, and nurses performed and participated in procedures which were not always pleasant. But those days were gone and the remoteness of her professionalism had faded. Each jab and poke and prod done to Cora seemed to resonate with something deep inside her. Throughout her career she had carefully guarded herself against this very thing, and had moved on when she felt the slightest confusion between compassion and empathy. But not so with Cora. Cora had stolen her heart sometime when she wasn't looking, and there was no way she could wrest it back and walk away.

Dr. Sykes would be arriving soon. Cora didn't leave the house for appointments any more—going out had stopped about eight months ago when she no longer had sufficient control of the muscles in her back. She could have been delivered by ambulance for each consultation, but Julius flatly refused to endorse such ignominy. He was happy to pay the extra to ensure Cora would remain in the relative comfort of her home.

Sykes was Cora's spine surgeon. He had been consulted when Cora's vertebrae had started showing signs of deterioration. Early on, before Cora's condition had been diagnosed by Dr. Garret, Sykes had fused four of Cora's discs in an effort to return some mobility. She walked, rode a stationary bike, and swam frequently to aid the bone grafts and to restore the lazy muscles. But she continued to weaken. The inability of her body to respond to the arthrodesis was a major factor in leading them to Dr. Garret and his diagnosis—and for that they were grateful.

Dr. Sykes did not make many house calls, but for Cora he made an exception. His practice was a busy one. Because his major expertise revolved around spinal injury and back problems, he was also trained in pain management, since pain was so intricately involved with spinal issues. It was Cora's pain management that brought him to her this day. He sat in the well-worn chair beside Cora's bed and enquired, "Well, ma'am, I need a full report on your pain for the past week. Everything since we last met. Leave nothing out." His authoritative and no-nonsense-today tone totally mocked by the smile that caused deep wrinkles around his eyes. She shifted a little, being careful not to allow the grimace to show. Sykes knew her stoicism and saw the pain flit across her face. Letting her know he knew, he said, "And how about yesterday?" Cora didn't want to admit she had had a very bad day, so she looked at Sheri and shrugged.

Sheri stepped in, "Yesterday was one of the worst in several days. Not counting the bedsores, which we treated in the usual manner, it seemed every movement caused her some sort of pain. We worked hard at trying to pinpoint its source, but weren't successful. It was as though the internal pain found a different route to the outside each time she stirred. But then she had a reasonable sleep last night." She related this to Sykes as if *she* had owned the pain, recoiling as she described what she had observed; Cora's suffering reflecting on her own features.

Sykes examined Cora carefully, his trained finger tips gently prodding her internal organs to determine if there were any lumps or enlargements signifying trouble. He measured her breathing, lung capacity, and heart beat with his stethoscope, all the while chatting idly with Cora as if they were enjoying a cup of tea in the local park. Whatever his fingers and ears were seeing, nothing of it showed. When he was done, he gently pulled the covers over Cora and rubbed her arms vigorously to restore what warmth she had lost while her skin had been exposed. His gentle bedside manner and his obvious care for Cora's well-being always moved Sheri.

He checked the chart meticulously kept by Sheri, noting fluid outputs were slightly low, but wasn't concerned. After a moment of thought, he charted some mild reactive cardiomegaly in response to his finding Cora's heart slightly enlarged. He told Sheri that if this progressed, it would indicate Cora's muscle degeneration had started affecting her heart—something to which he would have to begin paying close attention. Having finished writing up his findings, he prepared to leave.

When the front door closed behind him, the thought flitted through Sheri's mind that Dr. Sykes must have experienced deep pain at some point in his life; otherwise he could not possibly be as attuned to Cora's struggles as he appeared to be.

Chapter 22

JULIUS EMITTED A MUTED SIGH AS HE SLOWLY LOWERED HIMSELF into the chair opposite Rikki's desk. She was absent-mindedly opening and closing folders, seemingly lost in thought. Her furtive glance at Julius told him she was evaluating the story he had recounted.

"How did it go with Patterson?" she said.

"OK, I guess. There wasn't much about the accident he didn't already know. And," he flicked his eyes over to where Rikki was settling into her desk, checking her reaction, "I didn't tell him anything else—about this other stuff, I mean. He wanted to hear my side of the story directly since I wasn't in any shape to tell him much last night."

Rikki threw him a glance without raising her head, and continued to arrange her desk in preparation for what clearly she thought might be a long discussion. Julius fidgeted in his chair and asked, "Since I've already taken a lot of your time, do you want the long version or the short version?"

Rikki pushed a straggling curl back from her face, locking it behind her ear. Julius noted a sprinkling of grey he hadn't seen earlier. "The long version. If I'm going to help you I need every detail you can give."

"OK. I'll do my best," Julius replied, concern honing a sharp edge to his voice. His trust of Rikki was based solely on the thin thread of Marty's recommendation, and, when it came down to it, what did he really know about Marty? But what choice was there? He was in a position where he had to place his confidence in someone, and with Rikki, for some reason, he sensed she would hear him out at a minimum, perhaps even champion his cause and help him get it resolved—if he were lucky. On his part, he was determined not to leave her office until everything was on the table and she had promised to help, and maybe, in the process, provide some kind of protection. The terror that had gripped him so tightly the day before had settled somewhat, leaving him with an aching sense of dread shadowing his thoughts.

In the ensuing brief pause they both sat back, ready, so they thought, for the story to unfold.

Julius took a deep breath, looked down at his hands and began.

"I'm a software guy. I write algorithms—formulas, if you like—in computer code which are used in a variety of disciplines. I even have some patents." He lifted his head to see her response. Rikki was stalwart; not impressed ... maybe impressed ... but nothing showing either way. Feeling a little disappointed, Julius continued. "I write for the government, the Department of Defense, medical companies, defense contractors, businesses, and others. Six months ago I was asked to do some work on data security, so I took a course on hacking—perfectly legal, I assure you. Part way through the course we were given an assignment in which we were asked to create a harmless virus, put it out there, and document how it fared. I created a hitch-hiker virus to hunt around for a vulnerable server then back-pack out some data—not a lot, just something to show it worked. I wrote and tested the virus, releasing it one evening not expecting it to return anything. Because I write algorithms for a living, I built some high-brow stuff into the virus, just for fun, and I was a little less restrictive on the volume of data to be back-packed than I had originally intended. I really didn't expect anything to come back due to the stringent search criteria I had built into the formula. My plan was then to dumb down the virus and send it out again, repeating this until I finally had a hit. It would give me an idea of how secure the servers are in this area, and that would just be a cool bonus.

"I was astounded, and somewhat ashamed, when I was success-ful the first night. When I checked for results the next morning, my virus had returned to me a full pack of data. I was floored, really. At just a few seconds after two in the morning, the virus had located a vulnerable server, pirated a bag-load of data, and shipped it back to my computer. The virus told me where it obtained the data, or at least the IP address, so I did a little research and discovered it belonged to the Parks Hospital for Children."

Rikki's eyebrows shot up and her mouth appeared to begin saying something, so Julius continued, not wanting to be interrupted. "At first I didn't want to even look at the data because I felt so guilty about stealing it. But my curiosity got the better of me. I have a Top Secret clearance, and figured there couldn't be anything in the data above my pay grade, so to speak, so I took a peek. Recognizing patterns immediately, I went insane. I just had to figure out what the data meant. It was like a Rubik's Cube sitting on the shelf with the colors all messed up. I just couldn't leave it alone.

"I don't know how much you know about the way computers store data, so I'm going to briefly enlighten you, to help you understand my graduation from one level of this mess to the next. I'll apologize up front for it being a little tedious … OK … boring … but you wanted the detail, right?

"Computers configured to handle large amounts of data use databases consisting of rows and columns. The columns are the data elements, like a name or a phone number. Rows are like the names and phone numbers of different people … like your address book for email. Most databases are constructed so data is not repeated—or at least, if repeated, then repeated in controlled ways. For example, your cell phone company has an account for you, and it keeps track of phone calls, texts, invoices and so on. It would be crazy to put your name and address on the record of every phone call and every text, so it keeps a *table*, so called, containing your name and address, which is assigned a unique identifier, and then that identifier is placed on each of your phone and text records. If your address changes, it is changed in just one place and doesn't affect the hundreds, or thousands, or millions, of other records in your account. Well, I noticed a pattern in the data my virus had collected, and it looked to me like rows and columns—a database almost certainly. But a database of what?

"I wrote a few programs to scan through the data looking for more elusive patterns, and the short of it is that I was able to reconstruct the database to some degree. It consisted of billing records. It wasn't complete of course, so I was able to reconstruct only a limited amount of consistent data, but enough to keep me digging.

"Several years ago I did some work for a medical company and had to work with the Healthcare Common Procedure Coding System or HCPC, as it is known. I found some codes I thought I recognized and wrote a program to cross-reference them with the HCPC database. I located a column in one table that was clearly just codes, with associated columns handling dates and reference identifiers, probably links to doctor's names or patient names. I also located a table with very few columns, so it was clear it had been built for a very specific purpose. It contained a reference identifier and a date and a few flags—yes/no types of information.

"It became clearer than ever the data I had stolen were billing records from the hospital. The short table I mentioned a moment ago intrigued me, so I looked at it more closely. I should mention at this point that many database tables have a common stump—a block of columns replicated in every table—typically containing a link to who created the record, when it was created, who modified the record and when, and so on. All the tables in this database had a stump. None of the records in any table had an entry in the 'date-modified' column except *this* small table. I thought it was odd. If you were to ask a database administrator what the dearth of modified dates meant, you would likely be told these were records permitting single entry only, and could not be modified once entered. Such would be typical of billing information, I suppose. The software would simply not allow it. So why was this one table different?

"I'll skip ahead a bit since how I arrived at the next anomaly was entirely coincidental. Being a hospital where sometimes people die, I had my computer look in the local online obituaries to see if there were any matches to the dates in this short table. There were none, but some did fall within a few days. In fact I was able to match every date in the short table with an obit date just off by two and sometimes three days—always *after* the obit date. Coincidence perhaps? But I thought not.

"The obit gave me names, all children, as you would expect, with family names and funeral homes, so I made a few calls. I didn't want to seem insensitive so I researched only a few of them. I called the funeral homes to verify the date of death and each confirmed the obit.

"The only conclusion I could come to was the date of death had been altered on these records, and hence a *modified* date existed. So why would the date of death be modified on so many records—any for that matter? Determining what I thought to be the patient identifier, I checked it with other tables, and found a match with what I assumed to be the billing. And this is where things really went off the rails. I discovered billings were made for HCPC codes *after* the date of death reported by the obit, and before the date of death on the short table.

"I know this isn't forensic level proof of fraud, but it certainly looked like it to me. So what was I to do with this information? Initially I thought of reporting it, but then the data was obtained in a manner some might construe as sketchy at best, and I didn't have the whole picture, and it could well be just coincidence, or I may be misreading the data, so why should I get in the middle of it. If I had had real proof I certainly would have come forward, and I regret now not doing so, but I thought at the time I was doing the right thing. So I created a file in an encrypted format, took it to a friend and had it put on a tiny micro-chip. I thought of simply destroying the data, but in an egocentric moment of concern about self-preservation, I thought if the hospital discovered I had stolen the data, I could negotiate my way out of prosecution by handing it over and letting them know that I knew about the scam. Now, thinking about it more objectively, it was probably a really dumb thing to do.

"Anyway, what do you do with a micro-chip of sensitive data? Well, here's where it gets weird. I was having a crown put on a molar, so I asked my dentist to drill a small slot for the chip and embed it in the crown."

Opening his mouth wide, he pointed to one of the upper molars on the left hand side of his mouth and mumbled, "Ith righ u' th'r," then closed his mouth again.

Rikki, leaning over her desk listening intently, not the least bit amused, was making notes on what looked to Julius like the fifth or sixth page of her yellow pad. He hadn't noticed her taking many notes before this moment, and was oblivious as to how many she had actually taken. He was much too engaged in the story, reliving the emotions, and second-guessing the decisions he had made.

Julius paused, inhaled, and was going to start again, but decided it was enough for now. He sat back in his chair, letting his breath out slowly, crossed his arms, and waited.

It took Rikki a few moments to finish writing. When she looked up, her expression said it all. "I don't even know where to begin," she said with an audible sigh. "What I *do* know is I need something to eat. Let's head out for some fresh air and lunch—a late lunch by the look of it," checking her watch as she rose from her chair.

They left the Sheriff's office, working their way North around the Square to the corner of Rusk and Washington, where once resided the Weisman & Co. mercantile which served the community from 1878 until 1990, when the pressures of modern merchandising forced it to close its doors. The building had changed hands several times over the years, and was now an up-scale antique mall. Neither spoke until they were facing the order clerk at the Deli situated in the North quarter of the historic mercantile, when Rikki said, "It's on me today. You need to be *paid* for a story like that."

The Deli clerk stared at them both for just a moment too long, a hint of fear crossing his features. A cop and a guy with a mangled face must have been a bit much to handle. Julius wasn't comfortable with the scrutiny and looked around for a private spot to sit.

Waiting for their food to be prepared, they chose a table for two on the mezzanine, against the railing, from which they could gaze down on the wide variety of antiques, collectibles, gifts, and furniture, gathered into groupings like nests. Each was lost in their own thoughts, unable, or perhaps afraid, to say anything.

It took only a few minutes for their food to be delivered.

As they ate, Julius began to wonder what Rikki's silence meant, but there wasn't much he could do at this point. He had told his story for the very first time, and the reaction it invoked would be what it was—there was no going back.

Julius looked around, soaking in the ambiance of the old mercantile. The various patterns in the embossed tin ceiling tiles reflected what would likely have once demarcated departments within the store, but now, stripped of its original purpose, simply provided a variety which was pleasing to the eye. The central staircase of polished walnut was breathtaking as it curved graciously, spilling onto the mezzanine that stretched full-width along the back wall. The walnut continued in the wainscoting of the mezzanine, attractively sculpted into panels of varying sizes and orientation.

Julius could almost hear the din of shoppers as they scurried about the mercantile, refreshing their household larders, obtaining parts for their buggies and wagons, buying nails and metal sheeting for the new barn, searching for a harness to replace the one that separated while breaking the ground for this year's crop. On the mezzanine he could imagine the support staff at their desks, pounding out invoices and orders on old typewriters, and entering miniscule numbers into large leather-bound ledgers.

Rikki broke into his thoughts, her voice coming from a block away, "The guys in the Lincoln were hired by someone at the hospital to get the data back or eliminate the risk of it being disclosed. Is that what you think?"

It took Julius a moment to return to reality. He slowly replied in a whisper, panic threatening at the edges of his mind, turning his last bite to dust in his mouth. "Yes, exactly. I had a feeling in my gut when I found out the controller was injured—and I'm convinced it was violent—and a bogus controller was working the field, that I was the reason they were there. When they chased me into the bayou, it was very clear to me I was right. This story has lots of weird twists and turns, and perhaps the weirdest of all is that the Jeep I was driving hit their car. We were just inches away from each other, but I immobilized *them,* when they were trying to immobilize *me* … or worse. I had no idea they were in the other car until I looked in to see if I could be of any help after the accident."

"And you claim there were three of them, not the two found in the car?"

"Right," Julius continued in a very soft voice, his heart beginning to pound as he relived the previous day's events. He leaned over the table so his face was very close to hers, "so we have a hired gun out there looking for me …trying to kill me. But we don't know if he's injured or incapacitated or what. We just don't know what we are facing. I don't know if he will go after my family or—"

Rikki interrupted, "Don't go there quite yet. Let's get this into the hands of the right authorities."

She glanced at Julius' plate, noticing he had been pushing the last forkful around, but hadn't the least interest in eating it. She stood up. Julius followed and they headed back to her office, cloaked in silence once again.

Chapter 23

DR. GARRET ARRIVED AT TWO O'CLOCK. CORA HAD BEEN ABLE TO rest a little after Dr. Sykes' visit and had enjoyed a light lunch. Sheri was pleased with how the day was going. She greeted Benjamin—he insisted upon being called by his first name—at the door. As a nurse, Sheri struggled with this informality, but she understood that from the patient's point of view, it made his visits seem more friendly; less cold and clinical. "Allo, Cora, luv. 'ow's me favorite patient this arvo?" he bantered in the cockney accent he reverted to when the occasion permitted. He didn't really expect a reply; it was his usual greeting. He went right to Cora's chart and studied it for several minutes.

Sheri considered Dr. Garret for a moment. He was much too young, or at least young looking, to be a man of his education and experience. His youthful appearance stemmed from his long, lanky frame with drooping shoulders, thin arms, and finely shaped hands. He could have been a concert pianist—perhaps he was one. He wore his hair longer than most, and its length, together with its full rich chestnut color, took years off his age, the smattering of grey hinting at maturity. His face, on the other hand, told a different story. His hazel, sharply intelligent eyes, spoke empathy to his patients, his genuine concern showing in the finely etched lines on his otherwise clear, almost ruddy, skin. His square, slightly cleft jaw, and some-what pointed nose, hinted at his British roots, with perhaps a touch of aristocracy, belied by his cockney affectations.

"Is there anything I can get you?" asked Sheri when she saw he had finished his analysis of the multitude of numbers and medical terms on the pages secured under the spring clip.

"If by that you mean, would I like a cup of tea, then the answer is very much a *yes*. If you meant scones and clotted cream, that also would be a *yes*. But likely it's not what you meant? ... Right, then! ... Tea it is." Standing over Cora, looking at her face, Garret checked her color, the condition of her eyes, and how frequently she attempted to distribute moisture around her mouth. He took Cora's hand as he spoke with her, his eyes intent on hers. He gently pinched the end of her index finger, and, almost imperceptibly, his eyes flitted to the released finger and back again, measuring the speed with which color returned to her nail. Sheri loved to watch him work. He seemed to have a kind of radar, an invisible MRI, which saw the inside of a patient by looking at the outside. His body signaled with a slight jerk that his mind had finished its analyses. He turned abruptly to Sheri and said, "I'll 'ave that cuppa now, if it's all the same to you." Before he left the room he shot a glance back at Cora and said, "I'll be right back, luv. Just getting my afternoon brew. You rest a few."

Sitting at the kitchen table, Benjamin, speaking in lowered tones, told Sheri that based on his analysis of the data on the chart, and, in particular, Dr. Sykes concerns, he thought Cora was entering the final phase of her disease. "How much longer do you think she has then," asked Sheri quietly and solemnly, squeezing the bridge of her nose.

Benjamin took a moment before he answered, returning to his professional voice, "You know I can't give you anything definite, Sheri. We know so little about Cora's condition, so anything I give you is pure conjecture. But once the internal organs are affected and begin reacting to the disease, the end is in sight, but how far off I have no idea—a week, weeks, months. The organs will try to compensate for damage they are sustaining, and we see exactly that beginning in Cora's heart now.

"I see Julius didn't join us for this visit. Could we chat with him? He has a right to know what's coming. If he's here, I would like to be the one to tell him."

"He's away at the moment, so I guess it will have to be me."

"Do you mean *away* away or just out for a bit?"

"He was in some kind of accident near Marshall yesterday and stayed overnight after getting checked out in a local hospital. He called this morning to say he was OK but banged up. He'll be home tonight after dealing with the local cops. I really don't know much more about it than that. I do know it seems to have Cora on edge, so maybe she knows or senses something she's not telling us."

"What was he doing in Marshall?"

"I have no idea," Sheri shrugged. He was supposed to have a meeting in Houston, but I don't think he made it."

"Do you know what time this happened?"

"Not a clue."

"We mustn't let this upset Cora. An anxiety attack run amok could be lethal at this stage, so keep your eyes open, please."

They sat in silence for some minutes, each lost in thought.

Benjamin slid off his chair. "Well, I should be on my way." Finishing his tea, he returned to check on Cora. She was sleeping peacefully, so he didn't disturb her. He headed for the door and took his leave of Sheri. Shooting her a parting glance, concern flickered in his eyes, followed by a silent appeal. She knew that look, and understood fully what it communicated. She would have a long talk with Julius when he arrived home this evening.

Once his car was out on the main road, Dr. Garret's thoughts travelled back to his conversation with Sheri. He had read a brief clip in the paper about an accident on Route 9, but no names had been mentioned. Could this have been the one Julius was involved in? It sounded serious.

Julius was a computer guy and the hospital was in Marshall. Could the two be connected?

He should never have attended the meeting Atchley had called a few weeks back, but how was he to know Atchley would go all squirrely about some data breach at the hospital—and it was a command performance after all. From the way he was talking and from the looks on the faces of the other four doctors, however, it seemed to be a very big deal, at least to *them*.

Once Atchley had started to rant and rave he had simply tuned out and so caught only snippets of the conversation. None of it seemed relevant to him. One thing did niggle at him, however. Once, during the meeting, when Dr. Gomez put on the glasses he kept in the vest pocket of his lab coat, the resulting face triggered a memory he couldn't quite place.

He knew Atchley was doing some magic with the billings, and he had contemplated having his office check it out, but he had never found a spare moment to explore it. He knew Atchley from a joint grad school project, and, when asked, had recommended him to Parks strictly on the merit of his medical talent. He was well aware of Atchley's prickly personality but blamed it on genius.

Blake was concerned about the data being from the billing server, so maybe this did have something to do with his little scheme. Shards of the conversation that wormed their way into his subconscious were returning to him. '...unlikely even an experienced analyst would be able to piece it together, and, even if it could be done, the data is going to look totally legitimate ...' So, this *was* about his tweaking of the billing. The fact that he was ranting at the other doctors meant they must be taking advantage of his scheme. '... it cost me a lot of money to have the reprogramming done ...' Perhaps this ran deeper than he had originally thought. He was aware of a programmer from the hospital who quit, and then went missing—it had been in the papers some months ago. And Blake had said something about blackmail and 'cutting it off'.

His hand became unsteady on the steering wheel. What kind of a mess had he stepped into?

Atchley had used the words 'untraceable', 'undetectable' and 'unbeatable', so this had to be something Atchley had practiced and perfected. He never once thought to check Blake's background for activity outside the medical field. Had he helped unleash a criminal on the children's hospital? When the meeting was over, he remembered the other doctors looking at Blake with a combination of reverence and disgust. Perhaps this should have been a clue.

His thoughts returned to Julius. Julius was 'an experienced analyst' who could 'piece it together', and he couldn't help thinking the accident and Atchley's scheme were somehow connected. What if Blake had tried to get to Julius by arranging a car accident which simply backfired? What if Blake used his influence to somehow get to Cora? What if Blake tried to use *him* to get to Cora? ... He would simply have to refuse and threaten to expose Blake's scheme ... but this was Atchley we're talking about.

His shoulders sagged as he revisited the times his lunch money had been stolen by bullies, and he had gone hungry yet again ...

Bah, this was all far-fetched nonsense! Blake knew about the data but had no idea who took it. In fact there was no indication anyone knew who had hacked their computers. So there's no way he could have targeted Julius. There was nothing in the news or elsewhere, as far as he knew, which would tie these things together, but it had caused his neck muscles to cramp, and he couldn't seem to let it go.

He reached his office, strode past the reception desk without comment, pulled out his office chair and sank into it, then stared at the closed door of his office unable to shake the lump forming in the pit of his stomach.

Chapter 24

AFTER THEY WERE SETTLED ONCE AGAIN IN DEPUTY CASTILLO'S office, she began, rolling up both sleeves, "Julius, insurance fraud and in particular Medicare fraud, if indeed it's what we are dealing with here, is a federal issue, and the FBI will need to be brought into this. Your story is believable only because it's unbelievable. I have no reason to doubt you, but bringing this to the Feds opens a different can of worms. You may well spend your time going through your story time after time, and in the end, they may tell you there is insufficient evidence to start an investigation. You need to be prepared for that disappointment."

"But, with one of those thugs still on the loose, fraud is no longer at the top of my list, Deputy. He, or they, know who I am, where I live, and my—our— safety needs to be the main focus," said Julius, his right leg bouncing involuntarily. "When I thought the three of them were dead it was a different story; I thought time might be on my side. But now—"

Rikki broke in, raising her hand in a calming gesture, "I'm sorry; you're exactly right. OK, we'll deal with your safety first, and since the wreck and the dead stalkers are in my jurisdiction, I think we can keep the case at home for the moment. If and when we make a connection, we'll consider handing it off."

Sitting back in his chair, Julius folded his arms, his breathing slowly returning to normal. He was beginning to be captivated by

Deputy Castillo, and he wanted to observe her for a while in an effort to determine why. Perhaps he was grateful for her listening to his story; well, he *knew* he was grateful, and maybe it was his gratitude talking. Or maybe she reminded him of someone. Or maybe he just liked her as a person. Whatever the case, he was going to stay quiet until she developed a strategy for what to do next.

Rikki sat deep in thought, her face changing expression several times, mirroring a rough plan as it began to form. She took a few moments to piece it together. Putting her hands flat on the desk, she spoke, her words hesitant at first, "I … have an idea … we should explore. As I said, I can live with not going to the Feds just yet. I'm afraid their hands may be tied with so little to go on. It's a judgment call at this point, since the evidence is sketchy at best. If it's the wrong call, I'll have some explaining to do, but I think it is defensible. … However at some point we have to involve them; you need to understand that. So … with just us in it for the moment, we can proceed at our own pace and in our own way without interference. We need to find a way of collecting the evidence necessary to get the Feds interested."

"And offer some protection in there somewhere…?"

"Yes, of course. But I think the two are going to be inseparable."

With the seeds of a plan on the table, Julius felt his dark mood lightening; the weight of his predicament beginning to lift from his shoulders. Does this mean you believe me and are hopping into this rowboat, so to speak, regardless of where it's sailing?"

The smile that twitched on Rikki's lips spoke of his botched metaphor and, relaxing her professional restraint momentarily, she replied in a sarcastic tone, "Of course. Your story is simple, straight forward, and easily verified, so where is the risk? We should have this matter concluded by the end of the day."

Julius caught the lightness of her tone and tried to appear angry, saying curtly, "Well, if you're going to be that way about it."

This break in the earlier somber mood surprised them both, and silence reigned for a few moments while each pondered its implications. The smile faded from Julius' face, "OK. I'm in your hands. So, what do *we* have to do to collect what's needed for the Feds? Hey, keep in mind, this is completely out of my league, and certainly way beyond anything I've ever done before, so clearly you have to take the lead. I'll offer what I can."

"As I think this through, there is someone else we should bring into our confidence. I've never worked with her personally but her name has appeared in briefings and case reports from other counties. She is an insurance investigator with the York Standard Health Insurance Company, a national carrier, and she would be able to give us some pointers. Oh ... but she wouldn't be able to help if her carrier is not involved. So I guess the first thing we need to find out is whether YSHI is a company who gets billed by the hospital." Her expression changed as the thought hit her. "But I can make that happen quite easily." She dialed the hospital administration and said, "Hello, my name is Brenda and I have insurance with York Standard Health and I wondered if your hospital can bill them directly if I bring my child in for some tests ... Right ... I understand, yes ... Thank you for your help. Bye ..." and she replaced the handset.

"And ...?"

"Yes, they do bill YSHI but only for very specific procedures, so, and I quote, 'I would have to check with my doctor to make sure'. So it isn't certain Ms. Jansen, the insurance investigator I spoke of earlier, will be able to help us, but I think we should get her involved anyway and see where it leads."

"Rikki ... are you certain we should bring a third-party in on this? What if my name leaks out and these guys come after me with a vengeance?"

"Hey, are you alright? Have you forgotten yesterday so soon? It seems to me your name has already leaked out. And they've already come after you with a vengeance."

"OK, OK, you're right. If you think we can trust her then let's do it."

"By the way, her first name is spelled, K-A-A-T-J-E. It's Dutch, and I'm not sure how it's pronounced, but thankfully she goes by Kate."

After a moment Rikki said, "I think we should call it a day. Behind those bruises you look totally wasted, and besides, I have to finish a few things if I'm going to dedicate my time to this. And I'll call Kate. I think you'll be safe for a while—but I have no idea for how long. You said the ring leader of the thugs who were after you was in the front seat, and unless there was some rapid seat switching just before the deputies arrived, I think we can consider him dead. I'm not happy there's a third man on the loose, but it is my professional opinion it will take time for him to regroup, get instructions, report back, whatever. Whoever they are, I expect their plans have been disrupted sufficiently to buy you some time. I suggest you make arrangements to be away from home for the next several days and take a room at the Forty Winks Motel just around the corner. I know it's corny and sounds like a flea bag, but we use it as a kind of low-level safe house, and I'm certain you'll be OK there. Its proximity will help us work together, and it saves the commute home each day which, if I were after you, would be the time I would make my move."

"Uh … well … risk or no risk, I can't stay … won't work for me. I really need to be home. I've already caused my wife enough stress being away last night and so much of today … as long as my body is still functioning I'll drive back tomorrow for the meeting. Say nine thirty?"

Rikki raised one eyebrow but let it pass. "Fine. It's entirely up to you."

She rose from her chair, leaned over the desk, looked Julius in the eyes and said, "We're gonna get these guys. The more I think about their cheating the system … on the backs of kids, no less … the madder I get. I'll see you tomorrow." Sitting back down, she began attending to the files on her desk.

Julius left her office. His day was not done yet. He still had several decisions to make and wasn't clear yet just what to do next.

As he reached the security door, Julius suddenly spun on his heels. Marching back to Rikki's office, he knocked on the open door. Rikki raised her head slightly as Julius entered. "Back so soon?"

"I need one more favor, Rikki. I would like to get my airplane back home. What better place to ambush me than at the airport, knowing I'm not going to abandon my plane. I'll also need some backup when I explain to the airport manager how I shortened his Jeep. Any chance I could have a deputy drive me to the airport and hang around until I'm airborne?"

"Mm, you may have a point there. I still think we're correct in assuming the third assailant will lie low. I doubt he will head to the Springhill airport to wait for you any time soon … but waiting at an airport so close to Marshall is a different matter. Give me a few minutes to scare someone up."

Fifteen minutes later Julius was sitting beside a deputy in a county cruiser heading for the Cyprus River airport.

Chapter 25

JULIUS BURST THROUGH THE FRONT DOOR ANXIOUS TO SEE CORA for the first time in two days. Going straight to the dining room, he took the chair beside the bed and sat facing her. Taking her hand he said softly, "Cora, I'm so sorry I didn't make it home last night. It just wasn't possible—but I'll tell you all about it in a few minutes. You had doctors today? Anything I should know?" As he was speaking, Sheri came down the stairs and caught his eye, giving him a silent warning. "Actually, all that can wait, Cora. Tell me how you're feeling." He had learned to be patient. Cora often took a few moments to gather her thoughts, particularly when she had been resting.

She turned her head slowly so she could look him in the eyes, and her mouth flew open. "Julius ... your face?"

"Now don't worry about me. I'm a little banged up but I'm really OK. Let's talk about you and your day."

With a softness returning to her voice, she sighed, "I'm not doing badly today. Bad day yesterday, worse in the afternoon, but Sheri has been great, and Brittany stayed with me last night. Sykes and Garret were in today, but you'll have to ask Sheri about it. I wasn't told anything new." The effort brought a glaze to her eyes, indicating she had already overspent her energy, and Julius took careful note.

He caressed her cheek with his free hand, leaning to kiss her lips. She tried her best to respond. "You rest a bit. I'll be right back."

Sheri motioned for him to sit at the kitchen counter where they could talk privately. She relayed to him what Sykes had discovered and Garret's interpretation of it. Julius took it in stride, but the extra color left by the air bag burns had drained from his face, and the creases on his brow deepened. "Any mention of how long?"

"I asked. Garret said a week, or weeks, or even months. Progression of the symptoms will be the key, and today was the first evidence … so we're right at the beginning—but it has begun—that's the bad news."

Julius paused for a moment of thought before he said, "Thanks, Sheri. I don't know what we'd do without you. Why don't you head home and I'll see you in the morning. I have to go back to Marshall first thing. Maybe I can conclude things there. I'll give you the whole story, I promise, as soon as I can."

"Julius, are you sure you need to go again? These last couple of days have been really hard on Cora and the doctors would have liked to talk to you," her voice pleading.

"I'm stuck in this mess now and I have to see it through, Sheri. I don't like it any more than you do, but it is what it is."

Accepting his dismissal, Sheri headed for home. Julius followed her with his eyes as she stepped through the doorway, then turned to look back. The frown on her face spoke of trouble that had entered their home, and was now loitering in the lobby, hands in pockets, just waiting for its chance to pounce.

Julius owed Cora an explanation for missing dinner, the night in the motel, and the color of his face. The little he had told Sheri was insufficient; the entire story would be too much. He had to find a balance between the information Cora deserved, and the details that would cause her additional distress.

Trying to keep the emotion of the last two days from his voice, he narrated the days' events as if reading a story. "When I left our airport yesterday morning and found the controller less than professional, I felt I had to question it. I called Shreveport ATC and asked them to look into it. When they responded with the news that Carlos had been assaulted, it set my entire day on edge." He told her of reaching East Texas and deciding not to land. He recounted backtracking to Cypress River, of borrowing the old jeep, and driving out to Caddo Lake to the bayou where he grew up. "I left the bayou just as the sun was setting, and was caught in a heavy rainstorm. Visibility was reduced to almost zero. Suddenly there was a car crossing my path. I hit it broadside, landing us both into a field near the corner. I was really shaken but I seemed to be intact, so I crawled out through the window and checked on the occupants in the other car. It looked to me like all three were dead, so I called 911 and started walking down the road looking for help. The only bright spot was Marty Goodman—do you remember him?" Cora nodded slightly, one shoulder raised briefly. "Well, he's a paramedic now, and he was on duty when the ambulance came to get me. It was great to see him after all this time, and it was comforting to have someone I knew working on me." He told of his stay at the hospital and their pronouncement that he was shredded and burned, but OK. He spoke of finding the motel and needing to get onto the bed to sleep for fear of falling asleep on his feet somewhere between the cab and his room. Cora already knew about the motel manager's call to them and his message that Julius was damaged but OK.

"This morning I went to the Sheriff's office to do the paperwork associated with the accident—it took most of the day—and then I asked a deputy to drive me to the airport to get the Navajo and help me explain to the airport manager what had happened to his vehicle. I was afraid he may not believe the story if the deputy wasn't there to back me up." He told Cora he would likely have to pay for the jeep, since the airport manager hedged a bit when asked if it was insured. "There will be fallout from the accident and loose ends to put to bed for the next week or so. In fact I will be going back to Marshall again tomorrow morning to meet with a deputy."

Julius felt a pang of guilt. Although he wasn't telling Cora any untruths—except maybe for the 'all day' part—he was ashamed of himself for not telling her the whole truth.

"But, Julius, why ... didn't you ... go to your meeting ... in Houston, I mean?"

If she were stronger, and certainly, as he explained to himself, if her condition weren't declining, then maybe he would have told her the whole story. But he just couldn't burden her with all the facts—not just yet—maybe never.

But she was no longer listening. As fatigue took control, her eyelids sagged and she mumbled through a yawn, "Please stay with me tomorrow, I need you here to help me understand what the doctors are saying … about …"

Chapter 26

Thursday

MORNING, RIKKI," SAID JULIUS AS HE ENTERED HER OFFICE. "SORRY I'm late. I took Route 43 thinking it would be faster, but it turned out to be a stupid thing to do. I guess I'll take I-20 next time and hope the traffic doesn't get me."

Not taking her eyes off the file she was reading, she asked, "How are you feeling after a night's rest?" Then she glanced over to see if his physical appearance had improved. "Your bruises look a little less fresh, but you really are a mess. How's getting around; you doing OK?"

Rikki's mood appearing to be all business, he had to assume she hadn't found out anything overnight that would curb her willingness to help him. He replied, "I feel like I've been hit by a truck, both physically and emotionally. They say the second day is the worst, and this is it." He paused briefly. "What do we have on our plates today?"

"Actually, the third day is the worst," she muttered to a file folder.

"I have Kate Jansen coming in for ten o'clock. I thought I would give you a little leeway, since you did have to drive a bit to get here, and I wasn't certain you would be able to get out of bed this morning at all. I pretty much expected a call saying you were staying put. Why don't you get caffeinated and relax until then."

"And where do I go to do that?"

Rikki showed him where the kitchen was, and Julius poured a coffee then sat at a lunch table waiting to be summoned. He was surprised at the coffee's quality; it tasted good and was nicely brewed. It was nothing like the stereotypical squad room coffee popularized on TV shows. In fact this whole Sheriff's office was not stereotypical at all. The kitchen was modern and clean, and the fridge where he found some real cream didn't contain age-old sandwiches ripe with mold. It *was* quite full, but of lunch-sized plastic containers, each with a name. Some cartons also had names or initials scribbled on them. Things looked organized and well kept.

At ten o'clock Rikki fetched Julius and led him to her office. On the way, Julius was trying to picture Kate. She was Dutch, so she would be tall, blonde, slender, and, being an insurance investigator—he couldn't quite decide—would she be dressed to the nines, or would she have six-guns on her hips?

As he walked through Rikki's door, Kate stood to greet him and it took him a moment to recover himself before he could say hello. Eventually he sputtered, "Good morning, Ms. Jansen. I'm Julius Barlow. Thanks for meeting with me today."

"Good morning," replied Kate as she peripherally examined the damage to his face, "I'm pleased to meet you. Let's use first names, it takes less effort, and we'll be spending considerable time together I expect. Rikki has given me a four sentence briefing of the situation, and, since she's vouching for you, I think we have some crooks to catch; how about you?"

Rikki motioned for them to sit. Julius had been so wrong about Kate's appearance. She was dark-haired, shorter than Rikki, and … how to put it? … frumpy. He thought likely she would clean up well, but in her relaxed working clothes she could easily be a waitress at the local diner or the secretary of a sleazy private eye. Perhaps that was her secret; she looked totally harmless.

Kate led off, "I need to know the whole story, Julius. No abridging, nothing left out … everything. Sometimes details may not seem important to you but they solve the case in the end, so be precise."

Julius began at the beginning. He thought this would bore Rikki to death, but he figured cops were used to hearing stories multiple times. He assumed it allowed them to search for inconsistencies and pick out obscure details. He continued until his throat was dry and he had emptied himself of all the details he could remember.

At last he said, "So that's it, I think. I don't know if I, or my family, are in any danger right now, but I'm certain we will be once these guys regroup. I don't know if putting them away will increase *my* safety since it's entirely possible the hit has been prepaid, but getting them behind bars sounds like a priority … as long as I live to be of assistance."

Rikki had scribbled a few notes, so Julius knew there were some things he had clarified—or she had thought of some additional questions, perhaps. Kate had made several pages of notes, which she was now flipping through.

"So the summary of all this is that it was dumb luck you stole this data, and, if you'll excuse me, it was dumb luck you discovered what it contained. Accurate?"

"Well, I suppose so. Perhaps we should say discovering what the data meant was dumb luck tempered with some clever analysis brought about by years of extensive experience."

"OK, you get a point there. But in the end this all boils down to bad luck for whoever is doing this."

Both Julius and Rikki responded with a brief nod.

"Lucky or unlucky," repeated Julius, "here we are, and as much as I want to stop any abuse of the medical system, my top priority is still the safety of my family. While I'm here in Marshall, my wife and family are back in Springfield with no clue as to what's going on, or the danger they're in. I'm not sure if I could actually protect them from whatever's coming, but I certainly know I can't do it from this distance."

Rikki threw him a look indicating she was on top of it.

Kate glanced over at Rikki to determine if she should go on, and then turning thoughtful she said, "In most cases I deal with, there is almost nothing to go on, but in this case we have the cold facts, so why can't we just shut them down?"

"Well, that's just the thing," said Julius, "We have the facts but we don't have the *who*. Even though the modified death date is stamped with the user id of who physically made the change, I'm quite sure they will be way down the food chain, and, more than likely, will be an unsuspecting clerk or secretary who is just entering data, assuming accuracy because it's coming from a doctor's request or a computer record. Since the hospital prides itself on its policy of being essentially paperless, the original request to change the date would very likely be strips of paper in a shredder somewhere. I think we'll have to devise a more creative way to do our job."

"And your suggestion?" responded Rikki.

"Well, I was hoping Kate could give us some ideas," shot back Julius. "Kate's experience with other fraud cases should provide some hints as to where we could start."

Kate was staring past Rikki at the wall behind her, appearing not to be listening. After an awkward pause she blurted, "I think you are right. The data uncovers the fraud, but it likely isn't going to send anyone to prison. What we do know is that they know you know something. They know you have the data since otherwise they would not be going after you with such vengeance. I would take this to mean they think you know more than you really do. It's quite possible they believe you not only have the data containing the date changes, but that you also have names of patients and doctors. We need to find a way to exploit the fact that they think you know more than you do."

Some time passed, as Rikki and Julius absorbed this thought and what its consequences might be.

Rikki broke the silence. "Perhaps we could put the case out to the media and let them create a firestorm to generate panic among those involved. But, if they panic, I would think they would simply stop doing it. If we can't trace the modified data back to them, once they stop, we'll never catch them. So that's not going to work."

Kate replied, "Yes, but remember they don't know how much we know. If they think we have names, amounts, procedures, and other details, simply not doing it any more will not help them. They will have to destroy the existing data, or lead us to a scapegoat, or create some other kind of diversion."

Julius jumped in, "Wait a minute. If we take this idea to its logical conclusion, it will be essential for them to get the data in *my* possession, especially if they try to delete the data from their servers. So they'll want more from me than information about what I know. They will want the actual data and some assurance there are no other copies. No matter how you slice this scenario, it means they have to find *me,* and deal with *me.*"

"Absolutely right. We have to be careful what buttons we push. I'd rather we handle this so it doesn't come back to bite any of us."

Rikki stepped into the conversation. "OK, so we let them think we know everything, and we make it public that Julius has the data, and then we just watch Julius, waiting until another thug attacks him. That shouldn't take too long. And then we interrogate the thug and get the names of those responsible for the hit." A streak of mischief crossed her face as she said this, and fortunately it caught his eye as Julius began to protest.

"You may have made that suggestion tongue-in-cheek," Julius parried, "But the reality is they may decide to torture me until I hand over the data, then kill me because they likely won't leave behind a witness. As I see it, there are at least two flaws in this suggestion. First, they kill me; second, the last bunch of hoodlums they sent for me weren't going to give anyone up. In fact, it is entirely possible they don't have a clue who hired them."

Giving them both a puzzled look, Kate said, "You guys are kidding, right?"

"Not entirely, I suppose," Julius offered, "There may be merit in the general idea. It also crossed my mind that maybe we could get names of current terminal patients and follow the paperwork until we find a death date that has been changed. But, again, we may not be able to actually catch whose hands are in the cookie jar ... unless we can get access to the billing records. If it worked, we could identify the bogus procedures and the doctors involved. But then we would get *only* the doctor or doctors involved in the cases we are monitoring, and that's not enough. We really need to find a way to fill in the blanks in the data we have now, and find out how deep this goes."

He paused as he thought about whether there was a way to actually carry this out.

Kate offered, "What if we place one of our guys in the IT department and let him snoop around?"

Rikki said, "Not a bad idea, but if this goes right to the top we won't be able to insert anyone into the hospital without raising suspicion. But, maybe we don't care about suspicion. Thinking about it a bit, it's not likely they would be able to erase the data already on the computers—given the way stuff is backed up these days.

And so what if they stop doing it; we'll get them for what they've already done."

Julius interjected, "Forensically this is all Greek to me, but it would appear such evidence would be strictly circumstantial. Whoever we say is responsible will hide behind underlings, and the buck will get passed all the way down the chain of command to the janitors, and we'll have nothing."

Rikki nodded, "Partially true. Yes, the case would be based on circumstantial evidence, but if we can piece together a complete transaction and then 'follow the money', as the saying goes, we should be able to develop an entire chain of evidence identifying the crime, those involved, the receipt of money for fraudulent services— then any jury I know of would be happy to convict."

Kate was staring at the wall again. Julius and Rikki waited.

Breaking the silence, Kate said, "Try this on for size. We put an auditor in the hospital to do a routine audit of billings. The guys who are doing this think they have all the bases covered and could easily survive an audit. In fact it's likely they have already survived various audits. But since we know what we know, we'll be looking for something specific. If nothing else, we could get doctor and patient codes, correlate them with the data Julius has, and put together a full profile. Our auditor could pass data on to Julius for analysis, and somewhere in the middle of it all we'll catch them red-handed."

Julius responded, "I like the concept. Just a technical FYI; the doctor and patient numbers on billing records shown to the auditor will be hospital codes, not the ones used by the database to link information. But if we targeted the billings for the patients I have already researched, we may be able to audit the procedures performed after the actual death of the patient. This way we get to use the stuff we know they don't know we know, if that was in the least clear."

After a moment of thought Julius added, "Would the auditor be able to get access to operating room schedules and other data without raising a red flag?"

"Sure", Kate replied, "the idea of an audit is to pick a few trans-actions and follow the entire path, making sure everything fits. We don't usually dig in to such an extent, but it is well within our mandate. I would be very interested in finding out just how they exploited whatever loophole they found."

Kate stared at the wall. Rikki looked at her notes, and Julius looked at Rikki.

Startling the others, Rikki abruptly concluded the meeting, "I like it. Let's get started. We'll modify the plan as we go and change direction when it is required. Kate, will you find an available auditor and let us know when we can all meet again? Julius, you keep thinking about whether there is anything else in the data we might find helpful. I'll keep this out of any official reports for now."

"Julius, I don't want you to be concerned for the safety of your family while you help us here, so I'll call the Sheriff in Springhill and make sure your street gets extra patrols—just in case. Will that help?"

"I suppose so. It won't protect my son, or my daughter and her family, but it's something I guess. My gut tells me these guys will find a way to get to me regardless of what we do."

They all stood. Julius and Rikki shook Kate's hand as she left the office. Rikki looked at her watch and inquired, "Late lunch?"

Chapter 27

JULIUS HAD SLEPT ON THE SOFA. AS A RESULT HE WAS MORE AWARE than usual of Cora's nighttime distress. He was concerned about her decline, its symptoms compounded by the story he had told her the previous evening. Knowing the extra strain could make her restless, he wanted to be able to attend to her if the need arose—and to perhaps atone for the guilt he continued to feel. In the end, he discovered he enjoyed sleeping downstairs. He reflected that he might well be counting the days he had with her, and wanted, no, needed, to be as close to her as possible during the remaining time. Sheri had been right to scold him for being away for two days and then leaving again. The reprimand caused him to regret being involved in the investigation—but then his life, their lives, may be in danger if he weren't. And who else would stand and fight against the nasty business going on at the Hospital. Knowing Sheri would take good care of Cora, he elected to head to Marshall and dispatch his obligation.

Sheri came in a few minutes early so Julius could leave for his nine thirty appointment in Marshall. Cora was sleeping peacefully when she arrived, so she busied herself with cleaning the kitchen and organizing Cora's supplies and equipment. She turned to the appointment calendar kept on Cora's rolling table, opening it to the current day. Making a mental note of the activities that were outside the normal routine, she put the book back in its place. A quick glance at the chart revealed the log entry indicating Cora's night had been better than expected.

Yakov Travkin sat in the old rental waiting for just the right moment. It had taken him the better part of the morning to drive to Springfield and locate Barlow's house. He sat studying the property and working out the details of his plot. There was only one car in the driveway, but he had no idea if Barlow was home or not. *Someone* was home, and it didn't really matter to him who it was; he could execute his plan quite nicely regardless.

As he contemplated his next move, he noticed a glint of light in his side mirror. Rotating his head slightly he could make out a car going much too slowly as it entered the intersection behind him. Pretending to be looking at some notes on the passenger seat, he kept the oncoming car in his peripheral vision. Unless it was Julius, he hoped it would just roll on by, but instead it pulled in behind him and stopped. No one got out, and as he studied the driver from his rear-view mirror, his pulse quickened, recognizing the computer between the front seats, and then the barrier separating the back from the front. His mood darkened at the realization that either his luck continued to get worse, or somehow Julius had managed to get police protection. Keeping his cool, he waited until the officer was engaged with his keyboard, then started his car and slowly drove away. His work was done here for today.

After lunch Cora called to Sheri. She would have missed it if her ears were not tuned to the pitch and cadence of Cora's voice. Dropping what she was doing, she went immediately to Cora's side and sat in the chair. She took Cora's hand and, looking intently at her face, asked what she needed. Cora couldn't always express her needs. Sometimes the pain ran rampant through her body and she could articulate just her pain and nothing else. Sheri had learned to read Cora's body, and in a flash she knew from a raised shoulder or twisted hip where the pain source was. This time there was no such evidence, and she looked quizzically at Cora who said, "I've been watching the street, and for the last hour or so there has been a car parked across there," she pointed, "just to the left. Do you see it? It took me a while to figure out why the driver was just sitting there.

Then I saw a police crest on his shoulder just for a split second." Sheri twisted her head around and confirmed her impression with a nod. "Do you know why it's there?"

"I have absolutely no idea. Do you want me to go out and ask?"

Nothing was lost on Cora who said, "Yes, right now, and if he's good looking, get me his phone number."

Sheri laughed, "I'll get right on that." She returned to her duties, but the car's presence bothered her. Attempts at convincing herself it could be out there for a million reasons, none of which had anything to do with the Barlow family, failed miserably; the timing of its presence seemingly too connected to the strange events surrounding Julius over the past several days. She concluded there was much more to the story than Julius was telling. Whatever it was, at least in her view, it wasn't as important as his being home with Cora.

Chapter 28

RIKKI AND JULIUS RETURNED TO THE SAME DELI THEY HAD VISITED the day before, ordered their food, and sat under the mezzanine at a table set for four. Yesterday the conversation was strained, with long periods of silence and introspection. In contrast, this time they were both animated, almost excited.

After a few minutes rehashing the meeting with Kate, Rikki said, "Julius, I have a proposal to make which you may not like. You have every right to refuse it, but I would like you to hear me out." She looked up to see Julius' reaction.

He stopped eating, his brow furrowed, and said, "OK, what's on your mind?"

Thinking out loud she said, "We know someone in the hospital put a hit out on you. Or at least we assume it's the hospital, but it could be someone else, I suppose …" She paused. "Anyway, let's work with the hospital idea for now. I would like us, you and I, to do a parallel investigation; take a different approach from the one Kate is taking. Kind of come at the problem from different directions, meeting in the middle, if you like. If we can let whoever is behind this know that you eluded their hit, and that we're coming after them, maybe we'll shake something loose. If nothing else, we may be able to rattle them to the point where they make a mistake and open a door wide enough to let the DA walk through."

"So ... there you go again sacrificing me for the greater good," said Julius with a momentary rise of his left eyebrow.

"Well, I'm serious, that's kind of what I'm thinking. I want you to call the IT department at the hospital and confess. Tell them you inadvertently obtained some data, you're terribly sorry, and you discarded it. You hope they're cool with that, and no one needs to mention it again as far as you're concerned. Or something similar. I don't think it matters who you talk to; it's going to get to the bad guys one way or another. They know you have something of theirs, or they wouldn't have put a hit out on you, so we know there is a line of communication somewhere reaching out to those who are profiting from this."

"Let me get this straight. You want me to flaunt the fact that their hit failed, confirm they have the right guy in their sights, and ask them to look the other way? Do I have that right?"

"Sort of. I think this may work in your favor. Till now the hit has been a big secret. If you turn up missing, or dead, no one will connect that event with the fraud. Once you have put your name out there, the benefit of secrecy is gone for good. Any harm coming to you will immediately be connected to the disappearance of the data. These guys are smart, and I bet they would come to the same conclusion."

"Hmmm, 'you *bet*' ... but you're 'betting' with *my* life here."

"OK, bad choice of words. But at the moment our theory indicates they will lay low for a while, at least until they figure out how to reorganize the hit. They lost their top player, and that's bound to have its ramifications. They don't know if you hit their car purposely or by accident. In fact they don't even know it was *you* that hit their car. Maybe they think someone had taken out a contract on *them* ... for screwing up, maybe. They may have concluded it's best not to mess with you. Maybe they think you are dangerous, or are connected ... whatever. I'm convinced we are right in assuming they're going to take a step back. If we use this opportunity to put you out there openly, it may stop them from reinitiating the hit and buy us some time."

Julius put down his fork.

"I'm thinking like a cop now. And I know I'm assuming these guys are going to use reason and logic, but it's my experience crimes like this are not executed by dummies. These guys are smart, have worked out all the kinks so far, or at least it seems like it to us and, I'm sure, will continue to think through their actions. They aren't interested in getting caught, particularly due to some amateurish move."

"But, Rikki, I'm not an undercover cop. I'm an analyst who spends his days sitting on his duff in front of a computer screen. Subterfuge is just not in my DNA. What if I say the wrong thing, or get caught in something I can't handle? I don't lie well."

"Don't sell yourself short, Julius. Look at how you handled yourself just the other day when they came after you. That worked out, didn't it? You were a superhero on Tuesday."

"Let's not go too far down that road, OK? A split second difference in the timing and it would have been me who was killed in the crash. I don't take any credit at all for that particular outcome."

"Alright, these are just ideas at this point," Rikki prodded. "We'll have to work out the details and make sure you get help from someone who is trained in this kind of thing, if you need it. Right now I just want to know if you agree to take this to the next level."

"What about Kate's investigation? Do we tell her we're doing this? Isn't it possible we'll screw up *her* investigation? I mean, if we alert these guys that we're onto them, they'll fudge the audit, and Kate's work will be meaningless."

"I don't think so. We don't tell her what we're doing. That knowledge could cause her or her auditor to act differently, or let something slip. No, we keep her in the dark on this. As for alerting these guys, I think the opposite will be true. If you confess, and remove any threat to them, they'll relax and put the whole thing behind them."

Staring intently at Julius, Rikki saw a flicker of acceptance cross his features, mixed, she thought, with fear and uncertainty. He remained silent for a long time, idly picking his way through the remainder of his lunch. Rikki kept him under her gaze.

Eventually the cords in his neck began to relax.

"Alright, I'm ready to take this to the next level. But I reserve the right to put an end to it if I think it goes beyond my pay grade. I hate what these guys are doing, but I'm not certain I'm committed enough to put my life on the line—again—at least not yet."

Rikki exhaled slowly. In not much more than a whisper she said, "Julius, *you* are the smoking gun, and we need to use every advantage we can. I'm proud of you for stepping up. I desperately want to nail these guys too, but I know I have to be careful not to put you or your family in any more danger than absolutely necessary." The details of her plan would have to be carefully conceived and executed for her to carry out this promise.

Julius hadn't quite finished his lunch, but he pushed it aside and they headed back to the Sheriff's building. There was silence between them as Rikki wondered just how far she could push without having Julius bolt. In each of their minds there would be a delicate balance, but their scales were calibrated in very different ways.

When they were both settled back in her office, Rikki began to unfold the beginnings of her plan. She knew it would adapt as it was enacted, and all she could do at this point was give Julius the outline and hope he had enough faith in her to fill in the details as they went. She took a deep breath and began.

Julius nodded in some places and frowned in others. Rikki tried not to let his reactions affect her presentation.

When she was done, she exhaled, crossing her arms as she relaxed in her chair. "So, those are the basics. The more I think about it, the better I feel about this being a great way to complement what Kate is doing with the audit. We'll squeeze these guys until they beg for mercy."

Julius remained pensive.

Breaking into his thoughts, Rikki said, "I heard back from Kate and she will have her auditor in the hospital as early as possible next week. We don't want to spook them until they feel secure about the audit, so we won't place any calls until, say, Tuesday next?"

Julius shook his head, "The tricky part here is to make sure they don't connect the audit with my phone call. They have to appear completely separate and entirely coincidental. Has Kate informed the hospital yet about the audit?"

Rikki replied, "Not that I know of—but I can check with her, if you like. I think she was going to find out when the auditor she is suggesting would be available, and from what I've heard of her—the auditor that is—I expect she's quite busy."

"Good. I suggest then I make my phone call right away. Different departments are involved, and it's likely the Finance folk won't even know I called the IT department since there is no real reason for that information to be passed on. The loss of data is, I'm sure, an embarrassment to the IT boys, and they won't be sharing anything with other staff members until they know exactly what's going on."

"Alright, I see your point. If the data loss has been kept between the IT department and the guys cooking the billing, then Finance may well not be in the loop. I can accept that. In fact, it occurs to me they would not want Finance involved at all, since they wouldn't want them snooping around their scheme."

"Yup, exactly what I would do if I ran the IT department and had what could be a serious data exposure. I'd hunker down, tell only those who seriously needed to know, and work it out before making it public. I've worked with companies where this kind of thing has caused heads to roll, and, not infrequently, within the executive suite."

"Ok … let's call it a day. I'll put some things in motion at my end and let's meet tomorrow, say, at ten for the phone call?" Rikki looked past her notes to gauge Julius' reaction.

He sat for a long time looking at the floor under Rikki's desk, shaking his head almost imperceptibly. Eventually snapping out of his introspection he said, "Nice of you to let me out of class early, Ms. Castillo; or is it Mrs. Castillo."

"That would be *Deputy Castillo* to you," said Rikki rather forcefully, but with a hint of a smile. She glanced at Julius then muttered to her desk, "But otherwise it would be *Miss Castillo*." A blush rose, then, just as rapidly, fell from Rikki's cheeks.

Julius gave her a wry smile, rose from his chair and headed for the door.

Stepping outside, Julius scanned the parking lot, not really sure what he was looking for, and slipped into his car.

He wasn't totally convinced. He was becoming very certain they were dealing with a case of inexcusable fraud. And he wanted more than ever to put an end to it. It really irked him that people, already wealthy, seemed driven to steal from those who had little. Health care costs were already too high for the average person, and these guys were jacking those costs sky high for their own benefit. However much this felt like Prince John and the Sheriff of Nottingham in old England, he was no Robin Hood … but he would do what he could, as long as it was over soon. Cora needed him home.

Seemingly in time with the dotted line, his eyes flicked to the mirrors, searching for something he had no way of identifying.

Chapter 29

GLANCING OVER HER SHOULDER AT THE POLICE CAR, EDNA Terwilliger stepped smartly up to the Barlow front door, and rang the bell. With a flip of her head, her dark brown hair fell evenly to the shoulders of the business pant suit covering her lean frame. Those who knew her best quipped that she ate, slept, and worked in a suit. Julius told Cora one day he thought he saw her in a sweat shirt and jeans, and Cora told him, in no uncertain terms, he had to be mistaken; Edna would never wear such clothing, and, if she did, it would be in private; she certainly would not do so in public. She wore her fifty-one years well, aided by good diet and lots of exercise; some suggested a little too much of both. She was president of the Glen Oaks Foundation, a position held by Cora for many years—until eighteen months ago. Their meetings had dwindled to twice per month. The philanthropic activities carried out by the foundation were complex, and while Edna was still learning, Cora was still mentoring.

Sheri answered the door. "Good afternoon, Edna. It's great to see you again. Cora has been looking forward to this for days." Although Edna knew the way perfectly well, Sheri escorted Edna to the dining room and called, "Cora, Edna is here."

"Edna, it's so nice of you to come. Julius is away again today and I'm starved for any kind of human contact. Please … sit down."

She wrinkled her nose just as Sheri was about to protest, stopping her short.

"Well, Cora, how have you been these past weeks? Things have been buzzing at the foundation and I have a lot of things to discuss." Cora knew Edna didn't mean this to be rude in any way; she was genuinely interested in her wellbeing but she also wanted to be sure Cora knew this was not just a social visit.

"I've come through a rough patch this week, but I feel much stronger today. Everyone around here is talking in whispers and having clandestine meetings with doctors and such, so even though they won't tell me anything, I'm certain the news isn't good." She said this with her voice just loud enough so Sheri was certain to hear.

Edna and Cora discussed various details pertaining to the many projects with which the foundation was involved. Cora took special interest in the projects oriented toward the children of her neighborhood, and those of Shreveport, where many underprivileged families struggled to meet their children's daily needs. When she was president, she was the driving force behind pro-active programs attacking bullying at its roots, and counteracting student attention deficit with increased nutrition and cultural activities.

As Edna gathered her notes, placing them meticulously into a thin, brown leather case, she said hesitantly without looking up, "Cora … I don't really know how to ask this. I've wanted to for some time … but just didn't have the courage." She looked up, and seeing approval on Cora's face, continued, "If I were to become ill, and not able to work with the foundation, I think I would become bitter, and blame someone … anyone … for punishing me unfairly … for something I didn't even know I did. How do you remain so positive, given the pain you face every day?" Her eyes were beginning to shine.

Cora reached for Edna's hand and squeezed it gently. "First off, don't think I'm always positive; that would leave a very false impression. But I have always been able to put my faith to work when things got tough. I still have a strong sense of purpose, even when I don't know exactly what that is, especially in my current state. Maybe your visit today, and asking me this question, is that purpose … who knows."

"I suppose so."

"In any event, over the last four or five years in particular, my senses seem to have awakened to the physical and spiritual stuff going on around me. Put it down to a general heightening of my awareness … I don't know. The slowing down caused by this illness has allowed me to open my mind to the beauty of nature, the spectacular design of life … the incalculable value of each individual."

"I don't know how you do it."

"Well, I guess I don't know either. What I do know is that my life is in the hands of my creator … make of it what you will … it is sustaining, and encouraging, and helps makes sense of all this." She swept the room with her arm.

"Edna, I think deep down everyone has a little bit of faith. The problem is most keep it locked away in a trunk in the attic, piled high with old boxes. When trouble hits they can't remember where they put it or they don't have the energy to search for it. It's better to keep it out on the mantle where it's easy to find; where it's part of daily life."

Edna studied Cora for a long moment. "Well, no question your attitude shows … you're peaceful … I guess … and I find it inspiring.

"Anyway, I hope you don't feel I was intruding. Thanks for your honesty. I'd better be on my way."

"Edna, thanks for visiting, and thanks for asking. Sometimes I wonder if anyone notices, let alone cares."

At the end of Edna's visit, Cora was exhausted. She could hardly keep her eyes open long enough to say a proper good-bye. But she felt fulfilled, and a little smug; once again she had cheated her body of its control over her mind, and she had done one more thing that had significant meaning for someone else.

Chapter 30

MADHURI KADAR WAS BORN IN THE CHANDRAPUR DISTRICT OF Maharashtra state in India. Although the caste system is not legally recognized in India, its practice was still in full bloom. Madhuri was raised in the Vaishyas caste in a strong family who supported themselves in the coal trade. The family spoke Telugu at home, but they all learned and used English as part of their daily routine. From an early age she loved working with numbers, and as a teenager she was fascinated by mysteries and their solutions. Her social status and the progressive nature of her family, permitted an education and, at the point where she had to make a career choice, she selected forensic accounting. After attending university to obtain her degree, she was certified by The Council of the Institute of Chartered Accountants of India in Forensic Accounting and Fraud Detection. She was immediately hired by the York Standard Health Insurance Company of India to work in their Department of Accounting and Audit. Having expressed an interest in visiting America, when the time was right, she was transferred to the Texas office. This was her fifth year in the States, just eight months from the point at which she must decide if she will go back to India or apply for permanent status in the US.

Her name was a problem in America. English speakers struggled to remember it, and spelling it seemed impossible, and inevitably, she was given nicknames; some to her liking and others not. She wasn't fond of being called Mad, nor was she fond of being called Hurry, but she accepted Huri as a compromise.

To many, she was a beautiful woman. At five feet four inches, she was slightly above average height for her native district, but short by North American standards. Her black hair, high cheek bones, dark skin, and full lips, made her stand out in a crowd, and, more often than not, turned the heads of on-looking men. Wielding her dark, piercing eyes as a weapon, she was able to pry secrets from those she audited. Her capacity to memorize and recall, caused the downfall of many who thought they were safe from her scrutiny. She was York Standard's secret weapon.

Kate contacted Huri's supervisor and laid out her plan, discovering, to her delight, Huri could be made available the following Monday.

Kate placed a call to the Chief Financial Officer of the Parks Hospital for Children. After a short ring, the connection was made. "Good morning. Finance Office. How may I help you?"

"Good morning. This is Kate Jansen from the audit division of York Standard Health. To whom am I speaking?"

The receptionist gave her name.

"May I speak to the CFO, please?"

"She's on the phone right now, may I have her call you back, or I could put you through to her voicemail?"

"I would rather hold, if you don't mind. I have a matter of some urgency to discuss, so it's important I speak to her as soon as possible."

"Please hold then, and I'll let her know you are waiting."

"Thank you."

It wasn't long before an all-business female voice came on the line. "Ms. Jansen. What may I do for you?"

"Good morning. I'm from the audit division of York Standard Health, and you have been selected for a non-routine audit. This does not signify a problem. Our audit division randomly selects member facilities for audits which are outside the normal schedule. Your hospital surfaced. Would you be able to provide me with a contact and a work space for next Monday morning at nine o'clock?"

"Certainly. How may I reach you with the details?"

Kate gave the CFO her cell phone number and her email address, thanked her for her cooperation, and replaced the receiver, then said to no one in particular, "Good, that will get things started."

Chapter 31

Friday

JULIUS ARRIVED AT RIKKI'S OFFICE JUST BEFORE TEN O'CLOCK. HIS mood upon leaving the house was barely on the up-beat side of despair. As he entered the Sheriff's building, his chest began to tighten, and he reached for the railing, the room spinning momentarily on its axis. It seemed as if they were about to toss his life around like a football, and he could not see it coming to a story-book ending. Yet he felt driven by the injustice of it all. He had taken it this far, and unless there was some kind of closure, he knew deep down he would never feel right again. Whether he had the data or not, whether he used the data or not, someone out there considered him a serious threat, and would not likely stop until the threat had been neutralized. Upon reflection, his logic, his analytical strengths, things he relied on most, were being overrun by primal fear.

As he stepped into Rikki's office, and the reality of what they were about to do was upon him, he felt ready to bolt.

One glance at him told Rikki Julius was having serious doubts. Hurrying from behind her desk, she was at his side almost as he cleared the doorway. She took his arm and gently guided him to a chair. "You seem really spooked this morning. Is everything all right?"

Julius did not respond.

She said in a sympathetic tone, "Look, I know this is hard. I'm asking you to do something dangerous, and for that I'm feeling a little guilty. I hate to say it, but it could even be deadly, I suppose. But I'm confident we can do this safely. I know I haven't done anything yet to really earn it, but I *need* you to *trust* me. We've put the audit in motion, and we need to put pressure on from *our* side in order to get these guys. You still want to put an end to this, don't you?" Involuntarily she had taken his hands in hers, crouching low beside him.

Julius was in no state to interpret Rikki's unexpected closeness, but he did draw comfort from it. He responded, "Yes, I want this to be over. Not just for me, but for everyone who is being milked by these guys. It needs to be stopped. I'm just not sure I'm your man."

She remained squatting beside him, her face level with his. She lowered her head, as she worked to overcome the color that had suddenly come to rest on her cheeks. With determination, she examined Julius' face for a moment. When her eyes reached his, she frowned, recognizing the depth of his fear. She pushed on, squeezing his hands tightly. "We can do this. You and I … together."

He felt the tension ease a little, and with a deep sigh offered, "OK … I'm on board … I think."

Rikki reluctantly removed her hands, stood, and, returning to her desk, sat down. She folded her hands in front of her and leaned forward, letting her breathing slow, staring unseeing at a file on her desk. She paused a few moments, then taking a deep breath, said, "Shall we make the call?"

Julius nodded hesitantly. Rikki dialed the hospital.

When the connection was made, Rikki said into the phone, using a very official tone of voice, "Good morning. This is Deputy Castillo from the Harrison County Sheriff's office. Could you tell me, please, who the head of your IT department is?" She made some notes, and said, "Thank you very much," as the call was terminated.

"Mr. Koehler is the Chief Information Officer. Sounds to me like a good place to start."

Julius interrupted, "Jim Koehler, by any chance?"

"Yes, why?"

"Jim is very active in the IT community in this area and I've attended several talks he's given over the years. If I recall correctly, he's both a technical whiz and a very competent administrator. If things haven't changed, he keeps the hospital on a very short leash— everything paperless and very advanced technologically; a stickler for security." Julius could feel a shift in his mood. The immense burden he carried through the door with him just minutes before seemed to lift, although the gravity of his situation lingered. But he was beginning to feel the return of his resolve. "This will be a little easier. At least I can put a face to the name, and I have considerable respect for Jim. From the little I know of him there is no way he's involved in this, so at least I won't be talking to the CCO—the Chief Criminal Officer." His mouth twitched with the beginnings of a smile. He *was* feeling better. "OK. I'm ready."

Rikki dialed the hospital again. After entering a code on her keypad, she covered the receiver with her hand. "We'll record this just in case." Speaking into the phone, she said, "Mr. Koehler, please." And she handed the phone to Julius.

"Good morning. Mr. Koehler's office," answered a business-like female voice.

"Yes … uh … good morning. My name is Julius Barlow. It's urgent that I speak with Jim. Is he available?" He hoped the familiarity of using Jim's first name might get him priority.

After a telling pause, and a delicate cough transmitted through the earpiece, the voice responded, "Certainly. I'll put you right through."

So they already knew his name. Maybe he was wrong about Koehler being involved. His thoughts were interrupted by the responding voice.

"Mr. Barlow, this is Jim Koehler." His voice sounded strained.

"Mr. Koehler, I have a confession to make, and the only way I know how to do this is to just get it out." He paused but it was met by silence. "Some weeks back, doing an assignment for a class in computer security, I inadvertently pulled some data from one of your servers. It was unintentional; it was a fluke that surprised even me. I've been struggling with whether I should tell you because it's quite possible you aren't even aware it happened. Anyway, in the end, I thought it best to come clean. If you want to discuss it in person I'm willing to do so. I'll tell you, from my end, how I did it, and maybe, through all this, some benefit will result, if only to your security protocols." He paused not wanting to give too much information, but wanting to sound sufficiently contrite.

Jim responded, clearly straining to withhold what he already knew, "I see. Are you saying you *hacked* our system?"

"Well, I suppose you could use that term, but I assure you it was not intentional. I'm not at all comfortable talking about this over the phone, so I'll let you decide whether you think this event requires more discussion—and that will have to be in person, or not at all," hoping he would take the bait.

After a pause, "Obviously security is ultimately my responsibility, and I believe it's important to investigate any alleged breaches, no matter how insignificant. So, yes, I think we should discuss this further. How about Monday morning at seven thirty?"

"It's a little early for me since I don't live in town. I could make it for eight thirty, I think."

"Unfortunately I have meetings beginning at nine. Perhaps Tuesday would be better."

"No, no … I want to get this over with. I'll be there at seven thirty, but I may need a strong cup of coffee." Julius wasn't sure that last bit of levity was appropriate once it had slipped out.

"I'm quite sure we can provide a coffee at the very least, Mr. Barlow. I look forward to seeing you then." The connection was broken and Julius replaced the receiver.

"So, seven thirty on Monday I march into the chamber of horrors," said Julius to Rikki who had been listening intently from the other side of the desk.

"Not *I* but *we*," rejoined Rikki. I'm going with you. I think, due to the severity of the situation, you should have your *lawyer* with you—just in case you decide to say something stupid or incriminating." A mischievous look crossed her face and, although she tried to suppress it, her mouth broadened into a wide smile.

Her smile was so infectious, in spite of his mood, he had no choice but to respond in kind, glad she would be there with him. He had dreaded facing anyone at the hospital alone, innocent or not. Although almost certain Jim would not be involved, there was still a chance, and he had no idea who Jim would invite to join them.

He suddenly felt immensely tired. His cheeks seemed to sag, and he had to find a seat on the arm of the chair. Stretching voluptuously,

"If you're done using me as a pawn in your game of criminal chess, may I go home and get some rest? I won't likely get much sleep this weekend anyway as my mind paints ten thousand scenarios for Monday—all of them ending in a tortuous death and my tattered body slowly sinking into the gulf with my legs weighted."

"Hey! Where did all that come from? Is that *really* what you think is going to happen?"

"I suppose not. But I am allowed to be afraid even if it is down-graded from the *terror* earlier. Thanks for volunteering to go with me on Monday. Your company will help a lot. But it likely won't stop the nightmares over the weekend."

"I guess. But you're doing the right thing. You know that, don't you?"

"I think so. Sometimes it's hard to get that information from the head to the heart. I'll be fine. But I know how my body works, and this will take its toll as the hour approaches."

"I understand. How about we meet here at my office at seven on Monday morning. We'll go to the hospital in your car and play it by ear."

"I'll do my best," Julius yawned again as he stood and headed for the door. "I'll see you Monday." Leaving her office, he walked briskly down the hall and out to his car. He simply wanted to get home to Cora, but he had a few errands to run first.

Chapter 32

FRIDAY NIGHT WAS DATE NIGHT. ALMOST WITHOUT FAIL JULIUS AND Cora made a point of being together Friday evening. They didn't accept other engagements, either business or pleasure; this was *their* night. When Cora's illness progressed to where she was unable to leave the house, Julius brought date night home.

Tonight would be no exception. His week had been incredibly stressful, and his body was still sore, his face mellowing to a blotchy yellow hue. Her week had been painful and tiring too. But they would spend the evening together allowing the love they shared to rejuvenate and refresh them. While Julius was driving back from Marshall, he had placed a few phone calls, setting the evening up. The news from the doctors this past week had him concerned, and he wasn't certain how many more Friday nights he would have with Cora, so he wanted to make those remaining as memorable as possible.

Julius arrived home with several packages which he placed on the kitchen counter. After chatting briefly with Cora from the bedside chair, he excused himself and returned to the kitchen. From the larger package, he pulled out two hamburgers from Five Guys Burgers and Fries, the meat patties dwarfed by the extras; for him it was mushrooms and peppers, for Cora, grilled onions and hot sauce. The fries were plentiful and fresh cut. Cherry Coke was a favorite of them both, so he had purchased two old fashioned bottles and packed them on ice.

During the week, Julius had tried to relax by mixing a play list of fifties jukebox music. He plugged the thumb drive into the music server in the living room; the sounds of Cliff Richards and the Drifters crooning 'Move It' began filling the house. After microwaving the hamburgers and fries briefly to bring them to temperature, he put them on trays like they did at the drive-in restaurants, then took them into the dining room. Putting Cora's tray on her bed table, he rolled it into place, then sat in the bed-side chair with his tray on his lap as they ate their meal, lost in the music and each other.

When they were finished, Julius put the trays away, allowing them to dance to the music, his hands in hers, swaying with the beat. From time to time he would lean over and kiss her, reminding them both of an earlier time when they could dance on their feet; reminding them both of how their relationship had matured and deepened over the years, and how much they meant to each other on this particular Friday night. They sipped their Cokes between songs.

Noticing Cora's strength ebbing, Julius folded her hands on the blankets and they sat side by side, tapping out the beat of the music, both content just to be together.

When their drinks were done, Julius propped Cora on her pillows, making sure she was comfortable. Slipping the DVD into the player, he turned on the television. They spent the next hour and a half watching 'Sleepless in Seattle'.

A pang of guilt scraped at Julius' emotions. He really should tell Cora the whole story—but not tonight. It could wait until some quiet moment during the weekend.

Chapter 33

JIM SAT BACK IN HIS CHAIR FOR A FEW MINUTES, HIS ARMS HANGING, while he tried to assimilate what had just taken place. The very man they were seeking had arrived on their doorstep, unannounced and unexpected. But just what did it mean? It could be one of many things: Worst case, he could be in possession of data that compromises the hospital—maybe he'll be looking for payment—blackmail perhaps. Best case, he knows nothing, isn't interested in the data, and just goes away. But there were hundreds of scenarios in between.

His thoughts immediately went to Blake and his bullying tactics. Worst case, Blake would lobby to have him fired. Best case, Blake would hold this over his head for years and make his life miserable. Maybe it would be prudent to resign now, to get out before anything further is known about this dumb luck data loss. He could leave without a major security failure on his resumé, and get a good job anywhere else—without the Blakes of this world constantly in his face.

He mentally shook himself out of this self-pity. Having been in difficult situations many times before, generally not of his own making, he had answered to men more difficult than Dr. Blake Atchley. With this reminder, his courage returned and his mood switched from one of resignation to one of exhilaration, as he began to relish the challenge. Pulling out his note pad, he began working through what he wanted to get from this Barlow fellow on Monday.

Once he had the interview organized, he dialed Dr. Atchley's number. In this case a good offense was the best defense. He would take Blake by surprise, gaining him some field advantage. Blake's assistant answered. "Erika, this is Jim Koehler. May I have a brief word with Blake, if he's in?"

"He has some suppliers in his office right now. Is it urgent?"

"Not really. It can wait. Tell him I'll call him later in the day, or have him call me when he has a minute to chat."

"Actually, Jim, he'll probably thank me for interrupting the meeting. He generally hates these vendor meetings, so let me give him a try."

A few moments later Blake came on the line. "Jim, thanks for calling. What can I do for you?"

Jim was almost speechless. He needed to file away this moment. Clearly the time to talk to Blake is when his office is full of strangers from whom he wants to hide his real personality. This is the all-business, kind, and gentle … fake … Blake, which very few people ever glimpsed. The suppliers must be offering trips to foreign lands, or something else of value, for him to want to impress them like this. "Blake, Mr. Barlow called today," there was a strange, strangling noise on Blake's end of the line, "and we have a meeting set for Monday at seven thirty. I know it's early, but I want you to be there so you can ask any questions I might miss." And, thought Jim, hear the story first hand so you don't second-guess me later on.

"Oh, I'll be there, don't you worry," emphasized Blake, trying to stifle the gasp that threatened to escape from his throat.

"I'll let you get back to your meeting. See you Monday." Jim set the phone down and exhaled as he leaned back in his chair, glad the call was over. He had mixed feelings about having Blake in the meeting, knowing he would be miserable, ornery, and rude. But he didn't owe Barlow anything. After all, Barlow had violated *them*, they had done nothing to harm *him*—he would get what was coming to him. If Barlow had stolen the data intentionally and was going to try blackmail, Blake would probably terrify him sufficiently to shock the thought right out of him. If Barlow had meant nothing by it, and didn't have a clue what the data meant, then Blake would be the first to hear it, making him feel like king of the information mountain, and he would let the matter drop, at least until it served him in some other way.

Closing his notebook, he moved on to other things. Although the matter did eventually recede from the forefront of his mind, it never did dissipate entirely. He continued to subconsciously ruminate on the meeting, how it should be conducted, who should say what, and how he could draw out the truth from Barlow.

Dr. Atchley couldn't wait to be rid of the vendors sitting in his office. His demeanor had suddenly changed from engaged, to distant and rude, making it evident to his guests he had more important work to do.

It took a few minutes to put the finishing touches on their business and to wish the vendors a good day and safe travels—Blake almost meant it. Alone at last in his office, he sat back in his chair, leaned his head against the padding, gathering his thoughts as he relaxed. Mumbling to the array of product literature and brochures left by his visitors, he spoke just above a whisper, "So … Barlow would be in the building on Monday. Surely if I personally hand Barlow over to them, they would be able to get it done right this time. He may have slipped through my fingers earlier this week, but he has just made his own appointment with the undertaker."

Rummaging through the bag under his desk, Blake located the new cell phone he had purchased at a corner store the week before. He hadn't needed it until now. He didn't usually get involved in the details of the assignments he had handed out to his overseas contact. He didn't need to know; in fact, at some deeper level, he didn't want to know. However, since it was obvious Barlow was still alive, meaning the job had not been done as instructed, he would have to take matters into his own hands … and this opportunity was too good to pass up.

He dialed the emergency number provided by the Russian chief … he considered this an emergency if ever there was one. The voice on the other end growled with a strong accent, "What do you want?"

"I have a meeting with Barlow Monday morning at seven thirty, done before nine. I'm handing him to you on a silver platter. Get the job done. Understand?"

"Da," the grunt sounding annoyed and dangerous.

Blake pressed the End Call button on the phone, then tossed it carelessly back into the bag. In an effort to save a few bucks, he used the phone two or three times before he smashed it and tossed the pieces into a storm sewer—a different location each time, of course.

Chapter 34

Monday

AT NINE O'CLOCK SHARP HURI ARRIVED AT THE RECEPTION DESK OF the Financial Office of the Parks Hospital for Children. She was dressed in a tan business suit, setting off the color of her skin, had her hair pulled back, and wore gaudy glasses. She had applied just a touch too much perfume. Having presented her business card to the receptionist, she was asked to take a seat while her escort was called.

Ellie Christianson poked her head into the Finance Office and, assuming Huri to be the auditor, said, "My name is Ellie and you are …?"

"Madhuri Kadar, but please call me Huri."

Ellie was not a 'plain Jane', but nonetheless appeared intimidated by Huri's seemingly natural beauty. She gathered herself and said, "If you would follow me, I'll get you established and provide anything you need."

They walked silently along the hallway, rounded a series of corners, and, passing a host of modest offices, eventually arrived at a small but nicely appointed board room with a large table and six rolling chairs. The room was brightly lit by windows facing the courtyard giving a beautiful, almost panoramic, view of the hospital campus.

Huri said, "Thank you very much. This is lovely … what a view! I'll be lucky to get any work done at all. I'll be very comfortable here. Could you show me where the washrooms are, and where I could make a cup of coffee, or put my lunch in a fridge perhaps?"

Ellie showed her where everything was, and returning to the conference room said, "I'll leave you for a few minutes to let you get oriented and set up." As she handed Huri a business card she continued, "You can reach me at any time at the number on this card. You can use the phone there on the conference table to call within the hospital, or dial *nine* to get an outside line."

Ellie left the room; Huri followed the sound of her receding footsteps until they stopped a short distance away in the direction from which they had just come. A door closed. So, she thought, Ellie is not just a flunky; she has her own office. My custodian has a measure of authority, and that could be good—she will have access to information—but that could also be bad—she may also be reporting my every move to someone above her, and worse, she may have the smarts to send me down time-wasting rabbit trails. Making a mental note to pay close attention to what Ellie offered her, she resolved to be very specific in her requests.

Huri opened her computer and started the audit program, then laid out a variety of papers and folders, putting her make-up kit on the table where she could easily reach it.

A few minutes later, Huri heard Ellie's door open, then close, so she quickly snatched the mirror from her kit, lifted the lid, and turned so she could see Ellie's reflection as she came through the door. When Ellie entered, Huri was powdering her chin. She spun around, closed her compact, and stuttered "Sorry about that."

Offering Ellie a chair, she began, "We usually start a regular audit with a meeting of a delegation appointed by the management team; in fact it usually involves the management team. We explain what we will be doing and what areas we will be auditing. This is not a regular audit. I suppose it could be called a *surprise* audit, but then we let you know ahead of time, so I guess it really isn't a *surprise*." Huri allowed herself a little giggle. She continued, "We call these *pop-up* audits because the computer *pops* them up." Another giggle. "The computer also suggests what we should audit in terms of scope and time frame. In this audit I'll be looking at billings to our company for the last three months, with small samples from a wide range of services. I don't have a feel yet for how many billings it represents, so I can't give you a specific time frame, but I would estimate from one to four days. As long as I can be done before the weekend, it will make my personal life so much easier. I know this is also an inconvenience to you, so I'll make it as quick as possible."

Ellie tried to suppress a knowing smirk but wasn't successful. So she forced a brilliant smile and said, "I'll be whatever help I can. You are aware that we are a *paperless* hospital—that everything is on the computer, and we don't keep paper records? So everything I provide you will be electronic."

"Yes, yes, good," responded Huri. "If I can import data directly into my computer it will save me a bunch of time and a whole bigger bunch of typing mistakes. Manual entry can be so tedious, don't you think." A deep sigh followed.

Rising from her chair, Ellie headed for the door saying, "I'll get right on it. I should have some data for you within the hour." She walked casually back to her office. The sound of her door closing made its way back to Huri.

Ellie hurried to her desk and snatched up the phone, almost dropping it in the process. She dialed, and without introduction said, "Nothing to worry about. A greenhorn if I ever saw one. Twenty something. It's an unscheduled audit … looks like a training session or first solo. Looking at the last three months … just to her company … yes, of course. She can't wait to get this done and get back to her personal life as soon as possible. She'll see only what I want her to see and she'll talk to only those I want her to talk to—and be assured it will include only a select few of our male employees … yes, she does look dangerous on that front, but it can be managed."

There was a long pause while she listened intently. "Yes, I understand. This will be a non-issue, I can assure you." After hanging up, she waited for a moment, allowing the anxious frown induced by having to talk to *him,* subside. Then she dialed the IT support group and made her requests.

Huri wandered the hall to the small lunchroom. It was hospital white with white steel cabinets, a glass-topped table, a white refrigerator, a white toaster, a white toaster oven, and a black microwave oven. The window-less room required very little light, yet it was brilliantly lit with overhead fluorescents. Everything gleamed. The room left Huri with the impression it was seldom used, so she opened the fridge door. The interior was white with glass shelves that could easily have come, within the hour, from the appliance store. She would meet no one here. She would have no opportunity to chat with the locals and get a feel for the hospital in general. She had been placed in isolation.

This was not unfamiliar turf to her. Auditors were often shunned, and treated with suspicion; as pariahs. She made herself a cup of tea, sat at the table and began making notes.

Thirty minutes later Huri headed back to the conference room, arriving just a few minutes prior to Ellie showing up with a thumb drive. Handing it to Huri, she said, "The IT guys were on top of their game today. Here are the records for the last three months of billings to York Standard. They include doctor's names, OR schedules, and patient identifiers. We don't usually provide patient names, for confidentiality reasons, you understand, unless you specifically request them."

Huri responded, "Thanks for being so prompt. I don't need patient information at this point. I can match your invoice numbers with data at head office and make those connections if I need to. I'll work my way through this data," holding up the thumb drive, "and call you if I need anything else."

Approaching the door, trying her best to sound sincere, Ellie said, "OK, I'm just down the hall, so don't be afraid to ask for anything you need." She clipped the last word in an effort to suppress a snicker.

Huri plugged the thumb drive into her computer, concentrating on the screen as she familiarized herself with the files and their contents.

It was entirely possible she would find nothing. Even though the hospital dealt with her insurance company, there was no guarantee any billings in this data would be contrived. But she would either find such a billing, or she would uncover a series of events that would lead her to one—this was her specialty, after all.

She had no intention of using the standard audit program issued by the insurance company. She had her own arsenal of diagnostic tools which she now pulled from the hard drive.

Identifying the layout of the data files she had been given, Huri typed this structure, or meta-data as it is called, into her computer.

It identified where the invoice number was, where the billing code was, and so on. This was the tedious part, but once done, the computer would be able to scan the data in a matter of seconds, pulling out information that could be useful.

Upon completion, she unleashed her first analytical program. Her computer had access to head office files, allowing her to cross-reference invoice numbers, and verify dates, billing codes, doctor id's and patient particulars.

Everything checked out. All the company billings were reflected in the hospital data, and all the billing codes matched.

She then asked the computer to show her the data just for those patients who were deceased. This gave her two hits. The first was a teenager who had overdosed on drugs and could not be revived. She found these cases sad, and just for curiosity, poked around in the patient files to determine the kind of family background the patient had. It was as she expected it to be: upper middle class, good insurance coverage, and parents long term clients. Simply a tragic waste. Huri forced her thoughts back to the audit.

The second looked promising; a seven year old trauma patient who received treatment for nine days prior to passing away. Pulling the patient's name from the head office files, she launched an internet search to find the obituary, located it, and noted the date of death. Oddly, no date of death was reported in the hospital files.

Huri dialed Ellie's number. "Hi, this is Huri. Could you help me with something, please … yes, here, if you don't mind … thanks."

Ellie arrived just moments later and said, just a bit too sweetly, "What can I do for you?"

Huri stammered a bit, fumbled with her papers, and eventually said, "I know it's an awful thing to ask, but I have billing records for a child who died, and I need to know the date of death for my notes. Is there any way you would have that information? Or should I maybe contact the family, or … I don't know … what do you suggest?"

Just as Ellie was about to speak, Huri interjected, "Sorry … actually … I have two of them. I was going to ignore the first one, but I guess I should be thorough."

Ellie struggled not to roll her eyes, and replied, "I can get that for you. Rather than asking IT, I think I can get it myself. Do you have the patient ID's?"

"Sure, I wrote them here somewhere," Huri riffled through some notes and said, "Ah, here they are." She gave the two numbers to Ellie.

"I'll be right back. I can get this for you from the computer in my office." And she was gone.

Huri sat back in her chair and tried to look bored.

Within a few minutes Ellie returned and said, "The first one was pronounced June 13 at 2:04 P.M., and the second was June 28 at 3:18 A.M. Sometimes death occurs a bit before these times because the appropriate person has to be called to do the pronouncement, and if they are busy, it could take several minutes, an hour at the most.

Huri made notes on her pad. "Thanks, I hope it wasn't too much trouble."

"Not at all. That's what I'm here for. Anything else?" Ellie chirped.

"Not right now. But thanks so much for the dates." Ellie left the conference room with a spring in her step.

Huri had hit the jackpot on the second death, so she checked the first one as well. She cross referenced the patient name, then researched the obits. Much to her surprise she had two anomalies. She wasn't sure why she had written off the first one so quickly; perhaps the tragedy of a senseless drug death would prevent someone from taking advantage. Apparently not.

Now came the tricky part. She had to expose the discrepancy in the dates without tipping her hand. She sat back in her chair, crossed her arms, spun her chair around to look out the window, and stared, lost in thought.

For as long as she could remember, Huri had been fascinated by the interaction between the left brain and the right brain, or at least those parts that were so labeled. She had taken a few psychology courses featuring the work of Roger Sperry, participating in a variety of experiments on her own cognitive powers. Using the terms left-brain and right-brain had not been a good way of describing what she had discovered; rather she liked to use the term L-brain and R-brain since doing so removed the physiological connotation, keeping just the cognitive. She had discovered that if she fed her L-brain with lots of facts and then put it into idle, her R-brain would process the data, posit a solution and then pass it back to her L-brain. What she found so amusing was that the L-brain always took full credit for the solution.

Staring out the window she was able to put her L-brain into neutral. She saw the beauty of the hospital campus, gently musing about the donors, trying to imagine what tragedy coaxed them to make such large financial commitments to the hospital. Noting the cloud formations, she pondered what weather they may signify, or whether they signified anything at all. She scarcely blinked.

Suddenly spinning her chair around, she began scribbling notes on a fresh legal pad. Her L-brain had presented a plagiarized plan and she needed to work through the details to make sure it was feasible.

Chapter 35

AT FOUR O'CLOCK ON MONDAY MORNING JULIUS ROLLED GRUDG-ingly out of bed. Because he had been sleeping fitfully for the past several hours it was almost a relief to hear the alarm go off. Showered and dressed, he thought about breakfast, but nothing appealed to him. After quickly reviewing the notes he had prepared over the weekend, he peeked into the guest room to assure himself that Eddie was really there to look after Cora in his absence.

He was in the car by four forty-five. Early, yes, but he wanted to get the miles behind him. If he should have a flat tire or mechanical failure, he wanted to have time to resolve it. Nothing was going to interfere with his morning meeting.

At six fifteen Julius entered the east side of Marshall and located a small diner. He was quite partial to diner food since it was basic and generally wholesome. Some were down-right like home cookin'. Not that he didn't like a fancy meal from time to time, but he always returned to the basics when he needed comfort. He had rehearsed in the car almost all the way from Springhill to Marshall, feeling prepared and about as calm as he was ever going to be. He needed some breakfast and, if he thought about it enough, he was actually starting to feel hungry. He ordered two eggs scrambled with hash browns, pea meal ham, and whole wheat toast. He wasn't sure if his digestive system was ready to take in that much food and keep it down, but he would do his best.

At six forty-five he left the diner, his plate almost dishwasher clean, and drove to the Sheriff's building anticipating, if no other part of the day, his meeting with Rikki.

As he drove around Whetstone Square to find a parking spot on Franklin Street, his eyes were drawn to the historic Harrison County Courthouse, glistening in the early morning light. He heard it was spectacular when fully lit during the Wonderland of Lights festival. Someday he would make a point of taking a trip to Marshall with Cora to join in the festivities, but he couldn't make himself believe it could be any more beautiful than it was this morning, illuminated with the golden glow of the sunrise.

Entering the office, he said good morning to the desk clerk, someone he hadn't met before, perhaps the end of the night shift, or maybe the morning shift—he didn't know—but he was surprised he was allowed to just waltz through reception into the office area. It occurred to him Rikki must have paved the way for him, indicating she was in her office. His heart-rate increased slightly, and he felt a drop of perspiration spring from his brow, but he quickly wiped it away and pulled himself together. He wasn't sure his reaction was due to seeing Rikki again or his subconscious associating his dread of the up-coming meeting with Rikki's name.

When he entered her office, Rikki was facing away from the door, looking at something on the front of her desk. She was wearing a business pant suit, clearly tailor made, in soft colors that set off her hair which was no longer tied up, but allowed to flow freely over her shoulders, extending about six inches down her back. Hearing him approach, she turned around. This time his heart *did* skip a beat—he felt it distinctly. Rikki was wearing just a touch of makeup and a cream silk blouse. Although she hinted at being pretty when in uniform, she was stunning when in civilian clothes, which, he estimated, took ten years off her age. She would drive Mr. Koehler nuts, he was sure of it, a distraction that could be turned to their advantage.

After a brief greeting they headed out to Julius' car. He couldn't help himself; he opened and held the car door until she was seated. Her expression indicated she didn't expect such chivalry, but appreciated it anyway. Sometimes chivalry had its perks.

It took only a few minutes to reach the hospital reception area where they identified themselves, indicating they had an appointment with Mr. Koehler.

They were asked to wait a few moments for an escort while the receptionist made the required call.

Shortly, an attractive woman appeared, introduced herself as Kathy, Mr. Koehler's assistant, and, yes, she would be pleased to take them to him.

They passed Kathy's desk, then through the large doorway into the CIO's office. They each took note of the technology displayed to their left while being led to a conference table situated on the right hand side of the ample workspace. At the conference table were standing two men. One in his late thirties, hair thinning at the temples, gently accented with gray. At just under six feet in height, his physique spoke of attempts at staying fit, interrupted, perhaps too frequently, by the demands of his job. His intelligent eyes greeted his guests with a smile. The other was in his mid-fifties, his bald head topping a pocked and craggy face that seemed somehow to speak of personal pain and its oft-attendant bitterness. His six foot plus athletic frame made him look very much like a boxer and, with very little effort to disguise it, ready for a fight. The younger man introduced himself as Jim Koehler, the Chief Information Officer, then turned to the older man and introduced him as Dr. Blake Atchley, Chief of Staff. Jim's eyes narrowed as a frown skimmed across his brow.

Julius wasn't expecting a second attendee even though it had crossed his mind. His thoughts spun, attempting to calculate what it might mean. Recovering quickly, he introduced himself and then Rikki Castillo, his counsel.

Politely Jim said, "I didn't realize you were bringing someone with you, Mr. Barlow."

Julius replied, equally as politely, "Nor did I realize you would have someone with *you*, Mr. Koehler. If you are comfortable with Ms. Castillo, I would appreciate your allowing her to stay, since some of what I want to tell you may have legal ramifications for me, and perhaps for the hospital." Rikki's eye was immediately drawn to the clenching of Atchley's jaw.

Kathy came to the table with a tray containing mugs, a carafe of coffee, a bowl of assorted sweeteners, and a small pitcher of cream, then disappeared into her office, closing the door behind her.

Julius aggressively took the floor. "Gentlemen, as I said to Mr. Koehler on the phone, I inadvertently harvested some data from one of your servers. I created a small virus as part of a computer security course I was taking. I didn't expect it to return any data whatsoever, and I was totally surprised when it came back with a bunch of data appearing very much like a memory dump. I took from Mr. Koehler's response when we spoke on the phone that he knew about the hack, if you want to label it as such, so I'm glad I contacted him. The data is incomprehensible to me, and I would be happy to delete it from my computer if that is what you would like me to do."

Rikki's eyes flitted between the two men with focused intent. A lifted eyebrow registered the fact that Blake's color was slowly returning. Jim turned to Julius and said, "Do you mind if we use first names around this table. I see no reason for things to be too formal." Everyone except Blake nodded their approval. "Now, Julius, I do have some questions I would like to ask you. I have a technical background, so please feel free to be as detailed as you want. If your answers need translation, I'll be happy to do so in order for Blake and Rikki to follow the discussion." Blake glared at him for a moment, sending the message that he was not to be placed into the category of the ignorant.

As promised, Jim proceeded to fire a series of questions at Julius. Where Julius felt particularly at risk he answered as technically as he could in the hopes of keeping some details just between them. However, Jim was true to his word and offered layman explanations for everything Julius was saying.

Eventually Jim said, "You indicated the data was just a jumble to you and was meaningless. But you are a respected analyst and would either have the tools to decipher the data, or you could *create* the tools to find some meaning in it."

Touché! Julius was caught in the web he was hoping to avoid. Jim had done his homework. Either he had to disclose what he found or he would have to lie. He thought for a moment, looked at Rikki as if for approval, then let out a gentle sigh. "Gentlemen, I have to admit I did put some effort into reconstructing the data. Jim is right, it's just what I do. It wasn't done with any specific intent, other than curiosity." He again looked at Rikki, seeing her nod almost imperceptibly. "I was able to determine it was a dump of some kind of database, but, as with most databases, the data consisted of pointers and numbers that had no resolving references. I was unable to figure out all the metadata and, in the end, I simply stopped looking around and put it aside. Let me also say, if I had found anything with meaning, I would certainly have informed you immediately, I assure you."

With each word, Blake's lips compressed into a thinner line. He was now sitting upright, as rigid as a rifle barrel. On the other hand, Jim sat relaxed and poised, ensuring those present that he had accepted the words Julius had offered, but was not entirely convinced.

Julius caught Rikki's glance indicating it was time to go. She said, "Gentlemen it's been a pleasure. Thank you for your time. If you have any other questions, please email them to me and Julius will respond through me." Julius and Rikki rose together, followed awkwardly by a surprised Jim. Blake remained seated as he scowled at them both. Regaining his composure and his manners, Jim shook Rikki's hand. Passing Kathy's desk they thanked her for the coffee and headed for the car.

Once in the car, with the doors closed, Rikki broke the silence, "You can breathe now, Julius. Breathe! … In! … Out! … In! … Out! … You did exactly what you should have. You gave them a plausible explanation. You didn't say anything false but you left them with doubts. That should stir the pot, and if I may mix metaphors, the hornets will be busy for a while trying to figure what just happened to their cozy little nest."

After struggling to get the car into reverse, Julius almost sideswiped the car next to him while backing from the parking spot. Rikki asked gently, "Would you like me to drive?"

Julius was tempted, but thought if they were being watched it would appear very odd indeed and may raise suspicion, so he continued toward the parking lot exit. As he was putting coins into the gate, his eyes caught a familiar face in the side mirror; a face in the second car back; a face belonging to the third man in the Lincoln. His stomach knotted as his breath caught. He had trouble fitting the last coin into the slot. He tried steadying his trembling hands on the steering wheel. Rikki caught his reaction immediately and asked what had spooked him.

"The third guy in the Lincoln! The car I crashed into! The one that went missing! He's driving the car two behind us. He must know this is my car. Now I'm *really* glad you're here; you wouldn't have believed this if you hadn't seen it for yourself. I hope you're armed." His voice had climbed an octave and sweat was beginning to soak the back of his shirt.

"Calmly, Julius. Drive normally. He's not going to do anything in this traffic. Maybe we can make this work for us." As her mind was spinning with various plans and schemes, she advised, "Drive to my office. Park as close to the front door as you can—take a cruiser spot if you have to. We'll both go into the building and straight to my office where we'll figure out what to do. I'll have someone watch your car so there is no chance of tampering."

Julius did as Rikki suggested. As he approached the small visitor's parking lot, a late model red Camaro was just leaving—probably paying speeding tickets, thought Julius. He quickly swung into the open spot. Leaving the car, they entered the building where Rikki spoke a few words to the deputy at the desk and then joined Julius as he hurried to the perceived safety of her office.

Once there, she said, "This could be a truck-load of trouble for us. If this driver is in contact with the hospital, he could report back that we drove here, which could be interpreted in a number of ways, none of them good. They could figure out I'm a cop, or they might think we went directly to the police after our meeting, maybe to make accusations—who knows what they will think … My suspicion is that this guy was contracted by a third-party who isn't local—a go-between who can't be easily traced back to Parks. So I'm going to go with the theory that our location will *not* be passed back to the hospital or whoever ordered the hit. What this *does* tell me is that it *is* someone in the facility, someone who knew about the meeting and gave this thug a heads up. I suppose he may be just clearing away loose ends, but I doubt it. This proves we're getting close, even though we don't know close to *what*."

Julius focused all his attention on her as she spoke, sighing involuntarily as he forced back the nausea that was beginning to take hold of him.

Rikki continued. "I think we should make an effort to arrest this guy. Maybe he can lead us to someone or something that will help in the case. In any event, getting him off the street will certainly guarantee your safety, at least for some period of time. Whoever hired him won't know right away we have him in custody, and for the duration you're a free man ... what you wanted, right? Hopefully we can get to the bottom of this in the meanwhile.

"Here's what I'm thinking—and try to stay with me until I get to the end. I propose setting a trap for him. Remember I said to you once that the best way to get to you would be while you're driving home? Well, let's hand you to him on a silver platter. We'll put it in motion and drop it in his lap. You and I will map out a specific route taking you through some lonely territory in the city. My guess is he will follow you and take the first chance he gets to run you down, or off the road, or something. I'll have four unmarked cruisers positioned at the first place that makes sense, so as you pass, they will box him in. You'll be long gone if shots are fired, and we'll bring him in, dead or alive."

Julius' face had taken on the hue of ashes, and his breath was coming in short gasps. This was way, way out of his comfort zone and he wasn't in the least prepared for a high speed chase through the streets of town, pursued by a cold-blooded killer. He wished he was just being dramatic, but this was the reality—maybe not the high speed part.

Suddenly his legs made the decision for him. He bolted for the door leaving a trail of words behind him. "I can't do this! Find somebody else!"

Rikki's training kicked in. She shot out of her chair sending it careening into the file cabinet behind her desk. Reaching the door just as Julius was about to pass through it, she grasped him by the shoulders and spun him around, kicking the door shut at the same time, signaling to her colleagues that she had the situation under control.

Just inches from his face she pleaded, "Listen to me, Julius. Yes, I *could* get an undercover to impersonate you. Yes, there *may be* other ways of doing this. But I want ... I need *you* ... *not* some stand-in. This is *our* case. You are still the smoking gun. We're in this *together*. I need you to do this with me."

The adrenaline, the fear, threatened to undo him; threatened to make a mockery of his integrity as he felt the impact of her words wash over him. He desperately wanted to look directly into Rikki's eyes as she appealed to him—but he couldn't, staring at the far wall instead.

He had almost forgotten what it was like to have an attractive woman so close, so utterly alive. He drew in a deep breath, the warmth and scent of her boring into his soul. For a split second he allowed their eyes to meet, and he let his gaze fall to the curve of her lips, her mouth just an inch from his, maybe two. There would be no going back; the stain would be permanent. Cora had always been the love of his life, but she could no longer do for him what Rikki could.

With great effort he gently pushed her away and slumped back into his chair, accepting defeat on every front. Rikki retrieved her chair and rolled it over beside him so they were facing each other.

She sat looking at him, the flush all but gone from her cheeks. Eventually he was able to speak, his voice like cracked pavement, "What if he makes a move before we get to the other cops?"

She spoke softly as she offered, "I'll be tailing him. If he does anything unexpected I'll intervene immediately. If I *do* have to intervene, you get yourself as far away as you can, as quickly as you can. If you are in your car, drive to a populated area. If you're on foot for some reason, find a crowd of people, a local store, anything where you have cover. Don't just hide behind a rock somewhere; that may work in the movies, but not in real life." She paused for a long moment. "Just think about it, Julius, that's all I'm asking. … I'm going to change back into my uniform. Be back in a bit." She stood and walked out of her office into the curious gaze of the officers who had witnessed Julius' melt down. "Nothing more to see, guys," she declared, "Back to work."

With nothing to focus his thoughts, they began to spin through all the ways this could go wrong.

Immediately upon Rikki's return, she studied Julius carefully, then, trying to lighten the moment, commented, "You must be feeling a bit better about this. Your white-as-a-sheet complexion has a tiny bit of pink in it now, or is it yellowish-purplish-pink. … How are you doing, really?"

"A little better, like you said. I've worked this through, and although I'm not happy about it, I can't wait to get this last assassin off the streets. Maybe there will be others to come, but at least we'll be rid of the ones we know about."

"Attaboy, now let's go over the plan. After I changed I worked out the details with my boss, and I have been assigned four of the best deputies in this county. For your own protection I'm not going to introduce them to you or tell you what they're driving; the less you know the better. We'll be ready to roll in fifteen minutes; I have to get you out there before you change your mind." Her features took on the hardness of flint, convincing Julius she had the resolve to see this through.

They went over the course he was to take, choosing very prominent land marks, making it unlikely he would get disoriented. The route led roughly back home for Julius, so his pursuer would not get suspicious. But the road would lead them both through a very old part of town with many abandoned buildings, a perfect place for an ambush—or two.

Rikki instructed, "We need to wait another ten minutes to give the ghost cars sufficient time to ensure they can get hidden from sight and prepare to move in. Now, be sure you drive only twenty miles an hour through the target zone. Look lost. Look around as if you are trying to find something or someplace."

"I think I've got it. Mind if I catch a hot tea in the lunch room before I head out. Maybe it will help settle me down."

Julius brewed his tea without hurry. When the ten minutes had expired, he left the building and walked at what he thought was a normal pace to his car. He had been told not to look for the assassin's vehicle but he couldn't help himself. He glanced around as if checking the cloud cover. It was at the curb just down the street. Settling into his vehicle, he started it without haste, and left the parking lot, trying very hard not to look in the rear view mirror to see if he was being followed.

As he approached the target zone he began looking around and slowing down. He caught a glimpse of his tail poking around an intersection just a split second too soon. But he ignored it and continued on. He slowed to twenty miles per hour. Something would happen soon but he wasn't sure what. As he passed a side street he saw two older model cars parked about one hundred feet from the intersection, one on his left, one on his right. They were well disguised, looking like abandoned relics left to rot. He hoped they ran better than they looked. As he approached the next intersection he saw two other old vehicles. This time one was a rusty pickup. As he rolled slowly past he saw them pull out in a cloud of dust and block the road behind him. He could no longer see the first two cars, but he assumed they had pulled out as well to close off the rear of the trap. He immediately pressed on the accelerator, rapidly gaining speed, turning back into town toward the Sheriff's building. He would wait in the safety of Rikki's office, hoping his trembling knees would regain their strength.

As Julius accelerated away from the intersection, Yakov Travkin floored the gas pedal in an attempt to overtake him. Suddenly two cars emerge from the crossroad ahead of him, stopping abruptly. He instinctively hit the brakes, swerving to miss them. His old rental crossed the road, jumped a laneway, and hit the corner of an abandoned warehouse before coming to a complete stop. Exchanging instinct for training, he opened the driver's door and rolled onto the cracked and scarred laneway, causing his previously damaged shoulder to shoot darts of pain through his body. He landed on his feet, sheltered by the open car door, gun in hand. At that moment two more cars came to dusty stops about fifty feet behind him. He was surrounded.

He weighed his options. He could simply give himself up—he had no idea who these people were; they could be cops, but worse, they could have been commissioned to exact revenge for the botched hit on Barlow. He could shoot his way out—but he was significantly outnumbered; it was four vehicles to his one, and he had no idea how many occupants were in each. He could run into the alley and find somewhere to hide until they tired of searching. He elected to run. Staying low, still covered by the open car door, he ran in spite of the nagging pain in his shoulder which had started to inch its way down his side. He tucked the pain away and ran for his life, head down, watching for obstacles that would trip him or slow his progress.

"*Stop right where you are!*" commanded a voice with sufficient authority to make him stumble, recover, then raise his head warily. Standing a few yards in front of him was a uniformed female sheriff's deputy, gun leveled at his head, rock solid jaw, and unflinching eyes. Yakov's gun was in his hand, but aimed at the pavement. "You can drop your gun or you can raise your arm. Doesn't matter in the least to me. But, if your hand moves even the slightest in my direction, you will not live to pull the trigger. *Drop it! Do it now!*"

Her tone and stance made it very clear to Yakov that it would be in his best interest to believe her. He squatted and placed his gun gently on the ground.

"On your stomach, arms above your head! *Do it! Do it!*"

Rikki kept her distance, knowing the other deputies were on their way; she was interested only in keeping her collar incapacitated. She would not give him a chance to overpower her or to retrieve his weapon.

Within seconds the deputies arrived on the run, halting abruptly at the scene before them. The driver was sprawled face down on the pavement with Rikki standing twenty feet further into the alley, gun drawn and pointed firmly at the driver's head.

One deputy holstered his gun, approached Yakov cautiously, unceremoniously yanked the Russian's arms behind him one at a time, and securely hand-cuffed him. He pulled an angry Yakov roughly to his feet, and they marched as a group to the ghost cars. Rikki turned to her right, walked along an adjoining alley, and climbed into her own vehicle. She would meet them at the office.

Rikki arrived at the office several minutes before Yakov was brought in. Wanting Julius to be present at Yakov's processing, she retrieved him from her office, asking him to stand where he could see Yakov but not easily be seen.

As Yakov was being held at the booking desk, Rikki glanced at Julius to see if he could confirm Yakov as one of his assailants. Julius nodded slightly, then strode back to Rikki's office to sit down. Every few minutes his body began shivering; it took all the willpower he could muster to settle it down.

Rikki joined him a few moments later with a container of Yakov's personal belongings. They went through it together: there was a passport—Russian, a package of Camel cigarettes, an engraved lighter, an expensive leather wallet containing a disarray of papers almost all in Cyrillic script unintelligible to them both, a cell phone, a small amount of change, and a motel keycard. The keys to the rental had been left in the ignition awaiting the towing service, and his gun had been confiscated and bagged by one of the officers.

Idly picking up the cell phone, Julius looked at the call list. There were several numbers, all local, except for one. His curiosity got the better of him. He dialed the first one on the list—it was indicated as an incoming call—and let it ring. There was no answer. He dialed the second one—it had been used for several outgoing calls—and the receptionist at the motel whose name was inscribed on the keycard answered. Julius ended the call. He dialed the third—it, too, had been used for multiple outgoing calls—and it was answered by a clerk wanting to know what kind of takeout he required. The fourth was a long distance number—it had only one incoming call. Julius did not call it, having a pretty good idea of the country the area code represented and what type of person would answer it. He was tempted, however, to place the call and identify himself as Julius Barlow, expecting the person on the other end to be very displeased.

Looking up from the phone, he found Rikki staring at him. "So you want my job now do you? Since when do civilians participate in forensic phone analysis?"

Julius gave her a sheepish look and replied, "My curiosity overcame me. Sorry. But in case you're interested, there was no answer at the first number, the last number is likely his handler, and the numbers in between are the motel and the fast food joint. Would you be able to find out who owns the first number?"

"Certainly. I can do a search right here on my computer. What's the number?"

Julius recited the number from the display on the phone.

"Well … actually, I can't tell you who it is. The number is assigned to a pre-paid cell phone. We might be able to trace it through the seller, but to do so will take a bunch of time, and most often such phones are paid for in cash. There is likely no record of who bought it, unless we can find some security camera footage … and I highly doubt we'll be so lucky."

Julius relaxed, tossing the cell phone onto Rikki's desk among the other belongings. "Where do we go from here? I'm relieved knowing this guy is in your custody. But what do we do now?"

"Once again we've gone way past lunch, and with all this excitement, I bet you're hungry. I suggest we get something to eat, then contact Kate and check on how the audit went this morning."

Food sounded good to Julius. He rose slowly from the chair, emitting an involuntary moan as tense muscles heralded the stress of the day. He headed toward the door, holding it for Rikki to pass through. As they walked past reception, he glanced over at Yakov now sitting at the booking desk, and wondered just how much Yakov knew about him … his family … his life. It felt very strange to be so close to one's killer—but then he had been considerably closer once or twice before.

Chapter 36

EDDIE SAT BOLT UPRIGHT IN BED. IT TOOK HIM ONLY A HEARTBEAT to be past the guest room door and down the stairs. Cora had knotted a roll of bedsheet and clamped it between her teeth to suppress her cries, but she couldn't stop the whimpering coming from her throat. The violence of the seizure unnaturally arched her back, leaving only her shoulders and hips touching the mattress, and her face hardly recognizable as the pain drained its color and contorted its features. It took him a moment to get his mind focused. Running to the kitchen cabinet where they kept the emergency medications, he snatched a vial after checking its label, and a sterile syringe package, tearing it open with his teeth as he swung back into the room. By the time he was at Cora's bedside he had the syringe loaded.

Cora's body responded almost instantly to the injection. Her muscles relaxed, allowing her to slowly settle back onto the bed. Her jaws stopped clenching the wadded sheet, the whimpers quickly replaced with irregular gasps of relief. She didn't open her eyes or acknowledge Eddie's presence as he gently took the wad from her mouth, then rearranged the bed clothes. Turning her head to the left, she slept.

When Sheri came in at six thirty, Eddie still sported the sweat pants and T-shirt he had slept in; he hadn't left Cora's side, content to sit in her bedside chair and monitor her breathing, afraid each breath would be her last. Before long, the rise and fall of her chest regulated and became stronger. Before Sheri had her jacket off, Eddie was pacing the floor recounting the episode, his words stumbling over each other in a rising crescendo.

Rushing to Cora's side, Sheri took her vital signs, then logged Eddie's story in the chart along with Cora's numbers. After a quick check to assure herself Cora was safe, she returned to the kitchen in an effort to help Eddie calm down before he returned to the guest room to prepare for his day.

She called to report this episode to Dr. Garret, but he wasn't available, so she sat, idly pushing a string around in circles on the counter, immersed in a brooding silence.

Chapter 37

HURI DIALED ELLIE'S NUMBER. "HI, ELLIE? I KNOW THIS WAS KIND OF quick, but I pretty much have what I need. I'd like to meet with some of your senior staff to report my findings before I leave; then there are no surprises when my, you know, official report is filed. I think we should have the CFO, yourself of course, and the Chief of Staff. I know these people are very busy, particularly the Chief of Staff, but I like to involve him or her because the doctors whose activities we are auditing are their responsibility … but of course you already know that, don't you. Could you arrange a meeting for me for as soon after lunch as possible? If I can be out of here by midafternoon then I can keep my evening commitments."

Ellie rolled her eyes and replied, "Of course. I'll try for one o'clock, and if there is any change I'll let you know. Shall we meet there in your conference room?"

"Certainly. Meanwhile I'll eat some lunch and relax a bit, maybe take a short walk."

Ellie responded almost too quickly, "If you are going to leave your area you will need an escort both in and out of the building—.

Huri jumped in, "Oh, no then. I don't want to be any trouble. I'll wait here and read a bit and have my lunch in the coffee room. I brought a few magazines with me. Don't worry about me; I'll be fine."

"OK, if you're sure you don't need to go out for any reason."

"No, really, I'll be fine. But thanks for the offer."

At twelve fifty Ellie popped her head into the conference room and announced, "We are on for one. But the Chief of Staff, Dr. Atchley, insisted on it being in *his* office. If you want to gather your notes I'll take you there. Feel free to leave your other things in this room and we'll come by for them later … or take them with you, whatever is easiest."

"Maybe I'll just pack everything up. Then I can head out right after the meeting." Huri maintained her I-don't-care attitude for the time being.

Huri stuffed her things carelessly into her backpack, papers and cords jutting out at all angles, slung it over her shoulder and followed Ellie through a maze of halls, through a glass-walled walkway to an adjacent building, up an elevator, and along another maze of halls. She would definitely need an escort to find her way out.

Huri was led through an assistant's office, empty, probably still out for lunch, and then through large doors which opened into the office of Dr. Blake Atchley. He was sitting at the head of a mid-sized conference table situated on the left hand side of an ornate office, decorated more with art and artifacts than medical paraphernalia. Clearly Dr. Atchley liked looking and feeling important. This ought to be fun, thought Huri, as Ellie began the introductions.

"This is Megan Johnson, our CFO. And Dr. Atchley, Chief of Staff. This is Madhuri Kadar," she turned to Huri and said, "Did I pronounce your name correctly?" Huri reluctantly nodded. "But she goes by Huri."

After taking their places around the table, Dr. Atchley jumped right in. "Ms. Kadar, I'm sure you appreciate we are extremely busy at this hospital," implying her other audits were obviously with less busy, or perhaps less important, hospitals. "We have had to do some rearranging to put this meeting together, for, I believe, *your* convenience. So let's get right to the point." He started this statement in full control of his emotions, but by the end of it his voice was raised and his teeth were bared like a wolf protecting her cubs.

Huri had him on edge already, and that was exactly where she wanted him. Making no attempt to be subtle, she took a moment to scan her surroundings, to piece together a fuller profile of this man. She had already been impressed by the expense of his surroundings. Perhaps expensive wasn't quite the right word. Maybe opulent, or powerful, was better. Some of the trappings may not have been costly, but they represented importance. The African mask displayed prominently on the credenza, the art on the walls, the ivory lamp, the tiffany lamp shade, the inlaid desk, almost bare except for a digital phone and a laptop, the polished cherry conference table at which they sat with Dr. Atchley at the head, accompanied by his notepad computer and his cell phone. All this smacked of an important, busy man with many demands on his time—likely true in some respect, she mused. She waited until she saw the red rising further on Dr. Atchley's face as he shouted, "Well?"

"Yes, I understand. And thank you for putting this meeting together on such short notice. As I said to Ellie, I like to let my clients know my audit findings before I leave, just to ensure there are no misunderstandings when I file my official report." She looked around the table at each face, gauging their reaction. Ellie's left eyebrow slowly rose as she stared at Huri in response to this unexpected authoritative tone and no-nonsense manner. This was not the Huri she had worked with in the conference room. Huri continued, "It is the policy of our company to do irregular audits from time to time to assure our senior management and, by extension, our shareholders, that what your doctors are billing is legitimate. Billing fraud is on the increase and takes a wide variety of forms, not all of them obvious to a regular audit." She paused again to study each face in turn. Ellie continued to stare, her left hand finding an earring to play with. Megan's face was imperceptible but calm. Blake began to fidget like a child about to get his first injection. He knew something. "I have inspected your billings to our firm for the last ninety days—"

A cell phone chirped. Huri followed its insistent ring to somewhere around Blake's desk, perhaps under it. She said politely, "Do you need to get that, Dr. Atchley. We can wait for you, if need be."

Blake instantly went bright red, and mumbled in an angry tone, replete with expletives, the essence of which sounded something like, "I'll deal with *that* later." The phone rang five times and then stopped.

Heads eventually turned back to Huri and she continued, "As I was saying, I did a thorough audit of all your billings to us during the ninety days I specified earlier. I examined the hospital records associated with patient care and surgeries, and I'm satisfied the services were performed as billed. However, I have questions on two billings." She watched the faces around the table intently. Blake was sitting forward in his chair, his hands folded on the table, redness dissipating, face drawn, jaw set, attentive. "Each of them involves the death of a patient." Blake began an arrhythmic tapping of his lower lip. "The date of death you have on file is different from the date I found in the obituaries—out in the public, if you like." Blake's eyes turned dangerous. "I discovered, in each case, a billing for surgery just hours before the specified date of death. Now, this is not unusual of course, since last minute efforts to preserve life are expected. But I was puzzled by the inconsistency in the death dates. Can you suggest to me how such a discrepancy could occur?" Pausing, she continued watching each face around the table in turn.

Ellie was listening, but her glazed eyes broadcast that she wasn't engaged. Either this kind of inconsistency didn't matter to her, or it was a common occurrence. If the latter were the case then Huri had more to worry about than she thought. Megan had moved forward in her chair and was listening intently, likely understanding the implications of what Huri was saying. Blake, on the other hand, became furious and his rage finally got the better of him. "What does this have to do with us," he spat, "we can't help what the funeral homes print in the obits. We all know they get names and dates wrong. Sometimes they can't even get the family members straight. Why are you coming to *us* with this, like it's our fault?" He was barely under control.

Megan looked over at Blake and drilled him with a glance, instructing him to calm down. He struggled to regain a little composure.

Huri ignored his outburst and continued, "Because we have a date discrepancy and because there was a surgery just prior to the date you have in your records, I dug a little deeper into the surgery itself. I looked at the operating room records for those particular surgeries and found them to be in order." The purple of Blake's anger quickly faded to pallor and his jaw began to slacken. "Based on your records, and others I talked with, there were doctors in attendance, equipment used, and supplies consumed—"

Blake stared at her and interrupted, "What … did you just say?"

"I said the OR was used appropriately for the surgery specified on the billing. Is that a problem?"

"Uh … no, no, of course not," Blake sputtered, "I guess I just misunderstood what you said." Blake's lips were compressed into a thin line, and with wide eyes he looked at the edge of the table, deep furrows etching his brow.

Huri threw a questioning glance at Blake, then continued, "My report will show everything is in order for the time frame audited. I would like a response from you regarding the date discrepancy and, if I get a plausible explanation from you before tomorrow at the end of business, I'll not mention it in my report." She saw relief on each face around the table. "Thank you for your time, and Ellie, for your hospitality. I apologize for the inconvenience of this audit, but I'm sure you would agree that stopping fraud is important to us all."

Everyone nodded appropriately as they shook hands, and all but Blake left the office. Megan turned to the left while Ellie and Huri turned to the right. Ellie said coldly, "I'll guide you to the main reception area so you can be on your way."

They walked side by side in silence, each having completed their task.

Contempt wafted from Ellie like a scent as she recalled the transformation in Huri. The more she thought about it, the more she concluded it had been intentional. Glad that this part of the audit was over, and that it had been done so quickly, she sincerely hoped she never had to set eyes on this woman ever again.

Huri was pleased Atchley had been so unwittingly cooperative. His reaction at the ringing of the cell phone seemed extremely odd—but then he seemed to be a man of extremes. His surprise that the OR had been used for its intended purpose was something she would have to think about.

Her report would contain some interesting evidence.

Chapter 38

HURI DROVE BACK TO HER OFFICE, SETTLED IN, AND DIALED THE phone.

"Kate. Hi. This is Huri."

"Yes, Huri. I gather you are still in one piece? How did it go?"

"Extremely well from our perspective … not so well from theirs. I discovered two death date discrepancies, so I'm convinced Julius is onto something. However, when I inspected the surgeries billed after the obit date of death, they appeared legitimate. I went through the OR records and everything seemed to be in order. In each case the operating room was booked by the doctor who submitted the billing. I spoke briefly with others who were in the operating wing on each occasion, and they indicated the OR was in use. I don't know what that means yet, but it could mean the obit dates are wrong—but I doubt it based on what Julius found."

"Mm … odd. I would have thought the OR would either not have been booked properly, or it would have been left unused, or cancelled at the last minute … or something."

"Me, too. I expect this will take a little more investigation before we really know what happened."

"I agree. How did you leave it with them?"

"I asked them to provide me with an explanation for the date discrepancies. I suppose it's not really their responsibility, but I thought I would give it a try. I told them everything was in order and I would not include the date issue in my report. I'm sure they'll be scurrying around trying to find some kind of explanation no matter how inane."

Huri paused, and then continued, "Two other things happened that I thought were a bit odd. In the middle of our meeting a cell phone rang somewhere under Dr. Atchley's desk. I assume it was in his bag—not so unusual, I guess. But he had a cell phone with him on the desk, and what I thought was most curious, he seemed, uh, let's say, distraught about it ringing—like it wasn't supposed to. Anyway, it may have been nothing. The more important event was Dr. Atchley's reaction when I told everyone I had inspected the OR and found it to be used, and used appropriately. He was surprised, genuinely upset. It was almost as though he had no idea it had been used—particularly for what was intended. Through the whole meeting his emotions were all over the map. Perhaps he's just hot-headed, but I think it's more than that."

"Great. Thanks for the head's up. I'm going to try to meet with Rikki this afternoon, if possible, and see what she thinks of all this. I'll get you involved if they have specific questions. Thanks for your help."

"OK, Ciao, chat later."

Kate paused for a moment, then dialed the number for Deputy Castillo and waited.

After several rings Rikki came on the line, "Deputy Castillo."

"Rikki. It's Kate. Has your day been good to you so far?"

"Actually, it has. We took the third hit man into custody around noon, allowing several of us to heave a large collective sigh of relief. How about yours?"

"Mine, too—"

Rikki interrupted, "I'm putting you on speaker. I have Julius with me."

"The audit is done. Ms. Kadar, the auditor we sent in, has verified what Julius had discovered. We haven't made any moves yet. We will need to launch a more extensive investigation and see how deep this goes. Ms. Kadar noted two specific things I want to pass on to you. I'll let you decide if they have any meaning or not."

"OK, what are they?"

"She met with the CFO, a Megan Johnson, the Chief of Staff, a Dr. Atchley, and her host for the day, Ellie Christianson, an assistant of some kind. They met in Dr. Atchley's office at his specific request … demand, really." Kate told them of Atchley's surprise at learning the operating rooms had been used. "Also, according to her notes, about one ten or so a cell phone apparently in a bag under Atchley's desk, rang four or five times, and it appeared to upset Atchley. He had another cell phone beside him at the meeting. It may be nothing, but Ms. Kadar—let's call her by her nickname—Huri, found it odd. It could have been his personal phone while the one on the table was his hospital phone, but why would it upset him? It was as if he didn't expect it to ring and its ringing annoyed him."

Julius sat bolt upright and interjected, "That would have been just after we arrived back from the sting, going through Yakov's personal stuff. Remember the one number where I didn't get an answer. Kate, how many times did Huri say it rang?"

"Four or five."

"Exactly what I heard on this end as well. Would this not directly connect Atchley with the hit on me?"

Rikki responded, "It sure would. But if our scenario is correct, it is a prepaid, untraceable phone, as we suspected. His surprise at its ringing may indicate it is supposed to be used only for outgoing calls. If we are even close to being right, he'll dump it on the way home tonight, if he hasn't done so already."

Kate said, "So what do we do. It sounds like we have to do something right away if this is going to be of any use to us—I guess, really to *you*, since it has nothing to do with the fraud angle, best I can tell."

Rikki thought for a moment. "Let's try this. Kate, I'll get our tech guys here to patch you in to Dr. Atchley's line and record the call. You keep him on the phone for a while. I'll redial the number and we'll see if we can hear it ringing. If we can be sure it's his phone number, then we'll have to take action right away … I just don't know quite yet what that would be. But let's be sure we aren't dealing with a coincidence here."

Kate and Julius both agreed. It was a simple solution, a giant step forward with no downside.

Rikki placed a call to the Sheriff's tech group and assembled the various pieces of her plan.

When everything was ready, Rikki told Kate to wait for the beep and then treat the call as if she had just dialed it herself. She told everyone they would be able to hear Kate's side of the conversation, but Dr. Atchley would not be able to hear what was going on in Rikki's office. Kate was told to press the # key when she wanted to break the connection with the hospital.

Several moments passed, then the beep.

An assistant answered, "Hello, Dr. Atchley's office. May I help you?"

"Yes, please. My name is Kate Jansen. Madhuri Kadar, you may know her as Huri, did an unscheduled audit this morning at my request. May I speak with Dr. Atchley to get his feedback?"

"Certainly. I'll put you right through."

"Dr. Atchley speaking."

"Dr. Atchley, my name is Kate Jansen. The auditor this morning, Huri, works for me and I wondered if I could get your feedback on her audit and the post-audit meeting. We don't do this for regular audits, but these unscheduled audits sometimes take unusual turns."

"What specifically do you want to know? Unless you're stupid, you have to know this thing has been a gross interruption, and a big waste of time for all of us. So make it short," he snapped.

Rikki pushed the Redial button on the cell phone.

Kate said, "I'm sorry for any inconvenience. ... I understand Huri questioned you on two death dates in your system that didn't match with those in the newspapers. This is the first time in my career such a thing has been referenced in an auditor's preliminary notes, and I wondered what you thought this could be all about. I'm looking for your guidance on where to take this—"

A cell phone was ringing somewhere in Dr. Atchley's office—it was faint but distinct. Rikki counted with her fingers: one ... two ... three ... four.

Kate heard Blake's voice as he droned on about how incompetent the funeral homes were, broken only by a brief hesitation when the cell phone rang, but she didn't listen to his words. When he came up for air, Kate said, "Thank you for your time. I'm sure that's all it is. Have a good day." And she pressed the # key.

Rikki and Julius were beaming. They had proven to themselves Dr. Atchley had hired the assassin, or at least was involved in giving him information. How else would Yakov have known about the timing of the morning meeting and where it would be held?

"Now we have to decide how we obtain evidence strong enough to stand up in court," said Rikki, "Any suggestions?"

Just as Rikki was finishing her sentence, Yakov's cell phone rang. They each looked at the other wondering what to do.

On the second ring Rikki handed it to Julius and said, "Be Russian."

Julius was too stunned to refuse. He punched the Accept Call button, answering in as deep a voice as he could muster, "Yes?" As he did so he shrugged at Rikki and grimaced.

The voice they had just heard talking to Kate, or, more precisely, the same voice raised an octave, raged on the other end of the line. "You are never to call this number. Understand! Never! It was obviously a mistake to contact you directly; I should have gone through your handler. If I knew *who* you were and *where* you were I'd remove your liver while you watched. How can you be so stupid? I expected—"

Julius was holding the phone off his ear so Rikki could hear the conversation. She mouthed to him, "Just hang up."

Julius brought the phone down and pressed End Call.

Rikki immediately jumped in, "He'll assume his hireling just hung up because of his abuse. There's no way he knows we have the phone."

Kate was still on the speaker but she hadn't heard much of the cell phone call.

"Hello," she chimed, "I'm still here. What's happening?"

Rikki apologized, "Oh … sorry, Kate. We weren't ignoring you; we just forgot you were there." There was no mistaking the warmth in her voice. The speaker phone let out a short chuckle.

"We're back to where we were. We need to find a way to make use of this turn of good fortune."

Julius said thoughtfully, "Let's take the show to Dr. Atchley. He has no way of knowing we're involved. He was in the meeting I had this morning with the CIO, and maybe he would like to talk to me directly."

Kate chimed in, "OK, let me call his assistant. She will recognize me from our earlier conversation. I'll find out when Dr. Atchley will be in the office."

Rikki and Julius may have said something in response, but it didn't matter. They heard Kate's cell phone beeping out a number followed by a muffled conversation in the background.

Kate said excitedly, "He will finish his rounds and be back in his office at three thirty. I think we should be waiting for him."

Rikki replied, "Are you suggesting *all* of us should go? I think it would be better if only Julius and I go. After all we were a team earlier today."

Kate's voice was suspicious, "What do you mean, you were a *team* earlier today?"

"Oh, I guess we didn't tell you. Julius and I went to see the CIO and Dr. Atchley this morning. I went as his lawyer. It was very amusing, really."

Kate was aghast, "You took Julius to the hospital to meet the guys who are trying to kill him? What were you thinking?!"

Rikki responded quickly, "It's all good, Kate. We wanted to confront the hospital brass and confess to the hack just to see which stones rolled over. Watching Atchley, it was clear he is involved."

Kate went silent for a moment, then she said, her voice taut with concern. "Whatever you say, Rikki. It's not a choice I would have made."

"Well, I propose to do it again. If our suspicions are right, I'll arrest him on the spot."

"OK, then. I'll let you go and wish you luck. And I thought I was tough."

Rikki terminated the call.

"OK, my brave friend. I'm going to get changed into my lawyer clothes once again, and then we'll drive to the hospital. I don't want Atchley going home until we see him. We can't risk him dumping that cell phone."

Although they had a few minutes to spare they headed for the hospital, stopping for a quick coffee along the way.

At ten minutes after three, Julius and Rikki arrived at the hospital, identified themselves, and asked reception if they could speak with Dr. Atchley's assistant in person. Erika arrived in the lobby a few minutes later with a very puzzled look on her face.

"Hello, I don't seem to have an appointment for you. What is this about?" she said tersely.

Rikki took the lead, "Erika—may I call you by your first name?—there is one thing Mr. Barlow didn't mention in our meeting this morning that pertains directly to Dr. Atchley. We took a chance on coming in person because it's urgent we speak with him, if only for a few minutes."

Erika was still puzzled, but she thought she had better let them see Blake. If it was important and she shielded him from it, he would take it out on her personally. "Please follow me. Dr. Atchley will be back from his rounds in about fifteen minutes. You can wait in my office until he arrives." She was silent the rest of the way to Blake's office.

Julius and Rikki sat quietly in Erika's office looking at papers they brought with them, feigning preparation for an important meeting.

Eventually, the outer door burst open and Dr. Atchley stormed through. Perhaps his rounds hadn't gone so well. Or maybe the earlier stress of the day was taking its toll. He stopped dead in his tracks, staring at Rikki and Julius, his eyes turning dangerous as they lingered on Julius for just a moment too long. Then he turned on Erika who took the brunt of his anger as if she alone were responsible for Julius being alive. "What in the world is *he* doing here? I don't have time for any more of his stories—or anyone else's for that matter. Get them out of here."

Erika tried to explain but was unsuccessful at calming Blake's rage.

Rikki stood, taking charge while Julius rose hesitantly to his feet, "Dr. Atchley, we apologize for arriving unannounced. But in my discussions with Mr. Barlow, some things have come to light I felt should be for your ears only. It will take only a few minutes of your time."

This stroking of Blake's ego worked its charm. He calmed considerably, and reluctantly suggested they go into his office. Directing them to the cherry conference table, he offered them two chairs, one on either side, while he took the chair at the head. Rikki ignored his offer, sitting in the chair next to him, motioning Julius to sit on the far side of her. She didn't want Julius close to Atchley when he realized what was actually going down.

Color rose briefly on Blake's neck at Rikki's blatant disregard for his instructions. He forced himself to sit erect, planting a look of expectation on his face. "Get on with it!" Rikki sat looking intently at Atchley and waited. Julius reached into his pocket, stood, excused himself, and walked to the far end of the table facing away from Atchley who was scanning from one to the other and back again. He pressed the Redial button. Moments later a cell phone began ringing under Atchley's desk.

Rikki continued to look intently at Atchley until the third ring, and then said authoritatively, "Aren't you going to answer your phone?"

Blake looked at her curiously, and in a carefully controlled tone replied, "No, I'm sure it can wait until later."

Rikki said, "No, please, I insist, answer your phone. If you don't it just may continue interrupting our discussion."

Blake stared at Rikki with narrowed eyes, and the muscles in his jaw worked as he rose from his chair, went over to his desk, and rummaged in the bag under it. He fished out the cell phone, punched the *Accept Call* button and said in quiet tones through clenched teeth, "I'm in a meeting. I'll call you back." He took the phone from his ear and was about to press the *End Call* button when he heard Julius say behind him, "I think you really want to take this call." The words echoed from the cell phone with just a slight delay. Atchley looked at Julius, looked at Rikki, and then his face contorted into that of a gargoyle. Knees visibly weakened, he reached for the chair-back to steady himself. He tried to speak, but it came out only as a sputter.

Rikki leapt across the room like a jaguar. She gripped Atchley's left arm, causing the phone to drop and bounce on the carpeting, then twisted it behind him. A split second later she did the same with his right arm. Blake didn't have a chance to react. By the time he realized what was happening, Rikki had him handcuffed and subdued. He found his voice and began bellowing abuse.

Erika came bounding into the office, the door slamming on its stop. She demanded to know what was going on, but her words trailed off when she saw Blake's arms behind his back and heard Rikki reading him his rights.

Chapter 39

IN THE END, SHERI CALLED DR. SYKES, RELATED THE MORNING episode, and discussed with him the vital signs she had been monitoring each hour during the day. Sykes said he would drop by mid-afternoon.

Cora was still groggy from the morning injection when Sykes arrived. He wasted no time reaching the faded chair standing beside her bed. Gently he urged her to describe what had happened the night before, needing to understand the source of her discomfort; something ... anything ... that would help him determine how to alter, and hopefully correct, her pain regimen. After their brief discussion, Cora was fading again as he asked her in a whisper if she could hang on just a bit longer while he completed his examination. She nodded weakly.

Dr. Sykes checked her back muscles, prodding her vertebrae trying to find out why she had experienced a seizure during the night. Cora winced at some of his actions, and he apologized, but continued until he was satisfied. He made several long notes on her chart, then let her sleep.

When he returned to the kitchen he called Sheri to the breakfast counter. They sat side by side, talking in hushed tones. "There seems to be an accelerated deterioration of the intertransversarii muscle. I don't understand why it should have been so rapid. I did a full work-up of her spine just last week. It appears the disease is gaining speed and wreaking havoc as it progresses. I don't like her having such large doses of Valium, so I'll work on getting a cocktail ready as soon as I can, to do the job but not be quite as dangerous to her respiration.

"Keep her as comfortable as possible today. If you can get back to regular routine it would be good for her mentally—at least give it a try. Don't let her sleep the day away or she'll have a bad night." He retrieved his bag and his keys, and left for his car.

Julius arrived back home much too late to catch Dr. Sykes. Sheri was sitting on a stool at the kitchen counter, her head cradled in her hands. The sound of Julius opening the front door startled her, snapping her back to reality as she sought confirmation, "Julius?"

"Yes, it's me," his tone weary and low.

A quick look at Sheri brought Julius out of his introspection, his voice suddenly alert, "What's happened? Is Cora OK?"

"She's settled down a bit now but it's been a horrible day." She began by relating the morning episode Eddie encountered, and ended with Dr. Sykes' comments. "We really needed you here today!" she blurted.

Seeming to gain courage from the unexpected bitterness in her tone, she continued, "It's been a week Julius, and I know it's not my place, but there can't be anything more important than Cora's well-being, so what's making you leave her … us … alone so much. You're needed here, not somewhere else. You've been away this past week more than I remember you being away for the last many months all put together. Cora's getting worse, the doctors want to talk with you, and you just vaporize." Her voice cracked, tears threatening to spill onto her cheeks. "I'm sorry for having to say it, but someone has to remind you of what's important," she said between sobs.

Julius had never seen her this upset; her professional demeanor had never wavered for all the years she had been assisting him—well, maybe it had cracked a little at times, but it had never fallen completely apart. How could he make her understand that what he was doing *outside* the house was necessary for the safety of those *inside* the house? How could he explain to her that *he* had put everyone in danger; though unintentional, danger nonetheless? How could he give her a sense of how torn he was between the two responsibilities he felt weighing so heavily on his shoulders?

Sheri let out a long breath and through a sob said, "I hope you aren't messing around with some other woman while Cora is suffering here alone in this house. All this secrecy makes everything look *very* suspicious."

He began slowly, trying to catch her eye. "I'm not messing around, Sheri, so you can give that idea up." He fought the color threatening to stain his cheeks. "I'm just not able to give you all the details right now. What I *can* tell you is that I've become involved in a police investigation sparked by the accident, and it involves all of us, you included. I had to see it through, and today everything kind of came together. It's over, and I'll be home from now on to help you with Cora. I keep trying to explain this to her but there just doesn't seem to be a good time. I don't want to worry her but I don't want to keep her in the dark either." He was finally able to search her eyes. "I'm sorry this has upset you, but it's over now, and we can get back to business as usual around here. If you want a break and take a few days, go ahead. I can handle things on my own for a bit if you like."

"A break is not what I'm looking for. Don't you get that?" sniffed Sheri, "I've been worried about *you*, and Cora has been doing so poorly. I guess it finally got to me, but I won't apologize for what I said; someone had to say it."

She packed her things in preparation for leaving. "I'm sorry, Julius, for the outburst. I really do trust you, but things just weren't adding up. I may not know what's going on in Marshall, but I *do* know what's going on here. Cora needs you now more than ever." Dabbing at her tears she left the house.

Chapter 40

ATCHLEY WAS NOT THE MOST PLEASANT OF GUESTS AT THE SHERIFF'S office. He spluttered and cursed and loudly proclaimed his innocence and the lawsuit he would file against every cop across the nation. He flaunted his position, his importance, and his education; all of which fell on deaf ears.

When he calmed somewhat, he demanded to see his lawyer, and was left in isolation waiting for his counsel to arrive.

In the next interrogation room, Yakov sat, body erect, cuffed hands resting on the table. He was a soldier, and now was the time for him to act like one. He didn't care one ruble for the American justice system. He had been trained for times like this. When he signed onto the team for this mission, he had been given a package of information to memorize and then destroy. In the package was the name of an American lawyer who would be there if he found himself in trouble. The mission had been to enter the country on a legitimate tourist visa, execute his orders, and leave the country, leaving behind no trace of himself or his mission. The other two members of his team, including the team leader, had not carried out the terms of their mission—they were leaving behind their corpses— but *he* intended to leave no trace, but *only* after completing what he came to do. However, it appeared that unless something changed, he was also going to fail. After exercising his right to counsel, he sat waiting.

As the day neared its end, two lawyers found spots in the visitor parking lot behind the Sheriff's office. They arrived several minutes apart but came with the same purpose in mind.

Dr. Atchley had summoned a senior partner from the law firm that represented the hospital. A corpulent man wearing an expensive suit and carrying an ornate briefcase labored up the front steps after rolling out of his rare sports car, leased, naturally, at a cost of some $3400 per month. The license plate cover on the back of his car said 'My Other Car Is A Ferrari'. He looked like a lawyer, gave off the scent of a lawyer, and would apply his well-worn tools to get Dr. Atchley home for supper. His name was Cecil Perkins. He was white and thoroughly southern.

Yakov's lawyer was trim, in slacks and an open-necked shirt, wearing running shoes with no socks. He stepped from his late model Corvette then jogged up the stairs two at a time. His name was James Lofton. He was black and thoroughly southern.

Perkins was at the reception desk, having pompously introduced himself just moments before, asking for his client, Dr. Blake Atchley. The deputy at the desk was preparing to escort Perkins to Atchley's interrogation room when Lofton planted himself beside Perkins and boomed his name across the counter demanding to see Mr. Yakov Travkin. Perkins stepped to the side, Lofton having entered his personal space uninvited. Returning to his desk, the deputy shuffled through some paper work, saying, "I can take you two gentlemen together, if you just give me a moment to get the necessary papers." Perkins looked Lofton up and down not making any effort to hide the sneer that lay behind his affected smile. He took another step sideways putting more space between them.

The three men marched to the interrogation rooms. The deputy was in the lead, with Lofton right on his heels, Perkins two or three paces behind, laboring to keep up, looking unhappier by the second. The lawyers were ushered into the appropriate rooms and introduced to their respective clients.

Rikki had a plan for Yakov. Although he had stalked Julius and had drawn a weapon when cornered, he hadn't fired it and no harm had come to Julius. He couldn't be legally connected to the death of his two partners. Dr. Atchley was the fish she wanted to catch, and the sooner she was finished with Yakov, the sooner she could turn her full attention on the good doctor, something, she was certain, he would find quite unpleasant.

As Rikki entered the interrogation room which now housed Travkin and Lofton, James stood, introducing himself. Yakov tried to stand but barely made it to a squat, being restrained by the ankle chain binding him to the chair. He didn't much appreciate being treated like a caged animal. It brought back the nightmares he relived for years after his capture during the war. He sat back down heavily, somewhat subdued by those memories.

Lofton took a seat next to his client. Sitting across from them Rikki said, "Gentlemen, I would like this to be quick and easy. My proposal is simple. On camera and in a signed statement I want Yakov to listen to the recording of a voice. I want him to tell me truthfully if it belongs to the person who called him Friday morning with information on how to locate Mr. Barlow, and who then instructed him to assault Mr. Barlow. In return, Mr. Travkin will be allowed to leave the US, under escort, and he will be placed on the no-fly list. He will never be allowed to enter the US again for any reason. Is this understood?"

Lofton began doing his job, "Uh, before we go off half-cocked here with snitching and banishment and the like, perhaps we should take a look at the charges—"

Rikki cut him off. "I thought I made it clear, Mr. Lofton, that I wanted this to be quick and simple. However, if Yakov does not take my offer, as it was presented, I will charge him with reckless driving, stalking, possession of a concealed weapon, resisting arrest, violating the terms of his visitor's visa, attempted murder and conspiracy to commit murder. I expect I can stretch his trial out over, let's say, a two or three year period. Meanwhile he will be held in custody since he's clearly a flight risk. In the end, nothing may stick, but his career will be ruined. A good Russian hit man doesn't want incarceration in a US prison on his resumé. He can ply his trade all over Europe—around the world for all I care—but not on US soil. Do I make myself crystal clear?"

James asked for a few moments alone with his client, something Rikki was more than happy to provide.

Lofton called Rikki back into the room, beginning before she had a chance to take a seat, "We will agree to the terms, with one stipulation. Yakov wants to meet his client face to face."

Rikki raised her right eyebrow, thinking for a moment. If Yakov ever met Blake somewhere, sometime, he would likely kill him on the spot, but as desirable as that might be, it was never going to happen. Blake would be spending a very long time as a guest of the state or, more likely, a guest of the federal government. Age changes people, and, although Yakov may have an image of his face now, he would not likely recognize him in ten or twenty years. She said, "Agreed. In fact we will add to Mr. Travkin's written statement that he talked with his client and that he confirmed, in person, that the voice on the recording belonged to him. I'll have a deputy prepare the paperwork and the recording device. When everything is ready, Yakov can visit his client and then sign the last of the statements." She left the room and gave instructions to a deputy sitting at a desk along the windows at the front of the building.

Entering the next interrogation room, housing Dr. Blake Atchley and his lawyer, Cecil Perkins, Rikki interrupted the conversation being held in low whispers. Perkins tried to stand but he had trouble moving his bulk past the edge of the table. Atchley didn't even try. Rikki sat across from them. She had all the time in the world. She waited.

Cecil opened the conversation, his smooth voice and southern drawl lending authority to his words, "My client believes he has been falsely accused, and you are putting the lives of his patients at risk by detaining him, keeping him from his duties at the hospital. He and I *demand* that he be released immediately, and that we work out any misunderstandings which may have occurred at a time of our … uh … mutual convenience."

Rikki looked intently at them both and waited. She watched as Blake chewed his tongue and his breathing began to rasp.

Eventually, Blake exploded, "You can't do this to me. I'm a respected surgeon at the children's hospital and you tricked me with that cell phone caper you pulled this afternoon. I've done nothing wrong and I demand my release," the pitch and volume of his voice mounting as he spoke.

Cecil turned and glared at him, then whispered something in his ear. Atchley looked like he could eat a rock pile and then some, but he remained silent.

Rikki took her time and measured her words carefully. "First off, Dr. Atchley won't be going anywhere for a while. He is being charged with attempted murder and conspiracy to commit murder, and in a few days will likely be charged with insurance fraud." At the mention of fraud, Blake's stomach let out a vicious growl. "I don't think Dr. Atchley will be practicing medicine any time soon. Perhaps I should begin addressing him as Mr. Atchley just so he can get used to it." She paused.

Blake was about to pop again so Cecil put a hand on his arm to calm him. Cecil said coolly, "Based on what *Dr.* Atchley," he strongly emphasized the title, "has told me, all the evidence you have is based on a cell phone trick you performed this afternoon in his office. Such a performance would hardly hold sway in court given the standing of my client in the community. The phone you say belongs to my client could easily have been planted or left by the cleaning staff or any other number of things. I suggest you might want to rethink holding *Dr.* Atchley before you go any deeper into the grave you have dug for yourself."

Unwilling to take the bait, Rikki countered, "The trick, as you so incorrectly put it, simply verified it was Blake, here, who called a hired assassin and gave him instructions on how to find his mark. In fact, we have the assassin in the next room, and he's swearing both on video and in writing that the voice we recorded earlier in a conversation we had with Blake is the same voice as the one that gave him the instructions. In fact, he wanted to see Blake face to face since he had never had a chance to meet him, so we are going to oblige him in just a few minutes. I'm not sure why he wants to see Blake, but I can only assume he will consider Blake directly to blame for his imminent extradition. Should their paths ever cross, your hired thug may just teach Blake a lesson we are not permitted to teach him here within our judicial system."

Cecil pounded the metal table in front of him and tried to stand, "You can't do that. You're supposed to uphold the law and protect our citizens. Y'all are sworn to guard and protect!"

"This is quite true. But since Blake has had at least one conversation with this gentleman, we feel it is only proper that he actually meet him. Think of it as bringing two old friends together—and at the taxpayer's expense."

Cecil's face contorted and his lips twisted into a snarl. "Then this interview is over, and I demand Blake be taken to a private cell with your promise of protection, immediately … right now, girlie!"

"All in good time. I may have a few more questions for *Mr.* Atchley. I suggest you count on being here for another, oh, two or three hours." With a smile forming on her lips she stood and left the room.

Chapter 41

THE NEWS OF ATCHLEY'S ARREST TRAVELLED THROUGH THE HOSPItal like a brush fire. Within the hour the hospital CEO, Noah Jackson, had assembled his leadership team: Megan Johnson, CFO; Jim Koehler, CIO; Adrian Jessop, Deputy Chief of Staff; Armoni Beech, Director of Operating Room Logistics; Nakita Goldman, General Counsel; and Olivia Edeson, Noah's assistant.

Mr. Goldman began, "Ladies and gentlemen, we are having this emergency meeting to discuss the arrest of Dr. Atchley this afternoon. I spoke with the arresting officer and with Cecil Perkins, who is acting as Blake's attorney, and it appears Blake has been charged with attempted murder and conspiracy to commit murder based on his supplying certain information to a professional assassin whose target was Julius Barlow, the computer guy who confessed this morning to hacking our computer systems. At this point we have no idea why Blake has been considered a person of interest, and, if Blake should be guilty, why he would be so involved. Given just this information, it would be proper to assume this was something affecting Blake only, and does not involve the hospital, unless Blake and Barlow are connected. What is highly alarming to the hospital is Cecil's report that the arresting officer mentioned they were considering the possibility of insurance fraud charges against Dr. Atchley. This *does* involve the hospital.

"For those of you who don't know, Mr. Barlow and his attorney met with Jim early this morning to discuss a security breach of our computers. Later in the morning we were subjected to a surprise audit by the York Standard Health Insurance Company. The audit reported back to Jim and Blake indicating there were irregularities in the death dates of some of our patients. Then, of course, the incident with Blake's arrest in the afternoon. It seems too much to be coincidental so it is my opinion we need to consider all these events related, and, accordingly, devise an appropriate strategy."

Adrian asked, "Did the insurance company indicate they were pursuing any further investigation of the discrepancies they found?"

Jim replied, "Not really. They did ask us to respond to them with any explanations we may have for the discrepancies, but I left the meeting thinking it was not a significant issue. Perhaps I was mistaken."

Megan jumped in, "I suggest we take a look at this internally. Rather than just providing explanations, let's dig into the deaths cited by the audit and find out what the facts are."

Armoni retorted belligerently, "If the insurance company wants to investigate, then let them do so using *their* resources. We are busy enough without having this thrown at us—"

Megan cut him off, "No, I don't agree. Something like insurance fraud needs to be resolved from the inside out, not the outside in. I would much rather admit to a problem and fix it, or be fixing it, than to be blind-sided with a problem of this potential magnitude."

Noah spoke for the first time. "I'm with Megan on this. Whether it's embarrassing to us or not isn't the question. If there is insurance fraud going on in this hospital under my watch, I want it rooted out and stopped. I know full well if it's wide spread then we will have a staffing problem in the short term, but it's a risk I'm more than willing to take. The alternative? We all find ourselves in court, and then off somewhere collecting litter on the side of a road ... since we *are* supposed to know what is going on ... and that includes fraudulent activities. We may not like it, but the buck stops here in this group, and, ultimately, with me.

"Adrian, I want you to look into these death dates. And go beyond today's audit. Look back, say, a year, and we'll see what you find. If we need to go back further we'll do so.

"Megan, you will look at all the billings immediately preceding the deaths of any of our patients, and then cross reference each with the OR schedule.

"Armoni, for each billing Megan flags, at least for those which involved the OR, I want a full workup on what room was used, who booked it, who the personnel were that performed the surgery, what supplies were used, and anything else you can think of.

"Jim, continue working this hack, and get to the bottom of what took place and what was stolen.

"Olivia, please call the insurance auditor and tell her we have taken her concerns very seriously and, rather than offering explanations for the death date discrepancies, as was suggested, we are going to look into our records for the past year and find out if there are any anomalies of any kind.

"Nakita, I would like you to research any cases in, say, the last five years in which a major hospital was involved in fraudulent activities. I need to know how the courts perceive this and whether the judgments, if any, have been fair and impartial.

"Team, I don't want any of this to leave this room. You may task your staff for assistance but do so in a way that looks totally routine. If we do have stuff going on behind our backs, I don't want anyone getting spooked."

After a brief hesitation he added, "I'm having Olivia take careful notes of all of our discussions. I will *not* be distributing them in the usual fashion. We will meet frequently on these issues, and we'll review the notes, approving them at each meeting … here … in my office."

The team left the conference table, each face stoic, eyes downcast. It was enough of a challenge to run a large hospital in the world of competitive health care, but to face the possibility of fraud charges, and murder of all things—that was something else entirely.

Tuesday

At eleven the next morning the management team was again sitting around Noah's conference table. There was less tension in the air but all the faces were drawn and tired. Olivia had provided fresh baking, coffee and orange juice.

Noah opened, "Judging by the dark circles under your eyes, a lot of extra hours were put in last night, and I want to offer my appreciation to you. Some of you may have missed breakfast so please help yourselves. Adrian, what did you find out about death dates?"

Clearing her throat several times, she said in a voice huskier than usual, "Over the past year, out of 48,600 patients, we have had 263 deaths. Of the 237 we could track, there are 142 death date discrepancies."

Everyone around the table let out an audible gasp. Brows furrowed and the color drained from several faces. Nakita choked on the swallow of coffee he had just taken.

Between involuntary coughs he said, "How can this possibly be? What are we running here?"

Trying to get the mood under control, Noah said, "I admit this is a shock, but let's take it one step at a time. Let's get the whole picture before we jump to any conclusions. Megan, what did you find?"

Adrian answered instead, "Megan and I worked on this together. We didn't do exactly as you asked, since it seemed more efficient if Megan looked at the billings just for those deaths where the dates didn't match. As I found a discrepancy, she examined the billings. In every case we looked at, and we didn't quite get finished, we found a billing between the two dates, always for a surgery that looks legit; like it would be an appropriate surgery to arrest the progression of a documented condition, and which, if not successful, would be terminal. It's puzzling because everything we found looks to be within standard protocol."

Noah said, "Sounds like a pattern developing here. Armoni, what about you?"

"Well, I've been working with the cases handed to me by Megan and Adrian, so I'm one step behind them. However, I've been able to look at 46 cases so far, and in each case the OR was booked by the doctor doing the billing, gowns and masks were used, medical supplies were consumed, medical equipment was used, and the cleanup crew report was as expected. There is only one thing that struck me as being odd, but not totally out of the ordinary. No cases I looked at had an attending anesthesiologist. By itself, it isn't anything to be concerned about, since the logs indicate there were two doctors in the OR for each surgery. However, I would expect this to be the case in a *percentage* of the surgeries, not in every one of them. So, I have nothing conclusive, but just a lingering concern which may be nothing more than my current and, hopefully temporary, paranoia."

Noah concluded the meeting with a thank you to each one. "Keep working through the data. Sounds like you're on the right track. The larger the sample we have, the more certain we will be of any conclusions we reach. Let's meet again, same time tomorrow. Adrian, would you stay for a few more minutes, please?"

The other team members left the office, and Adrian moved closer to where Noah was sitting, waiting for Noah to say what was on his mind.

He started right in, "Adrian, what do you make of what Armoni was saying about these surgeries not having an anesthesiologist? Is that unusual? Is there something here I should worry about?"

"Noah, I can't give you a definite answer but I'll give you my opinion. Let's confine our discussion to the *last resort* surgeries, a term I think would classify the ones we are talking about. The patient is in critical condition and death is imminent. Often the patient is unconscious and usually on life support. Providing *general* anesthesia to a terminally ill patient, particularly a child, is a complex task requiring an appropriate balance between adequate anesthesia and hemodynamic normality. As a result, in cases such as these, it is not uncommon to use *conscious sedation,* in which two medications are normally given. The first is a narcotic analgesic—usually Demerol or Sublimaze. The second is a benzodiazepine or sedative/hypnotic—usually Versed or Valium. This type of anesthetic is commonly administered by one of the doctors doing the procedure. I would conclude then, it would not be unexpected for such surgeries to proceed without the assistance of an anesthesiologist."

"Thanks Adrian, that helps. I'll see you at tomorrow's meeting."

Adrian left, and Noah sat for a few moments mulling over the information presented to him by his staff. Pulling the phone on the conference table over to where he sat, he dialed Jim Koehler. When connected, Noah said, "Jim, one thing we didn't talk about in our meeting today was how the date of death could be different, from a technical perspective, between the hospital records and those kept by the funeral homes. It seems to me at the time of pronouncement, the date and time would be entered into our computers. Would not the same date be registered on the death certificate?"

"You're right in principle, Noah. In fact our practitioners are required to sign the chart immediately following pronouncement, then the nursing staff enters the date, time, and cause of death into their computer right away. Within minutes our system is programmed to transmit that information to the Texas Electronic Death Registrar. We have been doing this since 2007 when the new rules came into effect, and, as far as I know, without incident. Our system is programmed to protect certain information, such as the date and cause of death, from being altered without going through multiple levels of administration—much like releasing a nuclear weapon, although that's stretching it. To satisfy my own curiosity, I checked last night and there have been no formal requests for death date changes—ever."

"So what is going on then, Jim? This can't be happening on its own, surely. And best I can figure, from the results of our investigation so far and my conversation with Adrian, the surgeries performed between the two death dates are legitimate. Forgive me for my next statement, you know I don't mean any disrespect, but it's highly improbable we would be performing surgeries on dead children. Needless to say, this has me quite perplexed."

"Me too, Noah. I'll keep digging and I'll let you know if I find anything else."

Each rung off and paused to reflect on the odd events piling up like accidents on an icy freeway.

Jim's phone interrupted his thoughts. He answered it with his standard greeting.

"Jim. Tess. I have some things from the research you asked me to do. Do you want to discuss it on the phone or shall I come up?"

"Let's do it on the phone. Given the arrest of Atchley and the hospital being in such an uproar, eavesdropping on our conversation may actually *stop* rumors rather than *start* them. What did you find?"

"I wrote a small program to analyze each element of the billings for each of the doctors who made submissions between the two death dates I obtained from Megan. I compared each element with the corresponding element of other billings for those doctors. For example, I analyzed the invoice numbers, reference codes, and date formats. My twisted analytical mind wanted to know if anything was different. In fact, I did find some differences in one of the elements; the billing reference, to be exact. You know these well yourself. Since each doctor has his own billing system, and since we require all invoices to be submitted in a standard format, the reference is the link the doctor provides between his bill to us and his own internal system. All the between-deaths billings had a very complex reference while the other billing references were quite simple. Of course, almost all the doctors had a different *type* of reference. If they were the same then I assumed, for the moment anyway, they used the same billing software. But the complex references were very similar in many ways—not exactly the same, mind you, but similar. It caught my attention, but, of course, it may be nothing in the end."

"Tess, you don't believe that for a moment, or you wouldn't be calling me. Why does this bother you?"

"I'm not certain yet. I thought I would let you know it was bugging me, and get your take on whether I should pursue it a bit further."

"Well, you probably already know my answer. If it bothers *you*, it bothers *me*. Your sniffer has seldom been wrong, so spend some time looking, and see what comes of it. Keep me posted, please." Jim replaced the receiver and returned to the budget he was working on.

Jim plodded his way through the preliminary departmental budget spread sheet he had developed to help him determine trends in the costs his department was incurring. In the middle of typing the employee benefit percentage increase suggested by the administrative office, he snatched up the phone, dialed Tess's number and exclaimed, "Code injection, Tess! Check for evidence of code injection or something similar. Those odd references may contain rogue commands. Let me know what you find."

"Good thought, I'll look into it."

Jim tried to return to his budget spread sheet but couldn't concentrate. His intuition told him he was onto something, but he had no idea what. If the references had contained actual code, Tess would have spotted it immediately. But maybe his suggestion would send her in the right direction.

Wednesday

Noah began their third meeting with a greeting and started right in, "Let's just go around the table and see what we have discovered. I don't think the sequence is important here. Nakita, if you don't mind, I'll have you report to me privately after this meeting. Who wants to start?"

Jim and Megan started to talk at the same time. Although Jim was eager to tell the group what he had found, he said, "Megan, you go first, I insist. What I have can wait."

"Adrian, Armoni, and I have joined forces and continued our research on billings and death dates and OR activities. Since each of our responsibilities hinged on the other, we pooled our resources and have continued to work as an ad hoc committee. Summarizing our findings: out of 48,600 patients seen last year, 263 died at the hospital and there were 151 death date discrepancies. We verified the death date with the Texas Electronic Death Registrar which is updated, per Jim Koehler, automatically by our computers, and it registers the latter date, agreeing with our computer records. Each one had a billed surgery between the obituary pronouncement date and the TEDR pronouncement date. They are almost always 2 days apart. Each surgery has a fully documented OR. None of the surgeries involved an anesthesiologist. Those are the facts. Each of us have our theories on what is going on but we don't agree, unfortunately."

Jim took the floor next. "I've had my top analyst, Teresa Rivard, working on this, and she has some interesting theories. More research is needed, but I'm laying this out to you as a highly probable hypothesis. Each billing between the two death dates had a doctor's reference code different from those generally used by that doctor. Teresa has floated a theory suggesting these unusual references are somehow triggering the computer to change the death date in our system. Although well hidden in each reference, and not always in the same sequence, she was able to determine a short set of characters common to all references. The probability of this happening randomly is extremely low. She then looked for a date sequence or something indicating what the new death date would be set to. She didn't find what she was looking for. But, in each case, when the death date was moved two days, there was a 2 somewhere in the reference, and for one day, there was a 1, and in the very few cases where it was moved three days, there was a 3. Now, this is not proof, of course, since single digits could be used simply as part of the reference. But both Teresa and I think it is significant. She is running some tests in the software lab now to see if she can predictably force the change in the death date using these triggers.

"I have no idea what the implications of this are. However, it would explain how someone bypassed our safeguards on protecting the original death date entered. There is a very disturbing note in all this. Someone had to alter our programs in order to make this happen, and we have found no unlogged software changes in the billing system. Where this is intriguing news on the one hand, it is highly disturbing on the other.

"As for the TEDR records agreeing with ours; it's to be expected. The computers have been programmed to recognize when the death date is changed and to fire off a notice to the TEDR. Our intention was, and still is, when the death date is changed from *nothing* to *something* then the TEDR is notified. We didn't think we would have to deal with dates being changed *post factum*. However, I will contact the TEDR and find out if they keep a record of change notices.

"If this hypothesis is correct, we are dealing with an extremely clever conspiracy, totally invisible to the unsuspecting eye. If this kafuffle with Blake hadn't happened, we never would have come across it."

Adrian then spoke. "I'm afraid I'm the bearer of bad news. While Megan, Armoni and I were going through the billings, I made a list of the doctors involved. Based on the sample we've looked at, they are Drs. Torres, Perry, Reed and Gomez. Noah was right when he said at the very beginning, if this were wide-spread it could seriously hurt us professionally. And it looks just that way. These, together with Dr. Atchley, represent some of our top surgeons. They are primary physicians to many, many patients. Their expertise is critical to the life, or at least quality of life, of many of our children. This could develop into a *serious* problem for the hospital."

Noah wrapped the meeting up. "Thanks once again. For those of you who have finished your analysis, you can go back to your other duties. If you still have some research to do, please finish it *before* you resume your regular responsibilities. We won't meet again until I notify you. Nakita and I will work out a strategy and we'll discuss it with you before anything is implemented. Nakita, you were going to stay to give me your report, but I think we'll talk about it later. I would like you to stay anyway, and Adrian, I'd like you to stay also, if you can. The rest of you … keep this under wraps. Need to know only! Understand?"

Each member of the team nodded as they left the room, each with shoulders stooped, lips compressed into a thin strand.

When the others had gone and Olivia had closed the office door, Noah began. "Frankly, I'm surprised by the list of doctors you reported. I suppose, at a stretch, you could see Atchley doing something like this based on his miserable personality, but I would never have thought it of the others. Do you think that's the extent of it?"

"It is, based on the billings we studied. Perhaps if we went further back we would find others, since we don't know yet when this all began."

"For the moment, let's let sleeping dogs lie. We have enough to figure out right now. We'll leave any others to round two. Nakita, I need your input on this. I'm going to summon these doctors to my office and in the presence of both of you I'll question them about what we have found. I'm looking for information at this point. Accusations may come later, although I think I'll be prepared for that eventuality. Can I do this without prejudice, Nakita?"

"Yes, certainly. This is well within your powers as CEO, and I think it's a wise thing to do."

"I'll let you both know when this will take place. Until then continue to develop any theories that may come to mind. In all this confusion there is the truth … somewhere."

Nakita and Adrian left Noah's office as he moved to his desk to make some notes and work out his approach for interviewing the doctors.

Chapter 42

SEVEN OF THEM WERE SETTLED AROUND THE CEO'S CONFERENCE table late in the afternoon. Noah Jackson sat at the head of the table, Nakita Goldman at the foot. On Noah's right, sat Dr. Bastile Torres; Bas to his friends. Next to him was Dr. Anthony Perry, and to his right, Dr. Adrian Jessop. To Noah's left was Dr. Carmen Reed and, to his left, Dr. Pepe Gomez.

Noah was about to speak when Gomez leaned forward stiffly in his chair and demanded, "What's this all about? Does this have something to do with Atchley screwing up?"

Adrian interjected firmly and with authority, "Pepe, enough. Before you jump to conclusions let Noah tell us what's on his mind."

Gomez relaxed just a little, but he stayed forward in his chair, ready for battle.

Noah broke in, looking straight at Dr. Gomez, "I'll ignore your outburst for the moment." He then scanned the group and began, "We have a serious situation on our hands. Yes, this does have to do with Dr. Atchley, who, as you all know by now, was arrested several days ago. Adrian tells me you have been briefed in your meetings as to his status. His arrest and an audit by an insurance company caused us to examine some of our hospital records." He paused to look at each face, assessing its response. "We have uncovered what is very likely a serious case of fraud, but there is a great deal of confusion surrounding the facts. I called you here today to help us get to the truth."

Several eyebrows lifted around the table. Everyone was quiet except for Gomez who interjected, "Out of all the doctors and interns in this hospital, why single us out? And why isn't Garret here?"

Noah wondered about the logic of Pepe's comment and retorted, "Why do *you* think Dr. Garret should be here?"

Reed had turned sideways and was staring dangerously at Gomez. Perry and Torres as well had their eyes fixed on him with a glass-shattering stare.

Gomez took the hint and backed down. "I just thought he should be here, is all."

Noah made a mental note of the interruption and continued, "It appears Blake was modifying the date of death in the hospital records and then performing a surgical procedure after the death of the patient—or at least he was *billing* for such a procedure. It appears the OR was booked and used appropriately. If the later pronouncement date is correct, then the surgery was necessary and the billing was appropriate. But, if the date has been changed somehow, then it could be the billing was fraudulent. I need to know if any of you have even the remotest knowledge of this."

The room remained silent. The four doctors stared straight ahead at the table in front of them, faces blank slates, hands fidgeting. Noah waited, looking at each one in turn. As their new boss, Adrian scanned each of their faces, her eyebrows raised expectantly. Nakita focused his drawn countenance on one man, then the next, and back again, the vein bisecting his forehead beginning to bulge. The silence spoke eloquently.

Adrian broke into their thoughts. "Gentlemen, I'm going to take your silence as your answer. But now is the time to step up. If you have anything additional to say, now is the time to say it."

After a long pause, Bas broke the silence and exclaimed, "Guys, it's time to come clean. Atchley said this thing was fool proof, except it appears we were the fools."

Gomez interrupted, his voice sharp as a dagger. "Blake is to blame for this. He put it all in motion, and, yes, we knew it was going on but had nothing to do with it. Isn't it so, Tony?"

"Don't get me involved in this, Pepe," blurted Tony gruffly, "I've got nothing to do with it. If you guys are involved in some scheme or other, just leave me out of it."

After an awkward pause, Carmen looked around as if for approval and, finding none, tried to speak between swallows, his voice resigned and rough. "Blake ... came to this hospital after researching it thoroughly. He was looking for a place with a strong commitment to a paperless environment and an IT department with unusually tight security. He selected Parks Hospital for Children for just those reasons. After he was installed as Chief of Staff, he called a meeting and told us about his plan to bill for surgeries we didn't perform." The heads of the other doctors around the table shot up to stare squinting at Carmen. "He assured us no one would, or could, find out. It was our impression, although he never came right out and said it, that he had done this at other places, and it had worked flawlessly. We listened only because he was our boss. What else could we do? If we had told you about it, he could have made our lives extremely miserable. You know Blake as well as we do ... you either get on board or you're an outsider and pay the price dearly. Our only crime is keeping our mouths shut. Besides, you hired him, Noah, so we have you to thank for this mess."

The others began to relax a little.

Dropping the bomb shell, Noah said, "We have records of suspicious billings from *all* of you sitting around this table. You have *all* profited from this 'scheme', as you have called it."

After a long silence, during which each doctor seemed to be giving their knees a full and careful examination, Carmen again acted as spokesman, his voice weaker now. "Ok, you are right. We never knew how the scam worked. We were told by Blake to put some special codes into our billing reference for specific types of surgery when he notified us. We would get paid by the insurance company and he would cross-bill us for services rendered, so to speak. *He* made some extra money and *we* made some extra money; so what."

Adrian contradicted him, "Carmen, you aren't doing yourself any favors by lying to us. The patients involved were *your* patients. The OR was booked by *your* scheduling nurse at *your* request. *Your* staff did the billing initiated by *you*. How can you sit there and say you didn't know what was going on? You're up to your eyeballs in this." The pitch of her voice was rising, and by the end of her statement she was on the verge of shouting. "*How could you have been so stupid? All of you!*"

A light seemed to come on, and Gomez reacted with hostility. "If you have this all figured out, then why did the OR schedule check out? If we didn't need the OR, and didn't use the OR, and billed for a surgery we didn't perform, who do you think was in the operating room. Those billings are legitimate. I don't know anything about pronouncement dates being moved, but none of this is on my head. Carmen, maybe *you've* been involved in a nefarious plot but don't try putting this on me."

Noah broke into the conversation, his tone elevated and terse. "*Alright!* … It appears we have a wide variety of opinions on what is actually going on in this hospital … *my* hospital. We thought we would give you a chance to help put this behind us, but it appears it won't be quite so easy. I suggest you all retain good lawyers. If you have your passports with you, you will voluntarily surrender them to the Chief Deputy who is currently waiting in Olivia's office. If you don't have them with you, then one of the other Deputies Olivia has invited to her office, will escort you to your home where you will voluntarily surrender your passport. Your privileges in this hospital are suspended for two weeks, starting right now. You won't leave the city and you will be available for questioning 24-7. If these conditions are not clear to you or are not acceptable to you, you can remain behind, and I'll have a Deputy read you your rights and charge you right here and now. Then you will be able to spend the night in the county jail, rather than at home with your family, to whom, I advise, you tell the *whole* story—the *truth*—because it *will* come out in the next few days."

No one remained at the conference table. Olivia met them at the door, handing each off to a Deputy. She seemed to look right through each one as if he no longer existed; her anger for bringing a blemish of this sort to this hospital resting on her cheeks as a red stain.

When the doctors and their escorts had gone, Olivia reentered Noah's office, sagging into an easychair opposite the conference table. She muttered, more to herself than anyone, "I just can't believe it. Five doctors have thrown their lives away and have denied thousands of people their hard-earned gifts of healing—and for what?

… Some extra cash? … I guess we all have our demons, but these guys are intelligent, educated, wealthy—what more do they want? … What was the attraction?!"

Noah fell exhausted into the chair next to hers, and replied pensively, "You really have to wonder, don't you. But greed has started wars, deposed monarchs, and ruined countless lives. It's always there in our faces. And, in spite of what they think at the time, it seldom ends well for anyone." He paused for a long moment. "After you've settled a bit, please call the officer who arrested Blake. I would like to meet with her as soon as possible, either here or there."

Noah rose sluggishly, looking and acting as if a decade had been added to his age. Regardless of his weariness, he knew the nightmare was just beginning.

Rikki elected to meet Noah at the hospital, knowing he would have the opportunity to be more open, resulting in her learning more about what made Blake do what he did.

Noah offered Rikki one of the lounge chairs after introducing her to Olivia who would be seated next to her, and Nakita placed a chair to the right of Olivia for himself. Noah sat on the sofa across from the chairs. He wanted their discussion to be informal, expecting it to be a very difficult one.

Rikki proceeded to set the tone for the meeting. "Mr. Jackson, I want to express my appreciation for calling this meeting. I need to say right at the outset, at this point we are not investigating the hospital in any regard. We are currently interested only in Blake Atchley because we believe he ordered an assault on a Mr. Barlow. However, I must also state we believe Dr. Atchley was motivated by actions centered here in the hospital, so I would anticipate an investigation in that regard sometime in the near future. I recognize this meeting is voluntary, in fact it is at your request, but I still need to warn you: anything said at this meeting can and will be used should a subsequent investigation arise. With this understanding, do you still want to continue?" This last statement was directed at Nakita who nodded to Noah.

"Yes, Deputy Castillo—"

Rikki broke in and said, "Please … call me Rikki."

With a nod he continued, "We understand the terms. We have started an internal investigation and I want to tell you what we now know, and then establish a direct line of communication between this office and yours, so you are fully aware of what we find.

"I don't know if you were involved in the request we made to the Sheriff's office for deputies to escort four of our doctors to their homes and collect their passports? … At this point it is an administrative action initiated by me. They have been relieved of their duties for two weeks while we sort this out.

"It appears from what we have uncovered, that Dr. Atchley and four other doctors have been involved in a scheme to defraud the insurance companies by billing for surgeries they did not perform. This type of crime is not new, of course. But it was remarkable, the lengths they went to to cover it up and protect their plan. This has been going on for at least a year, and, we suspect, closer to two years, ever since Atchley joined our staff and, until a few days ago, there were no hints of any kind. There has been talk of Dr. Atchley doing this at his previous positions, but there was certainly no evidence of such in the interviews we conducted prior to his hiring.

"This brings me to one of the reasons I wanted to meet with you. There are two items we have uncovered which we find puzzling. The first relates to a fifth doctor, Dr. Garret, who seems to be involved, but we don't know how, exactly—there were no billings from him in the events we uncovered, but his name keeps getting mentioned by the other doctors. The second is regarding the operating room use during procedures we now think were the subject of fraudulent billings. This has us mystified. It appears the operating rooms were used to perform the billed surgeries, but we suspect the patient had already been pronounced dead. We would like to open our hospital to a Sheriff's investigation, both to confirm our suspicion of insurance fraud, and to solve the operating room mystery."

Rikki looked around, finding each person watching her expectantly. Clearly Jackson was not big on small talk. Her head was mulling through the facts he had presented and she searched for the proper words to say. "Less than a week ago evidence came to us indicating the possibility of fraudulent activity within the hospital. *We* initiated the audit several days ago to confirm our theory. Our auditor was also confused by the OR usage. Atchley's involvement in an attempted assault seemed related, so it piqued our interest. We are in the process of gathering the resources needed to investigate the possibility of insurance fraud by Atchley, since only his name appeared in the mini audit we just performed. The information you have given us will allow an expansion of our investigation along parallel paths, and will save a great deal of time and expense. Your confusion regarding the operating rooms confirms *our* uncertainty, so we will create a team to concentrate on just that aspect." She paused to gather her thoughts. Perhaps there wasn't much else to say. She didn't want to bring Julius into this discussion but she suspected these clearly astute professionals would be able to read between the lines.

Noah looked at each of his staff questioningly. With no further responses forthcoming, he rose, handed Rikki a business card, and said, "Rikki, please establish whatever line of communication you deem necessary. My office will be the focal point at the hospital's end. You can contact me any time of night or day while this issue remains unresolved."

His guests plodded out of the meeting, leaving behind the odor of fear and disappointment.

Chapter 43

Thursday

SITTING AT HER OFFICE DESK, RIKKI PREPARED HER THOUGHTS before making the call. She dialed Dr. Garret's office, only to find that he was making a house call and wouldn't be back for several hours. She said she would call back and didn't leave a message.

The mystery surrounding the operating rooms at the hospital was driving her crazy, so she made a mental note to call Kate Jansen and see what opinion she may have to offer.

The work Kate's auditor had done, and the information offered by Jackson, both pointed to the operating rooms being used for their intended purpose; surgeries were performed and they corresponded to the billings in question. Atchley certainly had his bases covered. If she could not prove the operating rooms were idle, she didn't think there was a case. The statements made by the doctors to Jackson weren't admissible until she presented more substantial proof; information they were not likely to readily confess. The evidence seemed against her, but she knew, *she just knew*, the key lay in the OR, but she had no idea of how to find it.

The case would have to be worked by the book, and see what popped up. She would interview the OR organizer—what was his name? Beech, yes, Armoni Beech. She may not find out anything about this particular case, but she would at least learn how the scheduling is done, and maybe it would lead her somewhere.

She picked up the phone and made an appointment to see Mr. Beech.

Two hours later she was sitting in Beech's office having been introduced and offered a cup of coffee. She had declined.

"Mr. Beech … may I call you Armoni?" He nodded slightly. "Armoni, Mr. Jackson has asked the Harrison County Sheriff's office to investigate the fraudulent billings alleged to be taking place within the hospital. You will agree, I'm sure, this is a very serious issue. If we develop a solid case, it will have to be turned over to the FBI." She studied his face. It was like stone; he would be giving nothing away.

Choosing her words carefully, she continued, "At the moment we have conflicting stories about the use of the operating rooms required by the doctors during the surgeries being considered as fraudulent. Clearly, if the operating rooms were used as specified, then the billings are legitimate and there is no fraud. If this were the case, I would be able to report no wrong-doing, and the hospital and its staff would be exonerated, and we could all move on to other things. However, I'm not hopeful of such an outcome." Rikki tried penetrating him with her gaze but was getting nowhere.

Armoni's stone face broke into a slight, almost gratuitous smile as he said, "How can I help you?"

"Mr. Jackson indicated to me you had looked into each potentially fraudulent billing and you reported everything to be in order; you did not find anything amiss. Is that true?" She was hoping to pry something from him; anything at this point to get him to open up.

"Yes, you are correct. Megan Johnson and I worked through the billings in question and determined that the records we have on file indicate our standard procedures were carried out properly. We could find nothing irregular."

Becoming frustrated with his attitude, Rikki decided to take a harsher stance. "I don't mean to be insensitive, but are you saying these rather complex operations were performed on the corpses of dead children?"

Beech's face grew hard again. Beginning in a flat monotone, "Perhaps the children you refer to weren't dead after all. Perhaps the early death date everyone is concentrating on is an error. Perhaps, as you say, these procedures and the associated billings are perfectly legitimate," his voice rising as he made his point.

So, thought Rikki, he does know about the two death dates, but of course he would have learned that from his part in the internal investigation. His defensiveness and apparent lack of cooperation bothered her. However, to this point, the only evidence of OR protocol being properly observed was *his* word, and *that* would have to be explored more thoroughly.

Attempting to set Armoni at ease, she said, "Perhaps you are right. I may be grasping at straws. I would certainly like that to be the case. Let's move away from deaths and dates and the like. Would you walk me through how operating rooms are booked and personnel are scheduled, just so I have a feel for what goes on in your department?"

Without changing his expression he replied, "Sure. Would you like me to just tell you, or would you like me to give you an actual demonstration on our training system?"

Rikki had to mull this over. She would like to know every minute turn of procedure, because the devil was going to be in the details, but she may not understand it all. An idea sparked. "Just the verbal overview would suffice. I would probably drown in the details."

Beech began with what appeared to be a well-rehearsed presentation. "Let me be clear at the outset, our hospital runs an almost totally paperless system. Everything is done on the computer. When a surgery is required, the office of the doctor requiring an operating room requests the OR using the computer. The requesting doctor, the patient id, requested attending physicians, and the procedure to be performed are entered; as is, of course, the anticipated length of time it is needed. This request is automatically assigned to the first available scheduler on my staff, who makes the arrangements for an appropriate room, scrub nurses, anesthesiologist, medical equipment, and non-standard supplies. The doctor's office is notified of the scheduled available time, and the pagers of the various required staff are notified automatically. If requested, texts are sent to cell phones.

"When the surgery is complete, the doctor's office staff retrieves the OR booking by doctor or patient id, and indicates the surgery as complete. Again the computer notifies one of my schedulers and the cleanup crew is dispatched, generally, again, by pager or text message."

Rikki responded curiously, "Why do you do some pager and some text notification?"

"Cell phones are not generally permitted in the hospital, and particularly around some medical equipment, because they are active devices; that is, they transmit a signal potentially detrimental to, or incorrectly interpreted by, certain medical equipment. However, some staff may not be on hospital grounds, such as scrub nurses or cleaning staff; they may be called in from home or from other duties as needed. Pagers, on the other hand, are passive devices; that is, they only receive signals, so they are totally safe around medical equipment."

"So you are saying no one really knows whether the room is used or not. All you have is the computer records of what is *supposed* to have happened."

Beech flinched involuntarily. "No, such a conclusion would be totally wrong, of course. Other data act as a cross-check for all this. For example, the billing coming from the doctor's office that booked the OR verifies the event. If a billing is not established within a specified period of time, then we are notified, and we investigate. We can't have rooms booked and not used since such inefficiencies could cost lives. The scrub nurses use a time collection system to record their activities associated with a given OR booking. Then the cleanup crew reports on medical equipment, supplies and room cleanup. These all dovetail into a single, consistent event."

"And you are saying the billings we are questioning have OR events consistent with the procedures performed, and have not flagged any irregularities?"

"Exactly, but those facts don't seem to be registering with you."

Rikki was thrown right back into the dilemma. Perhaps her gut was wrong on this—a fact she doubted very much. Too many things have pointed to anomalies, yet everything appeared to be as it should. She thought for a few moments and asked, "Would you allow me to talk to the scrub nurses who worked during one of the events in question?"

"Certainly. When would you like to get together?"

"Send their names to this email address," she said, handing a business card to him. "If they are available, I'd like to see them first thing tomorrow morning, say eight thirty or so? Perhaps we can conduct the interviews in your office with you present, if that's possible."

"I guess I can organize that for you."

Rikki thanked him for his cooperation, although she didn't feel much like doing so. Wishing him a good day, she headed for her car. So there we have it, she thought. This little mystery is going to play hard to get.

Friday

The next morning, Rikki reentered the office of the Director of Operating Room Logistics, and was introduced to two nurses, one in her late twenties and one in her mid-forties; both trim and professional looking. The two looked at each other as if they had never met. Noticing this, Beech said, "I'm sorry, I assumed you knew each other." His left eyebrow flicked up.

Recovering, Beech began the meeting by saying, "Deputy Castillo is here today to ask you some questions about your roles in the specific surgery I referenced in my email. Your cooperation is entirely voluntary."

Rikki thought she'd better jump in before Beech created so many caveats and wherefores and why-nots that her time would be wasted. "Actually, I would like to be a little more general at first, but I *will* have some questions about the specified surgery. Tell me please, what are your duties in these surgeries?"

The two women looked at each other briefly, the older one taking the lead. "We do general nursing duties but we have specialized training in preparing doctors for surgery. Some doctors ask us to perform the scrub for them, others do the scrub themselves, but then need us to apply their gloves, and check the ties on their caps and gowns and such. Sometimes a nurse is required in the operating room to assist with equipment, tools, and so on, but I, for one, am not trained to do that. I assist only with the scrub." She looked over at the younger woman who was nodding her assent.

"What was your participation in this particular surgery?"

The older nurse continued, "We have a list, which becomes second nature after a while, of which doctors require what assistance. We offer what they have specified they need. But there are certain surgeries where the doctor's name is not disclosed to us, but we are told what services are required. The surgery you mentioned was one of those."

"Regarding the surgery in question, would either of you be able to identify the doctor you prepped as being Dr. Atchley, or whoever his assistant was in this instance?"

The younger one spoke up this time, "I was going to say that usually I could for sure, but when I think about this surgery, I'm not certain I could. Generally by the time we meet the doctors they are gowned, masked, and have their safety glasses on already. Other than general body characteristics I don't think I could tell one from another. If there had been any conversation, it would be a different matter, but in this scrub neither the doctor nor I spoke a word."

"Clarify something for me. You two don't know each other?"

The younger one continued, glancing at the other nurse for confirmation, "No. Other than today, we hadn't met before. We've seen each other around the wards, but I don't think we've ever met in person."

Rikki pressed, "Didn't you work together at the surgery we are dealing with?"

The older nurse said quickly, "Until I saw your email addressed to two of us, I had no idea anyone else was involved. I wasn't aware there was another doctor scrubbing for this surgery, although often there *is* an assistant present. I prepped my doctor and left."

The younger one agreed, "Yah … me too. I saw only one doctor, and assumed he was alone. I never really thought much about it."

"Did anything stand out to you as unusual or different about this scrub?" asked Rikki, still trying to get a picture of this event.

"Not really. I was instructed to wait in the outer room until someone knocked on the door to let me know the doctor was ready," said the older nurse.

"I received the same instructions," repeated the younger one.

"You said the only features of the doctors you prepped were general body characteristics. What were they in this case?"

Seeming eager to be finished with this interrogation, the younger nurse replied hastily, "Medium height, Caucasian, more football hands than piano hands, but, surprisingly, that's true of many doctors." She turned to the older nurse as if to pass the baton.

"Six two, large build, black, large hands, strong but skilled, if my memory serves."

Beech glanced at Rikki as if to say they'd had enough. Rikki, taking the hint, nodded, then Armoni thanked them for their help and excused them.

Rikki stood and thanked Beech before leaving for her car. Discouragement threatened to overwhelm her. She had been sure meeting with staff who took part in the surgical events would provide more information; better clues. But it hadn't, and she wasn't sure what to do next. There was no evidence the primary doctor was *not* Atchley but, then again, there was no evidence it *was*. She may have to interview every crew from every questionable surgery in order to unearth something that would point to fraud. But at the moment it looked more and more like the surgeries took place as the billings stated; in which case, the death-date issue was just a computer glitch, and she had been wasting everyone's time. If there was anything encouraging in all this, it was that she had not taken the case to the FBI. If she had, crow would be on her dinner plate for the next month.

She swallowed the constriction in her throat, sighing involuntarily. Retrieving her cell phone from the passenger seat of the squad car, she redialed Dr. Garret's number. The receptionist indicated he would require just a few minutes to finish with a patient. She was happy to hold.

Chapter 44

DR. GARRET STEPPED THROUGH THE BARLOW FRONT DOOR AT seven thirty in the morning. He was generally an early riser, and based on the call he had received late yesterday from Sheri, he knew the family would be getting a prompt start to their day.

The early morning chill convinced him to wear a light jacket, which he took off and hung on the back of a kitchen chair. He went straight to the chart hanging at the head of Cora's bed. Although she was awake, he didn't greet her this morning. He was intent on feeding his mind with the week's events, so his mind could begin working on trying to understand what had taken place. He studied the numbers and comments for several minutes before he lifted his head, his hands absently replacing the chart on its hook.

"Good morning, luv. I wasn't trying to ignore you … really. But you've been doing such interesting things this week. I figured I should get caught up a teeny bit. I hear you've not been quite your-self." He signed to Sheri it would be good to have a cup of tea—he indicated two fingers. "I'll have Sheri make us both a nice, hot cuppa', and we'll talk about what you've been doing with yourself."

He didn't usually sit when examining Cora. Normally he stood, studied and touched, and somehow knew exactly what was going on. But this morning he elected to sit in the chair which had supported family and friends and caregivers as they shared Cora's waning life.

Sheri delivered the tea, then helped Cora get situated more comfortably in her bed. For more than an hour Benjamin and Cora chatted. Garret asked some questions; Cora gave some answers. They talked about family and friends, politics, and religion. It could have been a social call, given the chatter they exchanged. Yet, to Benjamin, this was a way of getting Cora to relax, step outside herself for a few moments, allowing him to accumulate a mental picture that would be invaluable in assessing and then diagnosing her current state.

"OK, luv. I have to go now. It was such fun chatting with you. Take it easy on yourself today. Try to stay away from the heavy house work … if you can." He patted her hand and left. Sheri followed him to the kitchen where he said, "Is Julius in, by any chance. I would like to talk with him briefly if at all possible."

"Certainly. I think he's in his office … I'll get him."

The men shook hands and Garret suggested while retrieving his jacket, "Could we get a breath of air on the front steps by any chance?"

"Certainly!" Julius pulled a windbreaker from its hangar in the front closet.

As they went through the door, Garret glanced back through the kitchen to the living room where Sheri was watching curiously, her face reflecting the queasiness settling into the pit of her stomach.

"Julius, Cora's condition is getting significantly worse. As I indicated when we last spoke on the phone, her internal organs are continuing to react to the disease. This is a turning point, suggesting we should start making palliative arrangements. There's nothing else the medical profession can offer her. I'm so sorry."

Reaching for the railing, Julius leaned heavily against it, Garret's words hitting like a sucker punch. Staring at the doctor, his mouth opened as if wanting to say something, but no words would come.

Garret took a step toward him, putting a hand on his shoulder. There was so much left unsaid between them. After a few moments Benjamin removed his hand and walked slowly to his car, not looking back.

He had so many questions for Julius, but none seemed appropriate. He had been briefed on Blake's arrest and he was aware that investigations were ongoing at the hospital. He knew Julius had been present when Atchley was arrested but he had no idea in what capacity. He thought maybe there was a connection between Julius' accident and Blake's murderous plot, but it was all conjecture, and, in any event, there's no way they would have risked Julius being present at the time of the arrest if he had been involved.

He snapped out of his reverie as his car maneuvered into his reserved parking spot, his memory of the drive eradicated. He had to pull himself together if he was going to be of any use for the remainder of his day. Checking his texts, he saw a call from the detective who was leading the investigation, but no message had been left. How would she even know about him? Could she be interviewing all the doctors associated with Parks? He greatly doubted it. Somehow, by someone, she had been given his name.

Chapter 45

DR. BENJAMIN GARRET WAS A HIGHLY TRAINED SPECIALIST WITH privileges at a variety of hospitals. He maintained a small suite of offices in the Medical Park just to the east of the Sacred Heart General Hospital on the south side of town. His staff of five shared the responsibilities involved in coordinating his various hospital, clinic, and rare home care appointments, doing the filing and submitting his billings. With his services increasingly in demand, he was becoming *too* busy. He had vowed several times to take on less cases and reduce his load a bit—mostly for the sake of his *own* health—but he was finding it a difficult thing to do. The patients he saw, both adults and children, suffered from rare diseases, or rare combinations of diseases, which proved difficult to diagnose, and even more difficult to treat. His personality, his interests, his training, and his experience, combined to allow him insightful and accurate diagnoses, and brilliant, if sometimes innovative, treatments, frequently leading to an unexpected cure or remission, and oftentimes resulting in a sustainable palliative solution.

Rikki arrived at the appointed time, introduced herself to the receptionist, and was ushered immediately into Dr. Garret's office. She was surprised that at first glance, physically he was an unremarkable man. She had expected otherwise based on his credentials. Although, at a distance, he looked somewhat younger, he was likely in his mid-forty's, standing six feet tall, weighing in at 180 pounds or so. He had a full head of neatly trimmed dense hair, lightly accented with grey, which seemed to gather at the back and flow down his neck. His sideburns reached almost to his jaw line, perhaps a left-over from early days besotted by Elvis, she mused.

After a brief period of introductions and small talk, Rikki said, "Dr. Garret—" He interrupted her and asked if she would call him Ben, if it didn't make her uncomfortable. "Ben … I think you are aware of the investigation going on at Parks. It is focusing on Dr. Atchley and four other doctors who appear to have been billing for services they did not render. During our interviews with them we were told you attended at least one meeting where this fraudulent scheme was hatched and executed. We have gone back a full year, and so far we have not uncovered any questionable billings from your office. When we do the research for Atchley's *full* term, will we find any of *your* billings in the list?"

Garret observed her with a grave expression, amazing Rikki that he could look her in the eye after the kind of question she had just asked. But then there was clearly more to him than was obvious at first glance. After a pause, during which he seemed to struggle with his emotions, he replied, "Yes. That is the truth. I was aware of, but never participated in, the scheme and I suppose I believed Blake when he said they would never be caught, so I just let it be. At some gut level I knew it couldn't be foolproof, but I was busy with regular stuff and just let it slide." He continued with a sigh, "This day was bound to come, I guess.

"Doctors are generally a close-knit group, particularly in a small town like ours. We often consult on difficult cases, particularly those of children … like at Parks. We follow, to some extent, each other's careers and sometimes professional jealousy or rivalry arises. Every now and then someone like Blake will come along who is put in a place of authority, and then bullies his way into the lives of everyone he works with. I recognize it was my responsibility to report him, but, if I am to defend myself at all, there was never any evidence offered to indicate anyone was actually carrying out his scheme. Some doctors who attended the meetings took exotic vacations and owned expensive toys, but nothing, in my estimation, beyond what they could afford based on their regular practice." He extended his hands toward her, palms upward. "Please, I'm not trying to make excuses; I'm just telling you how I felt about it."

"Ben, at the moment we don't have the case sewn up. There are several loose ends that frankly we can't figure out, and until we do, we cannot press charges. There is no evidence pointing to your involvement in their potentially lucrative scheme, so I'm inclined to believe you, and I accept, for now, your regret at not taking the action you should have. However, if we develop this case to the point of prosecution, I need you to know you will not escape mention, and I would be surprised if the DA did not find some book in her kitbag to throw at you. Please do me a favor and don't skip town; that will be on *me*." She paused to catch her breath and let the seriousness of this sink in to them both.

"Since you were in meetings where the fraud was discussed, do you have any information useful to our investigation? Strictly voluntary, I might add, since anything you say can and will be used against you, if it comes to that."

His face went ashen and his eyes shone. "I wasn't interested enough to pay close attention, but I'm sure I could help you with some of the ways in which Blake *intended* for it to be accomplished."

Rikki broke in, "Anything will be helpful. But I'm not interested in that today. I just wanted to meet you and find out how you would play this out. Knowing you will help us, helps me help you. I know you do valuable work in our community so I'll let you get to it."

Rikki stood, shook Ben's hand warmly wanting to seal their deal should she need to call on him.

"Uh, just one thing before you go. After I heard about Blake's arrest, a bunch of stuff was running through my mind while I was driving, and one thing still bothers me. In a meeting a while back, Dr. Gomez fished a pair of glasses out of his coat pocket, and when he put them on, a spark of recognition flashed through my brain, but I never gave it much thought before this. He had his glasses on for just a moment, and then abruptly put them back in his coat— like putting them on had been a mistake. I've tried to reconstruct that moment in my head, but I can't seem to get it right. It's likely nothing, but maybe it will mean something to you."

As she walked to her car she thought there was no middle ground with Dr. Garret. Either he was penitent and was truly embarrassed by his involvement, or he had applied his considerable intellect to throwing her off the trail. She sincerely hoped it was the former, but she would keep the latter in mind.

Leaning back in his chair, Garrett stared at the ceiling. He had much too much to do to let this sordid business get under his skin. What was done was done, and he would deal with the consequences when and if they arrived. His thoughts travelled back to the last meeting he was in with Atchley, replaying Blake's disclosure about the programmer, and his callous attitude over the whole thing … like he was discussing how to make a better pot of coffee.

He pushed the issue from his conscious mind, knowing it would niggle at his subconscious, hoping it wouldn't affect the quality of the delicate work he had yet to perform in the next few hours.

Chapter 46

Monday

THEY MET IN THE HOSPITAL VISITOR'S PARKING LOT AT TEN THIRTY, each with a coffee in hand. Julius threw her a sheepish smile and a cautious greeting. "You think we can take these into the meeting, or do we need to chug them right here and now."

Returning his smile and laying her hand lightly on his arm, Rikki replied, "Hey, you seem a little better today. I guess your week away from this mess did you some good." He nodded. "Let's take them in as an act of defiance—just in case such a rule exists."

They both chuckled, sensing the company of each lightened the burden of the other, quickly falling back into the cadence established during the last few days they had spent together. They proceeded to reception and asked to see Armoni Beech. Yes, they had an appointment.

While they waited, Rikki said softly, "Julius, I'm sorry I was so insistent on Friday when I called you about this meeting. I knew you were reluctant to make another trip, but I felt it was important to understand how all this hospital scheduling stuff works, and I can't do that by myself."

"I know. I kind of thought we were done when we exposed Atchley," he replied, "but this OR thing has me fascinated, and, well, I just couldn't say no."

Armoni arrived, terminating their conversation and escorted them to his office.

Rikki had planned on taking an aggressive position in this meeting and wanted to get started right after Mr. Julius Barlow had been introduced, but didn't get the chance.

"What's *he* doing here? Isn't he the guy who started this whole thing; stealing hospital data and then trying to pin it all on us?"

Rikki deflected his choleric comments. "Mr. Beech, I indicated in my email I would bring a specialist you could take through the process of booking an operating room. Julius is that specialist. The backstory is really none of your concern. My hope is he will ask the right questions, and the answers to those questions will lead us to a break in the OR mystery we've been facing … something, if I need to remind you, your boss commissioned us to do."

Beech seemed to set his suspicion aside for the moment as he slowly began his presentation of how a doctor books the OR on the computer, and then how the computer notifies the required personnel, equipment, and supplies, exactly as he had done with Rikki earlier. His mood warmed as he moved into familiar territory and continued.

Julius asked what data the computer used to notify the personnel and other resources.

Armoni replied, "Each procedure is associated with a list of personnel, equipment, and supplies. It is similar to a shopping list of items for making a specific recipe, for example. In the manufacturing sector, it's called a *bill of material*, if that helps at all. Each resource has a unique identifier linking it to a profile of attributes such as, in the case of personnel, a name, pager number, and so on. An availability schedule of each such resource is retained so the computer knows who's available when. Also priorities are assigned and frequency of use is retained. All that to say, the computer wades through a pile of data and arrives at the best resources for the procedure. This information is fed to one of my schedulers for review and approval. It then pages or texts the personnel, and requisitions the equipment and supplies. Demands are handled by the appropriate department, and, if it all works as it should, people, equipment, and supplies all arrive at about the same time in the specified operating room. Sometimes this happens almost immediately, as in the case of an emergency procedure. Others take weeks or even months, if the procedure is less urgent or is elective.

"All the procedures I reviewed, based on the billings we are investigating, were flagged as emergencies, and everything was assembled within a few hours of being requested. Oddly enough, none of these occurred at night, but some *were* in the late evening. Most were during the regular work day."

Rikki asked, "Why do you find such a thing odd?"

"Simply because I would have expected a more even distribution. Tragedy doesn't usually cotton to a schedule."

One thing niggled at Julius. "I've worked in the manufacturing sector where bills of material and labor were not always applicable to a specific production run. In those cases the scheduler was able to make modifications to the bill, but these were always segregated so QC could identify differences in the items produced. Does the hospital system permit this kind of variance?"

"Certainly it does," replied Armoni. "It's probably more frequent in a hospital setting since an individual's response to a given disease may be quite different from that of another. I would say, off the top of my head, unless the procedure performed was *very* standard, such as a colonoscopy, it would most likely have variances."

Rikki jumped in, even if just to stay in the conversation. "How do they, the variances I mean, get entered into the computer, and could we see them for some of the billings in question?"

Armoni clicked a few keys on his computer while he was saying, "The doctor has access to a computerized form, allowing entry of any type of resource desired. There are a bunch of dropdown lists which provide the choices, and the doctor selects what he wants. When they are all in place, the doctor can review the list, and then commit it to the procedure—not the general one, just the specific one, you understand."

He spun his laptop around to show them the non-standard resources requested for one of the billings he and Megan had researched.

It took a few moments for Julius to get comfortable with what he was seeing. His face suddenly brightened, and pointing, he said, "There are two doctors listed here, but neither is one of the five doctors we are investigating." He looked over at them, his face like that of a knight who had accidentally stumbled over the Holy Grail.

Armoni allowed himself a brief moment of amusement, but he controlled his grin. "I don't mean to deflate your deductive prowess, but the physician of record is always included by default, so does not appear in this list."

Julius was silent for a moment. "Of course, I should have considered that. But it does give us someone who could help us find out what is really going on in those operating rooms. Till now we haven't had any clue as to who was involved, other than the physician of record, as you say, but we are convinced he doesn't have anything to do with it—otherwise there is no scam and the billings are likely legit." Julius was still animated. "I don't know about you, but this sounds like a breakthrough to me."

Rikki admitted, "I think you're right. We need to talk to one or both of these people and find out what they're doing in there."

Beech said, "If there isn't anything else then today, I'll arrange the meetings and let you know by email. Do you want to meet them both together, or individually?"

Rikki thought for a moment, "Let's try them together this time. We have others we can question if they need to be separated."

Rikki and Julius prepared to leave, shook Armoni's hand, and left for their cars.

Rikki motioned for Julius to get in the passenger side of her car, and they sat for a few minutes pondering the events of their meeting. Rikki said, "That wasn't earth shattering, but I think it inches us along the road to finding out what is going on in those operating rooms. The secrecy intimated by the scrub nurses and the bogus billings twists my stomach into knots … this isn't going to turn out to be anything good, I'm certain of it."

Julius nodded absently in agreement, absorbed as he replayed and analyzed what he had just learned.

Breaking into his silence, Rikki said, "I haven't had a chance to tell you yet. I met with the fifth doctor yesterday and he seems genuinely upset by all this. If you recall, he's the one the other doctors said was in the meetings but his name didn't show up in the billings. I'm not sure I buy his 'all innocence and goodwill act', but he was indeed in at least one of those meetings, and he knows some things that might be helpful—if we ever assemble a solid case, that is. I want to keep that channel open if I possibly can. If his attitude is not an act, then he is the closest we have to a man on the inside of this case. Unfortunately for him, his knowing about this and not reporting it could cost him his career."

"Perhaps I'm not supposed to know this, but can you tell me his name?"

"Hey, we're partners, you and me. Aren't we?" shot back Rikki. "Seriously, I shouldn't tell you, but since you're up to your neck in all this I will … but with a warning. If our case falls apart, anything said about this on the streets could be considered slander, so it can't leave this car." Julius was looking at her intently and he nodded his assent. "His name is Dr. Garret, he's a spec—"

"You don't mean Dr. Benjamin Garret, do you? He's involved in this?!"

"Yes, why? Do you know him?"

The carefree tone had left his voice and he clenched his fists. "Know him! … He's the only doctor in this area who can provide any decent level of care for my wife."

"Julius, slow down. You're not making any sense."

He stared at the dashboard for what seemed like minutes, his throat working vigorously. He swallowed hard and began, "OK … I guess we haven't talked much about her, but Cora has several rare conditions that make her life very difficult. Garret is the only doctor who has ever come close to understanding her problems … and to finding her some relief." He gulped a breath, his willpower defeated. "He just *can't* be involved in this. Without him my family is in deep trouble." He paused to regain a little composure but it was short-lived. "This changes everything. If I had known he was involved, I wouldn't have told you about the data in the first place … I'm sorry, but I wouldn't have told you any of it!" Covering his face with his hands he murmured just above a whisper, "Rikki, tell me I'm dreaming; tell me this isn't happening!"

She tried to calm him. "First off, we don't know if there's a case here at all. Second, his involvement appears minor—"

"But enough to get him jail time or maybe lose his medical license, right? He turned his face to look out the passenger window and repeated, "I wouldn't have been involved in any of this, if I'd known. This is worse than having that Travkin guy after me … then it was just me … but now Cora …"

Rikki watched his reflection in the side window and couldn't help noticing the moisture in his eyes, threatening to spill over, being held back only by Julius' waning resolve. This was a totally unexpected turn of events and it left her inexplicably speechless.

"Listen, Rikki," Julius continued as he turned back to face her, trying to control his emotions, "I mean it. If I'd known this is how it would turn out I would never have come to you. I would have reported the accident and only the accident. If they came after me again I'd have dealt with it. If they'd killed me, at least Garret would still be there for Cora."

Reaching across the console, Rikki took his hand. She wished she could simply *will* comfort into him. They sat for a long time, each lost in their own thoughts. She wanted desperately to say everything would work out, but she knew it wouldn't. She wanted to somehow erase her knowledge of Garret's involvement, but then she would be doing exactly what *he* had done, and then *she* would be the guilty one. In the back of her mind she vowed to find a way to keep Garret in the medical profession, at least as long as Julius, or rather Cora, needed him.

Finally Julius seemed to reconcile with himself. He squeezed Rikki's hand briefly and said, "At least if we have to be in this mess … well … I'm glad it's you who's in it with me." As he opened the door he sighed, his eyes never leaving the ground, "Let me know when the interviews are and I'll be there. But for now, I just want to go home."

Chapter 47

IT WAS TEN FORTY-FIVE AND SHERI HAD FINISHED CORA'S MORNING routine. This morning had been more difficult than expected since Cora expressed little interest in her food and was complaining of more fatigue than usual. Her concern that Julius was gone again to Marshall seemed to banish any lingering determination to disguise her discomfort. She was grateful he had been home most of the last week, but she couldn't help but wish that all the business with the accident and its fallout would be over so things could be back to the way they were. Today, in particular, she felt she needed him near.

Brittany rang the doorbell and lumbered in, greeting Sheri with a hug, then went directly to the chair beside Cora's bed. "Good morning, Mom!" she said with an upbeat lilt in her voice, placing her two hands on the chair back and leaning on it heavily. Her youthful energy was like a tonic to Cora and she responded immediately.

"Good morning, dear. Shouldn't you be at work?"

"Not any more, Mom. I'm off now … on maternity leave. Actually, I've been off for a few days now—I was done last Wednesday—and just now have my house in order, and felt I should spend some quality time with you … just us girls." Brittany filled Cora in on the busyness of the past week and the activities planned for the weekend, including putting the final touches on the nursery. "The baby is really low and I've had some twinges, so I decided to take on the motherhood thing full time."

"Well, good for you," said Cora as she reached for Brittany's hand. "Sit down. You look like your feet aren't enjoying the extra weight."

Brittany went through the comedy routine of trying to sit, and was successful in the end. They chatted about the baby, the nursery, work, Jim, and Julius. They were just getting around to discussing how Cora was doing when Brittany's hand flew to her stomach, grimacing in an attempt to hold in the cry that wanted so desperately to escape. She breathed deeply and willed the cramp to pass.

"Are you alright, Brit," asked Cora looking very concerned.

"Sure …. I think so. The twinges I experienced over the weekend were nothing like that. Mm … glad that's over."

Cora called Sheri in and told her what had just happened. Brittany made light of it, brushing it aside with a sweep of her hand. Getting back to her duties, Sheri glanced at Cora and saw her stare fixed on Brittany. Sheri didn't want to see Cora burdened with any more anxiety, but she also knew worrying about Brittany and thinking about the imminent arrival of this new baby—the first grandchild—would keep her mind off her increasing weakness. She made a mental note to keep her ears tuned as she went about her duties.

Although it wasn't in Sheri's job description, today she made lunch for the three of them and set it out on the dining room table. Brittany slowly moved to one of the upholstered chairs as Sheri placed Cora's lunch on her rolling table then sat at the end facing Cora. They could all see each other easily and the conversation was free and relaxed. If someone were to peek into the room unannounced, it would appear as if three sisters, or perhaps three old friends, were enjoying an infrequent lunch together. Having Brittany there seemed to cheer Cora to the point where she was almost animated, the earlier fatigue seemingly gone.

Suddenly Brittany pushed her chair back from the table and doubled over, her sharp cry ringing through the house. It took Sheri less than a heartbeat to be at her side. Slowly Brittany straightened up, her hand on her stomach. "Woe … that was either a field goal or a contraction. Either way I'm not looking forward to any more like it." Sheri and Cora both glanced at her with one eyebrow raised, and she shrugged. "Ok, I get the point. At the very least, how about I get a postponement," she said through gritted teeth. Both Sheri and Cora continued to give her a maternal look, silently communicating she would certainly *not* be done with the contractions, and would likely not get a postponement, either.

They both returned to their seats, Sheri's eyes fixed on Brittany. As Brittany relaxed, so did Sheri. They resumed their conversation and sipped their drinks, the mood returning to one of camaraderie and solidarity. Eventually Sheri returned to her duties leaving Cora and Brittany alone.

"Mom, what do you think is going on with Dad? He said last week he was done with … well … whatever it was. It seems strange to me a car accident should require him to go back and forth to Marshall so often. And the police car parked out front …"

"I'm not certain what all is going on," replied Cora wistfully. "I have the sense now and then he is about to tell me something important, but then it passes and he'll talk about something else. As far as I know he isn't working on a project at the moment, so I don't think it's work related. I get the feeling it *is* related to the accident somehow but there's more to it than just the accident. Every now and then he talks about a deputy he's helping there, but I have no idea with what." Cora's voice trailed off as she stared out the living room window lost in thought. She shuddered as her mind returned to their last conversation. "I expect it's something he doesn't want to worry me with—but that doesn't mean I don't. In fact I've shot several videos in my head with Julius as the hero, chasing the bad guys and eventually bringing them to justice." This last statement brought a wide smile to her face. Brittany found her mom's smile very contagious—albeit too infrequent these days—and couldn't help but break into a warm smile of her own. The two of them giggled for some time as their minds embellished Cora's image of a husband and father enacting a hero's role, cape and phone booth included.

"A likely story," they said simultaneously, spawning another wave of giggles that overcame them.

Chapter 48

Tuesday

BATH DAY HAD ROLLED AROUND AGAIN, AND CORA WAS GLAD Julius was home. Her body seemed to be devouring her flesh, and any contact with her skin seemed to penetrate to the very marrow of her bones. She tried to put her feet under her when lifted from her bed, but this morning they simply wouldn't support her. It was as if her limbs had turned to rubber and her muscles no longer communicated with her brain. Julius pulled the wheelchair from the closet and opened it up, placing it behind Cora so she could fall backward into it. She hated the wheelchair. It embodied everything she loathed about her illness. It symbolized her inability to get around on her own, her total dependence on others. It mocked her, saying in a loud voice for all to hear that she had been defeated by some organism or genetic flaw she couldn't see, couldn't battle, couldn't confront … it galled her.

Her eyes brimmed with tears, periodically leaking onto her pajamas. Julius recognized their source immediately and crouched beside her. Taking her hands in his, he looked straight into her eyes. His voice need not participate in this communication. He willed strength to her; she drew strength from him. Her face cleared somewhat, and she nodded almost imperceptibly to Sheri who began pushing her to the bathroom. Cora loved her bath. Her momentary self-pity had passed, and although she despised her body for betraying her, she had reconciled her total reliance on Julius and Sheri to do for her what she could no longer do for herself.

Julius prepared the bath pad while Sheri ran the water. Together, as if they had been a team their entire lives, they offered Cora a brief respite from her pain; a time of warmth, relief, and pleasure, feelings Cora somehow reflected back to her 'team'. As she relaxed and her pain calmed, both Sheri and Julius became participants in her reprieve, each of their faces beaming. Words were seldom spoken during these times. Perhaps it was because there were no words that could describe how Cora felt, and how her almost constant pain was defeated, if only temporarily. These were Cora's moments, and neither Julius nor Sheri wished to usurp them through idle conversation.

When they had Cora back in her bed, as comfortable as possible, Sheri left for the kitchen, and Julius sat in the chair by her bed—perhaps, of late, his favorite chair in the house. Screwing up his courage, he began, "Cora, there are some things about the last few weeks—actually about the last few months—I haven't told you. They aren't bad things—well, not really, anyway—but I think you have a right to know why I'm spending so much time in Marshall. Several months ago—"

Cora's eyes were closed when she interrupted him, "Julius, bring Eddie into the house, would you. He's been in the back yard all morning batting into that net, and he must be burned to a crisp. I'll get him some iced tea. Let's convince him to stay in for a few minutes where it's a bit cooler." Her eyelids flickered. "Brittany, turn the hose off. There's enough water in the pool already for you and your friends to get cool." Her body jerked slightly. "Julius, is everything all right? I don't remember the ride being this rough before. Is the airplane OK?" Finally, Cora's body relaxed as her breathing slowed and deepened. She had fallen fast asleep, surrounded by her dreams.

Chapter 49

JULIUS HAD BEEN VERY RELUCTANT WHEN RIKKI CALLED ASKING him to meet her at the Sheriff's office at two that afternoon. The email she had received from Armoni with the names of two doctors willing to be interviewed had offered a time and place to meet. She couldn't turn it down.

They climbed into her squad car then headed to the hospital. Little was said between them. She wouldn't hold it against him if he blamed her for the fiasco with Garret. Although he may think so, she didn't consider him weak or spineless for reacting the way he did; anyone would do so, if it meant protecting family. Each in their own way, they were comfortable with the silence—for now at least.

Julius and Rikki were introduced to Dr. Bernard Huber, a resident at Parks, and Yun-seo Pang, an intern. They were all asked to be seated, and Beech gave them the background for the meeting and his assurance this was entirely voluntary on their part. The two men looked at each other quizzically.

Rikki began by asking each man if he remembered the surgery they had done on the afternoon in question. As each nodded their assent, the other's body stiffened, eyebrows raised.

Rikki's eyes flitted from one to the other as she pointed to each one in turn. "You two know each other?"

They both nodded in unison.

"But you had no idea you were partners in this surgery?"

They both shook their heads.

Then she asked while looking at them both intently, "OK, then. … We would like to know what type of procedure you were performing during the surgery in question."

With just the slightest of glances, perhaps looking for consent, Dr. Huber began. "First of all, let me confirm I had no idea Pang was my partner. We are told to remain anonymous, and we gown in such a way as to ensure we don't know who our partner is. I always thought it was strange, but since we were operating on a child at the end of life, perhaps it helps to keep emotion out of it.

"To answer your question directly, we were harvesting vital organs. We executed the procedure and preserved the organs in their designated containers as outlined in our—"

The simultaneous gasps of Armoni, Rikki, and Julius stopped him in his tracks. When Rikki was able to make her voice work again, she said haltingly, "Did I understand you correctly—you were *harvesting organs* from those children?"

Pang leaned forward in his chair, frowning severely, "Yes. But what's with your reaction?" He looked at Beech directly. "*You* issued the orders. How could you not know what the surgery was about?" He scanned back and forth among those present, waiting for an answer.

The entire room fell into an awkward silence.

Eventually, Rikki's investigative curiosity got the better of her. "How … did you … receive these orders?"

Bernard stepped into the conversation. "Nothing unusual. We received a page giving us the room number and the time, along with the procedure ID. As always, we dropped what we were doing, headed to the OR to scrub, and did the harvesting."

"Are … you saying … this is a common occurrence?" stuttered Rikki.

"Me? … I've been asked to harvest about twenty times, always in precisely the same way."

"And are you paid to do this?"

"Yes, a modest fee for the procedure. It goes a long way to helping with my education costs."

Pang was silent, fear playing across his features.

Rikki asked, her voice barely above a croak, "Tell us what happens after scrub."

Bernard again spoke. "When we enter the room the body is on the operating table, freshly off life support, and draped. We never see the child's face. The organ transfer cases are on a rolling cart, and all the supplies we need like sterile ice, infusion pumps and so on are there ready for us to use. We do the harvest and activate the transfer cases. Then we enter into the computer the time we finish, then clean up and leave. We never know who our partner is, who the scrub nurses are, or who the patient is."

"And you've never thought of this as a bit odd or unusual?"

"Not at all. Organ harvesting is relatively straight forward. We are taught the procedure in our courses and then we practice it in the lab. Something I do find a bit odd; the organ transfer cases are never the same. The intern is responsible for them, so maybe Pang can be of help there."

Yun-seo cleared his throat, and when he spoke he did so with a rasp. "Every time I've done a harvest, and I've done five or six of them so far, the transfer cases have been unlike any of the ones we used previously. Sometimes the infusion pump is different, or there isn't one. Sometimes the cases contain regular ice, and others, dry ice. The solutions we use are almost always different. But that isn't really my concern. We have no knowledge of where the organs are going or how long they need to be preserved."

"What do you do with the cases when they are completed?"

"We leave them on the rolling table just like we found them … except, of course, we place a seal across the crack between the lid and main case. The seals come attached to each empty case, telling us what organ goes in which one."

Rikki hadn't quite recovered from their disclosure, and apparently neither had Beech. She tilted her head toward the door and he nodded slightly. She said, "Thanks, guys. If we need anything more we'll be in touch." The two doctors left the room without further comment or even a parting handshake.

After a few minutes, Rikki shook herself, bringing her thoughts back to the moment. She murmured her thanks to Armoni and tapped Julius on the shoulder indicating they were leaving. In silence they left Beech's office and returned to her car.

With the doors closed, she said, "Wasn't expecting that. So Blake is not only making money on bogus billings, but he's selling organs on the black market. This is really getting sick."

Julius shook his head and stretched, willing back his ability to think clearly. "I'm not sure it's Blake." Rikki snapped her head around to look at him, her wide eyes asking what he meant. "Do you remember the audit report Kate gave us. Huri told her Blake looked surprised and angry when he was told the operating rooms had actually been used for something. I think he expected them to be empty and the resources cancelled. I don't think Blake knew someone was piggybacking on his scheme, and it made him mad."

"You're right; I'd almost forgotten. So as the mystery unravels it also gets more mysterious. I don't think the doctors doing the harvesting have anything to do with this. There must be a whole army of them, none of them knowing the others were involved. But someone has to be arranging all this somehow. It just leaves me cold and nauseous. I simply have no idea what's going on. What I do know is that this is the strangest and most macabre case I've ever worked on. … I think I'll keep this from the hospital administration—at least for the moment. We don't know where the orders are coming from, and we certainly don't want whoever it is to know that we know."

As they drove to the Sheriff's office, each offered various plausible scenarios, but by the time they arrived, they had not landed on one that really fit the facts.

Julius directed his thinking toward the transportation of the organs. This had to be a very specialized process, to keep the organs alive—whatever that meant—and undamaged for a period of time, and likely over some distance. He had heard of special organ flights that picked up a heart, for example, by helicopter in one location, and whisked it off to another where the recipient was prepped and ready. Time had to be of the essence. In the midst of his thoughts he muttered mostly to himself, "Someone has to take them from the hospital and get them into circulation."

Rikki looked at him quizzically and asked, "What are you talking about, or are you just mumbling to yourself?"

"I was trying to figure out how the organ containers get to their destination. They need quick handling and rapid transportation. If the doctors left them in the OR, and, assuming the cleaning staff didn't deal with them, or otherwise it would be in their reports, there had to be someone who took them away or moved them to some other location in the hospital." He stared out the window as he thought this through.

"Let's go back to what the doctors left in the room. Other than tools and equipment they would have left the child's body on the table and the organs preserved in special containers. Both had to be retrieved by someone."

"Bingo," shouted Julius, "That has to be it. Either the body is taken to the hospital morgue, or the body is collected directly by the funeral home. Either the containers are taken by the same person who moves the body, or it is someone else. So we have only four options to consider. We have morgue and one person, morgue and two persons, funeral home and one person, funeral home and two persons. Based on what we know about the operations and the secrecy surrounding them, my bet is there are as few people as possible involved, and it is done with as little fanfare as possible, which leads me to think it is one funeral home and one person. ... Now that I say it out loud, I guess it isn't quite so obvious. ... It's unlikely the same funeral home removed *all* the bodies—but I still think it's worth exploring, if, for no other reason, than it will eliminate that one possibility."

"I like where this is going ... mostly, if you'll forgive me, because we don't have anything else. I'll find out the funeral home of record for one of the patients and we'll make a visit." Rikki pulled out her phone and dialed the hospital, working her way through the layers to Armoni. Outlining the information she needed, she requested that he text it to her as soon as possible.

They arrived at the office but stayed in the car. Rikki figured it wouldn't take Armoni too long to get the funeral home name, so she asked Julius if he minded waiting a bit longer. In just a few moments her phone chirped. After a quick read of the screen she said, "Looks like we're heading to Meadow Falls Funeral Home and Chapel. Should only take a few minutes to get there."

Whipping her car out of the parking lot, she headed east, not being particularly observant of yellow lights or stop signs, finally arriving under the portico of a red brick funeral home with a tall sloping roof. Leaving the car in the 15 minute parking slot, they walked into the reception area. Flashing her badge, Rikki asked for the senior administrator in charge. It took a quick phone call to make the arrangements, after which she was told they would be speaking to Mrs. Marsi Fucinus; it would be just a few minutes, if they would like to take a seat, please.

True to her word, Mrs. Fucinus arrived bringing with her an air of calm and sobriety. It crossed Julius' mind that she likely thought she would be meeting a new client. She ushered them into a small anteroom containing an oval table and six comfortable rolling chairs.

"How can I help you," she asked in the smoothest of tones.

"My name is Deputy Castillo and this is Mr. Barlow. We understand your funeral home collected the body of a child from Parks several weeks ago." Rikki looked at her phone, reciting the child's name from the earlier text. Can you tell us how this is done—what your protocol is, and physically how it takes place?"

"My pleasure. It used to be much more difficult, but now it is very simple. We get a priority email from the hospital indicating a death has occurred, outlining the circumstances. This allows us to create the death certificate. We then email Haymore Stanward who removes the body and delivers it to us. Oh yes, the email tells us the room number where the body is located, and of course, some body attributes like age and weight; all of which we pass along to Haymore."

"You say you let someone else do the pickup? Another funeral home?"

"Yes. As I said, it is much easier now. Until Haymore established a centralized pickup service, each funeral home had to retain particular personnel to do the pickup. Not everyone has access to the hospital, and it takes special training to handle the body prior to the preparation done here."

Rikki stood, followed abruptly by Julius. "Thank you. You have been very helpful. We won't take any more of your time." They shook Marsi's hand and left the building.

When nearing the car, Julius said, "Correct me if I'm wrong, but I expect we're off to Haymore Stanward?"

"Yes sir. I expect part of our mystery is buried there." Rikki chuckled at what Julius took for an intentional pun, albeit morbid.

Haymore was clear across town, but Rikki knew how to avoid heavy traffic areas, so it took under ten minutes to get there. They announced themselves and were asked to wait in an anteroom refurbished as a civil war tactical center, complete with rifles, maps and other paraphernalia. Five minutes later Mr. Stanward Jr. arrived and closed the door. He immediately noticed their interest in the room and said by way of explanation, "This building is pre-civil war, and my father and grandfather before him kept this room much like it was in the day. We use it as our *personal* conference room for meetings unrelated to grieving clients. What can I do for you today?"

Rikki introduced herself and Julius. She outlined her need to find out how the centralized pickup worked and, in particular, who collected the body of the child whose name she retrieved from the text she had read earlier.

Stanward began haltingly, "About three years ago we hired a young mortician, about five years out of school, by the name of Eric Donola. He was certified to do removal, so we introduced him to the hospitals in the area, and used him almost exclusively for that purpose for about a year. He came to me one day and said he met staff from other funeral homes doing pickups and they appeared to be awkward, some of them expressing an aversion to doing it, particularly at Parks. So he asked if I would organize a centralized removal service. He would do all the work to get it going and advertise it. And so it started. He talked to the other funeral homes and to all the hospital administrators, and they loved the idea. Within the first six months we had hired 3 other specialized staff to do pickups around Marshall and surrounding municipalities. We do the paper work and deliver the body to the funeral home of choice.

"As for the body in question … let me look …? He opened his notebook computer and tapped a few keys. "Eric did that removal himself. In fact, I think he does most of the pickups at Parks. He has a soft spot for the kids, and seems to handle himself well if he bumps into parents or other family members."

Rikki queried, "If I send you a list of patient names, would you be able to identify who did the pickups?"

"Certainly, any time."

Rikki and Julius stood, shook Stanward's hand, and left the building.

When they were out of earshot, Julius said, "So, let me get this straight. Mr. Donola blows into town, creates a centralized collection service, and then does Parks all by himself. This sounds like a perfect opportunity to extract both body and containers. It doesn't help us with how all this is organized, but it appears we have the back-end solved. What do you think he does with those containers? I'll bet there's a lot of money involved, particularly for children's organs."

Rikki shuddered, then wondered out loud if there was any paperwork signed by the family indicating their consent, expressing strong doubts based on how this whole thing was set up. It appeared Parks was truly paperless, perhaps more so than anyone really knew.

They drove back to the Sheriff's office without speaking further, each face exhibiting their disgust at what had just been their misfortune to uncover.

Chapter 50

Wednesday

EARLY THE NEXT DAY, ON A WHIM, RIKKI WENT TO THE HOSPITAL TO speak with Beech. Perhaps he would know something about this Eric Donola. As she was walking through the main lobby, Armoni spotted her and called out asking if she was there to see him. She nodded, so he beckoned her to his office.

Rikki asked, "Do you know an Eric Donola from the Haymore Funeral Home?"

"Only to recognize him, but not personally. Almost everyone in the hospital knows him to some extent or other. He does a necessary but unsavory task, particularly in a hospital like Parks. But after he's been in, everyone is just a bit cheerier. I see him around town sometimes hanging with the younger crowd. Come to think of it, I've seen him chatting with Teresa, our analyst. Perhaps she knows him better than I do." Without waiting for a response, he dialed Tess's number. His conversation was brief. "She'll be right down. Would you like a coffee?"

As the coffee arrived, so did Teresa. She sat opposite Rikki in front of Armoni's desk, looking at both in turn quizzically.

In a tone that would put her mind at ease, Armoni said, "Tess, Deputy Castillo is asking if you know Eric Donola. I've seen you talking to him in the hallways, so I suggested she speak with you."

Tess replied hesitantly with some concern on her face. "Yes … I know him … a little, I guess … is he in some sort of trouble?"

Rikki wanted to calm her and said, "No, no. We are following every lead, no matter how small, in our investigation of the Dr. Atchley affair, and his name surfaced, so we're checking around. What can you tell me about him?"

"As I said, I don't know him well. What I *can* tell you is everyone around here likes him. He seems to have a demeanor that is comforting to the families he deals with. I don't know what he does that's different. It may just be the way he talks with them; he seems to be able to empathize with their loss. I don't know the whole story, but I heard he's not a stranger to grief. About a year ago he had a roommate who just disappeared. In fact, he was a programmer here at the hospital just before I came on staff. He resigned his position in our department, then about a month later he vanished."

Rikki was vaguely familiar with a similar case and prodding to find out if it was the same one, she asked, "Does the name Joel Beaufort mean anything to you?"

"Yes, that's the name, I believe. Eric took it really hard."

Armoni stepped in, "I knew Joel quite well. He implemented much of the OR scheduling software, so we worked side by side for several months. He was very bright, and had absolutely no interest in the corporate ladder or office politics; he simply loved programming—it's all he really wanted to do. He resigned rather suddenly well over a year ago. I didn't hear why. One day he was here and the next he was gone. It seemed to be totally voluntary, so maybe it was something personal, but it struck me as strange. As far as I know Koehler was very happy with his work. I know *I* was impressed by his skills."

Rikki's mind began fitting the final pieces into the puzzle. She was frustrated at having very little proof for her theory, but the theory was looking as solid as any she had prosecuted in the past.

Excusing herself from the meeting, she thanked both Armoni and Tess for their help. Her thoughts were racing as she reached her car. Before starting it she called Julius and told him the news about Eric, finishing by saying, "I think we have a working theory here.

Eric rooms with the programmer who knew the OR scheduling inside and out. Eric starts the centralized extraction, so he's the one who gets to remove the containers along with the body. Somehow they both profit. He's up to his ears in this thing, I just know it. I'm going to pull the video feeds from the entrances and hallways of the hospital to see if he slipped up anywhere. Meanwhile, I think we should visit him, you and I, as soon as possible."

"If you can catch him this afternoon, I'll arrive at, say, three o'clock? It shouldn't be a long meeting."

"OK, I'll call if the meeting is off. Otherwise, see you then."

Rikki's frustration with the case was beginning to turn. There were lots of unanswered questions, but she was beginning to get a general, albeit fuzzy, image of what was going on. Once the basic facts were complete and made sense, she could fill in the details with old fashioned police work.

That triggered a thought. Perhaps she could reach out to the FBI and get some information about the organ trade on the black market. But it would have to be carefully disguised. By the book, this case should have gone to the FBI a long time ago, but she wasn't about to give it over now—not until she had more proof, better proof, and certainly not until she, herself, understood what was going on. Stacy French, an old academy buddy, had taken a posting with the FBI. She would be a good place to start.

Back at her office, she located the list of FBI personnel in the Shreveport office, hoping she hadn't been reassigned. She located her name in the list, noted she had received a substantial promotion, and shot a thumbs-up. She put Stacy's phone number into her cell contact list in case she needed to call from the road. She pressed the call button.

"Special Agent French."

"Stacy, this is Rikki, Deputy Rikki Castillo. We met at the academy. I need some information for a case I'm working, and I thought of you."

"Rikki. Rikki Castillo? Yes, I remember you. You chose to work more at the local level, right? I'd be glad to help, if I can."

"Stacy, this may be a longshot, but do you happen to know anything about the illegal human organ trade?"

"Oh, this sounds serious." The pause was a bit too long. "Well, I know it's usually handled by the FBI …"

"Our case isn't about the organ trade exactly, but it may be involved. We're trying to get at our suspect by learning a little about it, and maybe going through that door. If we should uncover anything remotely resembling organ trafficking I'll give you a call, believe me." A slight half-truth, but it would have to do for the moment.

"I'm not the resident expert here at the FBI, but from what I've read and heard in briefings, it isn't much of a problem in the US or in North America, really. If I recall correctly, the first case cited was the Rosenbaum case back in 2009, which really rocked the nation's transplant industry. There are some who believe the trade is increasing with the donors being poor, and generally from emerging nations, selling organs to the wealthy of America."

"Stacy, are freshly harvested organs used for anything other than transplants?"

"Only one other I'm aware of, and that is by tissue labs who use them for bio research, drug testing and the like. However, this is closely controlled in the US by organizations like the California Tissue Consortium and others like it around the country … is this helping you any?"

"Not really, but it does give me some things to think about. Can I call you back if I need any more information, or perhaps the name of someone I can get further information from?"

"Certainly, call anytime. It was good to hear from you after all these years."

"Yes, you too. Take care and maybe we can chat again sometime."

Rikki ended the call. She didn't feel very much further ahead. But she would think a little about the tissue sample idea. Maybe Eric wasn't selling the organs outright, but maybe to organizations doing bio research—perhaps a very long list to work. She felt tired just thinking about it.

Julius rolled into the Sheriff's parking lot just before three o'clock. He had made this trip so often he had the shortcuts figured out, and any inaccuracies in the timing was strictly due to the number of red lights he hit. He took the front steps two at a time and strolled to Rikki's office. They were very comfortable with each other and their greeting was one between two friends; little formality remaining.

Immediately walking to Rikki's car, they left for the conference with Eric. Rikki chose the funeral home, thinking it might put Eric at ease. They met in the Civil War room where earlier they had seen Mr. Stanward. After introductions, they sat, with Eric at the table facing the door, Rikki and Julius across from him.

Eric was calm … almost too calm. He sat straight in his chair and seemed to purposely avoid small talk. He waited.

Rikki took the cue and started the conversation. "Eric, we are here as part of an investigation requested by the Parks hospital CEO. We understand you pick up the bodies of deceased patients at Parks, and we have a few questions we would like to ask you. You are here on a strictly voluntary basis and you do not need to answer any of my questions if you don't choose to. Do you understand this?" Eric nodded and remained focused on Rikki.

"I reviewed video tapes from around the hospital, and watched you come and go on several occasions. Each time you are wheeling a collapsible gurney, entirely covered in a white sheet, with what would appear to be an adult body under it. We also noticed the sheet went almost to the floor on the side of the gurney facing the camera, and in one shot there appeared to be the edges of boxes or equipment riding under the gurney. Since we have no idea how you do your job, perhaps you could tell us what we are looking at."

Eric was thoughtful, taking his time before speaking. "I do an unpleasant job. Each time I go to Parks I reach into the life of a family and extract their deceased child. Sometimes the family is still present, sometimes not. Although I try to avoid meeting anyone with the body, sometimes it can't be helped. I learned early on, that even though I had nothing to do with the child before the pickup and, in particular, I had nothing to do with the child's death, somehow, in the minds of those I meet, I was to blame. So I devised a way to help me and, at the same time, help the people I may meet. I never allow it to be obvious I have a child on the gurney. I suppose it's kind of silly, really, since it is a children's hospital after all—but it's the *perception* that counts in the minds of parents and family members. I load both ends of the gurney and cover it all with a sheet, so it looks like I'm transporting an adult, or just some equipment from one room in the hospital to another. I guess I never thought about how it might look like I was hiding something or stealing something. Is that what this is about? Theft of equipment?"

"No, no, nothing of the sort, Eric. But you have been very helpful by explaining what we saw in the video." Rikki paused a moment for effect. "Did you have a roommate a year or so ago who went missing?"

"Yes, I did." He straightened in his chair, his eyes brightening. "Joel was a great friend and even better roommate. He was quiet, worked all the time and was a great cook to boot. It killed me when he just up and left. I thought we had a good thing going."

Rikki interjected, "But you knew he had gone missing and the police were looking into it, did you not?"

"Yeah, I did. But nothing came of it. They didn't find him and I expect he just took off for a better job with better pay. A few weeks before he left he quit his job at the hospital and just kind of hung around. I got the impression he really wanted to be programming again, but he said he was working on something that would let him retire. I had no idea what he meant. He was young, very bright, and loved his job. It made no sense to me but it seemed to be what he wanted. I expect he went off to one of those high tech think tanks and was simply absorbed."

"Did he ever talk about his work when he was at home?" asked Rikki.

"Certainly. Programming was his life. When he wasn't cooking or sleeping he was at his computer working. He was proud of what he did, and often asked me to come and look at something he was working on. By the time he left, I think I had seen the entire operating room scheduling system he was installing. I didn't have a clue what he was saying most of the time, but it seemed to help him if I sounded interested and, from time to time, looked impressed."

"Did you have anything to do with his disappearance?" asked Rikki drilling him with those piercing eyes.

"Of course not," he replied indignantly, "As I said, I'm certain he's off making big bucks doing what he loves."

"When you came to Marshall you proposed, and then started, the centralized removal that is now a service offered by Haymore. Why?"

"Mostly because of who I saw in the various hospital hallways doing the job. When I finished school, one of my first jobs involved pickups. Everyone was highly trained and really expert at the job. When I arrived here in Marshall, I was upset by the lack of training, and I guess more importantly, the lack of professionalism, of those doing the pickups. They didn't know how to interact with families they might meet. They seemed ashamed of what they were doing. It just seemed wrong to me. I knew in a small town like this it would be difficult to get good staff into every funeral home, so I figured it would make sense to have one group of professionals do it all. Mr. Stanward saw the value in it and let me set it up. I'm proud of it. I think everyone involved would agree it's working very well."

Julius glanced at Rikki and received a nod of approval. "Eric, do you have any computer training, formal or otherwise?"

Eric suddenly stared directly at Julius. His face and voice had been a study in calmness and poise to this point. That veneer seemed to crack at Julius' question. The chords in his neck tightened and he swallowed hard attempting to clear his throat before he muttered, "No, not really. Why do you ask?"

"I was browsing through the Haymore web site this morning, and couldn't help but notice it was built by Eirikr Scand Productions. That's you, isn't it?"

Eric stammered, "Well … yes … but so what? How did you …?"

"How I know isn't important. I know lots of people who can build web sites for their friends, so maybe it means nothing. But they generally use templates, just fill in the blanks; drag and drop things. If they are good with color they can create a spectacular web site with very little effort. But that's not what you did, am I right?"

"Well, not really. I didn't use a standard template … but I guess you already have the answer, don't you?"

"In fact I do. The Haymore web site is code based. It is totally dynamic, each page created by computer code and then presented to the user. I would consider this well beyond the expertise of an armchair web creator … wouldn't you?"

"Uh, I guess so, but how do you—"

Julius cut him off again, "And didn't you major in database administration for the first two years of your college work—before you decided to become a mortician?"

He began to fidget as if he needed to be someplace else … and right now.

Julius continued to hammer at him, "And, having watched Joel work at home, did you not find a way to hack into the hospital databases?"

Eric lurched to his feet, sending his chair skidding across the floor on its side and muttered under his breath, "I need to be going." And he was gone.

Rikki was almost out of her chair in pursuit, but settled back down, staring at him as he punched through the war room door.

Rikki and Julius walked to her car. Inside, they discussed what had just happened.

"How did you know he had developed the web site?"

"The name gave it away. His name, Eric, is a derivative of the name Eirikr in Scandinavian. Hence the Eirikr Scand Productions. Since you are about to ask, I looked at the backend code for the web site—kind of an honest man's hack—" He looked at Rikki past knitted eyebrows and saw her mouth the question, 'Again?', "—discovered it had tags identifying it as having been dynamically created by computer logic. That's quite unusual and takes some significant computer smarts to do well. Once I knew I was onto something, I put Joel's and Eric's programming knowledge together, and took a shot in the dark. Oh, yes, I did a little research on him before I came here today discovering he had taken database administration in his undergrad education."

"Wow, since when did you become Sherlock Holmes? Makes me Dr. Watson, I presume?"

Julius shot back, "Well, if you really need to know, I have sleuthing in my blood. My great, great, great grandfather was a Pinkerton agent back in the mid eighteen hundreds. So I guess I come by it honestly. In fact, if the stories I've been told are true, I am his namesake. So what do you think of that?"

The chuckles came involuntarily, breaking the tension, offering a well-earned moment of relief.

As they drove back to the station Rikki thought out loud, "So, we like Eric for the setup of the surgeries and the removal of the transport boxes. He had opportunity and we can probably assume money is the motive, and he had the means. All we need to know is exactly how he did it. Somehow we have to find some proof to satisfy a judge.

"Oh, by the way, I spoke with an FBI acquaintance—"

"I thought we weren't going to bring them into this until we had some real proof?"

"Hold on there … let me finish. I spoke with an old FBI acquaintance and asked what value organs would have to anyone. She said either for transplants or for tissue samples for bio research. Perhaps Eric isn't selling them on the black market. Maybe he's selling them legitimately, or almost so, to bio labs."

"That sparks a thought," replied Julius. "It struck me odd when the doctors doing the harvesting said the organ transport boxes were all different, and had different fluids, and so on. I would think if Eric were working for a certain bio tech firm or even several, then the containers would tend to be recycled. But that isn't the impression the doctors gave. Or am I making more of this than I should?"

Rikki was silent for a long time, her brow knotting and unknotting. Eventually she said, "Now that you say it, I heard the same thing … but it didn't mean anything to me then … and I'm not sure it means much more to me now. I can't think of why it would be significant."

Julius said, "Somewhere deep down it feels important. I don't know why yet, but I'm going to put some time into finding out. Shall we meet tomorrow?"

Reaching the parking lot, they said their goodbyes, and Julius left for home.

Chapter 51

YESTERDAY CORA HAD EATEN ALMOST NOTHING. ALTHOUGH SHE seldom ate much at any one sitting, she always looked forward to meal times, generally cleaning her plate thoroughly—believing from childhood it was proper not to be wasteful. This nibbled at Julius' mind as he did his research on the Haymore website. He had trouble concentrating on either, his emotions divided.

Upon Sheri's arrival that morning, Julius told her he would be around all day, and could take care of Cora while she did her paper work and communicated the changes in Cora's condition to her physicians. At ten forty-five the call came asking Julius to be in Marshall at three o'clock. He would have to leave the house just before two. He found Sheri working at the kitchen table and said, "I'm needed in Marshall this afternoon so I'll be leaving shortly after lunch. I'm sorry. I expected to be here all day. Will you be able to handle the afternoon without me?" Swallowing the lump forming in his throat, he sighed, "I expect to be back late afternoon. I'll ask Brit to come by mid-day so she's here in case I'm home later than expected." He went to the next room and called his daughter.

As Julius left the house, the look Sheri shot him repeated the opinion she had so brashly laid on him the last time he had chosen Marshall over Cora.

True to his word, her Dad was back home by six. He helped her prepare to go home, thanking her for standing in. "Any more contractions today?"

"A few but not like the one I had on Monday. Goodness, that was something else," Brittany replied as she headed for the door.

"Say Hi to Jim for me. Oh, by the way, I'm doing some research tonight and I may have to head to Marshall again tomorrow. Would you be available to keep Mom company again for a bit?"

She began to open the door, but paused, then turned back toward Julius and slammed the door shut.

"Again, Dad?! You're leaving again? I thought you said a week ago this was all over and you'd stay home, and here you've left Mom alone again every day this week. I think *Sheri* is more worried about Mom than *you* are. What could you possibly be doing that's more important …?"

As she took a breath, Julius cut in, "Look, nothing is more important to me than Cora. Just because I'm not at liberty to give you the details of what I'm doing in Marshall does not mean I don't care. But it does require that you trust me, and I didn't realize until now that was an issue for you. I have a hospital full of kids getting ripped off by a bunch of sleaze-bag doctors, and I have to put a stop to it." He was shocked at his indiscretion and over-generalization; at the clarity of his words. He continued after an awkward pause, "Sorry, too much information. I hope you can keep it to yourself." Unable to look Brittany in the eyes, he focused on the closed door instead. "I don't want to fight with you, Brittany. Maybe you can't believe me when I say this thing is almost over, but it is, and that means we will all be much safer … including your Mom."

Slowly the icy silence separating them began to melt.

Exhaling a deep breath, she whispered, "OK, Dad," as she kissed his cheek. Before closing the door she looked at him inquiringly and said, "You really should tell us what is going on down there so we can stop letting our imaginations run wild."

"I'll tell you all about it very soon. You have more important things on your mind right now, Brit. It just seems every time we get one thing looked after, something else pops up."

Brittany gave him a crooked smile and left the house, noting the absence of the police car that had been stationed across the street for what seemed like weeks.

Chapter 52

Thursday

IT WAS EIGHT THIRTY IN THE MORNING, AND THE PHONE ON RIKKI'S desk rang three times before she could get to it. "Deputy Castillo. Good morning."

"Hey, I thought about the organ containers all being different and did some searching. I discovered that several large research hospitals around the country are spending a lot of time and money on designing containers and solutions for keeping organs alive for longer times across longer distances. St. Jude and Johns Hopkins are among those on the list. In fact, as it happens, there is a great deal of competition among them, each looking for patents to take their technology into the future.

"One really caught my attention: Texas Children's in Houston. I talked to an old friend in the technology department and found out they have an active research program studying the prolonging of organ viability. They are working hard on designing better contain-ers and preservative fluids. If I were to offer an opinion, I would say Eric was hooked into this research somehow."

"Julius, that's brilliant. It may well be Eric is not the scandalous black marketer we took him for. Actually … I think I'll take that back. If this were all above board, there wouldn't need to be the skullduggery that seems to be wrapped around this whole mess. I'm still convinced something illegal, or at least underhanded, is going on here."

"I agree, and I think I have some ideas on what may be going on. I suspect it isn't a good idea to talk about this any further on the phone, and since we didn't set a time for our meeting today, do you have a preference?"

They agreed on eleven o'clock.

After finishing some chores around the house, Julius headed out. The route to Marshall was so familiar by now the car took him there on autopilot. He found a parking spot and walked right in, greeting the various deputies he met on his way to Rikki's office where he sat himself down and slouched in the chair.

Julius was about to speak when Rikki rose to close the door. She returned to sit on the edge of the desk facing Julius and, looking at him intently, she said, "I know you're bursting with information; I can see it on your face. But I need to tell you two things before you get started. First, I feel really badly about Dr. Garret. I've decided I'll cut him a deal. If he provides us with information about Atchley's scheme, then I'm willing to leave him out of the report. If his name is mentioned during our investigation, I'll find a way to bury it. Puts me in the same camp as Garret, in a way, but I think it's important to leave him on the streets, for the sake of your wife, yes, but for all his patients."

Julius bounded out of his chair and hugged her. "Thank you so much," he said, his voice cracking. "This means a lot to me. Thank you, thank you." He released her reluctantly and she staggered toward the chair behind her desk, struggling to get her footing.

Clearing her throat in an effort to regain her composure, she continued, placing her hand on her chest as she caught her breath, "And second … based on your suggestion … I talked to Texas Children's … to their research department, and asked some questions about their work on organ preservation. They were very forthcoming—no secrets there, as far as I can tell—and they told me where they get their organ and tissue samples for testing." She paused for effect. "Now, what is it you wanted to say?"

"OK, now you know you can't get away with *that*…. you going to just leave me hanging? Where are they getting their stuff?"

"No, no, you first. You called this meeting," Rikki said playfully.

Julius gave her a look of feigned annoyance, shrugged, and took the floor. "I've been struggling with how Eric could possibly manipulate the hospital database in such a way as to force unscheduled doctors to do unscheduled procedures in a scheduled operating room. Given what I saw of the system from Armoni, I think I have it figured out—maybe not all the details quite yet.

"The OR scheduling system accepts procedure inputs from doctors, determines what is required, and is programmed to send out the necessary notifications. The scheduler, or doctor for that matter, can make any modifications needed, by adding one-off requests, like supplementary equipment or personnel or supplies. Armoni showed us where the doctors we talked to were in the *supplementary* section.

"Since Atchley and his crew didn't actually expect the OR to be used when they scheduled it for the bogus billings, I assume the personnel requests were sent with a standby flag. This would put them on alert, and then when the final page came they would be ready. If the final page never came, then they did nothing, and thought nothing of it.

"This is the trigger that puts the whole thing in motion. Eric has some way of being notified when this takes place.

"He then inserts personnel requests into the supplementary area *without* a standby flag, and as a result, they are paged and arrive almost immediately. Since the *procedure* can be overridden, I expect Eric did so at the same time. He would also be able to requisition appropriate experimental transportation containers from whomever he's working for."

He held out his hands, palms up, leaning back. "I know you are veritably busting at the seams to ask how he could do it remotely … Well, if my hunch is right, it's not very difficult. Have you ever heard of SQL injection?" Julius anticipated Rikki's shrug, but wasn't expecting her to ask if it was to ward off some kind of virus, and which arm did they inject. He scowled at her and continued. "It's pronounced like the word 'sequel', by the way. It's a technique hackers use to modify or destroy the databases of their victims. SQL is a method of talking to the database and telling it what you want done. If you are clever enough, and you know enough about the database structure, as Eric does, you can pretty much do whatever you like—as long as the web page, or application, or whatever you are using as an interface, isn't specifically programmed to block such things. Clearly the system at the hospital is not. That would have been where Joel came in. He removed this protection and left the security compromised.

"I think we should throw this theory onto Eric's proverbial wall and see if anything sticks."

Rikki responded, "OK, not a bad plan, but you didn't let me finish *my* story. I found out who the organ supplier was from Texas Children's ... as I was going to say earlier before you unceremoniously interrupted me. I suggest we track them, and, if we are right, it will also point to Eric, and we can get two birds with one stone ... since we are into overused metaphors."

Julius sat back in his chair in agreement while Rikki called the supplier whose name she had been given. "Can you tell me who owns your firm?" Julius sat forward, attentive at this question. "I see, thank you for your time." She looked across her desk at Julius and saw his anticipation. He shrugged a 'Well?' as she threw him a knowing smirk and dialed the phone again. She asked some questions about each doctor involved in the suspicious billings. She threw a mild fist pump when the supplier responded to her question about Dr. Gomez.

"... in Liverpool and then from Halifax, Canada, you say? ... Thanks. I'll call you back if I need anything more."

Julius exclaimed, "And ...?"

"You're going to love this. Texas Children's gets their tissue samples from a firm owned by Dr. Gomez, the same one who is currently employed at Parks, and, as *we* know, is one of the doctors suspended by Jackson. But get this! He is originally from Liverpool, England, but was at the Grace Hospital in Halifax, Nova Scotia, when he applied and was then hired here. This sounds all too convenient, wouldn't you say?"

"So, where is Eric in all this?"

"I expect Eric is Gomez's supply in Marshall." She thought for a moment and then added, "I wonder how we can prove it." Another pause. "Maybe it's not all that difficult." She pressed redial and said, "Hello, this is Deputy Castillo again. I have one more question for you. Do you know an Eric Donola?" Her face began to brighten and her smile told Julius all he needed to know about the response. Rikki thanked her source and rang off.

"I gather you just confirmed Eric is their supplier in Marshall?" asked Julius excitedly.

"Not quite, but the next best thing. They get their tissue from Haymore."

They both sat back in their chairs basking in this confirmation of their suspicions. They didn't have forensic proof yet, but as a theory it was beginning to show serious promise.

Rikki suddenly sat forward in her chair, scattering some loose papers in front of her keyboard. She began typing, and after a moment's pause she nodded to herself and said, "The thought came to me that maybe Gomez got his feet wet doing something like this in his native England. I just searched for the words 'organ' and 'England' and 'Gomez' and have some interesting results. Nothing on Gomez. But I did get a hit on an organ scandal in Britain.

"The article talks about a guy who worked at the Alder Hey Children's Hospital in Liverpool. They, and he, were deep in the middle of a controversy over the unauthorized use of organs, tissue, and bodies in a variety of British hospitals. He was fired, but they couldn't prosecute, it says here … because they couldn't link any specific tissue with a given patient. It might have been sheer volume, I suppose. The guy's name was … let me find it here … yes … van Belzen, who started this whole thing.

"Listen to this!

"When this went to public inquiry it was discovered there were over 2000 body parts, 850 from infants and children just in Alder Hey alone. … Wait, here are the final numbers! Over 100,000 organs, body parts, and bodies strewn over 210 hospitals in the national health care system. And this wasn't back 100 years ago; the inquiry took place in 1999." She read some more in silence. "Apparently van Belzen left Liverpool for … here it is … Halifax, but when all this came out he was fired by … here it is again … the Grace Hospital."

Julius was stunned. "Are you thinking what I'm thinking? … Gomez is Belzen? What kind of head hunter or personnel office would miss something like that? Surely Gomez, or van Belzen, or whoever he really is, wouldn't have been able to hide something as big as that?"

"Well, fortunately for us, hiring practices are not our problem. What *is* our problem, or better stated, our solution, is that we have a direct link between Gomez, who might really be van Belzen, and illicit organ and tissue supply. If we can put Eric in the middle of all this, we likely have the case we are looking for. I'm going to put a meeting together with the Parks' brass and see what we can shake loose." She dialed Parks, asking to speak to Noah Jackson. She figured it wouldn't hurt to start right at the top. "Good morning, Mr. Jackson, thank you for speaking with me. I have some information I want to share with you, and I will also need to see Dr. Gomez along with your new Chief of Staff. Could we meet this afternoon, if at all possible?" She worked out the meeting details; later in the afternoon would suit, so she asked, "Four o'clock?" as she looked over at Julius to get his reaction. He confirmed with a nod that he could be there. She thanked Noah and hung up.

"We have a four o'clock, then, at Parks. Meanwhile let's see if we can talk to Eric." Rikki placed the call to Haymore and, from what she was told, it appeared Eric would be in right after lunch. She set the meeting for one thirty.

Eric was transformed into a fortress of arrogant caution when he saw the two of them waiting for him in the War Room. Standing quickly, Rikki closed the door and stood firmly between it and Eric. Rikki's stare followed him like a laser as he took a seat, causing a look of fear to flicker across his face, almost imperceptible, but real enough. Julius began first, outlining with authority, as if he had irrefutable proof, how Eric had managed to coordinate the operating rooms, and had manipulated the doctors for his purposes. Rikki was proud of him. Eric's shoulders slumped as he began to wilt in his chair, his face, which had started the meeting with an air of defiant confidence, aged, with dark bags beginning to droop under his eyes.

Without giving him a chance to recover or to explain his actions, Rikki told of her call to Texas Children's, her tracking down Gomez, and of her discovery that *he* was Gomez's choice for organ supply in Marshall. If he looked defeated after Julius had finished, he looked next to death's door when Rikki was done.

Beginning to squirm in his chair, it looked like he may bolt again, or maybe do something else equally as stupid, so she strode around the desk, and ordered Eric to stand and place his hands behind his back. She applied the cuffs, and the three of them left the funeral home for the lock-up. Although protocol demanded she tell him the charges and read him his rights, Eric was in no condition to notice.

Noah Jackson greeted Rikki and Julius warmly as they entered his office. He introduced them to Dr. Adrian Jessop, Chief of Staff, and Dr. Gomez, after which they all sat at the conference table, with Noah at the head.

Noah began the meeting in his usual terse and precise manner.

He then asked Rikki to speak.

When Rikki asked Jackson if Parks was involved in harvested organ viability studies he responded, "Yes, but in a minor way. We have doctors who sit on the project committee at Texas Children's. We don't do any research here directly. Why do you ask?"

Rikki explained how she had contacted Texas Children's and spoke to a researcher there who informed her they obtained their samples from a variety of sources, one of which was in Marshall. "Does anyone in this room know who the Marshall source is?"

Everyone looked at her but Gomez. He looked down at the table for a moment, just long enough for both Rikki and Julius to take notice. Rather than satisfying their curiosity immediately, she moved on. "Mr. Jackson, how did this hospital come to hire Dr. Gomez?"

Gomez instantly sat erect, his eyes roving between Rikki and Noah.

Jackson looked directly at Rikki as he told her Gomez had been hired at the request of, and with the highest of recommendations from Dr. Atchley. When Rikki questioned the hospital's hiring practices, Jackson bristled with more than a shade of indignation. "Our personnel department is thorough and does due diligence for every applicant, particularly for our doctors. What are you driving at exactly?"

"But in the particular case of Dr. Gomez how was due diligence done?"

"I'm not sure just where this is going, but I'll oblige for the moment." He turned to Adrian and nodded. She immediately went to Noah's desk and dialed a number.

The remaining inhabitants of the room were engulfed in a tense silence. All eyes were on Adrian.

After a few moments of back and forth conversation, she returned to the table, sitting heavily in her chair. She took a moment to gather her thoughts, then, unable to look at anyone around the table said, "Apparently, in the case of Dr. Gomez, the personnel department was told by the Chief of Staff to rush the background checks, and since, in their cursory review, no red flags popped up, they went with the Chief of Staff's recommendation. The Gomez file is 'extremely thin'—their words, not mine.

Rikki thought she saw Gomez relax a little. She allowed Adrian's statements to hang in the air while she subjected Gomez to professional scrutiny. Dr. Garret's words about Gomez echoed in her mind. Garret thought something about Gomez was familiar, particularly when he put on his glasses. She dissected his appearance. She mentally removed the short beard. She brushed various colors through his black hair. She tried on various styles of glasses. She was becoming convinced. The set of the eyes and jaw, the looseness of the hair style, the straight, wide mouth, and the way he had crossed his arms when the issue of his hiring was brought up. Yes, she was absolutely sure and she was about to stake her reputation on it.

"Noah, Adrian, are you aware that Dr. Gomez, sitting right here with us, is not who he says he is? In fact, his name is Herman van Belzen and he was involved in the so-called Alder Hey Organ Scandal in England during the nineties."

Jackson slapped the table and shouted, "What?"

He turned his piercing gaze on his new Chief of Staff, and then on Gomez for an answer. Adrian sat frozen in time. When she sputtered that she had no knowledge of this, and that there must be some mistake, Jackson turned to Gomez. "Is any of this true, Pepe?" Gomez hung his head and remained tellingly silent.

Noah tried to recover the awkward situation. "I'm sure there's an explanation for this." He excused himself, went to his desk, and made a phone call. The tension around the table was palpable. Gomez was sitting on the edge of his chair swallowing rapidly. Rikki pushed the waste basket closer to him with her foot. She was totally prepared to cut him off before he reached the door, if he ran. When Noah returned he said, "My contact at the College of Physicians and Surgeons was very vague regarding the Alder Hey affair, but had no file on Gomez that would connect him to any improprieties." He looked directly at Pepe and asked, "Pepe, clarify this right now and we can move on." Pepe's mouth worked but no words came out. Noah faced Rikki and said, "Is this why you wanted the meeting with us? To question Gomez?"

"No, not entirely, but confirmation of our information was part of it. I wanted to tell you what we know, and how we know it." She and Julius took turns speaking for over half an hour. They exposed van Belzen and his tissue supply company, Eric, and his unauthorized use of the operating rooms, and finished with a graphic description of organs being harvested from unwilling children, of unwitting families, by unsuspecting doctors. "Dr. van Belzen has been up to his old tricks; that's what this amounts to. His actions caused a huge scandal in England, causing the government to overhaul legislation regarding the harvesting and use of human tissue. It took several years but in 2004 it was finally done. I won't give you all the details because it will turn your stomach. We already have protective laws in the United States, enforced by the Human Resources and Services Administration, and several others, but here, today, we have an example of someone ignoring the law, ignoring the wishes of families, and, in effect, stealing organs from children right here at Parks—right from under our … correction … *your*, noses."

Jackson began to tremble. The seriousness of the accusations and Rikki's confident tone would have communicated law suit to any corporate leader, and he began to sweat.

Everyone around the table was speechless. Pepe's breath was coming in short gasps. Rikki stood and moved behind van Belzen's chair. She took him by the arm and had to pull him up, his legs barely able to support him. Noah slid back in his chair and watched, his head shaking slowly, while she cuffed Gomez and led him out with Julius in tow. This was the second time today she had taken someone into custody without any formal charge, pushing the boundaries of her authority. But she didn't know if Gomez would cause trouble, and, knowing what he had done at Parks and in England, if he *did* resist, she wasn't sure she could control her disgust.

It was just before five o'clock when Rikki loaded van Belzen into the back seat of her squad car. As she closed the door she casually remarked to Julius about the brazen audacity of people like van Belzen and Eric, and how so many people are hurt for nothing but greed. Their conversation was interrupted by the ring of Julius' cell phone. After his initial greeting he said nothing for what seemed like minutes. Rikki waited, leaning on the hood. As Julius listened, his face paled momentarily, and then he broke into a wide smile. He said into the phone, "Is everyone OK? All the proper parts in all the right places?"

After he terminated the call, Rikki took a step toward him. "Is everything all right?"

"Yes, and no … mostly yes. My daughter just had her first baby, our first grand-child, and everyone is fine. The 'no' part is that she had it at our house while she was supposed to be looking after my wife. I have to get home," his voice trailed off to a distracted whisper.

She reached for his hand, but he turned quickly and headed for his car. Rikki wanted to shout after him to keep her posted, but she knew she didn't have any right to expect to be included in the joys and trials of *his* family life. The elation wrought by the day's successes paled in contrast, as she watched Julius pull rapidly out of his parking spot and enter the local traffic, knowing he was going home to welcome a new life, a new member into his family. She wanted to embrace him, to congratulate him, to wish him well, and tell him how proud she was of him. Her heart ached because she couldn't.

Chapter 53

HE WAS OUT OF BED BEFORE BEING CONSCIOUS OF HIS ACTIONS, awakened instantly by Cora's voice that had been enfeebled by the further deterioration of her condition overnight. A few strides across the living room and he was in the still-dark chair at Cora's side, taking her hands and stroking her cheeks as she murmured, the vocalization of some dream or nightmare. Just above a whisper, the assurances of his presence and care mingled with her unintelligible chatter. "There, there. No need to be afraid. I'm here. I'll get anything you need." Although Cora didn't respond directly, her voice softened and eventually diminished until just her lips moved.

Julius watched the dark sky take on the eerie light of morning, the dull glow suddenly ablaze with color as the sun split the horizon. The rays seemed intent upon illuminating his decision to go back to Marshall, a commitment he now regretted—but he had to finish what he started. Quietly leaving Cora's side, he dressed and made a light breakfast for himself. He laid out the ingredients for Cora's breakfast so she could eat as soon as she awoke. All he could hope for was a day better than the last few; she had eaten so little.

The few hours remaining were consumed with household chores and some activities related directly to Cora's special needs in preparation for Sheri's arrival.

As the gong clock struck eight, Sheri slipped quietly through the front door. From what she learned yesterday she was certain Cora would still be sleeping and she didn't want to risk waking her. Finding Julius working on his computer at the kitchen table, she said a quiet good morning. He pointed at fresh pot of coffee, told her in muted tones of Cora's episode early that morning and then excused himself to make a phone call. Sheri overheard bits and pieces; something about the Texas Children's Hospital, organ donations and containers, but she could make no sense of it. As Julius walked back into the kitchen he was saying, "... eleven o'clock. I'll have the rest of the information for you then." Apparently he was intending to head back to Marshall again, and this made her strangely uncomfortable ... and angry.

Doing her best not to wake Cora, she hissed through her teeth, "Really, Julius? You're actually going to leave again? I thought you said this was all over and done. Did I misunderstand you, or can I simply not believe what you say? In case you haven't noticed, Cora is getting weaker by the day and needs you more than ever ... *here* ... not *there*."

His response bordered on a snarl as the words she spoke mirrored the thoughts he had rejected just moments before, "I ... can't ... help it! We finally have a breakthrough in the case and I won't get another chance if I screw this up. It has to be today ... and the rest will be the responsibility of the police. I promise I'll make it up to Cora when I'm back. ... I have to go and get this done ... I've no choice, Sheri!" His last statement was softer, forming an appeal that he wasn't sure but may have been for himself.

Sheri looked for artifice in his countenance but found only sorrow. Turning away, she left him to the consequences of his decision.

Brittany arrived just after Julius was gone. If truth be told, she made two arrivals; first came her unborn child, and then the rest of her. It was a wonder she could walk at all, bent backward as she was to balance the weight of her baby. She was due in a week, but Sheri mused to herself as she shrugged off the black mood left by her exchange with Julius, that she wasn't going to make it. The baby looked ready to take on the world and wasn't going to abide by any rules, nature's or otherwise.

She plopped herself immediately on a stool in the kitchen and leaned on the counter. "This is getting ridiculous, Sheri. I can't walk, can't sit in a soft chair, I'm eating for two, and need the bathroom every ten minutes—and it takes me eight of those ten minutes just to *get* to the bathroom."

Sheri knew this wasn't a complaint on Brittany's part, just a statement of the facts. "Hang in there Brit, the awkwardness will soon be over, and then the fun will begin." Sheri couldn't help flashing Brittany a perceptive smile.

"You *know* I'm really looking forward to our baby, Sheri, and until a month ago my pregnancy was fascinating, almost fun, and I enjoyed playing games with our little kicker. But in this last month, his or her pending transition has been neither fascinating nor enjoyable. It has been just plain infuriating."

Sheri recognized no reply to this was expected or required. Brittany was just venting in her mild way; she was so like her mother in that. Brittany levered herself from the stool and waddled into the dining room to see her Mom. Recognizing immediately that Cora was still asleep, she turned around and planted herself again on the kitchen stool. "How is Mom doing?" she asked as she made herself as comfortable as possible.

"Your Dad said she had a bad morning. She was muttering and calling out, but none of it made much sense, probably the result of a dream or nightmare. It may just be—" Sheri stopped short of saying what was on her mind.

"Be what …?"

"Never mind. Cora is struggling a bit extra today, that's all."

Cora awoke just before lunch. Both Sheri and Brittany gathered at her bedside to determine her state of mind and whether adjustments were required to reduce her discomfort, but found her almost unresponsive. She seemed to recognize each of them but couldn't articulate what she had on her mind, her mouth working at forming words but without success. Sheri left the room deep in thought. She had taken Cora's vital signs earlier, as she did several times a day, and found them to be weakening, but not alarming, and was puzzled by the lethargy and incapacity of the moment. Reaching for the phone, she placed a call to Dr. Sykes and was put through immediately. She explained Cora's symptoms, reading to him the entries she had made on the chart. Sykes was quiet for several moments. Finally he said, "I have to admit I'm a bit puzzled. I have a full calendar today but I'll cancel my two o'clock and stop by. Perhaps seeing her in person will help me come to some conclusion." Sheri thanked him and replaced the receiver.

She headed back to the living room, stopping abruptly in the doorway, stunned by the scene before her. Brittany and Cora were having a quiet but animated conversation reminiscing about old times. She quickly interrupted to take Cora's vital signs again, wondering if something significant had changed. Nothing had. Her vitals were almost identical to those taken just a brief time before. What *had* changed was Cora's capacity for thought and conversation. She wondered if she should call Dr. Sykes back to cancel and thought better of it. The episodes related by Julius, and then witnessed by herself just a few moments ago, convinced her the doctor's opinion would be helpful.

They had lunch together as they had done many times before. Although Brittany was obviously uncomfortable, she was happily engaged in their banter, until her mouth flew open in a loud gasp as she stared at the edges of her chair and the floor beneath her. She was sitting in a puddle, her face flushed instantly. The conversation stopped abruptly. Sheri looked at her with wide eyes, suddenly realizing what had taken place. She leapt to her feet, knocking over her chair, and rushed to Brittany's side. The first contraction hit in less than a minute.

Sheri took control. Although she had not been trained specifically as a mid-wife, birthing had been on her nursing curriculum, and she had been involved in several over the years. She had never been solely responsible for a delivery, but she was sure she could handle it. One thing she was quite certain of; the baby had no intentions of waiting for the usual medical entourage. The appointment with Sykes flitted across her mind. Just to be certain, she picked up the phone and dialed 911.

Pulling towels from the linen closet, she made Brittany comfortable on the living room floor and headed upstairs for needed supplies. She rushed back downstairs and put together a makeshift birthing theater, drawing on her training and her limited experience. She could hear the wail of sirens in the distance and opened the front door just a crack.

Two young EMT's burst through the open door and came to a sudden halt when Sheri, as calmly as she could muster, asked, "Have either of you boys delivered a baby?" Both shook their heads and one let out an involuntary rough cough. "Then get your life support gear and help me when I ask for it. Otherwise stay out of my way!" The command in her voice sent the two scurrying to their vehicle. They returned with a crash kit, oxygen, and intravenous supplies. They returned for the stretcher and left it, wheels folded, just inside the door in case it was needed. Radioing dispatch, the leader narrated the situation, indicating they would stay until the baby was born and then transport both Brittany and the baby to the hospital.

An hour later, Brittany's baby was still struggling to make its entrance into the Barlow family.

At the sight of an emergency vehicle parked at the curb and the open front door, Dr. Sykes sprinted past the shrubs along the walkway and into the house. A quick glance told him it wasn't Cora needing help, but Brittany. His gaze lingered on Sheri, nodding his approval of her work so far. Rushing to the kitchen, he scrubbed quickly using supplies from the crash kit, then donned surgical gloves, and took over from a relieved Sheri. She plopped herself on the sofa and said with a long sigh, "I'm so glad to see you. I've never had to do this by myself, and my formal training falls into the category of museum-quality."

Sykes was totally composed. He replied with a bit of a smile, "Women have been doing this for many years totally on their own. We are here really as observers—here to ensure the welfare of Mom and baby once nature has done her work. From what I see, it looks like you've done a good job preparing for an event which appears … to me … as if it will take place almost any minute now."

Sheri forced herself off the sofa and knelt by Brittany's head, taking her hands, and coaxing her through the breathing and the contractions. A few minutes later Keira Tamara Evenson started breathing on her own, after making quite a fuss over the loss of her previous comforts. Sheri took the baby from Dr. Sykes and wrapped her in a warm towel. As he attended to Brittany he said to the EMT duo, "I'll have her ready in about a half hour. I don't want her moved just yet. All her vital signs are good and I see nothing unusual requiring emergency treatment. If you can wait, I'll have you take them both to the hospital to get them checked out, just to be safe." The team leader agreed and radioed the situation to his dispatcher.

Cora hadn't left Sheri's mind, but she had been too busy to even poke her head into the living room to see how she fared. Carrying the baby, she went into the living room and sat in Cora's visitor's chair. Cora was still bright, saying she had heard the commotion and the cries, and was able to hear most of the conversation, so she knew the good news, and was thrilled Brit had a new baby girl. Sheri showed Cora the baby's face and tears welled up as Cora met her grand-daughter for the first time.

Since the head of Cora's bed had been raised for their lunch and conversation earlier, she motioned with her hands for Sheri to let her hold the baby, and Sheri saw no reason why not. She made sure the baby girl was securely settled against Cora's chest, cradled in her left arm, then she raised the bedrail on that side to ensure Cora's arm did not have to support the additional weight on its own. When both were settled she asked, "Will you be alright for a few minutes while I check with Brit and Dr. Sykes?"

"Certainly, there's nowhere for the baby to go. She's so snuggled in … we'll have a grand time together."

Sheri left the room, going directly to Brittany to tell her the baby was safe with her grandmother. Sykes was still checking Brittany's vitals and the EMT crew was passing the time on the front steps waiting for the doctor to release mother and baby to them. Sheri busied herself helping Sykes with cleanup.

Twenty minutes later, Dr. Sykes had finished with Brittany and summoned the EMT's so they could prepare Brittany for the trip to the hospital. They radioed their intentions, requesting a neo-natal crew ready to accept the new mother and child. Since Sykes had come initially to see Cora, he thought he would have a quick look at her, and return the baby to Brittany after she was placed on the stretcher. He entered the dining room to find the baby tightly wrapped and nodding off. Cora had her eyes closed, both of them wet with tears, her face serene with the remnants of a smile. He couldn't help thinking she looked totally content. He said, "Cora, open your eyes for just a moment. … It's Dr. Sykes. … I want to check you over briefly and then I have to get to my afternoon appointments." He waited a moment or two before repeating gently, "Cora, I need you to wake up for just a few minutes and then I'll let you sleep." In light of what Sheri had told him of her morning episode, her lack of response concerned him. He retrieved her chart, read the entries Sheri had made during the day, then checked her vital signs.

Chapter 54

Friday

HER DESK SPROUTED MOUNDS OF PAPERWORK, TWO PAIR OF arrests, each opening the door for the other, but otherwise unrelated. The fact that Dr. van Belzen had weaseled his way into the hospital was chewing at Rikki's brain. It was abundantly clear he should never have been hired by the hospital in the first place. So, why had he? Atchley had pushed through his hiring, but why? And then there was Garret. He seemed to be clean, but why had he been involved in the meetings? Was there a connection of some kind, and, if so, what was it? Garret was not a hospital employee, so they wouldn't have personnel records for him. He had surgical privileges at Parks, but it would not follow that Parks would have his full profile. After doing an internet search she was no further ahead—quite the opposite of van Belzen.

Four arrests: Atchley was going away for a long time; Yakov would be exiled to Russia; Eric would receive a slap on the wrist— maybe he would do time, maybe not; Van Belzen would lose his medical license and would finally spend many years behind bars. The other four doctors would likely retain their medical licenses and would escape jail time, but they would have to pay back everything they stole from the system, with interest. The FBI would ensure appropriate penalties would be added, and the IRS would most likely get involved. Some of them may wish they *had* been sent to prison. Garret? She had been inclined to offer clemency, cut him a deal—information for his freedom—but if his involvement went deeper, she would have to rethink her position, and that would affect Julius. Uncertainty and indecision tugged at her mind.

She called Texas Children's, asking for the head of organ viability research. After several false starts, she was connected to Dr. Neville Rankin, introduced herself, and then asked if Dr. Garret had any involvement in the research his team was doing. She listened for some time before she stated, "You purchase some of your research organs from Dr. Gomez in Marshall. Do you know if Garret is associated with Gomez in more than a strictly professional way? … OK. … I see. … Yes. Are you familiar with the name van Belzen by any chance? … Oh! … Really? …In what way was Garret … instrumental, you say … helped expose him … in the UK?" Rikki's eyebrows shot upward and her face broke into a knowing smile as she listened to the remainder of Rankin's response. "Ah, OK. Thank you so much for your time. … Yes, you've been immensely helpful. Thank you again." They said their good-byes and she hung up.

Chapter 55

Sunday

THE FUNERAL SERVICE WAS HELD SUNDAY AFTERNOON—A LITTLE unusual perhaps, but fitting. The chapel at the funeral home was overwhelmed by those wishing to offer their last respects to a woman who had given so much of her life to others without counting the cost; a life that seemed, to most, cut short in its prime. But Cora would not have thought so. She made each moment count. She lived in concert with her principles. She gave birth to, and then helped raise, two loving children who were, themselves, making an impact on their generation. She loved, and was loved by, a very special man. She had held Keira, a brand new life, much too briefly— her labored breathing arrested by the weight of the bundle she adoringly cradled.

Only the immediate family accompanied the casket to the graveside. Julius had brought along the chair that once stood so faithfully beside Cora's bed, providing respite for those who came to comfort her, to care for her, to watch over her, to pray with her, to weep for her loss. The chair now held Brittany, whose body was weak with grief and new motherhood, and Keira, whose first public appearance was to witness the burial of her grandma.

"… dust to dust, ashes to ashes." spoke the pastor reverently, "Now to him who is able to keep you from stumbling and to present you blameless before the presence of his glory with great joy, to the only God, our Savior, through Jesus Christ our Lord, be glory, majesty, dominion, and authority, before all time, and now, and forever. Amen."

As the pastor stepped aside to allow the family access to the graveside, Julius caught movement just beyond the small ring of mourners. Rikki was standing in the middle of the access road, her hands thrust deep into the pockets of her dress pants. When their eyes met Rikki nodded, then turned and walked slowly back to her car.

Julius could no longer contain his grief. As the casket was lowered, and each family member dropped a token handful of earth onto the casket, the strength in his legs abandoned him and he sank onto the grass. "Cora …" was all that escaped his lips.

Glossary of Terms

THE INFORMATION IN THIS GLOSSARY WAS GLEANED FROM A variety of references including Wikipedia, Federal Aviation Administration publications, various flight manuals, online medical journals and online dictionaries.

AIM, Aeronautical Information Manual – **a** manual containing the fundamentals required in order to fly legally in the country of origin. It also contains items of interest to pilots concerning health and medical facts, factors affecting flight safety, a pilot/controller glossary of terms used in the ATC (Air Traffic Control) System, and information on safety, accident, and hazard reporting. Although the AIM is not regulatory in nature, parts of it re-state and amplify federal regulations.

Airport Facilities Directory – a pilot's manual that provides comprehensive information on airports, large and small, and other aviation facilities and procedures.

Anesthetist – one trained to administer anesthetics—compare Anesthesiologist.

Anesthesiologist – anesthetist, specifically a physician specializing in anesthesiology.

Arthrodesis – Lumbar spinal fusion, surgery to join, or fuse, two or more vertebrae in the low back.

ATC – Air Traffic Control, a service provided by ground-based controllers who direct aircraft on the ground and through controlled airspace, and can provide advisory services to aircraft in non-controlled airspace.

Attitude – An aviation term that indicates the orientation of an aircraft relative to the horizon. For example, if you are flying upside down when you aren't intending to, you are in a bad attitude.

AOPA – Aircraft Owners and Pilots Association, a Frederick, Maryland-based American non-profit political organization that advocates for general aviation.

Bayou – a Franco-English term for a body of water typically found in flat, low-lying area, and can refer either to an extremely slow-moving stream or river, or to a marshy lake or wetland.

CDI – course deviation indicator is centered when the aircraft is on the selected course as set in the VOR indicator.

CEO – Chief Executive Officer, a job title commonly given to the most senior corporate officer (executive) or administrator in charge of managing a for-profit or non-profit organization.

CFO – Chief Financial Officer, a corporate officer primarily responsible for managing the financial risks of the corporation. This officer is also responsible for financial planning and record-keeping, as well as financial reporting to higher management.

Chief of Staff – the chief administrative officer of the medical staff; the physician or other health care professional who is in charge of the medical staff in a hospital or health care organization.

CIO – Chief Information Officer, a job title commonly given to the most senior executive in an enterprise responsible for the information technology and computer systems that support enterprise goals.

Clearance – an authorization by Air Traffic Control (ATC) for flight into controlled air space. Each clearance follows a specific format:

- *Clearance* limit, the end point of the clearance (usually, but not always, the destination airport)
- *Route*, the route that the flight is to follow as part of the clearance (often the route originally filed, although ATC may change this)
- *Altitude*, the initial altitude to be maintained by the flight, plus, in many cases, a time at which cruise altitude clearance may be expected
- *Frequency*, the frequency to which the pilot(s) should tune upon leaving the departure airport
- *Transponder*, the transponder code that must be set for the aircraft prior to departure and during the flight. T also stands for time, as in void time, if one is issued. A void time is an expiration time, meaning, the IFR clearance is voided if the aircraft is not airborne by the void time.

Conscious sedation – Conscious sedation is a combination of medicines to help you relax (a sedative) and to block pain (an anesthetic) during a medical procedure

Departure, Center, Arrival, Tower – The departure controller is located in the TRACON facility, which may have several airports within its airspace (50-mile/80-km radius). He or she uses radar to monitor the aircraft and must maintain safe distances between ascending aircraft. The departure controller gives instructions to the pilot (heading, speed, rate of ascent) to follow regular ascent corridors through the TRACON airspace.

The departure controller monitors the flight during ascent to the en route portion. When your plane leaves TRACON airspace, the departure controller passes your plane off to the center controller (ARTCC controller). Every time your plane gets passed between controllers, an updated flight progress slip gets printed and distributed to the new controller

The arrival controller monitors the flight during descent to the airport. When your plane arrives in TRACON airspace, the center controller passes your plane off to the arrival controller.

The tower controller handles the final phase of flight which includes the clearance to land and the handoff to the ground controller.

DUAT – DUATS, or Direct User Access Terminal Service is a weather information and flight plan processing service contracted by the Federal Aviation Administration (FAA) for use by United States civil pilots and other authorized users.

FAA – Federal Aviation Administration, the national aviation authority of the United States. An agency of the United States Department of Transportation, it has authority to regulate and oversee all aspects of American civil aviation.

FBO – Fixed Base Operator, a commercial business granted the right by an airport to operate on the airport and provide aeronautical services such as fueling, hangar space, tie-down and parking, aircraft rental, aircraft maintenance, flight instruction, etc.

Flight Service Station – an air traffic facility that provides information and services to aircraft pilots before, during, and after flights, but unlike air traffic control (ATC), is not responsible for giving instructions or clearances or providing separation. The people who communicate with pilots from an FSS are referred to as Flight Service Specialists.

Glasnost – a Soviet policy permitting open discussion of political and social issues and freer dissemination of news and information.

Hemodynamic normality – the ability of the body's cardiovascular system to sustain itself without mechanical or pharmacological support.

ICAO – International Civil Aviation Organization is a specialized agency of the United Nations. It codifies the principles and techniques of international air navigation and fosters the planning and development of international air transport to ensure safe and orderly growth

IFR – Instrument Flight Rules, rules and regulations established by the FAA to govern flight under conditions in which flight by outside visual reference is not safe. IFR flight depends upon flying by reference to instruments in the flight deck, and navigation is accomplished by reference to electronic signals.

Infusion – the continuous slow introduction of a solution especially into a blood vessel. An **infusion pump** infuses fluids, medication or nutrients into a patient or an organ. **Pulsative infusion** indicates infusion with a rhythmic beat.

IP (Address) – Internet Protocol (Address), a numerical label assigned to each device (e.g., computer, printer) participating in a computer network that uses the Internet Protocol for communication. An IP address serves two principal functions: host or network interface identification and location addressing. Its role has been characterized as follows: "A name indicates what we seek. An address indicates where it is. A route indicates how to get there."

IT – Information Technology.

KGB – an initialism for *Komitet gosudarstvennoy bezopasnosti* (translated into English as Committee for State Security), was the main security agency for the Soviet Union from 1954 until its collapse in 1991.

Kneeboard – an accessory (usually made from cloth, plastic or metal) with various types of clips or mounts to hold objects for pilots during flight

Log File – the file to which a computer system writes a record of its activities.

Memory Dump – consists of the recorded state of the working memory of a computer program.

Navajo – Piper PA-31 Navajo is a family of cabin-class, twin-engine aircraft designed and built by Piper Aircraft for the general aviation market.

- a housing, separate from the fuselage, which holds engines, equipment on an aircraft.

ɔ – commonly applied to aircraft that have experienced a ɔ failure while flying.

ʃS – Omni Bearing Selector, the moveable scale around the utside of the instrument, used to set the desired course. When on-course the CDI is centered.

OR – Operating Room.

Phonetic Alphabet – more accurately known as the *International Radiotelephony Spelling Alphabet* and also called the *ICAO phonetic* or *ICAO spelling alphabet*, as well as the *ITU phonetic alphabet*, is the most widely used spelling alphabet. The International Civil Aviation Organization (ICAO) alphabet assigned code words acrophonically to the letters of the English alphabet so that critical combinations of letters and numbers can be pronounced and understood despite language barriers or transmission static.

Pilatus (PC12) – a single-engine turboprop passenger and/or cargo aircraft manufactured by Pilatus Aircraft of Switzerland. The main market for the aircraft is corporate transport and regional airliner operators.

PTA – Parent Teacher Association, an association composed of parents, teachers and staff, and perhaps student representation, which is intended to facilitate parental participation in a school.

Reactive cardiomegaly – enlargement of the heart in reaction to medication or deterioration of other organs.

Server – any computer or computerized process that shares a resource to one or more client computers or processes.

SQL – Structured Query Language, a special-purpose programming language designed for managing data held in a relational database management system (RDBMS).

TEDR – Texas Electronic Registrar Death Registration system.

TFR – Temporary Flight Restriction, a restriction on an area of airspace due to the movement of government VIP's, special events, natural disasters, or other unusual events.

Wilco – **Will co**mply (after receiving new directions).

Victor Airways – low-altitude airways established in the United States by the FAA for flight. They are defined in straight-line segments, each of which based on a straight line between either two VHF omnidirectional range (VOR) stations, or a VOR and a VOR intersection. Example, Victor Airway 13 would be designated as V13, pronounced as Victor 13.

VOR – VHF Omni Directional Radio Range, a type of short-range radio navigation system for aircraft, enabling aircraft with a receiving unit to determine their position and stay on course by receiving radio signals transmitted by a network of fixed ground radio beacons.

ZULU – an aviation term for UTC (Coordinated Universal Time), the primary time standard by which the world regulates clocks and time. It is one of several closely related successors to Greenwich Mean Time (GMT). For most purposes, ZULU is used interchangeably with UTC and GMT. Generally signified in a written time by the suffix 'Z'